the girl
in the
missing
poster

ALSO BY BARBARA COPPERTHWAITE

Invisible
Flowers for the Dead
The Darkest Lies
Her Last Secret
The Perfect Friend

the girl
in the
missing
poster

BARBARA
COPPERTHWAITE

bookouture

Published by Bookouture in 2021

An imprint of Storyfire Ltd.
Carmelite House
50 Victoria Embankment
London EC4Y 0DZ

www.bookouture.com

ISBN: 978-1-78681-695-5
eBook ISBN: 978-1-78681-694-8

To Julieanne, my friend & life twin
and
For all the missing – and those who are left behind

CHAPTER ONE

The face of a murdered woman stares back at me from the reflection of the high street shop window. One minute I was walking along the deserted pavement with my three dogs in tow, throwing a tired glance at the cheery displays in spring pastels, the next my eyes refocused so that I was no longer looking through the glass but at its surface, turned mirror-like by the setting sun.

There she is. Leila. Dead but alive.

Only it isn't her. It's me. Even after all these years, when I see myself it's my dead sister who looks back. My heart stutters. I turn away from the chocolate shop with its chick breaking free of a giant egg and its promise of an Easter 'egg-stravaganza'. The woman in the reflection has gone, long gone. Yet I still feel her presence as I turn the corner from the single street of shops onto a tree-lined avenue filled with Victorian town houses, which have all been converted into B&Bs or flats.

At the closest tree, I put my arms around the trunk, struggling to reach the piece of string I'm wrapping round. Pressing my cheek against it until the bark digs in, ignoring the tang of urine floating up from the base, concentrating only on reaching that damn string. Once the MISSING poster is secured, I try not to look at the photograph on it, at the features identical to mine that smile at passers-by. From above me comes a soft hushing, now that there are enough leaves on the trees for them to brush gently against one another in the breeze. It's the first time I've heard that sound since autumn, and I hadn't realised how much I've missed it. Spring is a time for change and new beginnings. Perhaps this will be the year someone sees one of the posters and comes forward to solve the mystery that has haunted me for over half my life.

It's been almost twenty-five years since my identical twin disappeared without a trace. No matter how much time passes the pain never lessens, only changes tempo slightly so that somehow it has become possible to live with it. It is the pain that drives me to make this annual pilgrimage around my hometown, covering it in pictures of my sister every single year in the run-up to the anniversary of the night she was last seen.

Beside me the dogs pant, bored by hours of having to pause every few metres while I attach posters to lamp posts, trees, noticeboards, whatever is available. With no hands to spare, the dogs' leads are clamped between my thighs every time. Buddy is starting to pull sometimes, eyes to the air, looking for birds to terrorise. Scamp is Buddy's opposite in size and temperament, a skinny cockapoo to his bear-like Alsatian-cross, and she has her nose to the floor. No doubt in search of food that will only flare up her allergies and make her itch if she scoffs it. Then there's Buster, a shi-tzu poodle cross with an unbowable spirit, his curly tail constantly wagging, his proud chest always pushed forward. All three keep looking longingly over their shoulders, clearly wondering why they aren't going to the beach.

'Come on,' I urge, ready to walk on again. 'We'll go home soon – apart from anything else, my feet are throbbing. Just one more street, kids.'

Some people might think I'm mad talking out loud to my dogs, but who cares? Their tails wag in unison as if they understand every word. The sight of their happiness puts a smile on my face and gives me the energy to cross the road and trudge on, chased by the smell of salt and vinegar, seaweed, freshly-cooked donuts and stale beer that permeates this seaside town. The dogs get a second wind, now convinced we're heading to Tower Gardens park across the way. When Scamp realises we're not, she gives a snort of annoyance while I pull another poster from my backpack.

Will the person responsible for Leila's disappearance see any of them? I wonder. Have they ever spotted any over the years? Perhaps they dread the anniversary as much as I do, hating the thought of seeing my twin's picture and having to relive what they did. Perhaps it makes them fear that this time someone will come forward to the police and they'll end up behind bars. Perhaps guilt will get to them and they'll finally come forward to reveal what happened to her, if only to put an end to their own mental torture. I hope so.

I want them to rue the day they ever set eyes on my sister, I think, giving a drawing pin a vicious shove and spearing a poster onto a wooden noticeboard.

It's not much revenge, but it's all that's left for me after decades of waiting.

When Leila first went missing, I was more confused than anything.

'She's gone. She's gone!' screamed Mum. 'Why didn't you realise?'

'I didn't know. It wasn't my fault.' I backed away from her grasp, not wanting it to be true, wondering how, after all these years of togetherness, I had no sense of Leila's loss. Guilt crashing over me like a tsunami, part of me wondering: *have I wished this into being?*

All the other, bigger emotions broke through the numbness of shock later, but in those first few days simply getting my head around the fact my big sister had disappeared from my life was impossible. She was older than me by mere minutes, but it was enough to make her the boss of me. Every breath I'd taken previously, I'd known exactly where Leila was. Every time I'd turned around, there she was, and vice versa. All that changed that night.

From the very beginning, it was obvious to all in our tight-knit family that something – someone – had happened to Leila.

Suspicion fell on everyone. The police scrutinised our parents and even me. We'd been prepared for that. As prepared as you can be.

But I always knew it was my fault that my sister had left our lives. Whatever had happened to Leila, I blamed myself as much as the person who had made her vanish.

I start tying another poster to a tree in my annual penance.

MISSING.
HAVE YOU SEEN THIS PERSON?
LEILA HAWKINS WAS LAST SEEN ON 24 JUNE 1994.
IF YOU KNOW ANYTHING, PLEASE CALL…

I smooth a hand over it just as a scream rips the air. I drop the poster, and it hits my toe, bouncing off and rolling across the pavement. Jumpy at the best of times, Scamp leaps back and her lead pulls free from between my knees.

'Watch,' I command.

Scamp instantly freezes, eyes on mine. I get her under control again and quickly feed her a treat.

Another scream shatters the peace.

It's close. Hearing it again, I know exactly what it is and where it's coming from. Posters forgotten, we all run towards the sound.

Another shrill shriek.

There's a terrified dog somewhere close, and I need to get to it. We burst into the park, round a bank of trees and the lawned area of Tower Gardens lies before us. In the twilight, I can see a squat man is aiming a white trainer at a French bulldog that shivers at his feet. The poor thing is flattening itself into the grass in total submissive pose.

'Hey! Excuse me, sir!' The polite words are forced out in a show of calm I don't feel. I slow my pace, trying to appear casual. 'Sorry, excuse me, sir, can I help at all? I don't want to intrude, but I'm a dog behaviourist and if you're having trouble, I might be able to suggest some ways of tackling it.'

From the depths of my soul I dredge up a smile. I need to break this man's concentration on his dog, and in my experience extreme politeness can often shock people in this sort of situation into responding in kind. Not always, but it's worth a go if it will stop him landing a kick.

He glares at me. He's only a couple of inches taller than me, short, wiry, balding, with a ferret-face. Seems to take in the middle-aged woman radiating politeness. My sensible walking boots teamed with scruffy jeans. The long-sleeved T-shirt that used to be white but is now grubby from a morning rolling around with dogs, playing and training them for my business before coming out to canvas the town.

Nothing threatening to see here, I will him to think.

Finally, some of the muscles loosen in his face and shoulders, making him look less feral. His dark eyes dart around as if a bit embarrassed.

It's the smile that gets people, I know. That, and my relaxed body language and easy tone of voice. I've spent enough time with aggressive dogs to know what to look for and how to calm them and learned that people are remarkably similar. This guy looks the type to happily kick the crap out of his dog because he knows it's too scared to fight back, but he won't pick on a person because he's too cowardly. With someone like him it's all about the power.

'She giving you a few problems?' I ask.

The dog still looks scared witless, but instead of bending down and protecting it, as I want to, I know the best thing long-term is to win this man's trust and calm him down – for the good of the dog.

'Nothing I can't handle. It doesn't listen. Stupid thing.'

'I could help there. Would you be interested in some training lessons?'

'Get stuffed. I'm not spending any money on that.' The words huffed out. Chewing-gum breath hitting me: mint with a hint of halitosis and lager. 'Come on!'

He yanks on the lead. The dog doesn't move, still hunkered down in fear, so she's dragged along the grass by her neck as he pulls the lead and continues walking.

'Hey, sir, there's no need for that. Why don't I take her off your hands, eh?'

He turns. 'Why don't you wind your bloody neck in?'

'How about you calm down?' This is called out by a third person, a man, approaching us. He holds his hands up, but the swagger in his walk is calculated to intimidate, I'm certain. All he's going to do is escalate the situation.

'Screw you!' The dog owner turns. Swings his arm hard, the chain lead arching and bringing the helpless dog with it. She squeals again as all four paws lift from the ground momentarily. I've never wanted to hit someone so much. 'You want a piece, eh? Come on then.'

There's a huge difference in sound between a dog that's barking to show off and one that's warning you to back off or it's going to rip you to pieces. This man's tone has just changed. Time for a different tack, I decide.

'Safe,' I warn my dogs, while pulling something from my pocket and stepping towards the aggressor. A new shriek rends the air, ten times louder than any animal can make. I've set my rape alarm off right beside the man's ear. The dogs are prepared, thanks to the command word they've been taught – the man isn't and drops the lead to cover his ears. Before he can recover, I scoop the trembling creature up, as light as a bird, and walk away. Buddy, Buster and Scamp are running beside me.

At a safe distance, I turn back. Both men shake their heads, trying to dislodge the tinnitus. The sun is dropping rapidly towards the horizon, the sky above us a blaze of red, and I want to be well away from the isolation of this park before darkness falls.

'Sir, you need to listen to me. My finger is on the button of my phone, ready to call the police, whom I've pre-dialled. I am taking your dog away from you so that a vet can check it over, after which I will contact you to let you know where you can collect her from. I'll get your details from her microchip.'

'What? Mind your own business, you stupid—'

'But I must warn you,' I continue as if he hasn't spoken, 'that if you do take her back, I will be contacting the RSPCA and police with a view to having you prosecuted for what I've witnessed today. There may be other charges too, depending on what the vet finds.'

He glares, but his body language had shifted again at the mention of the police. It's probably not the first time he's had a run-in with them. He spits on the floor. Shrugs.

'Do what you want. I don't want the stupid mutt anyway; you're welcome to it. More trouble than it's worth.'

Flinging his arms out to the sides and puffing out his chest in one last 'big man' gesture, he turns on his heels and strides off, swinging his arms. Mock confidence: I can spot it a mile off.

The other man stays where he is, looking between me and the person he was ready to square up to. He's handsome, with soft grey eyes that seem more piercing against his brown skin, and he's well dressed for around here. This is a budget seaside town that doesn't attract the wealthy. My knowledge of fashion labels could be written on the back of a stamp, but even I know his coat is popular with snowboarders, and his hat is one of those merino wool ones, because I recognise the label after looking into buying one myself for cold days when I'm busy dog training. When I'd seen the price, I'd instantly changed my mind – it was more than I spent a week on food for me and my dogs.

'Are you all right?' His accent is southern and well spoken, but more than that there's something about him that indicates he's used to people listening when he talks.

I nod, ask him the same thing. He rubs his ears and raises his eyebrows. 'I'll live.'

'Thanks. For helping. The Good Samaritan thing.'

'Not that you needed me. I can see that now,' he replies drily. Or perhaps he's annoyed but too polite to say. I don't have time to decide which because the French bulldog is trembling against my chest, not making a sound. She's in shock. I need to get her to a vet. Repeating my thanks, I hurry away.

Only after I've disappeared round the corner do I allow myself to acknowledge that my heart is beating fast and my hands are slick with sweat from the confrontation. Fear always seems to come after action with me.

CHAPTER TWO

By the time I arrive home I'm shattered and sink into the sofa, letting my body slide into the cushions moulded to my shape after so many years. Buddy jumps up on one side of me, Scamp the other, while Buster leaps onto the back and settles down with his head beside mine, all three assuming their usual positions. My shoes and socks – bugger, there's a hole in one heel – are chucked on the ancient pale green Chinese-style rug, and I groan in relief as aching feet slide into a bowl of soothing hot water. I'd been planning to put in some foot soak salts I'd bought myself for Christmas a few months earlier, but squirted hand wash in instead because walking upstairs seemed too far. My head rolls back, neck too tired to hold it up a second longer. There's a long cobweb in the corner of the Artex ceiling. I wonder how long it's been there? I really should do some cleaning and tidying, but the dogs don't complain so there seems little point.

After a few minutes, the silence gets to me. Groping around blindly, I eventually find the TV remote under Scamp's leg. The sound of people is comforting, even though I still don't have the energy to move to see the screen.

What a day! I probably shouldn't have risked confronting that man, but to my mind fear doesn't stop anything or change anything, and it is about as effective as trying to solve global plastic pollution by tap-dancing. So I don't worry, I take action. People who've had the worst already happen in their life tend to go one of two ways: worry about everything because they realise they've no control over anything; or let worry go because they know they've no control over anything. I've done the latter. I simply make sure I'm as prepared as possible for any situation and then get on with it.

That doesn't stop the dreams, though. Nothing stops the dreams.

The rescued French bulldog is currently curled in a tight ball in a spare dog bed I've dug out for her. She's been checked over by a vet pal of mine, Farrah, who's given me a care plan and five different medications for the poor dog to take.

The atmosphere at the veterinary surgery had been more subdued than normal as I'd waited to be seen. A man sat alone in the corner, his body boneless in grief, tears rolling from red eyes down grey cheeks. A glance at the receptionist desk showed a candle burning; they always did this to warn visitors that someone in the surgery was saying goodbye to a beloved pet. The realisation brought tears to my own eyes. It's embarrassing that I can't see someone crying without doing the same myself.

Farrah's door opened and although her eyes slid over mine, she didn't acknowledge me. Instead, she sought out the man and called him forward with a sad tilt of her head. Beyond her I could just make out what looked like a Staffie, its broad back to me, swaddled in a raspberry-coloured fluffy blanket. Then the man's back blocked out the scene and the door closed shut behind him. The sound of him saying goodbye, whispered messages of love and promises that everything would be all right, that the pain would be over soon, filled the air through the thin walls. Then sobbing. I buried my hands and nose in the fur of my own dogs and told them how much I loved them and soothed my new companion as she shivered and quivered.

I still had tears in my eyes after the man left. I'd tried to catch his gaze, to convey somehow that I was sorry for his loss and understood his pain, but he'd stumbled past me, thanking the receptionist in a thick voice then leaving.

'Pet' doesn't come close to describing the deep connection of the soul that happens between a person and their animals. They are best friend and family all rolled into one. They never judge or criticise, never steamroller over ideas, and never lie. There is no cruelty there. They simply live in the moment. They are utterly innocent. So how could anyone have hurt this poor little French bulldog? That's the question I asked Farrah after she'd examined her. Her reply was a long, lost shake of the head.

'She's severely emaciated and dehydrated. Recently given birth, too, so she'll need antibiotics for the infection she's picked up. She isn't even microchipped, despite that being the law now – which means she's probably never been near a vet before. Reckon she's about three, and has already given birth a couple of times, I think.'

'Poor mite,' I replied. 'She's only three? Look at her eyes, they're so sad; she seems so much older.'

'French bulldogs are fashionable right now. Means there's an opportunity for unscrupulous gits to provide dogs for people too impatient to wait for proper breeders to have a litter. They're not even getting the dogs cheap. Paying through the nose doesn't guarantee it's a decent breeder. People should just do their homework before they buy from someone.'

Farrah ran a soothing hand over the dog, her fingers bumping over the vertebrae sticking out, before carrying on speaking. 'A couple of years ago it was pugs – you couldn't move for pugs with all kinds of health problems: being overbred or raised in terrible conditions. Don't even get me started on cockapoos.'

We sighed in unison. We've been friends since primary school, along with Leila; bonded by a shared love of animals. Farrah had been there for me during the tough first years of losing my sister. Through the period where I'd refused to go out, had barely spoken, and smashed every mirror I came across. No judgement. No special tone of voice. She just carried on like normal. It was Farrah who suggested I became a dog behaviourist, which helped turn my life around. For all that, we rarely socialise. There's no time for friends – apart from the canine kind.

Now, the latest addition to my fur family watches me from her new bed as I roll my head upright and curl my toes under the soapy water.

'Bloody hell, that's better,' I groan.

My feet are throbbing a little less now, but tomorrow they'll have to do the same distance again and will probably protest even more. Barely a fraction of the town has been covered with flyers yet, and it will take another three or four days, at least, to get everywhere. The first time I'd done it people had volunteered to help. The local newspaper had done a big front-page splash about it, all the businesses in the area had been proud to display them, and neighbours near and far had put them in their windows. The whole town had asked: *Where is Leila Hawkins?*

Everyone else's lives have moved on, though, and now the only person interested in remembering Leila is me.

The landline rings, the dogs leap up, barking, and I jump a mile, sloshing water everywhere. Swearing gently, I hurry to the phone, doing a twisting motion across the carpet in a makeshift attempt to dry my feet. The phone is an ancient beige rotary dial one that was made before push buttons were invented, let alone caller display, so I've no clue who it is until I answer.

On picking up, there's an intake of breath at the other end. Expectant.

'Is that Stella Hawkins? My name's Penny-Sue Wolfe, and I'm calling about your missing sister. I think I can help you.'

My stomach does a little flip, but a few deep breaths soon calm me because no leads have ever come to anything so far. Still, I pick up the pen and notepad I keep by the phone, just in case someone should ever call with information – a rarity these days. There's an undertone of excitement in my voice while asking the woman to continue.

'I'm reaching out to you from a production company.' Penny-Sue says a name I barely catch and asks if I've heard of it. But before I can say no she's talking again. 'We make documentaries for Netflix – you know, the true crime ones? Very popular right now – and I stumbled across the tragic case of your missing sister and, well, it's heartbreaking, isn't it?'

The pen goes back in its place. Disappointment sinks through me. This woman doesn't know anything; quite the opposite, she wants information.

'From what I understand, you've campaigned tirelessly to raise awareness of Leila's disappearance. That must have been so tough for you – it was, wasn't it? Honestly, my heart just, oh, it melted when I saw your unending work over years and years. So that's what made me think this would be a perfect opportunity, and I wondered if you'd like to take part?'

'Take part?'

'In a documentary series investigating your sister's disappearance. Raise awareness of Leila's case. A tribute to her life, details of what's known about the case so far. Interviews with people in the know. It might bring some fresh information forward. It's the twenty-fifth anniversary coming up, no?'

'Um, yes. No, don't do that.' I wave at Buddy, who is drinking the soapy water I've been soaking my feet in.

'Excuse me?'

'Sorry, I didn't mean you. What were you saying?'

'The twenty-fifth anniversary would be the ideal hook, you see – it's a great excuse for us to revisit this cold case and, hopefully, warm it back up for you. Would the documentary be something you'd be interested in? There isn't the budget for a payment, I'm afraid, but the programme would reach an international audience. I appreciate it's a huge, emotionally charged decision, though.'

Screw my emotions; the thought of reaching so many people is all that matters. There's a potential reach of millions. Around the world. Which means no hiding place for the person responsible. Surely this will lead to the longed-for breakthrough. It's a shame about the lack of fee, but it doesn't make a difference compared to how great an opportunity this is. It would have been nice to get something, though. Printing thousands of flyers, phone calls, paying for the *Where's Leila?* website's domain name and upkeep, travelling around the country chasing (admittedly rare these days) sightings, it all adds up, and although I do okay as a dog behaviourist, I'm not exactly rolling in it. I only get by because I'm mortgage free after moving into Mum and Dad's house, left to me in their will. Technically, it should have been split two ways, as they'd never changed their will and taken Leila out, just in case. They never gave up hope.

This documentary could mean answers. Real, solid answers.

Still I hesitate. It'll mean in-depth interviews with journalists desperate to find a new angle to the story. They'll want titbits of information not offered up before, which plunge into my and my family's privacy. There will be a new wave of weirdos getting in touch, offering false leads and fake hope. Conspiracy theorists and whackos who tell lies about my sister for no other reason than their own entertainment.

None of that matters, though, not in comparison to the possible positives. It's too good an opportunity to pass on; probably the last chance of a breakthrough because not only has Leila disappeared but so has her story, considered old news not worth repeating. I need to find my sister's remains. For Leila. For our parents who died never knowing what happened to their eldest daughter.

The pen gets picked up again.

'Tell me more about what you want.'

CHAPTER THREE

My house has been invaded. A small team move in synchronicity, like a murmuration of starlings, around every nook and cranny, plucking and placing my things around to make shots more visually pleasing, taking light readings, and generally being busy doing things I don't have a clue about. Thank goodness I dusted away that cobweb on the ceiling and washed the dog blankets on the sofa.

I sit in a corner of the living room with my mouth desiccating at the thought of appearing on camera. This isn't the first time I've been filmed, of course – at one point it became an almost regular event – but it's been a long time now. Fifteen years or so, in fact; the last time any fuss was made about Leila it was the ten-year anniversary, and then it was only the local paper that ran a story.

It's not just the interviewing itself that's the problem, it's catching it on the television or radio later. Seeing myself, hearing myself, is too weird. Because for a moment that makes my heart jump so hard it actually hurts, my body and mind react as if it's my sister I'm seeing. Despite all these years passing, that will still happen. From whenever the moment of awareness began in the womb, we shared it. We were identical: one fertilised egg that decided to split in two to form a pair, and because of that there seems to be no way of overriding the instinct that my other half must be out there somewhere. It's a feeling that's always with me, but seeing myself on television makes it worse.

There's no point in worrying, though; the only solution is to get on with it, I remind myself, as I'm hooked up to a microphone by a blonde woman, who smiles with neat efficiency. This is Penny-Sue Wolfe. Younger than she'd sounded, and clearly fiercely ambitious and good at her job. She uses terrifying phrases like: 'I'll ping you an email', 'let's touch base', and 'end of play.' It's quite possible she does 'blue-sky thinking'.

Things have moved quickly since that first phone call just a fortnight earlier. Incredibly so. I'd always assumed television programmes took years to get organised, filmed, then transmitted, but that hasn't been the case with this production.

'Most crime docs get made at the last minute so that they're as up-to-date as possible at transmission,' Penny-Sue explained when I'd asked. 'The idea might be bubbling away for a year before but, by the time the channel has signed it off, it could be just a couple of months for us to organise. Pretty much everyone we contacted for interviews has agreed to take part in this one, so we'll definitely hit the anniversary and optimise coverage. It's perfect. Don't worry.'

One person who hasn't agreed to take part is Mary, my mum's best friend. She's been like a second mother to me since my parents passed away. She doesn't approve of the documentary because she thinks I already spend too much time living in the past and should instead embrace the future.

'Darling, I understand why you want to do this, of course I do, but it's time for you to let Leila go and grab life for yourself,' she said when I asked her about taking part in the documentary. Her diamond earrings trembled with passion as she spoke. 'Living in the past can make people stupid. It can trip you up if you're not careful. Spoils what you've got, making you blind to what's coming. I'm only telling you for your own good, sweetie.'

'But this *is* my chance to grab life,' I argued. 'Once I find my sister and lay her to rest.'

'And what if that never happens?'

I didn't have an answer to that – never do. We've had this argument so many times now and we're both entrenched in our views. So I'm ignoring Mary and doing this documentary, come what may.

Penny-Sue had been disappointed by the lack of involvement of such a close family friend, especially one who was a bit of a celeb back in the day, but she recovered quickly. As producer it's her job to pull things together no matter what, though, I suppose. Her team hang on her every word. There's researcher/assistant Keshini, camera person Pete, and sound person Josie. Ironically, Josie never seems to speak, just smiles and nods, while Pete pulls at his beard, looking lost without a lens to peer through. So far, the person interviewing me hasn't been around. Euan Vincent is his name and, although I've never heard of him, Penny-Sue assures me he's 'huge' in real crime documentaries. I'm more of a book person, myself.

Penny-Sue is currently eyeing up a framed photograph of Mary and Mum from the early Eighties. Mary, the ever-glamorous former singer who'd had a couple of hits back in the late Sixties and Seventies, is wearing an electric blue jumpsuit, with fluorescent bangles running up her arms. Mum is wearing a beige summer dress and no make-up. The picture is moved into the kitchen, out of the way.

They've been rearranging the family photos to make sure they're in shot and asking if there are others that could be put out. I pretend there aren't because over the years I've given so much of us away. It's important to hold a little back that's just for me. There has to be some privacy. Besides, half the photos of Leila and me as babies are black and white and make us look like ghosts because the Polaroids' contrast has faded. There are only a handful of us as newborns, but all that can be made out now are little blobs for bodies and heads. There is one I had specially doctored so that it's now crystal clear. It's of us aged about two. I'm sitting on an upside-down washing basket in the garden, gazing down at my dungarees, which are covered in ice cream. Leila is trying to wipe it off me to eat it herself. The framed picture is usually beside my bed, but I've hidden it away, along with snaps from our eleventh birthday, the year we were given a camera to share between us. There are so many photographs of us dancing around, showing off in front of the camera that birthday.

It seems silly now, in this age of cameras on every phone, but at the time it was such a luxury for kids our age. Every time Leila slid the button across to make the flash warm up it made a high-pitched whine that she always mimicked. Once it was ready a red light would glow. Then a photograph, snap! But you wouldn't know if it had turned out or not until you'd sent the whole film away and received the prints a few weeks later. At least half of them blurry and sporting stickers with quality warnings on, and you'd all stare at them trying to work out what on earth you'd been attempting to capture. Now everything is digital and instant, but back then waiting to see what you got was half the fun. Pictures are precious, and I don't want to share them with the world. Instead, I've removed all but the ones that the world has already seen. The one on the poster, the one the police used, and the one of the two of us taken that night. All the others are buried like treasure at the bottom of my wardrobe.

The assistant, Keshini, comes over and takes me from my thoughts by once again suggesting I put on make-up, despite my protests about normally only wearing moisturiser and maybe some mascara if my eyes are looking particularly piggy. She's worrying about the dark circles beneath my eyes, I bet. The dreams about Leila are always worse when the anniversary is approaching, and I often have to cope on a couple of hours of sleep.

'I don't want to look like I'm going nightclubbing or something,' I say. 'This is meant to be a serious documentary about my sister's disappearance, not a fashion show. If people think I look rough, I don't honestly give a toss.'

'You won't look too done up on screen, don't worry.' She prof-fers a mirror, but I shake my head. 'I take it you don't wear much usually?' She's quirky and kind, with black hair in a sleek bob, eyes outlined with blue eyeshadow and black kohl, her lips bright red to match her red dress with large polka dots on, like Minnie Mouse. The yellow Doc Martens turn it from kitsch to cool.

'Dogs are never bothered by whether my lipstick matches my outfit, so it seems a bit of a waste of effort,' I joke. The truth crowds, though, and comes blurting out. 'Actually, I rarely look in the mirror completely. If I'm doing my hair, I look at my hair. If I'm doing my make-up, I look at my eyes, lips, whatever, but I rarely look at the whole unless I want to see Leila.'

'Oh, gosh, I'm so sorry. I hadn't even thought how hard that must be. I wondered why you kept your eyes closed when I was brushing your hair.'

'When she was alive we'd sometimes sit opposite each other and have a good long stare at each other's face. It was better than a mirror. A mirror doesn't pull faces.'

'Sounds surreal!'

'Surreal and funny.'

Penny-Sue has paused beside us, listening. She squeezes my shoulder. 'Sorry, but would you mind repeating that on camera? It's just a lovely little touch. Brings home your pain. You know, as a lone twin. It'll really get the audience.'

She bustles away, leaving me blinking rapidly. Keshini shakes her head. 'Don't mind Penny-Sue. She's great at her job, but sometimes forgets that behind the story is an actual person.'

I decide to go after her to put my mind at ease. There's no sign of her anywhere, though. As I pass the door of the downstairs cloakroom, I notice the door is slightly ajar, as if someone has pulled it shut behind them and not realised it has a tendency to spring open thanks to a sticky latch. Through the gap I can hear a man talking.

'…bloody better work.'

'Don't worry, it's all in hand.' That's Penny-Sue. 'She seems accommodating. It'll be easy to charm her if we run into problems.'

'No problems. There's too much at stake for—'

A heavy thump overhead, then a crash as something falls to the floor upstairs. The voices go quiet. I take a couple of backward steps, so that when Penny-Sue peers out I don't look like I've been eavesdropping.

'Oh, Stella! There you are,' she gasps as though she's been looking for me, not the other way around. 'What on earth's happening?'

More thudding, heading down the stairs. 'It's Buddy, chasing flies. He always does this…'

Buddy races in. Ears twitching, eyes searching, panting but happy. Turns tail and races out again, leaving Scamp barking in his wake.

Penny-Sue leads me by the elbow away from the cloakroom and whoever she was talking to. 'I think they're going to have to go in the garden during filming. Okay?'

Clearly, it's not a suggestion.

'Okay. If we're lucky, they'll do a spot of impromptu gardening instead of barking and howling. If I'm *really* lucky, they'll dig beside that patch of thistles that's sprouting at the bottom of the lawn. But listen, I wanted to talk to you—'

A man approaches us from an angle planned to disguise where he's come from. Shame I saw him slide from the cloakroom and sidle around the room to the other door first. So, this is the man who's got 'too much at stake'. As I turn towards him there's something familiar about him. Maybe I've seen him on television. It's only when he's up close that I realise where I've seen him before.

'You? What are you doing here?'

'You recognise me then?' he smiles. It's a showbiz smile, wide and charming, and framed by a neatly trimmed beard that accentuates the whiteness of his teeth.

'Of course I do, what with me not being blind. Thanks again for the whole Good Samaritan act at the park.'

'No problem. I'm sorry my attempts to rescue you were so maladroit.'

I don't actually know what that means, but I'm not going to give him the satisfaction of asking, so I nod, smile, and tell myself to look it up as soon as I can.

Penny-Sue looks between the two of us. 'You've met Euan, then? He'll be interviewing you.' Something seems to catch her eye and she slides away, leaving us standing awkwardly together. Close up and without the drama of the other week to distract me, I can study Euan. He's younger than me by a good ten years at least and has the air of someone who has made it. Cool, calm confidence exudes from the large gestures, the straight back, the easy laugh, the cheeky winks that accompany the attractively wonky smile.

Interesting that his nails are bitten so badly.

'Where is the dog? Did it go back to its owner?' he asks.

'She's been with me for the last fortnight. The owner contacted the police, but when I explained what had happened they weren't interested, especially because I'd already given him some money.'

'You bought her? I'm amazed.'

As I explain it was worth it to shut the owner up and secure her for good after he'd tracked me down and started playing merry hell, Euan starts looking around. 'Where is she now? I'd like to say hello, given my part in saving her. A tiny part, but still.'

'Fifi – that's what I called her – is being looked after by a friend who's a vet. I thought the filming might upset her, as she's still finding her confidence. So… are you going to explain what you're doing here? Do you live around here then?'

He laughs. 'Gosh, no.' *It's not that bad here.* 'I was checking out the area, in case you said yes when Penny-Sue approached you. I wanted to do a bit of a location recce, get a feel for the place. I didn't realise it was you until just now. It all seems rather serendipitous, though, doesn't it?'

'Serendipitous or suspicious.' I'm only half joking.

He helps me herd Buddy, Scamp and Buster outside, though he seems wary of Buddy.

'He's the biggest, but not the one you need to worry about,' I say. 'It's the cute-looking fluff-ball who'll give you what for if you give her reason.'

'Really? This one? No, she looks so sweet.'

'That's what lets her get close enough to do damage.'

Once the dogs are shut outside, Euan invites me to sit on my sofa and starts talking through how the interview process will work. In professional mode, he smiles less but more genuinely. He speaks gently but not so quietly that it feels like I'm gravely ill, and he doesn't do the patronising head tilt of sorrow that so many do when discussing Leila. Although Penny-Sue has already walked me through the process, the journalist says he likes to do it, too, just to be sure that the people he's interviewing are comfortable before the cameras start rolling. He tells me for seven to ten days they will interview me here, in my home, as well as getting shots of me at various other locations.

'It will feel a bit tiring sometimes, as if you're going over things several times, but we need to be sure to get enough material, and to ensure you're at ease in front of the lens,' he says.

Discomfort twitches through me: that annoyance that the appeals somehow always focus as much on me, the left-behind twin, than they do on finding Leila. I have no desire to be the centre of attention.

He seems to sense my thoughts.

'I need to know how to get the best out of you so that you get the best out of the experience,' he says. 'We get one shot at this. Hopefully, it will solve the mystery of your missing sister. I'm going to be asking you lots of questions, but if anything gets too much for you and you feel like you need a break, just let me know. Okay? This must be so difficult for you.'

'That's kind of you, but I'm used to interviews. My technique is to always use the same words, as if talking from a script. That way it's possible to almost – almost – get through without thinking too much about what I'm actually saying… and that helps stop the feelings bubbling to the surface.'

That way there's less risk of breaking down and making a fool of myself in public.

'Good way of keeping the emotions at bay,' he agrees. 'Of course. Let me get you a cup of tea.'

Moments later he's back. He's even thought to get me a biscuit. It's strange: he's doing all the right things and saying all the right words, but something about his body language is off. Being a canine behaviourist means I spend a lot of time studying tiny clues in a dog's body to work out why they're doing what they are. I also work with owners who are often unwittingly the cause of their pet's problems. It all means I'm better than the average person at reading people. Sometimes it feels more like I'm training the human. Right now, I'm certain this journalist is trying to placate me but also has something up his sleeve.

Fair enough. The minute he tries, he'll realise I'm not the type to be manipulated or lied to.

*

The lights are hotter than I remember. Or maybe it's fear. Or my age. I'm in my mid-forties now, and probably knocking on the door of perimenopause. Perhaps this is my first hot flush, which will be yet another marker of time that is experienced by me and not Leila. The camera lens is scrutinising me. I rub at my eyes then Euan Vincent gives me another encouraging smile.

'Are you ready? We can wait, if you want.'

The room hushes.

'Rolling,' says Pete from behind the camera.

'Stella, tell me, what's it been like for you since your sister disappeared?' asks the journalist.

'Tough. Awful. When we said goodbye to my sister that night I had no clue I'd never see her again.'

'Uh-huh. What do you say to people who say it's your fault?'

I'm on my feet so quickly I knock my tea over. The ceramic bounces off the heavy wood of the coffee table with a sharp crack as the handle flies free of the body. Outside, the dogs bark, suddenly alert. Buddy's growl is low as a chainsaw and just as menacing.

'Get out,' I say. 'Now.'

CHAPTER FOUR

He holds his hands up like he's surrendering, but the apology is as fake as the designer handbags tourists buy on the seafront. Everyone in the room is frozen around us. Penny-Sue is gripping a clipboard so hard it might snap in two. No one speaks though, except for Euan.

'Apologies. Seriously, sorry for ambushing you, but I had to push you to see how you'd handle it. That's part of my job: to ask the tough questions. No point going ahead with filming if you fall apart too easily.' He shrugs like it doesn't matter, but his eyes can't meet mine. 'It was a business decision, pragmatic – and honestly, would make life easier for you, too, by saving you a lot of pain down the line, if you can't handle it.'

'I think you know exactly how tough I am, or have you forgotten that when you tried to rescue me like some knight in shining armour you discovered I wasn't a swooning damsel? Is that what asking the shitty questions is about? Punishment for me bruising your ego?'

'My ego has nothing to do with this.' Finally, he looks me in the eye. Smiles. Sheepish. 'Asking that question that way was a calculated risk to see how you'd react. Now I know. It *was* a shitty thing to do and won't happen again. I promise.'

'Oh, well, if you promise you must be telling the truth,' I growl. 'Do you know why I'm a dog trainer? Because dogs are trustworthy; people aren't.'

'You have my word I won't ask that question again, even though you know it's what a lot of people will be wondering.'

'A lot of people can go f—'

'You said yourself you always answer questions the same way, devoid of emotion. That's no good for this documentary, and if you can't handle showing people the raw emotion they need in order to connect with you then there's no point carrying on. Will you let us continue filming? Or do you think this will be too hard?'

I swallow. Seconds tick by, everyone watching me. Finally, I nod and the whole room seems to exhale. The threadbare apology isn't the reason why I decide to let the interview go ahead; it's the thought that I can't let such a huge opportunity to find Leila go to waste. No matter what the provocation. No matter the personal cost to me. Whatever it takes, there will never be too high a cost.

But I do issue a warning.

'I agreed to do a documentary with you about my sister. I didn't agree to make a window into my soul. Don't push it. You pull another stunt like that and I'll pull the plug on the whole thing. There'll be no third chance.'

Just before the cameras start rolling again, Euan leans forward.

'It's not too late to pull out. If this is too tough.'

'Why does it feel like that's what you want?'

'Not at all, not at all. I just… Look, I know I don't know you, but journalists have to be pretty good at getting a feel for people instantly and you're tough – I know that, it was obvious from the moment I first met you, and from the way you're refusing to back down now – but I get the feeling you're more vulnerable than you make out. I may seem like a pig but I promise you I'm actually trying to look out for you. But…' he leans back, pauses for a heartbeat, 'but of course I respect your decision.'

He nods to the cameraman, who starts filming.

'Why are you taking part in this documentary?' he asks. 'Do you hope to find Leila and be reunited with her?'

Folding my arms, I glare back at him. 'There's no hope. I keep going because what else am I supposed to do? I can't stop.'

For the next few hours Euan questions me. He's gentle, persuasive and not at all judgemental. I'm thrown by him, I admit. One minute he's a gentleman coming to the rescue, the next he's trying to sabotage me, then claiming he did it all for my good; he's got more sides than a Rubik's Cube.

When we break for lunch, I go to the kitchen to start making tea for everyone, but Keshini explains with a smile that it's her job. Happy to leave her to it, I wander into the living room. Domesticity isn't my strong suit. Euan goes to help her and from my sofa vantage point I notice Keshini stiffen. Is there a problem between them? I remember that whispered conversation between Penny-Sue and him and wonder if the person they were referring to was Keshini, perhaps about to make a complaint of sexual harassment. That would explain whatever nerves are causing him to bite his nails. But then she starts touching her hair, constantly tucking a loose strand behind her ear. Her cheeks are glowing chestnut, and she seems almost giddy. It doesn't take a body language expert to work out she fancies him. He can tell, judging from the way he is extra polite and maintains a professional distance between them, uncertainty hovering behind the smile. Smirking to myself, I wonder if an office romance will blossom during the time it takes to film the documentary.

It's times like this I miss Leila. I still find myself planning to tell her things and imagining how we'll laugh together, then lurching into reality.

To take my mind off it, I try to work out the Euan puzzle.

*

We've filmed every single day for a week. Thanks to the crew being so lovely, I'm feeling comfortable in front of the camera now. Most of the time has been spent in the house, capturing me tiptoeing through memories and trying to avoid the sharp ones that will cut me. Looking through old photographs; standing in the bedroom Leila and I used to share, the one I slept in until my parents died; sifting through old newspaper cuttings of the original investigation.

We've all been rubbing along quite nicely. Keshini started sitting beside me during lunch breaks, probably told to keep an eye on me in case I got rebellious ideas again, but she's a lovely girl, easy to talk to, and I've begun to look forward to our little chats. She's crazy about Euan, asking my advice on how to get his attention, but what can I tell her? I'm terminally single.

'How did you end up in this job?' I ask when I find out she lives in Mereford.

'There was an advert in the local paper online for a researcher and general assistant. It's only for a couple of weeks while they film here, but it might turn into more. I want to work in TV – behind the camera not in front.'

'Ah, so this is your big break, hopefully.'

She crosses her fingers and grins in reply.

Being forced into company has taken some adjustment, but I'm starting to enjoy it. In breaks I've been putting the radio on, as I'm not keen on silence, and somehow we've all ended up playing a game where we try to be the first to name a song from the opening notes. Even Josie, always listening but rarely speaking, joins in. The station I put on plays a lot of club classics from the Eighties through the Noughties, and it surprises me how many the team know because Pete and I are the only two old enough to have danced to them when they were released. Euan and I are the quickest by a long shot, and it's become a point of pride to beat him because I'm not going to have some kid beat me at my own game.

Today is the last day of filming, as we've got through everything faster than expected. It's been a long time since the house was full of laughter and going back to the quiet will be odd. We're not inside at the moment, though. I'm in Tower Gardens pretending to put up the MISSING posters. Penny-Sue and Euan explained last night that they need it to be caught on camera. I'd frowned.

'They always go up immediately before Easter,' I'd explained. 'I need to be sure they're seen by as many tourists as possible, so I always put them up at the start of the holiday season, even though it's a couple of months before the anniversary.'

'We'll still need the sequence, it's too important to miss out,' replied Penny-Sue.

'Trust us; this is an important scene.' Euan nodded.

So while I stroll up to the bandstand, the crew hide in the bushes, trying not to trample on the recently emerged bluebells, and film me from a distance like a stalker. Penny-Sue says they'll be doing these shots from a couple of different angles to see which looks best when it's all edited and cut together.

It's strange making a show of putting up the MISSING poster. Leila is smiling back at me, as ever, and without the urgency of having to get round an entire town as quickly as possible, I find myself lingering. Stroking a hand over her face and letting my mind drift back to the last time I saw her. My flesh goosebumps despite the warmth of the day. If only I could go back in time and change what happened.

The photo on the poster is beautiful – her chin down, as ever, but the eyes and smile are confident. The police had cropped out her two pals, who'd been standing behind her grinning. It had been taken that last night. Dad's fiftieth birthday party. The last birthday the family ever celebrated.

A movement in the corner of my eye comes at the same time as a shout of warning. I look up to see Euan striding forward towards Fifi's former owner. Tommy Rogers doesn't break his own stride, though, and saunters over to me, shoulders back, a swagger that would make Liam Gallagher jealous. His bright white trainers shine in the sun's rays. He leans in towards me. So close I can smell him. Chewing gum, lager, a hint of dog that makes me suspect he has a replacement for Fifi. There's also a layer of cheap aftershave, and I wonder which poor unfortunate he's trying to impress.

'Got your guard dog with you,' he whispers in my ear as he reaches past me, intimate as a lover, and pulls the poster down. 'I know who you are. I know all about you. You want to watch that what happened to your sister doesn't happen to you.'

Vicious brown eyes sparkle. He feels totally confident and in control, despite the crew coming towards him. If he were a dog, right now he'd be dry humping me like a Yorkshire terrier showing a cushion who's boss.

'How's your hearing? Recovered?' I smile.

Euan and everyone else arrive by my side before he can answer. He looks around at them and laughs.

'I think you should leave,' says Euan.

'Just catching up with Stella here. Asking how my dog is.'

'*My* dog, the one I bought from you after you overbred and underfed her to the point of malnutrition, is doing just fine, thanks.'

He chuckles, shakes his head. 'Be seeing you, Stella.' Makes to hand the poster back to me. I don't reach for it and am rewarded with a twitch of disappointment before he covers it with a smile as friendly as a hacksaw as he tears the paper in two. He walks away without a backward glance.

Finally, Euan speaks. 'He knows your name?'

'How else would I have bought his dog? Anyway, I'm not exactly difficult to find. I make it easy, in case anyone has information about Leila.'

Keshini scoots between the two of us and turns her back on me. 'Euan, you were so brave confronting him. My heart's racing, here, feel.'

Penny-Sue claps her hands together. 'Right then, are you okay, Stella? Good, in that case let's crack on. If we're lucky, we can get finished early today.'

*

Filming is over, for me at least; although the crew have another week ahead of them, interviewing various people around the country. The dogs are overjoyed to have their home to themselves again. The first thing Scamp does is rub her face all over the rug, bum up in the air, making huffing noises of joy. Buddy and Buster jump straight onto their spots on the sofa, while Fifi follows me around. I turn on the radio, but there's no one to play name that tune with, so I turn it off. Life is back to normal. Now all I can do is wait and hope the documentary creates a breakthrough.

CHAPTER FIVE

Documentary Transcript
Title: *Missing: The Twin Who Never Came Back*

[White writing on black background.]

*The following is an investigation into true events. Past events and
accounts have been dramatized but all interview testimony is real.*

*[Fades to elevated view of the seaside town of Mereford. Camera is
moving from the seafront along the roads to the town, the houses, then
the fields beyond, so flat you can see for miles.]*

Voiceover – archive news broadcast. Reporter 1: Police in
Mereford are investigating the disappearance of Leila Hawkins.
The 19-year-old probationary police constable, who is well-known
in the town, went missing on Friday and hasn't been seen since
leaving her father's 50th birthday party. Family say it's out of
character.

[Cut to archive image of a line of police searching sand dunes.]

Voiceover – archive news broadcast. Reporter 2: Hope is
fading for identical twin Leila Hawkins, who has been missing
for a week now. Volunteers joined police to search the area. There
have been no sightings of her and a source close to the police told
us they are now treating the case as a possible abduction. They are
said to be "extremely concerned" for her welfare.

[Cut to archive clip of news interview with Detective Inspector John Glossop.]

DI Glossop: It's frustrating that justice has not yet been done, despite four months of hard work by the team. But we will continue to work hard to find out what happened to Leila. She was one of our own, and we won't rest until the truth is uncovered.

I would urge anyone with information, no matter how small, to come forward. Loyalties and relationships change over time and there may be someone who didn't feel able to speak to police at the time, but who may be in a position to do so now.

[Cut to piece to camera. Euan, walking on Mereford beach as he speaks.]

Euan: "Loyalties and relationships change over time." That's one of the reasons why I've decided to investigate this tragic story, in the hope that after twenty-five years someone will finally come forward with new information. My name is Euan Vincent, and I've spent my entire career as an investigative reporter. I'm hoping to lend my expertise to crack this case.

So, what are the known facts?

In June 1994, Leila Hawkins mysteriously disappeared. No arrests have ever been made. No body has ever been found. What happened to her?

Someone goes missing every ninety seconds in the UK. It rarely makes the news. But something about this case caught the media's attention across the world. Perhaps because Leila was an identical twin, leaving behind her mirror image to go on without her. Or the fact she was a police constable (albeit a probationary one) at the time she went missing; someone who was training to keep others safe; someone strong, capable, and aware, who had received training in defending herself, wasn't able to stop something terrible from happening. Perhaps it was because she and her sister were photographed together living life to the full, just an hour before she was last seen – a photograph that has now become etched on an entire nation's psyche.

Most likely, it's because of that famous mistake that everyone links to this case. A silly, innocuous mix-up that happens to any one of us from time to time. It's that human element of "there but for the grace of God" that always captured my attention and ensured this case stuck in my mind for all this time. My fascination with it is one of the reasons I decided to become an investigative journalist myself.

Now I've come to the traditional seaside town of Mereford to look into the unsolved case. I've spoken to Leila's remaining family, her friends, and officers in the original investigative team and uncovered an explosive tale. Were crucial mistakes made by detectives from the very beginning? Could the pressure of living two lives have led Leila to run away to start a new life – or even end it? Or did someone in her tight circle of friends and family have reason to kill her?

After twenty-five years, I'm going to try to discover what really happened to Leila Hawkins.

[Euan turns and looks out to sea. Camera pulls back. Fades out.]
[Fades in. Interior of Stella's home.]
Stella: My childhood? It was great. Mum and Dad were always singing and laughing, and they played practical jokes on each other a lot. Just silly little things. They had both been performers at one time, so had quite big, confident personalities. And obviously, Leila and I were inseparable. People couldn't tell us apart; not until they got to know us well. We always did things as a family though: ice-skating, swimming, football, kite-flying on the beach. Baking cakes was a big thing: one of my earliest memories is of Leila and me in the kitchen with Mum, stirring a bowl of cake mix and making a wish – Mum always made us make a wish. She said food should be made with love. There was a lot of love in our house.

We'd been very much wanted. Mum and Dad had been trying for a good few years and almost given up hope of having a baby when suddenly she got pregnant with two. They chose names for us that complemented each other. Leila because it means "night"; it's Arabic, I think. My name, Stella, is Latin or some such for "star". So you see she was the night and I was the stars; different parts of the same thing, one never without the other. That sums us up, really.

[Cut to camera panning over bathroom cabinet's contents.]

Voiceover – Euan: The clutter in the house, the half-empty box of St John's Wort replaced by two bottles of 5% CBD Oil, spoke to me of mild depression managed by someone too strong or too stubborn to ask for help. Someone used to coping alone. Stella is the identical twin left behind to cope with the disappearance of her missing sister. She's found it tough.

Stella: My being a twin-less twin made life harder for everyone. I developed claustrophobia. Around twelve months after Leila disappeared, we held a memorial and also I started seeing a therapist, though not for long. I was told my claustrophobia was a result of trauma of loss.

It was painful in its own unique way for my parents watching me change and get older, and so by association, my sister with me. There was no: "We'll never hear her voice again" in our house because we did, every time I spoke. For bittersweet split seconds they could kid themselves that she was still with them. Later, every time I laughed, there was Leila's throaty laugh.

Did it make it better or worse for them having me as a constant reminder? I never could decide, and even now I have no idea what it must have been like for them. But the indecision made me quieter. I got into the habit of not speaking, and of trying to keep out of their way as much as possible, because the last thing they needed was to be hurt even more after what they'd been through.

[Footage of stormy sky.]

Voiceover – Euan: June 24, 1994 was a hot one, with the mercury hitting 31 degrees Celsius. There had been a flurry of electrical storms over the previous days, which continued into the following weeks. That Friday night was no exception. There was torrential rain from around 8.30 p.m., with squally conditions creating hazardous driving as winds gusted up to 60mph.

[Interior. Stella. The microphone has trouble picking up the words at first. Just off camera the voice of the interviewer can be heard, prompting Stella, encouraging her to carry on a little louder. She clears her throat, shuffles in her seat before settling again with a cough and talking again, this time louder.]

Stella: Dad had been really excited about his party. Mum had made a cake in the shape of a guitar for him because he used to play. That's how they'd met, actually, at a gig. All my parents' friends were there, along with cousins, uncles, everyone we knew. All celebrating together. Having a drink.

[The voice is still devoid of emotion, face blank.]

We had identical coats. Leila and me. Of course. We hadn't planned to, but we'd both turned up wearing matching brand-new coats, bought separately.

[The picture cuts to a different angle. This one shows Stella's hands. Clutching a tissue so hard her knuckles are white, her fingers almost blue at the tips.]

Leila took my coat by accident and I took hers. It was just a stupid mistake.

[The scene changes to a re-enactment by actors.]

Voiceover – Stella: When she got home by taxi, Leila reached the front door and must have realised she couldn't get into her flat. She and her boyfriend had only moved in there a couple of months before. She didn't have a mobile phone – people didn't, as a matter of course, back then. She probably tried to reach a phone box to call me, us. Or maybe she grabbed a passing minicab to get to our parents' place, which was, I don't know, about two miles away? We don't know what she did or what happened, really. We just know she was never seen again. Maybe she was daft enough to accept a lift, but I can't believe that. She was confident, but she wasn't stupid.

Back at home, I realised my mistake and got my boyfriend to take me to her flat, but that wasn't until the next morning. If I'd just realised earlier…

Euan: When you reached Leila's flat in the morning, there was no sign of her?

[Stella's head wobbles no.]

Euan: What did you do?

Stella: We rang the doorbell. Convinced she must've got in somehow because, otherwise, she'd have called us or got a cab home to our parents' house. Even if she hadn't had enough money, she'd have known someone in the house could cover it. When there was no answer we rang again, hammered on the door. Then I remembered, like an idiot, that I'd got the key and let us in. The flat was empty.

Euan: Did you know immediately something was wrong? Did the fact it was your twin give you any extra insight, do you think?

Stella: Did I get a psychic feeling, you mean? No, because we're not characters in a TV programme.

There was no sign of her. The coat was nowhere to be seen. The bed not slept in. The toothbrush and deodorant were still there, and the bags she used if she overnighted anywhere. After checks, the police always worked on the theory she never made it inside. I think that's right.

After two years the search was downgraded. The case left open but scaled back to the point of nonexistence. We knew then that it was down to us as a family to keep Leila's name at the forefront of people's minds.

Mum and Dad always said that when they woke in the morning the first thing they thought of every time was Leila. She was the first thing on their mind every morning, the last thing they thought of at night before they went to sleep. They died without ever knowing what happened to Leila, and I think that's the cruellest thing of all. I need to lay my sister to rest. Find her remains and say goodbye so she isn't alone any more.

I don't want her forgotten about.

I don't care about the killer, to be honest. It's gone beyond even getting justice – although that would be ideal, obviously.

No matter how small the body part – I know it sounds awful but it's true – it would be good to be able to bury it so there's somewhere to visit. To speak to her. To just be together again sometimes. I miss us.

Euan: You don't believe she's alive, then?

Stella: After all these years?

[Cut to the beach. Camera pans along the sand then around to the Clock Tower, finally coming to rest on a table where three people are seated.]

Voiceover – Euan: Leila's best friends, who attended the family party and were among the last to see her alive. We meet in a café on the seafront, and I ask them what she was like.

Emma: Oh! Leila was always ahead of her time. She had her shoulder-length hair cut in shaggy layers a year before Jennifer Aniston appeared with "The Rachel". Remember that?

Sarah: Suddenly we all wanted to look like Rachel from Friends; but it was also kind of freaky because, really, we were mimicking Leila, too. Ha, actually, Leila looked a bit like Rachel before she had the nose job – remember that? Leila and Stella were ever so pretty, with such bright blue eyes that really stood out against their black hair and pale skin.

Emma: Very Celtic. Gorgeous.

Together: But big nose.

Emma: They always hated their nose, didn't they? Anyway, so Leila had "The Rachel" haircut before it had even been invented, but Stella's was a bob, I think? She'd had it done at college a few months earlier. Think she wanted to look a bit different, you know? Stella was just starting to get into that scruffy grunge look, too, but Leila was smarter – I suppose because she was training for a proper job, while Stella was a student. I mean, students back then were scruffy, weren't they? But they both loved dark red lipstick and dark red nail polish.

Sarah: So cool. She was wearing it that night. It exactly matched the colour of the trench coat she'd bought; that's why she'd bought it that day.

Emma: The weather had been dreadful that whole summer, you see. So many electric storms. Even though it was June, she'd had to buy this new, lightweight coat, so she wouldn't look like a drowned rat at her dad's birthday party. And of course, it was that that started it all really.

Sarah: A stupid mix-up and…

[Clicks fingers.]

…gone.

[Cut to Stella's home.]

Stella: For a long time, we didn't do anything but exist and hope after Leila disappeared. We never had the chance of a funeral. We did hold a memorial on the one-year anniversary, though. I tried to be strong for my parents. Most of it's a blur, though. There were so many people there; the church was packed. Some in the crowd had clearly only come to gawp, though. At the time it made me angry, but I kept my head down and concentrated on thinking of Leila. Wishing she were there beside me.

One thing I do remember is a neighbour coming up to me and giving me a big hug. She said, "It must be worse for you." It was the first time I'd really thought of it that way, and I don't know if it was worse than my parents' loss – after all, they'd lost a child, and besides, I'm not sure you can compare grief like that. But Leila was identical to me; she was the person I'd shared a womb with; she'd been born only eight minutes before me. The relationship was utterly unique, and no matter how close I become to someone it will never be the same as the one I had with my twin. Getting used to being alone was hard, but I did it and I'm stronger because of it. It's why I've never let anyone else in: I've no desire to become two only to suffer the trauma of losing them. It's better being alone.

I still dream about Leila. Nearly always, I'm trying to save her from some horrible fate. But the very first time I dreamed of her, just days after her death, I remember particularly. She sat on the edge of my bed and said: "I will never leave you." She never has. Just like I'll never leave her.

CHAPTER SIX

The radio is on full blast in the kitchen, and I'm singing along to D:Ream's 'Things Can Only Get Better', that Nineties classic, while pouring a generous glug of red wine into the vegetarian goulash I'm cooking. I close my eyes for a moment and remember.

Leila in the middle of the dance floor. Arms open wide as she twirled, singing at the top of her voice. A kaleidoscope of colours flickering across her upturned face.

The documentary went live on Netflix today, twenty-five years to the day that my sister disappeared. No work has been done today; I deliberately didn't book anything in so that I could watch it, bingeing on all the episodes at once to get it over and done with, needing to know what it looks like and what has been said by others who've taken part in it. Hating it for muck-raking but hoping it's worth it. It's been tough, I'm not going to lie, so I'm distracting myself by cooking. It's this or cry and wallow and cooking at least achieves something.

The warming aroma of paprika fills the air. Comfort food is exactly what I need right now. I'm not one of those sad singles who lives on takeaways or beans on toast because I can't be bothered to cook for myself. While I don't watch much television I am addicted to any cookery programme and often experiment with recipes. What I don't eat tonight will go in the freezer in portions for other days.

I'm really getting into my groove now. The generous glass of wine I've drunk while cooking may explain why – I don't normally drink, so it's gone straight to my head. I point a wooden spoon dripping with goulash at Buster, who cocks his head on one side at the dodgy notes I hit while explaining that things can, in fact, only get better, particularly now I've found him. Scamp's too busy sniffing the floor for dropped titbits to give a toss. A knock on the front door halts my singing. Perhaps Farrah or even Keshini has come around: both offered to spend the day with me but I refused. More likely it's a neighbour come to complain about my caterwauling – the back door is wide open so the dogs can come and go into the garden, making the most of the warm June evening.

It's the last person I expect.

'Euan!'

He's holding a bottle of wine, and staring at the dogs, who are still clamouring behind me as he steps over the threshold. I turn to them.

'Quiet.' It's said soft and low and I put my finger to my lips. Peace descends instantly.

'Impressive.'

'Thanks. Can I help you?'

'Oh!' He looks at the wine like he's just remembered it's there. 'I brought you this and, er, these…' he produces chocolates, 'to say thank you for all the time you put into the documentary. You were great. Have you watched it?'

'You're thanking me? Now. Even though you've been round pretty much constantly since we stopped filming?'

His continued visits are odd. In the three months since filming stopped he's popped over roughly once a week. Sometimes it's to double-check facts, even though he could just as easily call me for the information. Other times he says it's to check on Fifi, who seems to have stolen his heart. I'd have thought he'd be long gone back to his London life by now, but he seems to be lurking in Lincolnshire.

'Oooh, something smells good. What are you cooking?' He ignores my question completely, nosing into the kitchen just as the opening bars of a song throb from the radio.

'"You've Got the Love", Candi Staton,' he says a fraction of a second ahead of me.

'Huh, that's why you've come round, really, isn't it? To beat me at this game again.'

'You guessed it.'

He stares at me. An awkward silence stretches. Normally, I'd ask him to leave because I'm about to eat. He's waiting for me to do that, I'm sure. He rubs his hands on his bare arms, a gesture of vulnerability that makes me relate, and suddenly I realise that I really don't want to be alone any more today. In a warm glow of red wine and desperation I ask if he wants to stay for something to eat.

'Only if you sit down and let me serve you.'

'I couldn't do that!' Despite my protestations I'm being led firmly to my sofa, and my wine glass topped up. He takes a sip from his own glass, and I do the same because it seems rude not to, somehow.

'Stay there,' he orders.

Instead, because it's getting quite dim in the room, I turn the fairy lights on that run across the bookshelves. They're less harsh than having the main light on. It sort of looks like I'm trying to create a romantic mood. I wonder if I am.

Clinking and clanking comes from the kitchen. Euan must be searching through my cupboards, looking for the plates. It makes me uncomfortable, and I haul myself from the sofa. It takes two goes; this wine is strong...

Before I go in, I hear him talking in a low voice to someone. Who? It reminds me of when I heard him and Penny-Sue in the cloakroom. I wonder if that problem they were whispering about ever got sorted. I edge closer to the door, keen to discover what he's saying.

'You're so beautiful. You've no need to be jealous, you know.'

Is he on the phone to his girlfriend? Perhaps pretty, quirky Keshini has finally got her man.

'Ah, who can resist those eyes?' Apparently not him. 'Okay, I'll give you a tummy rub, but not for long.'

Tummy rub? Peering round the corner confirms my suspicions. Fifi is on her back, stumpy tail a wagging blur, eyes almost rolling in ecstasy.

'Am I interrupting anything?' I smirk.

'We're just having a moment, while I try to find the plates,' he replies. He's got a tea towel slung over one shoulder and is looking utterly at home, crouched on the floor beside the French bulldog.

'They're in here.' I open a cupboard to the left and pull two out. 'You're good with her. She's wary of most people but trusts you.'

'Well, she knows I played a part in rescuing her. Even if it did bruise my ego not to be needed.' He's teasing, referring to our argument. There's that tension again.

'Prodigy, "Fire Starter",' I burst.

'What?'

'The radio.' I point unnecessarily. 'Beat you.'

He smiles the kind of smile that has me grinning back, then washes his hands and dishes up – just as there's a knock on the door.

'That'll be Keshini,' I laugh.

'You're expecting her? Sorry, you should have said…'

'Come off it, you must have noticed how she always "just happens" to pop over at the same time as you. Why don't you ask her out, already?'

'It's not just my imagination, then. Look, she's a work colleague, anything more would be inappropriate even if I did fancy her – and she is not the person I'm interested in. Can you do me a favour and pretend I'm not here?'

'Maybe I want to invite her to eat, too.'

'Do you?'

I look at the food. 'There's not enough to go around, or I would. But you still owe me for this.'

It is indeed Keshini on my doorstep. She jumps up as the door swings open. For a split second I think she was about to spy through my letterbox, before realising she's checking her lipstick in its reflection. She grins at me, the tips of her mouth seemingly attached to her shoulders, which also rise.

'Hello, chick, how are you? Tough day, eh?' She opens her arms to hug me, then lets them fall with an awkward laugh. 'Sorry, forgot you're not a huggy person. Do you want company? Or do you have it already?'

'Actually, I'm about to eat. It's lovely of you to come over, but I'm honestly fine. Do you mind…?'

'You all alone?' She actually starts to peer around me. My guilt morphs into irritation and with a 'have a nice evening', I close the door. She's a nice girl and I feel bad for her, but she doesn't really want to be my friend – she's only using me to get close to Euan and that's out of order.

Euan at least has the good grace to look sheepish and changes the subject to the dogs as we sit on the sofa and eat with the plates on our laps. Halfway through I wonder if I should have suggested the table, but it's got paperwork all over it, with a cleared space only large enough for my breakfast bowl.

With the last mouthful, Euan again raises the subject of the documentary, asking if I plan on watching it. He's careful to keep his eyes on the glasses he's refilling while he speaks.

'You can look at me, you know. I've watched it and I'm still in one piece.'

'It can't have been easy. Hopefully, we'll get a good reaction to it, though. Us hitting the anniversary has got it some brilliant publicity in the nationals – papers and TV news. We've a hashtag on Twitter that's getting some traction, too.'

He uses 'we' as if he and I are a team. I haven't been one of those since Leila. It took a lot to get used to being on my own, but after years of hard work, I excel at it. I wouldn't change it for the world.

'One thing's for sure, true crime is big right now,' he adds. Takes a sip of wine then taps the glass against his lips.

I sigh. 'Out with it.'

'What?'

'Whatever you clearly want to say.'

'Can I ask you something? Not as a journalist, just as… I don't know, someone who is interested. Someone who is starting to like you.'

'Talk about damning me with faint praise.'

'Okay, as someone who *does* like you.'

'Better.'

'Did you mean what you said that day, about not having any hope? It just seems so… sad. It's so very, very sad.'

There are no cameras recording. There can be no ulterior motive for the question. So I find myself wanting to tell the truth. Just once. Just because of the time we've spent together, him asking me questions about the worst time of my life. It's created a feeling of intimacy between us, no matter how fake and short-lived. Before answering, I take a large swallow of wine, noticing it doesn't seem warm now as it slips down my throat because the rest of me is glowing.

'When someone you love disappears there's no closure of a funeral. All you have is a person-shaped hole in your life, an absence that never stops aching. Even when my goals shifted from finding Leila alive to the search for her body, there was always hope – hope is a pain that never disappears. For my own sanity I refuse to acknowledge it, though. I tell people who ask about hope that it doesn't exist. I pray it has starved to death due to lack of attention, but then something will happen and there it is, rattling at its cage to remind me it's still alive and kicking. But with all my heart I wish there were no hope.'

'You're so brave.' His voice is low.

Seductively low, Leila might have observed if she were here. But what he's saying is bull: I'm not brave, I only ever do what's got to be done, from looking for Leila to tackling arsehole men who want to kick dogs.

His hand is on my forearm as he speaks. 'I was impressed with the way you handled yourself the first time we met.'

'Which first time?' Sarcasm. It's my go-to.

'Both, actually,' he laughs. 'You're very sangfroid.'

'What's that mean?'

'You keep your cool in danger or when under strain. It's impressive – and intimidating.'

'So's your vocabulary.' His thumb is drawing circles on my skin. His forearm has that muscular line down it that I've always found a turn-on. And he's definitely flirting with me. Despite being so much younger… It's hot in here and the room is looking suspiciously soft focus. 'I'm not much of a words person,' I add, pulling my arm away and reaching for the wine instead.

'You're more into body language.'

My laugh comes so hard I snort. 'Cheesy, Euan.'

He insists that he was talking about the dogs, but a flush creeps across the back of his neck. Embarrassment or annoyance. It's still hard to read Euan, but he doesn't seem angry: no clenched hands; no tension at all that I can see as my eyes trace over him to check. His marl T-shirt is tight, and he's got some decent muscles showing. It's also the exact same soft grey as his eyes.

The wine and muscles combination is making blood rush to unexpected places for a 44-year-old single woman. I haven't had sex in six long years. It's been a while since I've thought about it, but right now it seems bloody obvious that I miss sex. A lot. That sex would definitely take my mind off the documentary, Leila and the raging guilt.

Maybe it would stop the dreams. Worth a shot, for one night only. And it would be only for one night.

Alcohol lowers inhibitions and mine are so low a sausage dog would struggle to walk beneath them. Sod it. I lean forward and kiss him. He tenses for the briefest of seconds – is he going to reject me, have I got this wrong? No, he goes with it… just as Scamp jumps between us.

'Kids, bed,' I order.

Each goes to their respective beds, but don't look impressed as I take Euan by the hand and lead him upstairs. Maybe they've got a point. Maybe this is the worst mistake of my life. Another part of my anatomy is overruling my brain right now, and all I can hope is that I don't end up regretting it. My last thought as I go upstairs is: *I hope he doesn't notice my hairy legs.*

It's been several weeks since the documentary aired and I made that awful error of judgement with Euan, so these days, looking in the mirror isn't only tough because of Leila. Every time I catch a glimpse of myself, I groan in shame at what I did.

Currently, I'm staring into the wash basin as I clean my teeth.

It was fun, don't get me wrong, but it should never have happened. Worse, I feel as if I've betrayed Keshini – particularly as she's come around several times without Euan appearing first, proving my suspicions of her to be incorrect. Still, logically, I know I've done nothing wrong; she and he aren't together. It's not simply guilt that makes me continue meeting her for coffee and chats, though: it's nice to listen to someone… untainted. She's refreshingly open about her feelings, her attraction to Euan, dreams of moving to London and climbing the career ladder. I remember being like that once. I rarely offer an opinion, as I'm far too jaded, but it's nice being a sounding-board.

Then there's the man himself. Euan keeps calling me. Considering he's young, fit and successful, I'm amazed by his reaction because he can't possibly be seriously interested in me. Whether he is or not, I'm not up for a relationship and thought he knew that.

Luckily, I've been able to legitimately keep him at arm's length without being rude, as I'm busy making the most of the buzz about Leila. All my savings have been blown on more leaflets and posters and running an ad on Facebook to promote the 'Search For Leila' page I set up. I wonder what she'd make of social media? Facebook didn't exist back in 1994. No selfies! No one has come forward so far with any great breakthrough, but now's the time to push for it, and any leads the police haven't had the time to chase, I've checked out. Driving all over the country has been exhausting and fruitless – and made me completely broke. At least now it's mid-August and the school summer holidays are in full swing, work is busy for me, too. A lot of people put off tackling problems with their pets until they've got some spare time, so I'm getting a lot of calls, emails and messages from my website.

But before I check any of them, I'll go on to Twitter: my new morning routine. I spit in the sink and as I wipe my mouth with a towel, I see Leila from the corner of my eye. Whenever I see what's trending on Twitter it makes me think of her. We were obsessed with being trendy as teens, reading those 'what's hot and what's not' lists in magazines.

'Well, you're not trendy now but you are trending, Leila,' I tell her.

She smiles back at me from the mirror, before turning away. Eyes reddening with tears. I wipe the wet from my own cheeks. Perhaps one day I'll be able to look myself in the eye.

Seven weeks on from the documentary first appearing on Netflix there's an ever-growing amount of chatter on social media, all sorts of theories. Mostly mad. Some are still convinced that her boyfriend did it, and my heart fills with pity that by trying to raise awareness of Leila I've inadvertently thrown the spotlight back on Damien. Others claim I did it. My motive mainly seems to be crazed jealousy. I've read entire threads about it, pushing down the hurt and reading on in the hope someone, some time will say something relevant.

The sister deliberately took the wrong coat. It's obvious.

Yeah. Bit weird she 'forgot' she'd got the keys to Leila's flat when they went round next morning. Clearly stalling – but why?

Accomplice? Might have needed time to hide the body then dispose of it before the police arrived.

At the other end of the spectrum, are those seemingly furious with me for 'raking up the past'. They tell me 'get over it' and 'move on', while others think I'm doing it for 'the money'.

It's sick the way she's cashing in on her sister's death. Get a proper job you scrounger.

It's sad and all that but the body is never going to be found. Stop the obsession. Get a life.

Do they really think it's that easy? Could they simply move on if it were their sister? People sometimes say losing a loved one is akin to losing a limb, but it's more profound than that. I've lost part of my soul. We were two people with one spirit. At the time, my doctor told me that the loss of a twin is the hardest thing to get over. Living without her, being me and only me, still feels alien. We took our togetherness for granted, always assuming we'd be there for each other. It never occurred to us that we'd be parted. It was incomprehensible.

So, no, I didn't kill Leila, nor am I 'trying to cover my tracks by protesting too much'.

I scroll through while eating my breakfast, keen to see if there are any new theories that might be helpful. One particular tweet grabs my attention.

Leila killed Stella, and to throw everyone off the scent she is now living as Stella.

'Someone's been watching too many crime dramas,' I mutter, closing my laptop with a little too much force. Time to tackle the post.

It's not just social media that's brought the weirdos out. My house has received a sackful of snail mail. I go through it all, putting it into piles – I'm an old hand at such things after twenty-five years of it. *Useful. Well-wisher. Weird. Malicious.* I always reply to well-wishers. It's something Mum did and I now do it for her. Any threats go straight to the police. I'm no martyr nor am I stupid; they can deal with all of that, it's not my job.

Anything that looks promising is bagged in evidence bags I have for this purpose. Latex gloves are worn the whole time I'm opening post; I'm ever aware of how easily evidence could be destroyed.

The letter opener slices neatly through the top of the plain white envelope I've picked from today's handful of offerings. The front is printed, which makes me suspect it will be going in the weird or malicious pile.

Hey Fag Ash Lil,

Are you sure you want to rake up the past? I always was the stronger one after all, born first. Let things lie.

Leila x

A squeak of shock escapes me. Buddy and Buster instantly come to me, standing either side of my legs and pressing themselves against me. Scamp, ever desperate to give and receive comfort, jumps onto her hind legs and paws at me, reaching for my lap. Fifi doesn't stir from her bed but does gaze at me, questioning. Buddy's large ears swivel as if listening for danger.

There is no danger, though, only hurt that someone would be cruel enough to pose as my Leila.

But…

But the words taunt me, making me feel uneasy.

I'm trying to think it through.

Is this a piece of information I've given out during an interview?

Definitely not in the documentary; I can be certain of that because I watched it again the other day. Over the years, though, who can say? It's doubtful, though.

I could have sworn it was never made public that my sister called me Fag Ash Lil.

I stare at the note again, heart thumping. It can't be from Leila. It can't.

CHAPTER SEVEN

Is my sister really still alive?

My head reels at the thought. The dogs scatter as I stand and pace. Fifi whines, uncomfortable at the change in atmosphere, and that's what brings me to my senses. The dogs need me to get myself together.

Logic, not hysteria, is what has got me through the past years. Once again I wrap it around me and slow my thoughts.

'It's okay,' I soothe. A quick search of my pockets produces some liver cake crumbs that I dole out. That gets their tails wagging, which settles me, too.

Only family and close friends knew the nickname. It's possible they've told other people about it over the years. It's not exactly a state secret, the sort of thing people take to the grave with them. Maybe Damien knows, or even my old ex, Ryan. Damien got in touch a few days after the documentary went live, demanding his name be taken out of it. I wrote back explaining that it's impossible to tell Leila's story without mentioning him, and he's been bombarding me with demanding letters ever since, as if I've got control over what's included in the documentary. So the chances are he won't be in the mood for answering any of my questions.

Who else might know about my nickname of Fag Ash Lil?

It had come about when Leila and I were going through a short-lived period of smoking. We only did it because we were going to raves, aged 16, and everyone else was doing drugs. We were the goody-goodies who refused to so much as smoke a spliff, though, but we decided to smoke menthol cigarettes instead, in an attempt to make ourselves look older. I say we but of course it was Leila's idea, and she decided a practice run was needed.

'What if Mum and Dad smell it? They're only upstairs,' I pointed out.

'No one will notice,' Leila insisted, pulling the golden, crushed velvet curtain across the door. 'That should keep the smell trapped in the room.'

Mum and Dad had been going through a gold and beige phase in the late 1980s. The sofa was beige with gold and orange flowers, and the seats came in individual sections that could be moved around to fit the room as desired, and because they were made from polystyrene they were light to move. In fact, we were constantly having to push it back into a line because if you as much as looked at it the seating moved. Cheap furniture, but the best we could afford with Dad being on disability benefit because of his bad heart, and Mum working every hour in the local Safeway supermarket.

I lounged on the sofa, pulling my feet up beneath me, thinking. 'I'm still not convinced.'

'We don't need to inhale,' Leila said. 'Just hold the smoke in our mouths, like this.'

She lit the cigarette, then coughed and spluttered. I laughed so hard I almost rolled off the seat.

'Here, let me try.' I plucked the cigarette from her lips and put it between my own. Inhaled just enough to make the tip glow, then made a big show of blowing it out of my mouth, feeling terribly grown-up.

'Now me,' said Leila. She reached for it, but I batted her away.

'Get your own!' There was a fair bit of ash building up at the end of it. Where was I going to put it? With no other option, I held my hand out and let it drop into my palm.

'Bugger!' It was hotter than I thought. Flapping my hands, it dropped onto the sofa, along with the cigarette. The material melted, a hole opening up in the sofa. Then – tea soaking me and making the seat sizzle. Leila had chucked her cuppa.

We were lucky the whole thing hadn't gone up in flames. We got away with it because we insisted a spark had flown from the open fire and caused the hole. Mum and Dad didn't necessarily believe us, but they never stood a chance because we always backed each other up. Mum was probably pleased, anyway, deciding to redecorate and get a different sofa that adhered to the new flame retardancy laws. That was the last time the décor was updated, and I haven't changed a thing since inheriting the house.

As for Leila and me, we didn't bother trying smoking again. But after that, my big sister would often refer to me in private as Fag Ash Lil, and we'd both collapse in giggles at our silly secret.

Could my sister be alive? Living all these years just out of reach, and never missing me once? After all we'd shared?

Perhaps it was what we shared that made her do it. The thought makes me shiver.

No. It's impossible. She'd never be so cruel. This printed-out note, not even in her handwriting, has been sent to hurt me and I've been stupid to allow that to happen even for a second.

I should bin the ridiculous thing.

*

Much as I want to throw away that awful letter, common sense prevails. It's been placed into a plastic evidence bag and I've called the police so they can look at it. One of the officers who handled Leila's disappearance from the start, Dave Burns, comes around himself to pick it up. He was a DS back then and did all the running round for the remote Detective Inspector Glossop, who ran everything from a distance and never deigned to have much to do with the family. Since then, Burns has climbed the ranks to become detective chief inspector, but it hasn't stopped him taking a personal interest and we've become friends of sorts over the years.

He's a pragmatic man not given to overexcitement and hyperbole, which is why we get on well. Similar natures despite the age gap. Apparently back in the day he was a bit of a ladies' man, but I've never seen any evidence of it. If he were a dog he'd be a Labrador: the perfect nature for steadfast service. Although his hair, what little there is of it, is definitely salt and pepper rather than golden.

'The weirdos are coming out again in force, then,' he says, taking the bag from me and putting it in his own evidence bag.

'No surprise there. We can handle it, though, eh?'

'Me and you can take anything they chuck at us.' He smiles but there's a tightness around his eyes.

'What is it?'

He grunts. 'You should have joined the police force along with your sister; not much gets past you, does it? I've got a bit of news I've been meaning to tell you.'

'Another promotion?'

'Stella, I'm retiring. I wanted to tell you myself – it's why I'm here instead of one of the actual investigating team to pick this letter up.'

I sit down. Shake my head. 'But you're only, what? Fifty-five.'

'Sixty, but the job gets to you after a while. This is my only case that's still open. Hopefully, we can put it to rest before I go – we've had a fair few calls since the documentary aired.'

'No decent leads though, from the look on your face.'

'That obvious, eh? Well, in a last attempt to get this case cracked, I've got a new team together.' As he's talking, he walks to the front door and opens it, beckons to someone outside. 'Hope you don't feel ambushed, but when you called I decided to bring along the people heading it. Introduce you, like, so you know you're in safe hands, even though I won't be around any more.'

A man and woman come in. The man is a cool blond with a stern air and eyes as sharp as his nose, who shakes my hand with an almost over-firm grip. He touches his tie as if for reassurance. The woman, who has a chaotic energy, stands by his side but with her body turned to almost give the impression she's behind him. Deference. It's obvious who is boss with this duo.

Burns does the introductions, assuring me he's handpicked the brightest Mereford Station has to offer, but as I say hello to Detective Inspector Nick Fremlin and Detective Sergeant Alison Fox, 'bright' is not a word that springs to mind. Fremlin is smart in his suit and carries himself like a politician rather than a cop. It's a contrast to Fox, who is wearing a smart/casual short-sleeve top, black jeans that make her long legs look like a spider's, and silver trainers with a thick sole. She's got what looks like a piece of crisp stuck in a curl of her wild hair. Something else is bugging me, though.

'When you say you won't be around any more… you'll still be in Mereford, right? You'll keep in touch with the investigation?'

'Well,' Burns gives an awkward laugh, 'since you ask—'

'You're off to Cyprus, aren't you, guv?' He stiffens at the interruption by DS Fox. 'All right for some, eh? Sea, sand and sangria.'

'That's Spain, Detective Sergeant,' he says.

Cyprus. No more DCI Burns to share my frustrations with. Once again the sense that everything is changing hits me. He's been a constant in my life for twenty-five years, though admittedly in the background since those first flurried months of activity dampened down. It touched me that he never forgot. Every anniversary he'd text to let me know he was thinking of Leila too. Sometimes in-between times we'd speak with one another about updates, new sightings, new theories. The members of the investigating team had changed often over the years but Burns had given me a sense of continuity. All that ends soon.

He taps the bag that contains the letter supposedly from Leila. A ra-ta-tat of authority that brings all retirement talk to a close.

'You know this isn't from her, right? The chances are tiny. Everything points to it being from a crank.'

'I know it.'

'Just a cruel-hearted bastard messing with your head.'

'For a change.' I shrug.

Leila's disappearance plunged my family and me into a full-speed lesson in the extremes of human nature. There were those who supported and rallied round. Those who didn't get in touch, worried about saying or doing the wrong thing until eventually they let us slide from their lives. Strangers who went out of their way to send love and support and messages of hope. And those who were cruel. Who taunted us with false sightings and dashed hopes simply so they could get some attention for a while. This letter is nothing new.

But they know your nickname. How is that possible? I find myself thinking.

Despite the shock of DCI Burns's news, I feel better for having seen him. Of course, he's right and the letter isn't from Leila, but either way at least the police now have it and will run tests to see if they can find any forensic evidence of a connection between it and my sister. In the meantime, life continues as normal. I rush to my appointment and spend two hours teaching an owner how to get his boxer, Tyson, to walk to heel. He became reactive after being attacked by another dog a year ago. Ever since, John, the owner, has been hauling him away bodily from other dogs, which has reinforced his pet's fears. Two hours in he is so much more relaxed, and so is Tyson. John is one happy customer, unable to believe the transformation.

'I thought he'd end up attacking someone else's dog himself and then have to be put down,' he says, wiping tears from his face.

'This is why I love my job so much,' I beam.

As soon as I leave him my phone rings. Euan. My heart sinks faster than a puppy told there are no treats. I only answer in case he has news about Leila – which he doesn't. Desperate to avoid an awkward conversation about 'us', I end up telling him about the letter and Burns's retirement before making my excuses because I've another appointment to attend. Angry chihuahuas wait for no one.

*

By the time I return home I'm exhausted, so when Euan's name flashes up on my mobile I'm in no mood.

'You need to get a life,' I say when I answer the phone.

'Save the charm offensive for later, Stella. I did some checking, trawled through your old interviews – your parents', too – and double-checked with the researchers who worked on the documentary. There's just one mention of the Fag Ash Lil story, by a family friend during an early interview. The piece was small and took a long time to find, so…'

'So what are you saying? You think it's Leila?'

'It could be, but I wouldn't get your hopes up—'

'They're definitely grounded—'

An inhalation of breath, as if readying to say something momentous. 'I think you should be careful. It could be someone just messing with you, but what if it's the person who hurt Leila?'

'Trust a journalist to come up with a crazy story based on no evidence. Don't be ridiculous. It's someone who wants to play silly buggers, that's all.'

'Whoever it is they have knowledge and they have an agenda; they're warning you to back off, basically. Watch yourself. Journalists have instincts – and feelings,' he adds.

I end the conversation with an apology. His words stay with me, so when Farrah texts to see how I am I give a lengthy reply, explaining why I'm too knackered to see her. She doesn't come back to me. Perhaps I've accidentally trampled on her feelings, too.

Bloody Euan making me feel guilty.

Only when I'm tucked up in bed, Buster on the pillow beside me, Scamp snoring gently in the crook of my knee, Buddy by my feet, while Fifi rests in the space beneath the bed, do I wonder if there might be an ulterior motive to Euan painting such a dramatic picture. Might he want me to feel vulnerable so I'll turn to him?

Scamp suddenly growls. Buddy gets to his feet. Worried they've heard something, I strain my ears, trying to hear a sound in the darkness. Buddy jumps from the bed and paces to the bedroom door. I flick the light on and watch him sniffing the air before finally returning to his warm spot.

CHAPTER EIGHT

Documentary Transcript
Title: *Missing: The Twin Who Never Came Back*

[Camera shows the outside of the property where Leila Hawkins lived at the time of her disappearance. A two-storey house, each floor converted into a flat. It then pans to show the rest of the residential street, Glentworth Crescent.]

Voiceover – Euan: From the very beginning, the hunt for Leila Hawkins was dogged with problems. A huge storm on the night of her disappearance brought with it torrential rain. Generally, Mereford in late June is bustling with holidaymakers, but despite it being a sweltering 23 degrees Celsius that night, the heavy rain had driven everyone indoors – which meant no one was around to witness the young woman's fate. To this day, not a single eyewitness has come forward to give a clue about what happened after she was dropped off at her home.

Around twenty millimetres of rain fell that night – that's two weeks' worth in just a handful of hours. The severe conditions caused problems for minor shipping off the coast due to the gust front appearing so suddenly. And for police, the rain didn't only create a lack of eyewitnesses. Any possible forensic evidence was washed away in the downpour.

[Outside the house stands Detective Chief Inspector Dave Burns.]

DCI Burns: There are, I think, over two thousand pages of statements relating to this case, all of which have been checked thoroughly. But there's no smoking gun. We don't have an eyewitness to Leila being killed. We don't have the discovery of her body. It would be idle speculation as to whether a weapon was used. I don't… and I'm not sure that anyone has… a theory as to what happened. We say that all of the evidence points to there having been a criminal act, but there is no evidence of anything, really, and if Leila has been killed – which is my belief – we don't even know the motivation behind it for sure. So, yes, we have a strong sense of something bad having happened to her, but, discovering exactly what would be very difficult to prove. And we've tried; believe me, we've tried.

[Cut to exterior of seaside café.]

Emma: Oh yeah, that storm was terrible. Terrible! The sky went Armageddon black, it did. There was fork and sheet lightning, and the wind was kicking up. We watched it for a while, standing under the awning in the beer garden, having a fag, didn't we, Sar?

Sarah: That's right, yeah. The lightning was constant, like a, a bombardment, you know. Like those videos of cities being bombed at night and all you can see is flash, flash, flash. Enough to give you 'eadache. The sky looked angry. There was this cloud, big and black it was, and it kind of swirled until it almost looked like a whale mouth. I remember because I tried to take a photo of it.

Emma: 'Course, the storm's the reason why there was all that hoo-ha. You know. With the coats. If it had been typical June weather, there'd have been no need for raincoats. It's why some people – some stupid people with no idea what they're talking about – make comments about it all being Stella's fault what happened to her sister.

Sarah: Anyway… Come on, let's—

Emma: Oh, 'ey, and do you remember someone's car alarm went off because of the thunder? He couldn't shut it up.

Sarah: Ooh, now who was that? Can't remember. The alarm was blaring; all the dogs in the area were barking; the thunder was almost non-stop… Storms like that, you understand why people are afraid of storms, you know? We thought there'd be a power cut, but the music stayed on until midnight, which was when the party was ending anyway.

[Cut to the busy seafront at night, the nightclubs and cafés that line it are blazing with multi-coloured lights, and the many amusement arcades are a firework of flashing colours.]

Voiceover – Euan: The power cut hit at around the time Leila would have been going home. The streetlights went off for five hours, plunging the whole town into darkness. The drains were overwhelmed and there was local flooding on the roads and playing fields. By morning it had all but disappeared though – along with Leila.

[Cut to interior.]

Stella: Everything was guesswork from the get-go. We know Leila was dropped off by the cabbie, but the driver didn't wait to see her go inside, so didn't realise that she'd forgotten her key and was left stranded outside. What happened next? Was she attacked outside her home? Did she start to walk to the phone box? Or flag down an unlicensed minicab to get to our parents' house and was attacked by the driver? Did someone she know come along and offer her a lift? Perhaps she even started walking the two miles there; we always loved walking so the distance was nothing. Any of these scenarios could be right. No one knows. Her flat was only a five-, maybe ten-minute walk from the seafront, and right next to homes and B&Bs, but no one heard or saw a thing.

It's hard for people now to comprehend, but the world in 1994 was a very different place. We all take CCTV for granted now – you know, recent figures show the UK has the most CCTV cameras per head of any country in the world, right? One camera for every eleven people, supposedly. And that's not counting drones, body-worn videos, people taking non-stop photos and videos to post on social media. Now is the golden age of surveillance, digital eyes everywhere.

[She leans forward. Taps her finger on the coffee table.]

In 1994, the government launched the Partners Against Crime initiative, and between then and 1999 the Home Office spent over two hundred million on CCTV systems. Did you know that CCTV footage has proved crucial in ninety-five per cent of murder cases investigated by Scotland Yard? Ninety-five per cent!

[She flops back in her seat.]

Notice the spending splurge started in 1994. The year my sister disappeared. Round here there were a couple of cameras on High Street and along the main section of the seafront: the bit that has most of the nightclubs, cafés and arcades, but there was no coverage at all on any side streets.

Hard to imagine now, isn't it? But there's no CCTV footage at all of my sister from that night. The police checked the cameras at the train station in case she simply decided to leave her life. There was no sign, though – as if she'd do that to us.

[Stella's eyes, which have been pinpoint sharp as she reels off this information, suddenly soften. She smiles.]

As you can tell, I can bore for Britain on the subject. Sorry. It's just that it's something I've done a lot of research on since Leila went missing.

Euan: You campaigned successfully for CCTV in the town centre to cover more areas, didn't you?

[She nods.]
Stella: The community really got behind it; it was very much a team effort.

[Cut to Euan, piece to camera, walking along the beach.]
Euan: With no footage of Leila and no evidence of what happened to her, the police were struggling. The local force based in Mereford is set up for the small population in winter not the huge explosion of holidaymakers and seasonal workers that come in during the summer months. Although they do their best, they struggle to keep on top of the small-time thefts, assaults, and drug offences that create the majority of crime here. Disappearances and murder are so rare that the last one recorded in the town was three years ago. Before that had been another ten years. Critics say the force was clearly out of their depth, uncertain how to proceed with the complex investigation.

Leila's boyfriend, Damien Francis, was just 20 when his girlfriend vanished. Despite friends and family initially painting a picture of someone who was devoted to Leila, the trainee accountant quickly became the focus of police attention.

[Cut to exterior of Leila's house. DCI Dave Burns stands outside with Euan.]
Euan: Some people say the police developed 'tunnel vision', refusing to consider any other suspects apart from Damien. Would you care to comment?
DCI Burns: That's simply not true. DI Glossop and subsequent teams over the years have explored every avenue of investigation open to them and scrutinised every person who came into contact with Leila.

Initially, the obvious person to check out was the taxi driver, particularly when a background check showed he had a criminal record for breaking and entering and had a complaint against him by the mother of his children for violence against her – although she hadn't pressed charges in the end. We went over his timeline again and again. He'd dropped Leila off, then immediately picked up another fare. There'd been no time for him to do anything to the young woman.

At one point, Leila's disappearance was linked with another case in Essex. The investigative team there saw some initial similarities to their case. It's standard stuff and we were open to the idea, co-operating fully, but further checks – conducted by them as well as us, I might add – showed there was no evidence to back the theory.

Believe me, we did not pursue only one line of investigation to the detriment of all others; there simply weren't any other viable options that presented themselves. That's why Damien Francis became the prime suspect, and why he has never been ruled out. People don't want to hear this because in cases like this it's always easier to believe a total stranger swooped in from nowhere and committed a terrible crime, but the fact is that most crimes are perpetrated by those who are closest to the victim.

You have to remember that Leila was one of us. She may never have had the chance to serve more than a handful of weeks, but she'd gone through training and by all accounts had a good head on her shoulders. Showed potential to become a real asset to the force. When something happens to a fellow officer, the entire station is invested in finding the perpetrator – even more invested than usual.

Euan: Had you ever met her?

DCI Burns: It's possible we came into contact – Mereford isn't the biggest of stations. If we did I've no recollection, though, which is a shame. I've come to know her sister, Stella, quite well over the years and admire her fortitude in adversity. It makes me certain that Leila would have had a bright future ahead of her had things been different.

Our investigation from the start was frustrated by a complete lack of physical evidence. No body, no forensics, no witnesses. It was a tough case from the off. The only option open to us was to look closely at family and friends to see if they could offer any breaks. Immediate family were quickly discounted. All had alibis and no motive.

We did question closely Ryan Jonas, who had been dating Stella at the time, following some statements from others about him and his, shall we say, interesting hobbies. But again it came to nothing.

So we did concentrate on the boyfriend, yes. Do I regret that? No, not one bit. Damien Francis was our best lead at the time, and to this day is considered a person of interest to this case.

His alibi is shaky, at best. He reportedly told Leila that he couldn't make it to her father's party because he had to attend a weekend training course for work. That was a lie. Once you've been caught in a lie by the police, you're on shaky ground. Why wouldn't you tell the truth? That's what we have to ask ourselves. Why, when you know that lying could waste police time and you're supposedly eager to discover what's happened to the person you love? These are all questions you have to ask yourself when you're investigating a disappearance and possible homicide.

Damien Francis has never been able to prove where he was. However, at this present time there is insufficient evidence for anyone to be arrested or charged with the…

[Pauses.]

However, to this day there is insufficient evidence to bring charges against anyone in connection with the disappearance and suspected murder of Leila Hawkins.

[Cut to photo of Damien Francis, aged 19. His arm is around Leila as they stand on the beach, squinting into the sun. He is around five inches taller than Leila, with broad shoulders and skinny hips, and wearing a Take That T-shirt. His face is round and boyish; his hair short at the back and sides, while the longer top section is gelled forward into a fringe of small spikes similar to Gary Barlow's at the time.]

Voiceover – Euan: The police continued to scrutinise Damien. At one point he claimed he was being harassed by the police, although a Police Complaints Authority investigation into the matter at the time supported the force's actions.

[Cut to blurry CCTV footage. Voiceover continues.]

Damien Francis has always stuck to his story that he stayed at a hotel not far from Nottingham because 'he fancied a break'. His reasons for initially claiming to be at a work conference have remained unclear. This is footage of him checking in at reception on the Friday afternoon – here he is on the left, with his back to the camera – which corroborates his claim. He's caught on camera again on the Saturday at around lunchtime; here he's checking out, presumably following the call from Stella that Leila was missing. Given that this corroborates his story, what brought his alibi into question?

[Cut to DCI Burns.]

DCI Burns: At first, the team discounted Francis as we thought his alibi stood up. But when we looked more closely at him what we found blew it out of the water.

His room – a room he had specifically requested – was beside the emergency exit. The alarm on this exit was discovered not to be working. In fact, it had been tampered with. We believed at the time that he had lied to Leila about going away, tampered with the emergency exit so that the alarm wouldn't go off, and knew that he'd be given an alibi by reception staff and security cameras. Our hypothesis was that he then left the hotel via the emergency exit, ensuring that no one saw him and that no cameras caught him. He then drove to Mereford where he waited for Leila and attacked her. There's no evidence to suggest we were wrong in this line of thinking.

Euan: But he had a reason for asking for that room, didn't he?

DCI Burns: He said he'd asked for that room because he wanted a no smoking room, and that he needed to be on the ground floor because he has a fear of heights. The only room that fit that criteria was the one beside the emergency exit. It wasn't hard to find out that he was a regular smoker.

Euan: But what would his motive have been? They were, by all accounts, happy together.

DCI Burns: Sadly, in this world some people don't need much of a motive in order to take a life. Jealousy, a word said out of place, money problems, all can be enough reason to murder someone. Two women every week in England and Wales are killed by a current or former partner. According to the latest crime figures, around three-quarters of victims of domestic killings by a partner, ex-partner or family member are women, while suspects are predominantly male. So it's no surprise we scrutinised Damien – and we didn't like what we saw.

Euan: If police are so certain it's him, why hasn't he ever faced trial?

DCI Burns: I never said he was guilty. I just said that we still consider him a person of interest in this investigation. Presumption of innocence is a basic tenet of our justice system. For there to be enough evidence to bring a case against anyone to court would be nigh on impossible as things stand. In a case like this, where the victim hasn't been found, it's hard to prove that she's even dead. It's possible she could turn up next week or next month. Unlikely, but possible.

CHAPTER NINE

It's been a week since the letter arrived and disturbed my peace. The dreams of my sister, which were dispelled by my night with Euan, are back with a vengeance and shadows haunt my face, but I'm trying to push it to the back of my mind and get on with normal life. Well, my version of normal.

While the dogs feast on their own breakfast, I eat mine while checking emails. There's a contact form on my website for potential clients to get in touch with me, and when they fill it in the site emails it to me. My email address is also on there for those who prefer not to fill in the form, as is my mobile number, so most mornings start this way after I check social media for any talk of Leila. It's always a good feeling to hear from new clients and know that there will be money coming into the house for a bit longer – as a freelancer I live in permanent fear that my next client will be my last, even though the business has ticked over nicely for decades now, so I really can't complain.

There's a query from the owner of a rescue dog whose recall is awful. A mouthful of cereal, then I type a reply while chewing, suggesting a time and date to see them. Although I keep my reply neutral and make no promise, what's been described should be an easy fix. I love helping rescues. Seeing them come out of their shell and gain confidence is so rewarding.

I open another email. This owner writes that they're desperate because their dog, called Bunny, destroys the house every time she's left alone. Carpets are scrabbled at until even the rubber backing beneath has been strewn across rooms, cushions are gutted without mercy, and wooden furniture chewed. A photo's been attached of the back of the kitchen door, where they shut the dog in, which shows all the paint from one section of it has been clawed away. Instead of replying by email, I make a quick call to the number left at the bottom of the message. The frazzled owner and I are both keen to get started as quickly as possible, so we arrange to see each other at lunchtime today.

I'm almost at the end of my inbox as I take a sip of herbal tea – detoxifying nettle tea because as I've got older I've tried to become healthier, suddenly aware that if I don't look after this body of mine it's not going to last well. I'll check this final message, finish my drink, then walk the dogs before starting work proper.

Dear Stella,

Why am I writing to you? I keep asking myself this question and then deleting what I've written. You should see how many drafts I've done. I want to be as honest with you as I can, which also means being honest with myself – it's harder sometimes to do that than anything else. And so the reason I write is threefold: to confess, to apologise, and to ask a favour. Right now, all I ask is that you read all the way to the bottom of this message before making up your mind.

What an odd way of phrasing a request for help. I can't wait to hear what's wrong with the dog after all this build up.

First, the confession. I wrote to you the other day pretending to be your sister. As soon as I sent the letter I knew it was a mistake, but it was a terrible act of lashing out in order to protect myself. I can't begin to imagine the hurt I inflicted on you when you read it. It must have been torture.

You must be wondering what drove me to it, and here is my true confession. I am responsible for Leila's death.

How can you believe me after my first letter to you was such an awful lie? But I took the liberty in my pathetic attempt to throw you off the trail and used some personal information that your sister shared with me in her last moments. Perhaps that is enough to persuade you?

I mentioned earlier that I wanted to apologise for what I'd done, but how can I possibly? I stole your sister's life away, took her from her family. I didn't mean to, but things happened outside of my control and the next thing I knew she was gone.

For years I've replayed every moment that aligned to bring Leila and me together, wondering at how so many people's lives changed that night through sheer chance. A simple sorry can't make up for what I've done, but still I need you to know that if it were possible to go back in time and change what happened, I would. Her loss should not be something that is glossed over. In the brief time I spent with her, she seemed so strong and full of life, and the fact I watched that spark die, literally, in her eyes is something that will stay with me until the day I move from this world into the next.

Then the documentary came along, and despite all those fine-sounding feelings, the strongest one I felt was fear that my secret might finally be discovered. That's what made me panic and write that ridiculous note claiming to be your twin, hoping it would stop you from looking further into her disappearance. It was cruel of me, though, to give you hope even for the briefest of moments, and the fact it's not the worst thing I've done to you only increases my shame and horror.

I'm being torn in two by cowardice and wanting to do the right thing, by the dark and light that has ruled my life, by wanting to hide so my secret is never found out, and the urge to step forward into the light and face the music I've avoided for so long.

Having already taken so much from you, I'm afraid to come to the final part of my reason for contacting you: to ask a favour. How dare I? I don't honestly know, but as awful as it is that's exactly what I'm going to do. Here is my request:

Would you please write back? Tell me why I should hand myself in. Lend me the courage I lack to tell the police everything. I desperately want to but am too pathetic to face the music without a dance partner.

I need you, Stella; I can't do this alone. Please believe me when I tell you that.

If you're still reading, thank you for coming this far with me. With all my heart I hope you'll consider my request.

A friend

I stare in horror. I want to slam the laptop shut but can't seem to move. My eyes refuse to look away. The words stare at me. Full of malevolence.

Only they aren't. Actually, the email seems crammed with pain and sorrow.

A groan escapes me and I rub my face. I don't know what to do. I always know, but not today. Anger and uncertainty close in on me. *Shut the laptop, that will help.* The screen disappears from view. It's not enough. I need to get away from it.

As I clip the leads on the dogs, only Buddy looks keenly at me, his amber eyes seeming to question.

'I'm okay,' I tell him. 'A walk will help.'

Outside, I put my head down and the pavement blurs past my eyes, a ribbon of grey pulling us to our destination without any of us having to think about it. My mind is utterly filled with the message. The author claims he is responsible for Leila's death, but he wouldn't be the first nutcase to do so. At the last count, five people, I believe, have done so over the years. Three have entered the police station and claimed the crime as if it is a prize to be won. Of the two others, one called me and the other wrote a letter. All of the five were fully investigated and released because nothing they said added up, and what little did had been lifted straight from the newspapers. There may even be more whose confessions were so incredible that the police didn't bother informing me – I know of a group on the internet that is absolutely convinced Leila was the victim of an alien abduction, saying that there's evidence of scorch marks on the ground which have been covered up and removed from all crime scene photographs. The less evidence there is to back up their claim, the more they argue that it is its very absence that is the ultimate proof their theory is right. Some say I've been paid off by the government to keep the secret, others that I'm actually an alien replacement, while a handful think I'm an innocent victim in a huge cover-up and am simply too stupid to accept the truth of there 'being something out there', like something from *The X-Files*. Sometimes, I'll laugh about it with friends, gallows humour to hide my despair because this is not an entertainment programme but my life. My actual real life that they're desecrating with their ridiculous ideas and confessions.

I reach the beach and automatically turn right to head towards the nature reserve at Spear Point, as no dogs are allowed on the main section of beach at this time of year. The dogs are overjoyed to be let loose from their leads and chase each other across the flat golden sand, a barking mob. Despite the differences in their size, they're pretty evenly matched, though Buddy can outsprint his pals. He prefers to run by their side though, only occasionally teasing them with a blast of speed that leaves them in his wake. I pause for a moment to watch them and let their joy wash away a little of the tension. This is what I needed. The fresh air irons out my forehead as I stare out to sea. Scamp comes up beside me and starts digging a hole at my feet, but I set off again, a quick check over my shoulder confirming the dogs are following.

So, back to the problem. The writer could be someone with genuine mental health problems, or a sicko wanting to gain some notoriety. One thing he is right about is the fact that Leila was virtually forgotten by everyone outside the confines of Mereford, and a lot of those were only aware because of my annual posters. Until the twenty-fifth anniversary documentary, few people remembered or cared. Some oddbods have definitely come out of the woodwork since it aired. But perhaps the actual killer has, too.

CHAPTER TEN

I stand still, breathing the fresh sea air in deep to try to quiet my mind. My scalp prickles as though someone is watching me, every sense on high alert.

Is the author of the emails really who he claims to be? The only people who know about the letter supposedly from Leila are me, the police, Euan, and of course the sender. Yet the email referred to it. The sender of the email knows about the letter; the sender of the letter knows about my secret nickname; the links connect undeniably with Leila.

Scamp is whining for me to throw a stick she's found. As I turn my body to hurl it towards the sea, I notice someone in the distance behind me. Possibly a woman, though it's hard to tell from this far away. She's staring at me but turns away and disappears behind one of the shelters along the concrete walkway that runs parallel with the beach. My skin prickles again.

'Stella! Fancy seeing you here!'

It's Keshini, coming from the opposite direction, trying and failing to keep her hair from whipping across her face in the sea breeze. When she reaches my side, she tries to pet the dogs but they dance away. Scamp and Buster playfully chase Buddy, while Fifi presses her warm body against the back of my legs. Keshini tilts her head to one side, studying me.

'You okay? You look like you've something on your mind.'

'How are you doing? What brings you to the beach?' Hopefully, she won't notice the deflection.

'Actually, I was just heading to the café. Fancy joining me?'

An open smile, but there's tension around her eyes. A refusal hovers on my lips before Euan's 'feelings' dig surfaces, so instead I invite her to join me on the walk and ask how her job applications are going. We set off, heading into the wind.

'Not great. I'm trying to be picky about who I apply to; it's got to be right for me, not just any old thing, you know?'

'It's good to know exactly what you want. Is it bigger companies you're applying for, then?'

She faces straight forward as she replies, chattering about how smaller, bespoke companies are better so she can continue to focus on crime documentaries until she's more experienced. She doesn't look at me as I make a noise of agreement.

'Nothing's as good as my old job, though. Euan is the best; I need to be with him. I mean, he can teach me stuff.'

As she talks, my mind drifts to my own problem. The police have had the letter for a week now, but there's been no word yet about the results of any tests. As soon as I get home, I'll contact DCI Burns and ask for an update, and tell him about the email and… what? That I think the emailer is telling the truth? That my dream of discovering what happened to my twin may be within touching distance?

'But I've already sorted out what I'll wear to any interviews I get. There's this lush dress I've seen online.'

Keshini's words wash over me as I think. After all this time I can't let my imagination run away with me, but the questions rush in regardless. What happened between this person and Leila? How did they meet? Were they close? Was what happened to my sister an accident or something more sinister? And if it were an accident why didn't they simply call the police?

'Because red's supposed to be a power colour, isn't it? Or do you think it's too full-on?'

'It depends. Is it—?'

'Because there's a different dress I've seen…'

Then there's a final question, even more important than the others: where is Leila's body?

My eyes fly skyward as my brain tries to deal with the enormity of what I'm thinking. More than anything in the world, more than getting answers, I want to find her and put her to rest. She deserves a grave that I can visit, and a headstone. I already know where she'll be buried – beside Mum and Dad: so that they can be together at last and perhaps even know at some level what happened to her. I've never really believed in all that spiritual stuff, but Mum became convinced a few years after Leila's disappearance, when it became obvious we may never find her. She found a level of comfort in it which bewildered Dad and me, but as she wasn't being ripped off by spiritualists, we kept quiet about our own misgivings.

Mum and Dad would want to engage with this person. Just in case. I sigh and pause my walking to gaze again at the grey sea.

'Euan seems to like green. I think if I asked his opinion, he'd tell me to go for the green. Don't you?'

I literally bite my lip to hold in my impatience. 'Has anything ever happened between the two of you?'

'He's scared of looking unprofessional. You wouldn't understand.'

'Well, no. Mainly because if I'm interested in someone, I do something about it.'

'And have you? Done something?' Those big eyes turn sharp. Her head juts forward. She's about to lose her temper, and I check the tension in my own body language. Deliberately choose soft posture, soft words, to cushion the young woman who seems suddenly so aggressive yet so vulnerable.

'Keshini, your personal life is your own, so apologies if I've overstepped the mark. I'll be honest with you here: I think I've taken advantage of your kindness. The documentary made me long for the days when I was young and Leila was still alive. You befriended me and it was flattering being in your company; it reminded me of what I used to be like when I was your age. But maybe it's time for me to step away and be with people my own age again. You must be desperate to go out with your mates, drinking, dancing, talking about… whatever it is on the TV that people your age watch now. And best of all, maybe concentrating on your career, too. It's time to move on from me and the documentary and Euan—'

'Are you jealous?' She laughs. Incredulous. 'Do you think you stand a chance with him? Oh wow, you fancy him!'

'I think you'd be wiser looking for evidence that he's interested in you in anything other than a work capacity, Keshini, rather than worrying about any feelings I may or may not have for someone.'

'You think he'd want some dried-up old prune like you when he could have me? I've seen you with him, you know, throwing yourself at him. He just feels sorry for you.'

'Keshini, believe it or not I've got bigger things to worry about than this… childish drama—'

'Oh, you're telling me to grow up?'

I've never seen her like this before. Eyes bulging, veins on her neck straining as she shouts in a full-on teen tantrum.

'I'm leaving now. Good luck for the future,' I say.

I stride away, calling the dogs to me, but Keshini follows a few steps behind, still shouting. People on the beach are stopping what they're doing to look. Mums looking from us to their children to check we're a safe distance away.

'He feels sorry for you, Stella. It's a pity shag for the woman who can't get over her sister dying.'

Sand flies as I wheel around. My finger trembles as I point it towards her. 'Don't you dare bring Leila into this. If you continue to shout this nonsense, I'll have no choice but to talk to your parents. Do it again and I'll file an official complaint about your conduct with the production company. Third strike and I'll be informing the police. Be warned, Keshini. Leave me alone and we'll forget this ever happened – but you walk away now.'

The last I see of her, she's staring after me, all flared nostrils and gunning eyes.

*

Back at home, it takes a while to calm myself enough to open up the laptop, putting aside emotions. Trying to be totally rational as I read the email and analyse the written words while ignoring the awful turn my conversation took with Keshini. The first thing that strikes me is how often the sender apologises. Saying sorry will never make up for what they've done, they're right about that, but at least they're trying.

Far too little, and way too late, of course. But still.

I'll pass it to the police, as I do with anything vaguely suspicious, leaving it with them to hunt the sender down and solve the mystery. The fact it was sent to me direct rather than via the forms on my website will, hopefully, make it easier to trace the sender.

When I drop into the police station to show the email to DCI Burns, he isn't around, and the tech bod DS Alison Fox brings with her has other ideas. A few taps and DC Parker makes the sort of noise mechanics make when they're about to tell you your engine is falling to pieces and your brakes are buggered.

'See, your basic problem is that you can encrypt your IP address and do whatever you want via the Dark Web.'

'So… it's hard to trace who sent the email?'

'You could be in Dublin and a police trace would show your IP in Spain. With an encryption you can bounce your email off so many different hosts it would be nearly impossible to trace.'

'But it's not something your average Joe could do, surely. You'd have to be some kind of whizz—'

'Actually, there are loads of encrypted email services. A quick google and you'll find lots.' DC Parker sucks her teeth as if her point has been well and truly made.

'Is that what's happened here? Can't you go to whichever service has been used, serve a warrant, and force them to give you the information about the sender?'

'I don't know if that's the case with the email you've received. I'll have to do some checking, but if it is, the users are completely anonymous – that's the point of them.'

I bite my lip to keep the swear words in. It's not the officer's fault but what a ridiculous state of affairs. Sensing my frustration, she promises to investigate the email fully, and DS Fox pats my shoulder in solidarity when we're left alone.

'We'll get there in the end, eh?' I say.

'We will – we, the police. There's no easy way to say this, Stella, so I'm going to come right out with it: you need to take a step back. Your involvement in the investigation is—'

'If you're going to say unhealthy, I—'

'Unhelpful. I understand your passion, but the extent you've been included is highly irregular. Modern policing doesn't work that way.'

'Perhaps it should.'

'There has to be distance in order to be objective about the evidence. Of course, we don't want you to stop coming forward when things such as this email happen but leave the actual investigating to the professionals. Please.'

I'm ushered from the room like an annoyance. Stunned, I stand in the car park trying to decide what to do and call Burns, who comes out to meet me. The first thing he does is tell me to start trusting the team instead of relying on him, although he raises an eyebrow when told about the 'modern policing' dig.

'Just as well I'm leaving, if people think my ways are so ancient they'd make the Peelers proud.'

'Honestly, Dave, what's your gut say about these two messages?'

He looks at me in that way I've come to know so well over the last two and a half decades.

'Facts lead policework, Stella, not my stomach.'

'You – never mind. You don't think it could be—?'

'The killer?' He's never hidden the fact that, even without a body, he's convinced my sister is dead. Neither have I. 'Could be. You know we'll treat it seriously. But why on earth would the killer get in touch after all these years of getting away with it?

'Anyway, I'm glad you came in because I was going to call you this afternoon; we've got the test results back on that letter you received. There are no fingerprints on it and no DNA to identify the sender or link it to Leila.'

'What about the emailer knowing about the letter? What do you make of that?'

'Chances are they're from the same person.'

'My nickname being used…'

'Yeah, it's certainly made both items a priority for the team. Don't worry, we're going to do everything we can to find this person – and if they are, as they claim, responsible for Leila's death, they'll end up before a judge if I've got anything to do with it. I won't let you down.'

I look at the sky and blink rapidly until it's safe to meet the detective's eye again.

'Something about the combination of the note and the email has got to me like nothing else. They've burrowed under my skin like a tick,' I confess.

'You're expecting big results from the documentary and have put yourself under pressure in the process. Things have been quiet for a long time and now suddenly the world and his dog's on about your sister. It's natural to feel stirred up. But don't let a chancer get to you – and this most likely is just some bored person toying with you after binge watching the series.'

Burns promises to keep me updated, with the sort of look that tells me he's still in charge no matter what DS Fox says. And he asks that I do the same, especially if this person contacts me again and shows more personal knowledge.

We say our goodbyes, but once alone I do a couple of minutes of deep breathing in the car park. My world's been inverted and I don't like the sensation. My whole adult life I've been methodical, slow, steady, logical, in order to deal with the loss of my sister and keep a clear head for investigating her disappearance. Every time I think of the letter and email it's a jolt of electricity through me. It makes no sense that it impacts on me so much when it's almost certainly just a malicious prankster. But the airing of the documentary has stirred up a lot of emotions and there's a tension to everything I do lately. I can't squander this huge opportunity. But what if all we get for our troubles are blind alleys and the chance to chase our own tails?

I jiggle my shoulders as if shaking off my tension, then drive to my appointment with Bunny.

The front door is the colour of the face of a toddler having a tantrum, and the second I knock on it a dog starts rapid-fire yapping. I make a mental note to work on door training at some point. First, we need to work on that separation anxiety, though. It turns out that Bunny, a bichon frise, is every bit as destructive as her owner described to me. To her credit, the owner is determined to solve the problem.

'I'm mad about the destruction, of course I am, but I'm more worried about Bunny. She's clearly so miserable. I don't want to get rid of her, but maybe she'll be happier with someone else.' Tears roll down her face as she speaks.

'It won't come to that. We can sort this out. It may take a little time, okay, but we'll get there.'

It's clear Bunny adores her mum. Maybe a little too much, in fact. So the first thing I do is teach some simple training tricks in order to build the dog's confidence.

'It doesn't seem like much, I know, getting her to come when she's called, when she already knows that, but it's about making her feel good. It's an ego boost,' I explain as her owner gives her some cheese as Bunny trots confidently up to her when her name is called.

'Does she have her own bed, or does she sleep with you?'

'With me. I don't want her sleeping downstairs alone,' she adds quickly.

'Don't worry, that's fine. It's a good idea to get her a place that is just hers though, so that she can feel some confidence away from you. It may help.'

'Hang on.' The woman jumps up, disappears for a moment, then returns with a gorgeous, squidgy dog bed. 'Bought this a while back but she never used it.'

Perfect! We do half an hour of simple work of throwing cheese into the bed and encouraging Bunny into it. It takes a while as she's so nervous, but eventually she's sitting in her bed, proud as punch, tail wagging every time she's given cheese. She's a clever girl and won't take much training, I think.

'I've never thought of giving a dog cheese, but it's working wonders!'

'It's all a question of finding the right reward – do that and you can get anyone to do anything.'

At the end of the session, I recommend some trustworthy people I know who could pop in several times a day to check on Bunny. I also suggest longer walks, as tired dogs have less energy to be destructive. What I really need, though, is to see Bunny in action when she's left alone. The owner agrees to let me put a couple of little cameras around the house.

'They're only small, so they're discreet,' I explain, holding them out so she can examine them. 'When you leave the house switch them on here, see, and after that they'll record every time there's movement. When you return home, turn them off so you don't need to worry about me recording you. I'll get a couple of days' footage and create a full training programme based on it.'

As I leave the house, I can already see how much more confident both dog and owner seem, which puts a big smile on my face.

Still, I find myself checking over my shoulder unable to shake the feeling someone is watching me.

CHAPTER ELEVEN

The day has been so busy it must have lasted a week, but when my appointments are done, I nip home only long enough to get the dogs on their leads for a five-minute walk to see Mary, my mum's oldest and best friend. She'll cheer me up.

Mary is wonderful. She was a singer in a band back in the Swinging Sixties, and although she never quite hit the big time, she did have some mid-chart hits. The biggest by far was the Top 5 'Let Me Tell You a Secret'. That, and the fact she was absolutely gorgeous, with cheekbones to make Keira Knightley jealous and lips like Scarlett Johansson, was enough for her to be chosen as support act for a handful of huge stars – and linked romantically with several more. Even now that she's recently turned 77, she still has something magnetic about her; there's no ignoring Mary. She was part of the age of rebellion, fighting for peace with the 'ban the bomb' movement, putting the environment first, and becoming a vegetarian ('before Linda McCartney,' she always says). But to me she's always simply been 'Mum's best friend', and now mine, if I'm honest.

She sits in her high-back winged seat like a queen, greeting the dogs after I've leaned down and kissed her on either cheek.

'How are you, my darling?' she asks. 'You look well. Have you had sex?'

'Good grief, no!'

She keeps looking at me.

'Okay, yes, but it was weeks ago – so you're slipping.'

'Perhaps I've been waiting for you to tell me and have grown tired.' She laughs and her yellow diamond earrings swing, throwing sparkles of light across various music industry awards and black and white signed photographs of celebrities. 'Now, tell all. I have to live vicariously, these days.'

Despite it being summer, she's feeling the cold, but she wouldn't be seen dead in a sensible cardigan. A lot of the clothes she's been ordering off the internet lately are highlighter-inspired neons. They must be in – she's a lot more in touch with fashion than I am. Today she's sporting a thin cotton polo neck the colour of a tennis ball, with cropped palazzo trousers in cobalt blue linen, and some sneakers so bright white they remind me of the ones Fifi's original owner wore.

While making us a cup of tea each, I fill her in on Euan, while she leans on the back of a chair, listening.

'It was a one-off,' I finish. 'Biscuits?'

She nods, and I reach into the usual cupboard for some custard creams.

'Darling, it's about time you found someone to love and rely on and build a life with. Use this anniversary of Leila's to remind yourself that your life's been on hold for far too long. All your spare time's been devoted to your sister. You need to concentrate on yourself now – and getting a man would be a fine first step. It's like you don't want to be happy.'

'I hadn't wanted to end up alone. I'd wanted a husband. Children. A family. But after Ryan and I split up when I left university—'

'Oh, him! He was never a keeper.'

'Well, after we split I didn't even think about being single, much less mind it. My twenties disappeared in the blink of an eye and by the time I hit my thirties everyone I knew was settled down, apart from me and Farrah. The only singletons in town.'

'Don't give me that fatalistic rubbish, young lady. The decades disappeared because you were too busy playing detective all the time and trying to be both yourself *and* Leila for your parents. After Leila, you decided to never let anyone in again.'

'I do!' I bite into a biscuit. Crumbs fall onto the counter, and I scoot them around with my finger to avoid Mary's gaze. 'Oh, all right! Trust doesn't come easily to me – but I do try to keep my paranoia in check. I'm just… I'm always too suspicious of people, reading too much into everything they do. Besides, the whole "getting to know you" conversation is so complicated. They ask me if I have brothers and sisters and it's like: where do I even start?'

My gaze drops to the floor, feeling like a scolded child. Mary's house is always neat and tidy but is starting to show signs of neglect. The kitchen floor is dusty around the mats she's laid down to help stop her slipping, so she clearly struggles to bend. The carpet doesn't get vacuumed unless I do it on the pretext that it helps me think – I generally have to pretend there's a problem to mull over, though she probably isn't fooled. My eyes slide up to meet hers, gazing at me with her brows drawn together.

'Don't worry about me,' I say, taking hold of her hand. 'I've accepted it's going to be me and the dogs for the rest of my life, and believe it or not, I'm happy. I like my own company, don't need someone else to complete me.' *No one, except Leila.*

'There's nothing wrong with any of that, except you've said it that many ways in the space of one breath, it makes me think you're protesting too much. Just saying.'

'Erudite old devil.'

Mary inclines her head in regal agreement. 'Have a fling. Some fun. Remember that? Roger this young man senseless! I would, given half the chance…'

Laughing, I roll my eyes and promise to think about it. 'Now, do you need me to buy any food?' I ask, to change the subject.

She hasn't been the same since a fall a couple of months ago. Before that she was still doing yoga, but after breaking her hip she's barely moved from her chair. She eats like a bird, despite me buying all her favourite foods. She never had children, so there is only me. Not even any nephews and nieces, as she was an only child. She is not someone to be pitied, though, she's a kickass inspiration, whose body might be starting to let her down a little, but still has a mind as sharp as a tack and would probably thump anyone who described her as 'sprightly'.

Her fridge is running low, and a quick check in the cupboards confirms they're in the same state. I start to make a list, but she puts her hand over mine to still it.

'I have news. I'm moving house! I've found a marvellous place and the contracts will be signed next week.'

'What? That's – how? – it's so quick.'

'The magic of the internet, darling. I found it online, and my solicitor has sorted it all. I didn't tell you before because you'd try to talk me out of it.'

I shake my head in confusion as she tells me about the assisted living village she'll be in.

'But you could move in with me if you want someone to look after you.'

'You're… you're my friend, not my nursemaid. I won't be used as yet another excuse not to live your life to the full.'

Mary's always been just a couple of streets away from me. Why is everything changing suddenly? First DCI Burns, now Mary. I don't like it.

'You don't need to move. I can come here more often. We could even get some carers in, if you really feel you need the extra support.'

She's shaking her head and the look in her eyes is pure pity. I try again, desperation making me cruel.

'Isn't assisted living like accepting defeat, after living your whole life on the edge?'

'Did I ever tell you about the time I met Marilyn Monroe?'

'Mary—' Now is not the time for one of her anecdotes.

'Such wisdom! Of course, no one was interested in what she had to say; they were too busy looking at her. I was only 14 or 15 and trying to break into movies, and of course I thought the perfect way to get noticed was to be seen with Marilyn when she visited London for the premiere of *The Prince and The Showgirl*. I sneaked into her hotel by pretending to be a chambermaid and that's how I ended up in her room. She was incredibly kind, saying I reminded her of herself at that age, that desperation to achieve and be more than I was. She told me not to be afraid of change. "Sometimes good things fall apart so better things can fall together," that's what she said, and it's always stuck with me.

'So, my darling, accepting the inevitable and making the most of it isn't the same as being defeated. I'll be with people my own age – don't write us off as a bunch of boring old dears; I'll shake the place up a bit if it needs it. You'll see for yourself when you visit, but this place is amazing. It's not an old people's home, it's a village set up for people of retirement age. You know they've got a little cinema on site? There are book clubs, music lessons – I've asked if I can give some singing lessons, did I mention that? – art lessons, exercise classes, all on my doorstep. And if I need any help, it's there at the push of a button; I'm not as steady on my pins as I used to be.'

It does sound good. Perfect, in fact. The more Mary tells me about it, the more I know she's doing the right thing. Her eyes are wide as she speaks, her hands animated, and she leans forward. She's excited. To steal that from her wouldn't be the action of a friend, much less a virtual daughter.

'Did you really meet Marilyn Monroe?' I ask.

'Oh, yes. She was more ordinary to look at in real life but had something that glowed from within. I wish life could have been

kinder to her, but then I wish that for many people in my life.'
She lifts my hand to her lips and kisses it. Gives a sigh. 'The older
I get, the more I look back on life. Think about how I could have
done things differently, how hurts could have been avoided. It's
one of the reasons why I want to move: so that I have some life
ahead of me, not all in the past; otherwise it's too easy to dwell on
mistakes and if onlys and beat yourself up about trying to make
up for them when it's all too late.'

Her words make me think of the email. DCI Burns wondered
why the killer would get in touch after all these years when they're
in no danger of being found out – not really. Listening to Mary
talk, it makes a certain sense that they've suddenly had a fit of
conscience. Like Mary, I've found myself thinking about the past
even more than usual as I get older. It seems to be part of ageing.
Perhaps the emailer really is the person who took Leila's life, and
wants to atone for mistakes made.

I don't share my thoughts with Mary, keen to not do anything
to dampen her excitement. With so much to look forward to, I
don't want to tell her about the letter and email unless something
comes of them. After an hour we kiss goodbye, and I listen to
make sure she locks the door behind me before heading to the
beach so the dogs can stretch their legs properly. While they race
about like lunatics, barking with joy at one another, I pull my
phone out and check for new emails.

There's nothing from the possible killer. I can't help feeling
disappointed, even though I hadn't expected anything.

The sun is sliding towards the horizon before I finally call the
dogs to me and we wander home.

I push the front door open and Scamp surges forward, taking me
off-guard and almost unbalancing me.

'Hey! Give me a second to get your lead off!'

Buddy is giving little huffs. Not quite a bark, but something is disturbing him. The second Scamp's lead is unclipped, she puts her nose down and starts trotting around, tail wagging. She's following a scent, one that has got her excited. Buddy follows after her, still making his funny huffs, while Buster keeps looking between me and his brother and sister, unsure of whether to stay on guard duty or follow them. Fifi is the only one who acts normally and goes to her water bowl.

Someone has been in the house. While I was out walking the dogs.

The links of the chain lead dig into my knuckles as I wrap it around my right hand and make a fist. It makes a good makeshift knuckle-duster. The other leads swing from my left hand like an impromptu cat o' nine tails as I step cautiously into the house, watching the dogs. If there's someone still here then they'll find them first and alert me. Every sense is on high alert. I can hear nothing but the dogs walking busily around the sofa, sniffing along the coffee table. Scamp jumps up, running her nose along one cushion then looking at me and snorting. Her tail slows to a lazy wave, and the other dogs have a sniff at the cushion, too, then come to me.

'All gone?' I whisper.

I sidle further into the room and keep my back to walls so that no one can come up behind me. A check of the house reveals… nothing. Everything is in place. After everything that's happened over the last few months, perhaps we're all feeling a bit off-kilter. That's what I tell myself as I start to cook. But tonight, instead of having the back door wide open to let the hot air out and allow the dogs to trot around on the grass, I keep it locked.

CHAPTER TWELVE

Documentary Transcript
Title: *Missing: The Twin Who Never Came Back*

[Interior, Stella's house. She is sitting with Euan on her sofa, sifting through old newspaper cuttings.]

Voiceover – Euan: More women are killed by partners or ex-partners – sixty-one per cent – than by strangers. So it was inevitable that the investigation into Leila's disappearance initially concentrated on the boyfriend, Damien Francis. Even after he was ruled out, rumours continued to persist about him, and he and his family were hounded from the town. His house had been repeatedly targeted by vigilantes, and he was beaten up several times, according to police records I've obtained through the Freedom of Information Act. No one apart from Damien has ever been in the frame.

Euan to Stella: Why do you think no one has come forward with information? Do you think someone saw what happened and is too afraid to for some reason?

Stella: Possibly. Fear could definitely be a factor, but I also think that people don't like to speak out and make themselves look stupid. The other day, I read a news story about some neighbours who heard screaming coming from the flat next door. They didn't do anything because they didn't want to get involved in a personal matter and then have it be awkward between them and the woman next door – they barely knew her apart from to say hello to as they passed in the corridor.

Her boyfriend beat her to death.

Embarrassment stopped her from being saved.

In Leila's case though, maybe no one did see or hear anything. Look at the number of women who disappear every day. Look at the number of rapes that happen in broad daylight. Look at the abductions of children. If an attacker is confident, quick and most importantly obvious, they can get away with anything, pretty much.

Euan: What do you mean, obvious?

Stella: If an attacker is confident and obvious, it's easier to hide in plain sight, which means those close to them may not realise there's anything to be suspicious of.

Okay, it's like this…

[Tucks hair behind ears.]

If someone is looking shifty in the middle of the night, it catches your attention, doesn't it? It looks suspicious, so you're more likely to notice and call the police or check that the other person is okay. But if it's broad daylight and the people are smiling, and the person is being really blatant about what they're doing, then no one bothers them. But who's to say that one of them isn't holding a knife or a gun and telling the other person: "smile and look relaxed or I'll kill you right now"? Loads of burglaries take place in broad daylight. Someone near me got broken into once, in the middle of the day. The person who did it shinned up a pipe at the front of the house to gain access. A passer-by did stop – but only to ask if he wanted a hand. It didn't enter the person's head that the bloke halfway up the drainpipe might be lying because he wasn't even trying to be subtle about what he was doing.

Perhaps the reason why no one came forward in Leila's case is because they genuinely don't realise what they saw; they think it's too obvious to be of any importance – which is why police always say in their appeals something along the lines of: "no matter how small you may think it is, if you remember something please come forward".

Euan: Or perhaps they do realise now how important what they witnessed was, but don't want to speak up because they feel it makes them look bad that they've waited for such a long time.

[Stella nods.]

If that is the case, what would you say to them?

Stella: If you know anything about that day back in 1994, please come to the police. Maybe you were afraid to speak out at the time; maybe your situation has changed. Out of love and respect for my sister, I really need to know what happened and be sure that the person that took her from us will never hurt anybody ever again.

You know what, you don't even need to come to the police, contact me. It doesn't matter that it's taken you time to realise the truth, the only thing that matters is that you know – or suspect – it now. No one will think any less of you for waiting.

I just wish someone could explain to me – or a judge and jury – and tell me why they killed her. It makes no sense to me. It will never make sense to me.

[As she speaks a single tear escapes. The camera zooms in on it shakily, following it as it trickles down her cheek, until it is abruptly wiped away.]

CHAPTER THIRTEEN

My limbs are heavy with fatigue this morning. The dogs didn't stir in the night, and there were no further signs that anyone had come into the house, so I think I'm probably reading too much into their actions. I slept like the dead last night, but when sleep came so did the dream with its crushing darkness echoing with Leila's cries. This morning calls for a hearty breakfast to kick-start my day, and I'm just flipping my fried egg when a knock on the door makes me drop it on the floor, the yolk spilling out and into the cracks where the lino tiles are starting to break up. The dogs race forward, with Buster winning the prize. I pick up my rape alarm and hide it behind my back when I open the door.

It's Euan. 'Sorry I'm so early, but I wanted to be sure to catch you. Listen, I've a contact in the police telling me someone's been in touch claiming to be the killer. Is that right?'

'No comment.' I go to close the door.

'Hey, hey, hey. I'm here as a friend—'

'Sounds like it. What are you even doing here? You live in London, don't you?'

He's always popping up. Even before we did the documentary together, there he was, just happening by when I had that run-in with Fifi's owner. Coincidence or something more? Why is it that since I met him I've been haunted by the feeling someone is watching me? It could be paranoia – but it could just as easily be my animal instinct kicking in. No wonder my stomach flips every time I see him.

Euan's jaw is working, unsure how to answer me. I throw him a lifeline, but only so I can tow him further out of his depth. It's time I started investigating the journalist. 'Sorry – not a morning person. Come in. I'm doing a cooked breakfast, if you're interested?'

He smiles that easy smile of his as he comes inside. As soon as he's over the threshold he hunkers down to greet the dogs. Scamp generally distrusts everyone, but now gives her ultimate seal of approval by rolling over to show her stomach.

'Hussy. You should play harder to get,' I say.

The rest of the dogs are just as bad. Fifi gazes adoringly at Euan while he scratches the favourite spot behind her ears. I soften slightly. If the dogs like him it counts for something.

'Come on through to the kitchen. Don't worry, they'll follow you – you've made friends for life, there.'

But as he walks behind me, I hear him pause. 'I don't remember seeing this when we were filming. Is this Mary Bird? My granddad's got a couple of her records, you know. She's a family friend, right?'

Turning, I see he's holding a photograph of Mum and Mary, their arms around one another's waists.

'Penny-Sue knew; she hid all the photos of Mary; said they might be "distracting from the main message" if viewers noticed them in the background. My mother and Mary went to school together. Despite a two-year age gap, they were inseparable as children – they were jokingly referred to as "the twins". They stayed close, starting out as entertainment staff at Butlin's holiday camp just down the road.'

'That's where Mary formed the band with her husband, Joe, wasn't it? Like I say, my granddad's a huge fan.'

'Really? They never made it that big, really.'

'Toured with big names, though. I bet you've heard some hair-raising stories of sex, drugs and rock 'n' roll.'

'You're determined to winkle out everyone's secrets, aren't you? How about you share some of your own?' I keep my voice light. 'Anyway, she and Mum stayed friends through it all, despite their lives being poles apart. By the time of Leila's disappearance, Mary and Joe had long since split up and she'd been living back in Mereford for years, her high-rolling life well in the past.'

'Friends in high places,' he says quietly, setting the picture down. His fingers trace the frame, eyes distant. Then he's back in the room.

'I know all about you, Stella, so how about today I even our relationship out a bit and tell you about me?'

'Relationship?'

'Friendship. Acquaintance. Thing.' He smiles easily, but a nervous energy betrays itself in the briskness of the words. It makes Scamp give a quick shake off, to rid herself of tension as we all go into the kitchen.

'One egg or two?'

'You're changing the subject. Two, please. And can I smell bacon?'

I hold up the pack of vegetarian bacon. It doesn't seem to put him off, and he asks for two rashers.

He watches me bustling around, fetching tomatoes and popping bread under the grill, while he moves some papers to one side to make room for himself at the table, and asks if I cook a lot.

My mobile vibrates with a message. It's from Keshini, the beginning of the message showing.

'Can I come round? Need to see you to...'

I turn it over without opening it.

'I'm not answering questions today, remember? Do *you* cook much?'

He gives that charming smile again. He relies on his charm a lot as a deflection technique.

'I'm away too much chasing stories.'

'Come on, I bet you've a couple of tried-and-tested seduction recipes.'

'Ah, well.' A laugh. 'Don't spoil my game, but I do tend to order in from a local bistro and claim all the glory.'

'What?' It comes out as a shriek. 'So that explains why you seemed so at ease taking over my cooking the other week.'

Bugger, I hadn't meant to mention that night ever again. 'Least said soonest mended', to quote my mum. Or to quote Mary, 'Embarrassing sex is only made worse by talking about it.' Euan ignores the reference, though, thank goodness.

'Women seem to love a man who can cook.'

'They do. What they really love, though, is someone honest.'

He has the good grace to blush. Unexpected.

'Do you live in London?'

'Just outside, in Surrey, but within the M25. It's a nice little place, and work is going well so it's no problem to afford it.' His hand covers his mouth as he plays with his neat, espresso-coloured moustache and beard, scratching gently at the short bristles. I make a mental note.

'Lots of work for a documentary maker then? That's nice.'

'I often have to turn work down at the moment. Unlike women – who are definitely not throwing themselves at my feet right now. What I mean is, I think you seem to have the impression I'm some sort of clichéd Lothario from the Big Smoke, luring women in with my well-honed seduction techniques. Actually, I'm appallingly bad at affairs of the heart.'

'It doesn't matter either way to me.' I take a slurp of tea – strong and milky like a builder's. 'What's your flat like?'

'It's near a big park, which is handy for people with dogs. Not that I've got any.'

'You sound tempted.'

'Always.' He holds my gaze for a beat longer than is strictly comfortable.

'Sorry, but what's going on here? The slightly flirty comments, the lingering looks, and the frankly shameless attempt to get my dogs onside. The documentary is over, right? You've nothing else you want from me, so what's with the charm offensive?'

'I – look, I like you. I want to get to know you. Better. I'm crap at this.'

'You? Come off it.'

'Are you always this hard-hitting with people who fancy you?' Realisation dawns across his face, and I have a bad feeling I'm turning the colour of a sunrise. 'You are, aren't you! Of course you are. Listen, please, I'm here to talk, to get to know you and so you can get to know me. No agenda. No deep, dark secrets. You seem like someone worth taking the time to let into my life and, hopefully, you might do the same, eventually. As friends.'

I look at him. He holds his hands up in surrender.

'As more than friends, ideally, yeah, okay, but if friends is all that's on offer, then I accept that. I mean, I don't know, I just feel like – well, it's too early for feelings or declarations. I don't really know you, but…' There's a moment of pause before he changes tack. 'I lie about the cooking because I feel an idiot admitting that I'm 32 years old and burn scrambled eggs; that's the problem with a career where you're away a lot and often live in hotels. It sounds glamorous, and yes, when I was young it was a great line to hook-up. But now? My flat doesn't feel like home and I work more and more to fill the hours. I'm lonely, Stella. I want to have something meaningful at some point in my life.

'I'm a country lad at heart – grew up in the countryside and want to return at some point in the not too distant future. I'm getting too old for London. It feels such a young city. I'd like a slower pace and someone to share that with, maybe.'

I stay still, say nothing. It's been a long time since anyone showed interest in me, and I'm not sure how to feel or how much to trust myself. Lately, there's been a lot of blood rushing around neglected places, and lots of feelings churning around me that I thought I'd outgrown.

He takes my hand and I don't move. Leans forward as he talks. 'There aren't many people who capture me once I've scratched beneath their surface. I'm good at reading people, Stella; good at seeing what they're hiding – it's my job. It puts me off most people. But the more I get to know you the more I *want* to know.'

My hand slides from his gentle grip easily. I laugh to break the tension.

'A lovely speech but I'm not interested in romance, friendship or whatever. Thanks for the compliment. Anyway, grub's up, so why don't you sit down at the table?'

Turning my back, I take several deep breaths to clear my head. Serve the food on two plates inherited from Mum and Dad, which are bone china and have a pattern of periwinkles painted around them and a gold rim. For the first time I really look at them and realise that they're not to my taste at all. They're pretty, but incredibly old-fashioned. An urge to get new ones ripples through me, then I scold myself for being an idiot.

The romantic interlude seems to have passed, thankfully. We tuck into our food in uncomfortable silence, so I put the radio on and CeCe Peniston fills the void by singing about falling in love at long last. There's more I want to know from Euan.

'So, you're coming around all the time because you fancy me and we had banging sex a few weeks back,' I say through a mouthful of Quorn bacon, 'but that first time we met, with Fifi, wasn't a coincidence, was it? You knew exactly who I was.'

Euan chokes on his mouthful of breakfast. Until then, I hadn't known for certain, but it had been a theory that's bugged me from the beginning. He swallows, takes a gulp of tea, too, and makes a little gasping noise before replying.

'Honestly, Stella, I didn't go to the park that day trying to bump into you. How would I have known you'd be there? Like I said before when you asked, I came to Mereford to check the area out before we started filming – just in case you agreed. You've seen how tight the turnaround is on these things, so I wanted to be fully prepped.'

His hand moves to his mouth again.

'There's more to it than that.' I shrug, taking another mouthful and raising my eyebrows at him as I chew.

'Okay, yes, I admit that when I saw you and that man—'

'Tommy Rogers.'

'…when I saw you both arguing, I did recognise you. I didn't speak up at the time due to lack of opportunity, and when I saw you again, I felt an idiot about the whole thing, so didn't reference it.'

Despite trying to keep my best poker face, I feel my eyes narrow to scrutinise him. This time he seems to be telling the truth, though my speciality is dogs not humans so what do I know? I run my eyes over him again unable to shake the feeling he's still hiding something.

The opening bar of a song on the radio interrupts my thoughts.

'"Ebenezer Goode", The Shamen,' I say before Euan can even open his mouth. Beating him is more satisfying than it strictly should be.

The mind is a strange thing, the way ideas happen when you're thinking of something completely different. Just as I relax with Euan, I suddenly recall something from yesterday's argument with Keshini…

She said she'd seen me throwing myself at Euan. The barb about the pity shag shows she's aware he's stayed over. Which means she's been hanging around outside, spying on me. On us. Perhaps she's even been inside my home. The thought shocks me and I decide to have it out with her as soon as possible.

*

For days I call Keshini, but she doesn't answer despite her text message, which had been characteristically self-centred.

Can I come round? Need to see you to apologise. Please don't tell Euan what happened!

I typed a reply back:

Call me!

But she hasn't.

Euan stays away, and I settle back into a routine. Mornings are spent checking social media and emails, walking the dogs, work, then either straight home or a quick visit to Mary before another walk and more emails and social media. There are no fresh leads, no one is coming forward as an eye witness. It's hard not to start getting annoyed by the lack of progress, and it makes me realise how much I've pinned on the documentary. Apart from the letter pretending to be from Leila, and the consequent email from 'the killer', there's been nothing. DS Fox has been in touch, saying that the tech unit have had no luck identifying them. That was a blow, of course, but it's also not a huge surprise. After all these years, I hadn't really believed it would be so easy that within hours police would be kicking down a front door and making an arrest.

Today is Sunday, so I'm later than normal to go online. Twitter is quietening down now. Presumably, people are too busy with their children to have time. Facebook is dead, too, but at least the emails are busy.

There's one with a blank subject line. I open it and instantly my heart stutters.

Dear Stella,

How I wish you'd replied to me, though it's understandable you didn't. Yet I can't stop myself from contacting you again, selfish devil that I am, to make another confession to you…

I'm so scared of dying in prison. My whole life I've always believed in justice and know it's what someone who commits a crime deserves, but when I think of what being behind bars would do not only to me but my family, I know I can't do it. It's selfish and awful, but that's no surprise. Living like this isn't an option either, though, which only leaves one solution: I'll kill myself.

Me ending it is easier all round. I long for this pain to be over, and surely knowing I'm not in this world any more will give you the closure you need. Don't blame yourself for not getting back to me; the blame for this mess is mine alone.

Think badly of me. I deserve every dreadful thought.

I will remain always and for ever,
Your friend.

CHAPTER FOURTEEN

No, no, no! They think they'll make restitution for what they've done by killing themselves? No way! I can't let them do that. If they die now, Leila's remains will never be found. I need to email a reply right now! My fingers fly over the keyboard. Words spew across the screen, misspelled and out of order in my haste. From the corner of my eye I can see the dogs watching me, drawn by the hammering of the keys. As ever, they bring me to my senses, especially Fifi, who has started to yawn and pant. I clench my hands to stop myself writing anything else.

Think, think, think! Don't worry, don't panic, just think.

I drag my eyes from the screen down to the keyboard and breathe slowly in and out several times, staring at the worn keys, the way the printed letters 'a', 's' and 'n' have disappeared completely, and the space bar has an area worn smooth slightly to the right of centre. When my heart returns to normal, I allow myself to consider the message again.

This person is probably nothing to do with Leila, and the threat of suicide is just another twist in their cruel hoax. The sender not contacting me again is good news, right? One less nutter to deal with.

That's if they are playing tricks. If there's even the slightest chance the sender really is who they say they are, though, then the police need to track them down and fast. So I need to keep them not only alive but communicating with me because the more emails the greater the likelihood of this mystery person letting something slip that will identify them. Under arrest, they'll tell me where Leila's body is. By this time next year, she might finally be laid to rest.

My nerves tingle.

What to reply, though? They're on a knife edge; write the wrong thing and they might fall and end their life – taking with them the information I need. The messages are full of contradictions; this person is clearly tearing themselves to pieces trying to decide what to do. Keeping a secret for such a long time does terrible things to a person, I know. It wears away at you, like water dripping on stone. Getting them to reveal the hole in their soul won't be easy, though; I'd rather die than show anyone mine.

Putting myself in their place, it's perfectly understandable that Leila's killer (if that's who this person is) doesn't want to hurt their family by telling them the truth. And why killing themselves might feel like punishment enough. I understand it – but there's no way it can happen. They have to face up to the consequences of their actions properly, and that means telling me where my sister's body is. No matter the cost, I need to lay her to rest.

I make myself go to work – the weekends are always busy – and keep thinking of how to reply to the email. Animals are straightforward and honest, it's just a matter of translating what is making them happy, sad, scared, whatever, but people have so many layers and not all of them good. The day is spent feeling jangly and edgy, wondering if I'm too late and the 'friend' has gone through with their plan, wondering if rather than taking my time I should send back something, anything, to them. What?

Please, please, please don't top yourself, you selfish arsehole – not until you lead me to my sister's body. Then you can do whatever you want and no one will care.

It's what I want to write but it's not going to get me anywhere…

*

I drop in on Mary on my way to the beach and bring her up to speed about the letter and the emails, and confess I want to reply.

'Hmm, so I'm not the only one who's been keeping secrets,' she says when I've finished.

'There have never really been any between the two of us.' None aside from the one that's haunted my heart for my whole adult life. *The sound of the slap ringing out. The sting on my skin. The horrifying realisation…*

Mary's eyes, bright beneath lids drooping with age, bore into me. Even after all this time, it takes a lot of willpower not to tell her. If I were to confess to anyone, it would be her. Sometimes I wonder if it would be better to get the truth out, but much like the person we're discussing, I'm too afraid. Instead, I fill the silence with another thought.

'I don't know if they really know anything or not. I'm not even sure if my reply will arrive or if it will bounce around the ether for all eternity never to be read. Am I being stupid emailing them?'

'Do you feel stupid?'

My reply is a shake of the head.

'There's your answer, then. Darling, they don't call it women's intuition for nothing. There are some things we simply know – and when we do, it's ignorant to ignore it. The answer will sneak up on you when you're looking the other way.'

'In that case, distract me! If I think about it any more, my brain is going to explode.'

'You can help me pack? I've professionals coming to do the whole thing in one go, but some of my more precious personal things I'd like to know were packed with love.'

There it is again, that knot of horror at the thought of not having her round the corner from me. I pick up a photo of her and Mum, their arms wrapped around each other, cheeks pressed against one another, both in their Butlin's holiday camp uniforms.

'You read my mind,' she smiles. 'That's definitely one I want taken good care of. If anything happened to it, I'd be devastated. She was – and you are – the closest thing to family I have in this world. She could have been famous, you know, with that voice of hers and those legs! But all she ever wanted was a family.'

'I'm going to miss you so much.'

'I'm a twenty-minute drive away. You'll come visit, won't you, darling?'

I roll my eyes at her to show how silly she's being to even ask. 'When can I see this amazing new home, anyway?'

'I pick the keys up next Wednesday. Want to come with me?'

'Too right! You're not moving in without my seal of approval.' I'm only half joking. 'Anyway, what else do you want me to pack? I'd do the whole place for you, quite happily. You don't need to waste money on professionals.'

Mind you, it's a five-bedroom house and there are lots of trinkets, ornaments, memorabilia, and general… stuff. One room, the size of my living room and kitchen combined, is entirely given over to her clothes, shoes and handbags. Even only packing the precious things she wants me to will take me every night for a week, at least. I pick up a photo on the side that I've never seen before.

'Hey, who's this? He looks a total dude!' The man's long, black hair falls in waves from his centre parting. He's handsome, though his nose is a bit big, and he's wearing a tie-dye T-shirt, flares and platforms, and standing beside a well-used drum kit.

Mary looks at him and shakes her head. 'No one. I really don't remember.' Odd. She generally remembers everyone and has a story for them all. The shake of her head is curt. 'Anyway, do tell me all about your love life—'

'Packing! Not gossiping!' I laugh. 'There's loads to do—'

'It will all get done, a bit at a time. It's amazing what you can achieve in instalments. That's how I got a friend off drugs once, you know, by cutting it down and down and down just the tiniest bit at first so it didn't matter, but it added up over time, you see. Everything a bit at a time, that's the key. He had no idea at the time, of course, but Keith thanked me in the end, once he was clean.'

'Keith…' A suspicion forms. 'Hang on, you got Keith Richards off drugs? Is that who you're talking about?'

'Darling, I'd never name names.' She does, constantly. 'Let's just say his dad was what made me decide to act.'

I shake my head and laugh as Mum's face disappears under bubble wrap. 'Sometimes, Mary—' Then it hits me. I stare at her, mouth open. 'Oh my god, you're a genius! Ooh, sorry, didn't mean to hug you so hard, but you've done it! You've given me an idea of how to get this person to open up to me… bit by bit.'

She's frowning in confusion, but instead of explaining, I grab my mobile and start tapping something out. I read a couple of lines to her, and she makes a few suggestions, which I take in then start adding more until I've got something that's just right. Mary gives it the thumbs up. I try not to fiddle with it too much after that, despite temptation.

'Better to speak from the heart than try for cold perfection,' agrees Mary.

'Okay, here's the final draft,' I say. '"Dear Friend, Please don't do anything rash in my name. The last thing I want is for you to take your life. Just as I read to the end of your messages as you requested, I ask you to do me the same favour. If you are as serious about doing what I want as you claim, then you'll LISTEN to me on this. You must stay alive!

'"If you are who you say you are, then I believe you when you also say you're sorry; if you weren't, there would be little point in getting in touch with me. You aren't gloating about what happened. If anything, you seem haunted by it; in which case, let me help you. Perhaps we could arrange a date and time to meet, and we can walk into a police station together. I'll gladly be by your side, giving you the strength you need so that we can both reach an end to this nightmare.

"'If that's too scary to contemplate then don't worry. Don't even think of it right now. We can keep these conversations between the two of us and see where it leads.

"'It must be a terrible weight for you to carry such a secret for so many years. So let's tackle this as if you carry a suitcase full of woes on your back. Just open it up and leave one item of clothing with me to lighten the load the tiniest bit. A metaphorical sock. See if you can feel the difference when it's gone; I'm sure you will. Tell me one thing about that awful night. Only one, and it doesn't even have to be anything big and important, just whatever you can manage. Then see if unburdening yourself makes you feel better. I'm sure it will because I can tell that's what you really want. Sock it to me (see, we can even joke about things). Trust me, I'm here for you.'"

I finish reading. Silence. Mary's eyes sparkle as she reaches out and squeezes my arm.

'Wow, that's… that's powerful stuff. Send it, darling.'

I can't bring myself to sign my name as if we're friends. Part of me wonders if I should swallow my pride and do it, but it makes my skin crawl.

With a quick tap and a whooshing sound it disappears into the ether.

'I just hope it gets read,' I whisper.

*

Walking home I can't decide if I feel lighter for sending the email, or scared that it will make no difference and I'll never hear from this person who always claims to be my Dear Friend again. The dogs pad by my side, sensing my agitation and staying close by even when we hit the beach, mostly abandoned by tourists who have now moved on to restaurants and pubs for the evening. Clouds have gathered, lit from below by the setting sun. Buster stands on his back legs and waves his paws at me, and I pull a tennis ball from my pocket and toss it across the wet sand. Drops of water fly like sparks from his paws as he and the others race after it. Worry and fear are a waste of energy, I remind myself, and let them be washed away by the sunshine. The peace is prised from my grasp by that now-familiar feeling that someone is watching me. I turn, scanning the beach, but there's no one there but fellow dog walkers and a couple out for a romantic evening stroll. Like a dog, I shake the paranoia off physically, then call out to my pack so we can head home before it gets dark.

The sense of being watched reminds me. As I walk, I dial Keshini; not that she'll answer...

'Stella!' she cries. Then the sound of sobbing.

CHAPTER FIFTEEN

Documentary Transcript
Title: *Missing: The Twin Who Never Came Back*

[Piece to camera. Euan walks along the beach.]

Euan: When Leila went missing, she was just 19 years old, with her whole life ahead of her. What made her disappearance doubly tragic was that her identical twin had been left behind, and it's this that seemed to particularly fascinate the nation's media. That the fate of two identical young women should be so different – and it should all be down to a single item of clothing.

[Cut away to a police evidence photograph of a woman's trench coat in maroon, mock croc leatherette, with a belted waist.]

Voiceover – Euan: The coat became a key fixation with not only the police but the press and public. It added a tragic twist to an already evocative tale. The twins had, without one another's knowledge, bought identical coats and wore them for the first time that fateful night. How much did the victim being a twin influence the investigation – and what impact has the loss of her other half had on the twin that was left behind?

[Cut to interior, Stella's home. She and Euan sit at opposite ends of her sofa.]

Stella: I fell in love with the trench coat as soon as I saw it. Loved the colour. It looked vampish. Sexy. It matched my favourite lipstick colour, Amethyst Shimmer, which seemed like a big deal at the time. Back in the days when that was my biggest worry. It had been so wet lately. Hot – bloody roasting in fact – but we kept having storms. So I decided to buy the trench coat in case it rained again.

Beadle's About had just started when my boyfriend and I set off from home for the party. I'd wanted to make sure I set the video for it because we all loved that programme. We'd always watched it together, as a family, and loved laughing at people being pranked. That's how it felt when Leila went missing. Like it was a cruel prank. Like at any minute, Jeremy Beadle would come out with his massive microphone and snigger in our faces.

As soon as I got to the pub, the sky started to darken. It was so sweaty and humid that I chucked my coat off the minute I arrived; I almost had to peel it off my skin. The weather front came from nowhere. It was like an eclipse, that's how fast it happened. We were all outside, and a huge gust sent flying the glasses and paper plates we'd set up on a table outside. Then the rain started. Massive drops that quickly turned to a deluge. It was vicious. We were all running backwards and forwards, bringing everything in from outside. I remember Dad saying what a good job it was that he'd hired the room as well as the beer garden.

I could barely breathe it was that humid indoors. So many people were crammed inside, dancing. It created a weird atmosphere, a tension I hadn't expected. Almost like the weather was trying to warn us of something terrible coming. But even though it was so unbearable, we couldn't open any windows because it was raining so hard it would have flooded into the room, you see. There was no escaping the atmosphere and the sticky, overwhelming heat, just like there was no escaping the future that was bearing down on us but none of us could see it.

[Shudders, then gives a laugh.]

Sorry, got a bit melodramatic there.

Euan: What was it like being a twin?

Stella: What's it like not to be? That was always our reply when people asked us – and as far back as I can remember, Leila and I were asked. People have always been fascinated by us being identical, as if it's the only interesting thing about us. And can I just add something? You said "was: What *was* it like to be a twin?" I still am, always will be. There's a photograph of us when we were newborns in the cot, and we're sucking each other's fingers as if we don't know where one ends and the other begins. There's no destroying that connection, whether Leila's here or not.

Being a twin defined us, but it was also something we took for granted – like you take breathing for granted, you know? If I thought about it at all, I suppose I felt a bit sorry for the other boys and girls who didn't have a best friend like Leila; someone who knew exactly how I felt about everything without ever having to explain. Who understood all my thoughts and feelings: what made me laugh, what made me cry – it all made her feel the same. We were identical. One person split in two.

Neither of us knew there'd come a time when we were no longer together. That I'd look back on the past and realise, now I'm alone, just how amazing and unique it is to be an identical twin.

Euan: Was there ever any competition between the two of you? What about when you got older and fancied the same people?

[Shakes her head.]

Stella: We were never attracted to the same men. Leila preferred hers more quiet and reserved, whereas I always like the loud, overconfident, sporty types.

I think I was aware from the age of about five that we would be compared by our looks and that photographs would be pored over. We always insisted on being pictured separately in school photographs; the only time we liked to be apart.

People loved to find little differences in us. When we were nine, we got bikes identical in every way apart from our name, which our parents had stencilled on. One day we were racing each other when Leila's tyre hit something – must have been an unseen stone. She went flying over the handlebars! My stomach shared her weightlessness, then crashed down on the road beside her. I threw my bike down and, as I crouched beside her, saw blood pouring down her chin and knew she'd lost a tooth before she even opened her mouth. She spat it into my hand and burst into tears – not because of the pain, no; she was upset because we didn't look alike any more. Of course, she got a replacement tooth, but she was left with a tiny scar on her upper lip. She was always so careful to cover it with make-up as soon as we were old enough to wear any. In summer, it always stood out white against her tan. Everyone used that scar to tell us apart. Before that, Mum had used our clothes; she dressed us differently so that she could differentiate. Yet as we got older and started to buy our own clothes, we'd often come back from separate trips to the shops and discover we'd bought the same outfits—

[Pauses. Her nose and cheeks redden. She clears her throat.]

If one of us was pegged as more likely to survive than the other, from the start the smart money would have been on Leila. She was the firstborn – and like so many firstborn twins, she was the heavier at birth and the stronger. As we grew up, she was the leader while I followed, something that had been set from the moment she set off down the birth canal before me. She was always protective of me – to be honest, she was protective of everyone she cared about, but was particularly, fiercely, protective of me. It cut both ways, though. No one ever bullied us because they knew they were taking on a team, not an individual.

And then, suddenly, she was gone and I was alone. Trying to come to terms with that was…

[Long exhalation. Stella shakes her shoulders slightly.]

I'm lucky, though. There's no other way of looking at it. I had nineteen years sharing my life with Leila. There is nothing like having a twin, especially an identical one. We shared special feelings, secrets we never told anyone else, the personality we shared, the idiosyncrasies. Imagine that. Not having her is an impossible loss; but having her was the biggest bonus anyone could ever have. There are some things that simply can't be shared with others, only with your twin.

Euan: It sounds wonderful. It must have been tough getting used to being just you – a twin-less twin.

Stella: Understatement of the century.

[Shrugs.]

You just get on with it, though; it's not like there's any choice. I had to live in a totally different way and find unknown parts of me in order to survive. Yes, there's still a unique kind of loneliness, but keeping busy helps. I'm always busy. If she hadn't left me, would I have been less insular? Almost certainly. Part of me went with her.

Euan: You mentioned looking in the mirror previously, and how it makes you miss your sister. But I've noticed you avoid mirrors; is that because it's difficult for you?

Stella: Yes.

[She stares at him. Silence. Euan coughs.]
[Cut to footage of the police reconstruction of Stella playing Leila getting into the taxi on her last journey home.]

Voiceover – Euan: When police filmed a reconstruction, the obvious choice to play the missing twin was her sister. The footage was shown on Crimewatch in the UK and on national and local news channels, and while hundreds of calls were received by the police as a consequence, the longed-for breakthrough never came. I can't help wondering how walking in Leila's footsteps must have affected Stella.

[Cut to interior. Stella's home.]

Stella: Playing Leila was really screwed up, but it had to be done. Like I've said before, there's no point getting emotional about these things.

[Her hands tighten into fists.]
[Cut to Euan on the beach. Piece to camera.]

Euan: Despite police and Stella working tirelessly to find Leila, convinced something terrible had happened to her, no trace has ever been found. But the more I started digging into this incredible case, the more I began to wonder… In the next episode, I'll be looking at some startling new evidence and asking: could the pressure of living two lives have led Leila Hawkins to suicide? Could she even have decided to abandon the twin that adored her by running away to start a new life?

CHAPTER SIXTEEN

I try to understand what Keshini is saying as she cries down the phone, but only the odd word is decipherable. There's no point talking to her like this, so I ask if she can get herself together enough to meet me at the Beach Café and hope the choking sniff is a 'yes'. A neutral place will help the difficult conversation I'm bound to have.

By the time I've got the dogs home and settled, then come out again, Keshini is already waiting for me, the tip of her nose as glowing as the sunset she's watching fade out behind the Clock Tower. Her pretty fingers are wrapped around a mug she holds between us as a barricade. For all her tears, she's not so upset her manicure has suffered – she's sporting sky blue acrylics scattered with daisies, which are so long and pointed I don't know how she manages to pick up anything. A glance at her feet confirms her Doc Martens are the same shade of blue.

'Are you okay?' I check. A nod. 'Good. Let's keep this short, eh?'

'You haven't told Euan, have—?'

'Have you been spying on me? Did you break into my home, Keshini?'

Her mouth falls open, facial muscles slack. Then it screws up as yet more tears fall. 'Please leave Euan alone—'

'Enough!' I hold my hand up to try to quiet her, but her words descend in impenetrable sobs again. It's so bizarre I find myself reaching for her hand, and she stiffens at my touch but at least the tears slow. 'There's more going on here than just a crush, isn't there?'

Lips fold into her mouth, then her hand covers it for good measure. I'm right, I'm sure of it. My heart beats faster.

'Has Euan hurt you?' She jerks her other hand from mine and looks at me like I'm mad. Okay, I'm probably way off line, but still double-check. 'Because if he has, you can talk to me about it, or anyone. Even if he's made you promise to keep it secret—'

'No! What makes you say that?' A hiccupping sigh as her manicured fingers wipe at her face. 'Are you two—?'

We're not discussing my sex life again, and that's made clear in no uncertain terms.

'I didn't mean to upset you,' she sniffs. Her eyes skitter from mine. 'I just really like him and know if you left him alone something would happen between us.'

Her skin glows the same chestnut it always does when she's telling me about him, a blush of embarrassment. Although I believe her about Euan, I know she's not telling me the full story, but I've tried my best.

Over the following days, my brain feels like it may explode there's so much to think about – and it's all out of my hands, from Keshini to the mysterious Dear Friend. Over the years I've got used to the ebb and flow of expectation as solid leads disappear like footprints in the sand. Still, there is something different about this time. I'm more desperate, constantly haunted by the feeling that this is my last chance. Now or never. The MISSING posters have faded, been torn down or covered up with other posters, everyone moving on.

As the end of the week approaches, I check my email until it turns into an obsession. Even during training sessions I'm sneaking my phone out when the dogs should be getting my undivided attention. They're all doing so well, and Bunny in particular is improving massively. The footage from the cameras picked up her triggers and key behaviour, and the owner and I have been working together daily to stop her destroying cushions and carpets when left alone. Another couple of sessions and the little bichon frise will no longer need me – and that lack of challenge isn't helping me because I need something to distract me from the worries nibbling at my peace of mind. Is the Dear Friend emailer ghosting me, no longer wanting to engage for fear of letting something slip that will put them in jail? Have they taken their life, convinced they're doing the right thing for everyone? Or perhaps they are sitting at home, worrying themselves into a breakdown trying to decide what to do?

Friday arrives, and there's still no reply to my email. Each of those five days has felt like a year. I'm still checking in with the police, but there's never any news. Social media is still full of people with theories, but no new facts to share about Leila. I'd hoped that the documentary would end the circle my life's been trapped in; instead, it seems only to have tightened it into a noose that is starting to strangle me.

Desperate for distraction, I start thinking about the pesky journalist. Who am I kidding? It's not an active decision, Euan keeps popping into my head whether I like it or not. The sex may have been drunken on my part, but it was great, and memories of it sneak up on me often when I'm alone in bed.

So it's almost – but not quite – a disappointment that he's done as he's told and hasn't contacted me. He probably thinks he's 'treating 'em mean to keep 'em keen', but that's not going to work with me because there's no room for romance in my life. Another hook-up would be nice, though. More importantly, it's occurred to me that he is the only other person who knows about both the note pretending to be from my sister and the email claiming to be from the person responsible for Leila's disappearance. Then there's the complication of Keshini and him. For those reasons alone he's worth looking at more closely.

It's got nothing to do with fancying him. Okay?

Euan makes me suspicious. I live in a world of worst-case scenarios – because in my case the worst really did happen. Most people don't wait around long enough to get past my defences. Euan is waiting. It makes me uncomfortable. It makes me wonder why he's being so patient.

This is how I end up spending Friday evening sitting in the garden, hunched over my laptop, searching the internet for information about Euan in a not-at-all-stalker-ish way. I'd researched the company before I agreed to filming going ahead, but they were a start-up with little information about them. Leila's story was the first documentary they'd made. A bit of rooting around on Companies House quickly reveals that Euan actually owns the whole thing. That explains why Penny-Sue didn't give him what for when he clashed with me on the first day of filming.

I'm more interested in his private life, though. His Facebook page has tight privacy settings (good on him; they're the same as mine), so I can't see a thing, not even a friends' list. Twitter is all about his work. He's tweeted a couple of times about the documentary, but before that there was nothing for a couple of years, which is a bit surprising, but I suppose he's too busy to update social media all the time. His Instagram account consists of precisely four photos. One of him smiling into the camera, with sun flare looking artsy across the Palace of Westminster. The other three are pictures of coffee cups.

I sit back and stretch my arms above my head, twisting this way and that. My back gives a satisfying crack. That's better. Scamp looks at me.

'It's not t-r-e-a-t time yet.'

She settles her head back between her paws and sighs the sigh of the deeply disappointed.

I return to refreshing my email and getting annoyed, before returning to clicking on more Euan-related links. Most of them seem at least a couple of years old, though. I see he's written a couple of books about celebrities and give a little bark of surprised laughter because it's absolutely what I can imagine him doing – him and his love of big words and overlong sentences.

There are various images of him through the years, too. Younger. Fresh-faced. Hair a bit too long. He looks exactly the no-good, arrogant type I'd have fancied the pants off as a teenager. Good thing I'm older and wiser now. I look closer. Study him in a way I wouldn't dare if he were in front of me. His eyes have a slight downward slant that gives them a sad, soulful impression.

My stomach dances. Bugger. I wish Leila were here. I'd love to tell her that I've met someone and ask what she thinks of him because I can't make up my mind. No amount of wishful thinking has ever brought her back to me, I think, deciding to stop my research and grab a glass of orange juice. Another wild Friday night looms. I check my emails again – still nothing – and stand just as the text alert on my phone sounds.

'Talk of the devil and he appears,' I mutter when I realise it's from Euan.

'You free or busy? If you're at a loose end, I could come round for a couple of drinks?'

It sounds like a booty call to me.

I look at the dogs. They look at me. Buddy's amber-eyed gaze is particularly hard.

'Don't judge,' I say, then type:

'OK. Bring wine!'

Euan has manspread, face-down across the mattress, and is snoring gently. I'm cocooned in the light summer duvet, sitting up and having a bit of a letch at his tight bottom while chewing my nail, wondering how to get rid of him.

Sleeping with him definitely stopped me from checking my emails – boy, did it – but now I'm feeling guilty for using him. Then again, he's a young, fit bloke who is getting off with a mid-forties woman, so he's probably not in it for the love either.

Maybe if I make lots of noise while having a shower, he'll wake up and sneak out. I don't much fancy an awkward postcoital breakfast because I honestly don't know what to say to him. Sleeping with him once was a mistake, twice is unfortunate – and any more and he'll start to think it's a habit.

This is ridiculous. I'm a grown woman, for goodness sake. I reach my foot out towards him and… prod him. He murmurs, then his eyes open.

'Oh, you're awake!' I say. 'Want a cup of tea before you go?'

'I'll make breakfast if you—'

'Hang on, I'd better get this. Saved by the bell and all that…'

Rolling my eyes at the lameness of my own joke, I answer my ringing mobile. It's Jilly Prescott, one of my regulars. She started breeding dogs a few years ago, and often refers the proud new owners of the puppies to me for help if they feel they need it. Many do – and others call me later, in despair at their 'impossible to train' pet. Hopefully, she's got more work to send my way, which will be a far better way of keeping myself busy.

But when I answer, she's in a real state. I can't make out what she's saying through the tears.

'Someone's broken in and stolen the puppies!' she sobs.

'Bastards! What happened? Are you okay?'

'I am, but I should have fought harder. I should have stopped them. I just froze, couldn't think of a bloody thing to do, like I was held in place by one of those whatjamacalls that they have in sci-fi: a freeze ray. But poor Roxy has some terrible slashes on her muzzle. She's in with the vet now; they've had to put her under to stitch her up. She, she…' The rest of the words disappeared into incoherence.

'It's going to be okay. I'll come round right now.'

I end the call. Euan is already pulling on his clothes, almost falling over as he pulls his trousers up with a jump.

'What's happened?'

I'm too busy checking my diary to answer immediately. Great, there are no lessons booked until 4 p.m.

'Sorry, I've got to go. You'll have to have breakfast in a café – most of the ones along the seafront will be open now.'

He shakes his head. 'I'm coming with you.'

'It's nothing to do with Leila.'

'It doesn't matter – you look upset.'

I swear. 'I don't have time for this. If you're coming, let's go!'

CHAPTER SEVENTEEN

Running into Farrah's waiting room, I instantly spot the crumpled wreck of Jilly. She's doubled over her jiggling knees and looks pale enough to pass out.

Roxy is Jilly's absolute world. She only breeds from her occasionally – this is her third litter, and there's always been plenty of recovery time between. This will be the last litter she has. Jilly's priority has always been Roxy, rather than seeing her as a cash register to sell the puppies at the highest profit. She carefully vets the new owners, too, ensuring the puppies are going to a good, loving home. If a buyer does change their mind, she insists they bring the youngster back to her for a refund, rather than try to sell it on. She's a true dog lover.

One of the receptionists has her arm around Jilly and judging from the brimming bin beside her, she's gone through almost a whole box of tissues. Her face is blotchy red and swollen with tears, and my heart breaks for her. With a nod to the receptionist, we make an unspoken deal that I'll take over comforting my friend from here. She curls into my shoulder. Euan stands looking at us for a moment, like a spare part, then disappears without a word. I've no energy to be annoyed by his rudeness.

'Jilly, how's she doing? Any news?'

'I don't know. I can't think. It's all – how the hell could someone do this to Roxy? You know what those bastards did? When she tried to defend her pups from them they…'

I flinch. Hug my friend tighter.

'She's lucky to be alive. I stood there, about as much use as an aspidistra – but poor Roxy, she was amazing. So brave. You should have seen her. There was no way she was letting these strangers snatch away her babies. She stood at bay, growling and snarling. So they just, they, oh, it was awful. One of them – he must have been six feet four if he was an inch – he knocked her out with a machete handle. She didn't stand a chance. Then they just shoved the pups into two holdalls.'

'All six?' I gasp.

I feel her nod then disintegrate again. I'm furious, absolutely furious, but feel so helpless. Right now, the only thing either of us can do is wait and keep everything crossed for Roxy.

Euan returns, bearing another box of tissues, three large coffees from the café round the corner, and some sandwiches for us all in case we're here for a long time. I'm touched by how thoughtful he is. An hour later, Farrah's treatment room door opens. She's still wearing a surgical mask so we can't read her expression as she walks towards us. Jilly grips my hand. Then Farrah's eyes crinkle, and I know she's smiling before she even pulls off her mask.

'We've stitched up Roxy's face,' she says. 'None of the cuts were life-threatening; she's been lucky. She's in recovery at the moment, but I'll let you know as soon as she starts to come round from the anaesthetic.'

The room fills with gasps of relief and smiles all round. As I hug Farrah, she puts her lips close to my ear, reminding me of Leila, who couldn't whisper without it tickling me. What she says makes the smile fall from my lips, though.

'I just hope the police find the puppies soon. They're only five weeks: too young to survive for long without their mother.'

Those poor innocent creatures. Snatched on a whim and paying with their lives.

*

The house I stand outside is immaculate. Expensive triple windows, a pristine garden of white gravel and plant pots arranged tastefully, and a white Audi parked in the driveway. This is where my tip off has led me, but I'm wondering if there's been a mistake.

As we'd sat in the waiting room while Farrah operated, I'd made some calls, trying to find out who might have taken the puppies from Jilly. Unless they are tracked down soon, they will die. The police are doing everything they can, of course, but those youngsters are on a countdown, so I started asking around myself. Then one tip came through that sounded particularly interesting.

'I'll go check it out, and if it looks like there's anything to it, I'll let the police know,' I told Jilly.

'Well, just you be careful. I want the pups back but these guys are dangerous. Don't. Get. Hurt.'

'As if.'

'Bah, you always make out you're so sensible, but when it comes to looking out for others you always put yourself out. You're like a mamma bear: so protective over those you love, and always willing to defend us fiercely. You're like Roxy!'

'I've no intention of getting myself injured, don't you worry.'

'Don't worry, Jilly, I'll make sure she's safe,' Euan said.

'Erm, who put you in charge of me?'

'I was thinking more team member than manager.'

Once again Euan refused to take no for an answer, and he had almost had to run to keep up with me as I strode to my car. Now we're here, outside the address I've been given, and it looks like we've both wasted our time. It doesn't take long for the bickering to start again as we sit in my car, feeling like a microwave meal in the baking heat. Him asking if I've had any more letters or emails from 'the so-called killer' starts it and things go downhill from there.

'This doesn't look right at all,' says Euan. 'Machete-wielding dognappers belong in scruffy hideouts, not in middle-class suburbs.'

'I told you not to come,' I snap. The atmosphere in my ancient Ford Focus saloon, which recently celebrated its sixteenth birthday, is getting chilly despite the sun pouring in.

'Why are you so furious with me for wanting to help you?'

'It's patronising. I've been doing things alone for years, know how to handle myself.'

'You know what I think?' *No, but I've a feeling you're going to tell me.* 'I think you don't want to rely on someone else in case they disappear on you like Leila did. I think you're scared you're too fragile to rebuild yourself if that happens again.'

'Spare me the pop psychology. It's stifling in here; I'm going to have a look around.'

I slam the car door shut and stroll as casually as possible along the road. Hopefully, if anyone is looking, they'll assume we're a couple of lost tourists.

Bloody Euan, why did he insist on coming with me? I'm fine alone. Absolutely fine. All I'm going to do is check around, see what there is to see, and if there's anything suspicious then I'll call the police immediately. I want to help, but am not willing to put myself in danger despite Jilly seeming to think of me as some kind of crime-fighting superhero.

A glance at the car shows Euan is still sitting inside, the windows all wound down. If he weren't so stubborn, he'd be out in the fresh air instead of staying put in that sweat box. There's no way I'm getting back into it, so carry on walking. At the end of the street I turn back… and have a thought. Before I can change my mind, I'm marching up the driveway of the house. Knock on the door.

There's no harm in seeing who lives here.

A blonde woman in her mid-twenties, shoulder-length hair in two pigtails, answers the door and looks at me suspiciously.

'Sorry, I think I've got the wrong house. Danielle doesn't live here, does she? Danielle Peters?' I already had the name made up ready to offer.

The woman frowns. 'No, I'm really sorry.'

'Could have sworn it was this place or one of these,' I wag my finger left and right to take in the two neighbours either side.

'Can't help you, I'm afraid. I don't know the neighbours.' Even as she's speaking, she's starting to close the door on my cheery, 'Sorry to trouble you.'

As I turn my back and walk away, a grim smile appears on my face – because she didn't close the door quick enough. Two things happened before she shut me out. The distinctive smell of dogs, but particularly puppies, punched me in the face as soon as she opened the door – she's probably grown used to it and thinks that the huge amounts of air freshener she clearly sprays will overwhelm the smell. It doesn't. There are a lot of dogs in there, I bet. Secondly, a man padded through the hallway in shorts, glaring at me when he saw the door was open. Despite being barefoot, he is toweringly tall. Around six feet four and gangly, just like Jilly described one of the attackers.

It's not exactly conclusive proof, though. I call the police and decide to wait for them to arrive. Then I fill Euan in. He's not happy I didn't tell him what was happening earlier, and mutters something that sounds suspiciously like: so much for partners. We agree to wait for the police to arrive before going our separate ways and pass the time by playing the intro game. Euan cheers up a lot after thrashing me at it.

There's still no sign of the police after an hour. They're so overstretched these days that it could realistically take days before they get round to checking this tip off. I'm starting to worry a neighbour will report us for suspicious behaviour, so am about to suggest heading home when…

The door opens and the tall man and the blonde woman get into their car and drive away.

'Well, that's that. Even if the police arrive, there's no one in to talk to,' says Euan, throwing his hands in the air. 'Er, where are you going?'

I'm already sliding into the fresh air. The breeze hits me, feeling wonderful on my skin after being stuck in the heat for so long, but I don't pause to enjoy it. I jog across the road. Behind me comes the sound of a car door opening and closing. A whispered hiss of someone trying to shout my name and stay quiet at the same time. Running footsteps.

Euan catches up with me, bounding by my side as if the pavement were hot coals.

'Stella! What are you doing? You're not doing what I think you're doing, are you?'

I walk over to the house as fast as I can while still trying to look casual, and go to push open the gate to their back yard.

'Hey, now. Come on! Stop it,' begs Euan.

It won't give. Must be bolted shut. Well, I don't want to break in by climbing over their fence, so I'll have to make do with peering through the long, thin window on the side of the house, beneath an air outlet that must be for the kitchen. It's frosted, though, so I already know I'll be leaving none the wiser.

'What if they come back?!'

Still I press my face against it in desperation, my hands cupped around my eye; I think I can hear whining through the outlet.

Now, there are all kinds of whining. There's 'I'm hungry' whining, or 'I need a wee' or 'I'm bored, play with me'. Then there is the pitiful sound of a scared dog. I know them all – and what I'm hearing right now is the sound of at least one dog that is terrified. It's soft, though, as if used to going unanswered.

Indecision has me in its grip.

'Okay, you're thinking about something. What are you thinking? Did you see something? Out the way, let me look.'

But only for a few seconds. If there's a chance there's a dog in there that's in trouble then I'm going to check it out. A quick look around to see if I can make out any neighbours' curtains twitching, then I'm over the gate.

From the other side I can hear Euan swear softly. An arm appears at the top of the gate, then a leg, then with a grunt he's over.

'We're breaking the law. You know that, right?' he stage whispers. I put a finger to my lips. 'You don't even want to know where I've got a splinter,' he adds as I creep to the patio doors. The curtains are drawn. There is, however, a tiny chink right at the bottom where the two sides haven't quite met, and it's to this that I press my eye.

The room is full of cages. Full to the brim. They don't just cover the floor; they are stacked up against the walls almost to the ceiling. In fact, to around the height a six feet four inch man can see at eye level. Inside, are dogs. Many look thin and bedraggled, their eyes tired even in the half-light. Most are either nursing pups or pregnant, by the look of their swollen bellies. When I show Euan his eyes tear up.

As tempting as it is to smash through the lock, we unbolt the gate and go back to my car where I call the police again. They arrive within fifteen minutes.

'I thought I heard a dog in distress, and the gate was wide open, so I went into the back garden,' I say. Maybe they know I'm lying, but if they do they don't seem to care.

At first they keep me away from the scene, but one of them recognises me because he did some work with the police's dog unit a while back and I helped them out at the same time.

'The RSPCA are on their way to collect the dogs but…' He shakes his head.

'Can I see if my friend's puppies are there? They need to be back with their mum as quickly as possible or they're going to die.'

When he leads me inside, my heart breaks. The air vent I'd noticed earlier had been fitted to take away the rancid air of dog excrement from the lounge-cum-puppy-farm. The outside of the house might look neat as a pin but inside it is a house of horrors.

Whether the dogs are drugged to keep them quiet or so lethargic because of lack of nutrition I don't know, but they barely make a whimper let alone a bark. Certainly not enough noise to alert neighbours to an illegal puppy farm going on a stone's throw from their cosy family homes. Between that and the triple glazing, there's nothing that from the outside would alert anyone to the terrible cruelty inside.

Roxy's stolen puppies are quickly identified and rushed back to their mother. They're weak and will need to be checked over by Farrah, but their ordeal has lasted less than twenty-four hours, and I think they'll be okay.

'Why would they bother stealing Roxy's puppies when they have so many already?' Euan asks.

'We reckon they stole to order,' the officer says. 'Probably had deposits from a few people who had reserved puppies and then, when the pups died, rather than have to refund them these buggers sourced some replacements.'

'Money is the only thing that matters to these people,' I say. 'The welfare of the dogs doesn't matter at all. You know, the people who run them hire third parties to pose as caring owners who have bred their much-loved family pet and are now selling little bundles of furry joy. Often the truth is that the puppies have been born in filth, not given the correct injections, not fed properly and so are prone to all kinds of behavioural and physical issues. Some of the poor pups even die within days of arriving at their new homes.'

'At least you saved Roxy's puppies,' Euan says. His hand slides into mine and we walk back to the car that way.

*

Back at the house, I've an hour before my work day starts, and I need to walk the dogs and have a shower. But left to my own devices, having dropped Euan off at the B&B he's staying in for a few days, I can't help checking my email. There's nothing from my Dear Friend.

Euan was right to have a go at me earlier about climbing over the gate instead of waiting for the police. I don't regret it, but it's not like me. I'm normally sensible, meticulous. Something has shifted inside me since the documentary, though. Old wounds are bleeding, making me dizzy and foolish. I can't shake the feeling I'm being watched and wondering if someone has been in my home. It's been years since I've felt this vulnerable.

CHAPTER EIGHTEEN

Monday arrives. It's been over a week since Dear Friend contacted me. For all I know they're dead, taking with them the last chance of Leila's remains being found. Today is going to be a tough one; I could sense it looming for a few days now and tried to ignore it. A heaviness is clinging to me that threatens to overwhelm if I don't keep busy, keep moving, so it can't pin me down. An early morning walk, before the sun gets a chance to heat the day up, doesn't shake the feeling, so when I get back home I try a different tack and call DCI Burns. He sounds tired when he answers.

'We've no new leads, Stella. I'm so sorry. I'd love to give you some good news, especially tod—'

'Are the tech team still looking at the letter and email?' I interrupt.

'We've hit a dead end with those; there's nowhere else we can go with them. Try not to get too down about it.'

''Course not – it's just the usual, I'm used to it.'

'You're almost managing to sound breezy, but you don't fool me.'

'If you want to cheer me up you could do me a favour…' I explain that Mary's moving and I'd like the security checked over, if possible. 'If I know she's safe, then it's one less thing to worry about.'

'Consider it done.'

Still, when we say goodbye I sink to the floor and hug the dogs close, needing their comfort. Only the home phone ringing makes me move. I wonder if it's DCI Burns again, calling to tell me something he's just remembered. That makes me pick up quick, silently cursing the lack of caller ID on my old rotary dial phone.

'Hello?'

Silence.

'Hello? Can you hear me?'

No sound. I listen hard. Someone is breathing. Or perhaps it's my imagination trying to fill the quiet. I hold my own breath, listen closer. Nothing. Nothing until a click and the call is cut off.

Despite the heat, I wrap my arms around myself, wondering. I'm about to dial the code to find out the number the call was made from, when the phone rings again. I jump a mile.

'Who is it?' I demand.

'Not the friendliest way to answer.' Euan chuckles at his little joke.

'Did you just try to call me?'

'No – why? Is everything okay? Has something happened?'

With a 'fine, fine' I brush over that line of conversation and ask him how he is.

'Actually, I called with an ulterior motive. It's a beautiful day and… I happen to know it's your birthday, so… Fancy lunch together?'

Crap. 'I never celebrate it, try not to think about it if possible. Everyone who knows me knows better than to mention it.'

'That's a no, then?' His voice is quiet, dropping its usual confidence. There's disappointment there.

'I'm fully booked today, anyway. Thanks for thinking of me, though. Must dash – bye!'

Before Leila disappeared, our birthday had been a big deal in our house. We'd wake early and swap presents before our parents woke, savouring being alone together to celebrate for a little while. For our twelfth birthday I created a scavenger hunt around the house as Leila's gift. Watching her work out the clues was such fun, but she was way too fast because, of course, she knew exactly how my mind worked. One of my favourite memories is when we turned 14 and Leila gave me a jar full of 365 birthday wishes: one for each day of the year. A walk on the beach; having chocolate for breakfast; making my bed for a week; being allowed to borrow any item of clothing without asking (for one day only): each wish was unique and thoughtful. That was the most amazing present, making every day feel special, and because it was so thoughtful, I shared them with her, so that one morning I'd pick one, the next she would. We used to love our birthdays.

Perhaps it would be okay to have lunch with Euan. Not a celebration: that would be too much. My day is fully booked with work, but I do have to eat at some point, and a bit of company might be nice.

I pick up the phone, block out the voice whispering worst-case scenarios in my ear, and call Euan back.

'I've been thinking about the lunch invitation…'

We arrange to meet not for lunch but dinner, so I can relax after a day of work. When I ask him about his day, he gives his slick, showbiz smile, the one that hasn't appeared for a while, and replies: 'This and that.' Then he tops up my glass. We're sitting outside in the beer garden of the Vine Hotel, beneath a large oak tree, the canopy of which is already looking a less vibrant green than a week ago. Now that it's September the gentle slide into autumn has begun, and all too soon everything will be the colours of flame. But not yet, I remind myself, bringing myself back to the here and now. The dogs loll around us on the grass. It's touching that Euan's found a dog-friendly restaurant. The fact he's thought about my life and passions and bothered taking them into account means a lot.

He's managed to restrain himself from asking if I've any updates on Leila or the messages and is instead talking about us finding that puppy farm.

'Honestly, when I saw you shin over the gate I thought you'd lost the plot. But it was absolutely the right thing to do. You don't do things by halves!'

It's a throwaway comment, and yet it creates a ball of tension in my chest.

'A lot of people have said that to me over the years. They don't understand that it's the fact I'm now only half that pushes me on.'

'Ah, sorry, that was a terrible choice of words. Forgive me?'

'It wasn't intentional.' I take a long swallow of ice-cold Pino Grigio, savouring the notes of sharp lemon, mellow pears and smooth vanilla that spread across my tongue before the cool liquid is swallowed. 'Anyway, enough of me. As it's my birthday, I get to choose the topic of conversation. Tell me something about yourself – something you don't tell other people.'

His eyes widen as if I've shocked him. Then he suddenly becomes fascinated with the condensation on his wine glass and nods a couple of times. Psyching himself up for something, perhaps.

'My fiancée died.'

This is it: the secret I've sensed he's been holding back from me. I don't speak, don't want to interrupt. But I do reach across the table and take his hand.

'I was 26. So young, but absolutely certain that Adele was the love of my life. We had our lives planned out. A beach wedding in Mauritius, to live in London for a little longer before moving out to St Albans, where we'd raise the two children we wanted – a boy and a girl, of course. There are great schools in St Albans, you see, and Adele was a teacher so it was win/win. When the children were grown up and moved out, Adele and I were going to move to Brighton, to be by the sea. We thought we'd planned for everything, but you can't, can you? You know that.

'You know what killed her? Her teeth. Of all the stupid…! She had problems with her wisdom teeth. They were impacted –

growing along her gum instead of up. During the operation to have all four removed at the same time, she had an allergic reaction to the general anaesthetic. According to the inquest, the reaction is exceptionally rare. It's even rarer that her life wasn't saved in time.'

He picks up his wine glass and wags it at me. 'You can take every precaution in the world to make yourself safe but life's still dangerous.'

'I'm so sorry, Euan.'

He gets it. He knows exactly what it's like to imagine life is going in one direction only to be body-slammed off course and never fully recover. He knows there's no point in planning or worrying because they give us a sense of control that doesn't exist. I drain my glass then stand.

'Come on, let's go back to my place.'

His hand is hot as it encases mine and when we stand he has eyes only for me – but a flash of emerald green catches the corner of my eye. Keshini is standing in the entrance of the pub watching us, her eyes brimming with tears.

'What's wrong? Oh…' Euan gives a harsh sigh. 'Shall I go speak to her? Tell her once and for all I'm not interested?'

'Just for one day I'd like no drama. Take me home. We can lose ourselves in each other for a while – it's not a solution, but it's fun while it lasts.'

I'm sitting at my table, going through my emails, tired but relaxed. I don't allow even the disappointment of nothing from the creepy Dear Friend to bring me down. Euan stayed over last night and left first thing this morning when I took the dogs for a walk, after giving me the best birthday I've had in years. We feel closer after last night's revelation, and there's no denying the smile on my lips.

The next email I open is from a prospective new client. Great, I really need the cash. Skint doesn't begin to describe my financial situation; I really shouldn't have spent so much on leaflets and adverts, but what's done is done, and my warm glow stays in place. The dogs suddenly jump up in unison and race to the front door, barking, before someone knocks. It's the postman, holding a couple of envelopes.

'A'right, Stelz? Here y'are.' He hands me the small pile. 'This here was on your doorstep, so I thought I'd give you a knock and let you know.'

'Hand delivered?'

'Looks like. S'not Royal Mail, for sure.'

With a quick thanks, I shut the door while examining the padded envelope curiously. It wasn't there when I returned from my walk, but maybe it was delivered when the dogs and I were playing in the garden. Whoever it's from definitely didn't knock, though, or the dogs would have barked. Maybe it's a little surprise present from Euan?

It's too well taped up for me to open without scissors, so I wander into the kitchen, the dogs surrounding me, their tails wagging lazy circles. I sniff.

'Does someone need to go out? Go on, the door's open.' They're herded out. My flip-flops slap against the soles of my feet as I walk outside, scissors sliding through the tape and padding. I peer inside and the smell hits harder. The envelope tumbles from my fingers, landing with a splat as the contents spill out.

Excrement.

What the—? Someone's sent me dog mess. I run inside, grab a couple of nappy sacks I use to pick up my own dogs' business, and start to clear up. That's when I notice the corner of a white piece of paper, protected inside a clear plastic bag, poking out. When it's pulled free, the words written on it in black marker pen can be made out beneath the brown smears on its casing:

You're in deep shit, Stella.

There's no time for me to call the police, so I place the disgusting message in a plastic bag and put it to one side in the garden, so I can give it to them later.

The morning is crammed with four appointments, one after the other, then lunch is a sweaty cheese and onion sandwich on limp white bread, the only one left in the shop. It's eaten as I drive out to Fenmere, a village nine miles away from Mereford, and where my next appointment is. There was a big scandal there a few years ago, when a young teenager was attacked out on the marsh beside the village.

With all the windows down, it's a nice drive, the breeze ruffling my hair and cooling my skin as I enjoy the countryside. It's flat and wide around here, the landscape squeezed into a few inches of view that's dominated by the sky. You can see for miles in every direction.

When I find the place I'm looking for, I park in the shade of a hedge, and check my emails. Just in case. There's nothing new.

The next hour is spent with Glitzy, a Doberman that's too afraid to go outside after being attacked by another dog. We do some confidence-building work, but it's not going to be easy to get this dog sorted, not least because her owner is overprotective. I've got my work cut out changing his attitude, never mind the dog's, and trying to explain how things are going to work makes me late for my next appointment with Bunny, back in Mereford.

Bunny is doing brilliantly. There's no evidence of any destructive behaviour around the house, and the footage on my cameras confirms that she's now settling down when her owner leaves the house. She's doing so well that I take the cameras from the house and say we'll only need one more session of training.

There's twenty minutes until my next appointment, and it's ten minutes away, so I'm looking forward to a brief rest when I climb back into my car. The upholstery seats are hot, and the leather steering wheel is about the same temperature as lava. Windows down, I wait for the steering wheel to cool down enough for me to touch it. It's not long before I'm bored, so I pull out my phone, hop onto Facebook and Twitter, then check my emails.

Dear Stella,

I read. My heart jumps.

CHAPTER NINETEEN

A glance at the clock tells me I have five minutes before I need to leave for my next appointment. Long enough to read what Dear Friend has to say.

Dear Stella,

I was stunned to receive your last email. Sorry it's taken me so long to reply but coming back from the brink has been hard and the tug to return to it continues to be tough to ignore. Your offer of keeping things between us has helped so much, though.

Your suggestion of baby steps is inspired – when I read it I actually gasped out loud. I'll try to reply in the same spirit that you made the clever suggestion, so here's the first step: I can honestly state that hurting Leila was never, ever part of a plan. I was driving along the road that awful night, the rain hammering down, and all I was thinking about was getting from A to B safely. My biggest fear was aquaplaning because of the flooding – the drains couldn't cope with the deluge and the roads were like streams, full of puddles so deep they almost came over the top of the tyres. Do you remember? I'd never driven in anything like it. Then I saw her appear from out of the darkness, and both of our lives changed in that moment. Already, it was too late to stop what was going to play out.

You've no idea how often I've watched in my head that moment and all that came after it, wishing for different reactions.

In the documentary you spoke of her being literally your other half. I can't help wondering if you somehow felt what happened to her, despite you saying in the documentary that wasn't the case. I'm sure there are things you've kept to yourself about that night – perhaps you need someone to confide in as much as I do.

There is so much more I could write about it, but it's hard to face. I still can't help feeling that it would be better for everyone's sake if I ended it all. That will, I know, devastate my family, but surely realising their father is a cowardly criminal will be even worse?

Your friend

At last I know. They may not have gone into details, but…

I sit back and close my eyes, fighting to stay calm and focused. Imagining what happened and filling in the blanks.

There was an accident. They probably aquaplaned and hit Leila as she was crossing the road. I can see her in my mind's eye, stepping out, head down in the deluge. Maybe she was blinded by the rain pelting into her eyes. Perhaps she was so preoccupied with getting to shelter that she simply didn't look.

My imagination flies to the car so that I'm now the driver. I can hear the rapid thunk-thunk of the wipers working at maximum speed but not clearing the windscreen. The rain's coming too fast. Wind buffets the car and I'm fighting it hard, leaning over the steering wheel and squinting forwards into the darkness. There are no street lights because of the power cut. The glare of my headlights hits the surface water on the road and is thrown back up at me. The tyres keep losing grip, the car slip-sliding, I'm fighting to get the wheels under control again and again, then suddenly it's happening and there's no getting it back. Panic slicks my skin. I'm out of control. Then I see something. Red highlighted in the headlights. A sickening thud, a shudder of impact. Leila's face thrown against the windscreen; her body bouncing from the bonnet, flying through the air.

My eyes fly open. The summer sun warms my goose-bumped flesh, the sound of children playing in a nearby garden, a dog barking in the distance, everyday life continuing. But I can't pull myself away from the scene in my mind. *Oh God, I can't breathe!*

Whenever we were upset as children, Leila and I would hold each other's forearms and stand with our foreheads touching, breathing in for four counts and out for four counts, taking it in turns to count aloud, the rhythm soothing us. Now I grab my own forearms and rest my forehead on the slowly cooling steering wheel.

Breathe in, two, three, four.

The driver must have stopped as soon as they could. Run to Leila and held her as she died. She would have called for me; she must have spoken for him to know our secret names.

Breathe out, two, three, four.

But why didn't the so-called Dear Friend call an ambulance?

Breathe in…

That's what I can't forgive. No matter how bad he feels about what he did, by not calling an ambulance he made everything a million times worse. Anger starts to white out the horror. How dare this person ask me to write to him about Leila? He doesn't deserve a window into our souls – if he wants that he can watch the bloody documentary again.

Dear Friend might be behind the silent phone call last night, and the envelope stuffed with crap this morning, too. Perhaps it's someone who wants to make my life a misery because that's what I've done to him by digging up his painful past with the documentary.

Breathe out. A long, hard sigh that deflates the anger.

Telling this person to get stuffed won't get me what I want. As awful as this is, this sort of information is what's been needed for years. So I need to keep him on side, stop him from taking his life, and get him to come forward. I need to train him the way I do dogs, using encouragement and rewards to keep him coming back. With each piece of information given, I'll reward with praise and a little bit of information about me and Leila, to remind him why he's doing this and about the person the world has lost. Eventually, even if he doesn't come forward, I'll know enough to be able to track him down. I've learned so much already, just from this last email. Just a bit longer and who knows what will slip out? Nasty parcels through my door, silent phone calls and anything else that's thrown at me isn't enough to put me off – ever.

Right now, I need to get going or I'll be late for my appointment and really can't afford to lose a client. Money's too tight. But this is the chance I've waited twenty-five years for…

My fingers drum on the steering wheel as I think, then make a decision.

'Hi, Mrs Dickens? I'm so sorry but I won't be able to make it to your appointment. I seem to have got a bug – or perhaps it's a spot of sunstroke, but either way I woke up thinking I'd be able to battle through but am getting worse and worse. Can we reschedule for next week, same time? Thanks so much.'

Lying isn't something that comes easily to me, but I'm haunted by the image of Leila in the rain as the car speeds towards her, and can't just sit here acting like normal. Of course I could *not* reply to Dear Friend, save myself some pain, leave it in the hands of the police. But just like every time I've ever considered ignoring a lead, Leila eggs me on, saying: *What if this is the one? What if this time it really could lead to something and you're ignoring it? Maybe this time…*

Before typing a reply, I read the message again, trying this time not to get upset. Impossible, but at least I don't have a panic attack. My Dear Friend certainly loves words! Uses ten where one would do, a long one where a short one would work; but each word screams of desperation to have not only their guilt acknowledged but their suffering, too. That's my way in. By contacting me, a link between us has been forged, and if I can take advantage of it, I'll turn that link into a chain that will shackle them to justice.

Can I do it, though? Body language – canine body language – is my superpower. Words, particularly written words, are my kryptonite.

My fingers hover over the keys as I think. The words from my new friend's original email spring to mind.

I need you, Stella; I can't do this alone.

Slowly, agonising over each word, I type out a reply. Write a sentence, growl, erase it, and try again. Sweat is dribbling between my breasts and shoulder blades by the time I'm done.

Dear Friend,

It sounds as if your life was destroyed almost as much as mine, and all because of an accident. That night, with the rain driving down, is often replayed in my mind, too. Losing Leila was unimaginable. Literally. For those first few days afterwards, mainly I felt utter disbelief – not denial as such, but complete inability to imagine life without my identical twin. If there had been definite news on what happened it would have been easier to cope. The constant wondering, the unanswered questions dripped away at our minds and stopped us from ever healing. Despite hope, deep down I think we all knew the truth – that Leila was dead – because she would never have deliberately disappeared; it was too cruel a thing to do. But it also felt disloyal to think that. Mum never let us talk about Leila in the past tense. She said doing that was giving up on her.

A wise woman once told me that acceptance isn't the same as giving up. That's what I believe, too. I accept that Leila has gone but will never give up trying to get her back. If I were to be able to know once and for all exactly what happened to her and lay her to rest, it would mean everything to me. Please help me to do that.

Keep writing to me.
Stella

That will have to do. It's taken me almost an hour to craft those few lines. Baring my soul isn't something I'm comfortable with. I press send and pray I haven't held back too much, fearing I have.

The sky is a faultless dome above me. What was that word Euan used the other day for the colour? Azure, that was it. Chiffon clouds of peach drape across its edge. I'm lying on the grass, staring up, trying to let my mind drift. Concentrating on the sensations of the breeze on my skin, the stirring grass tickling me, the comfort of the body-temperature air. Listening to the sounds surrounding me, pulling them closer: traffic, children playing, a ball bouncing, birdsong. My fingers twitch as muscles unwind. Quieter, closer, leaves shushing, a bumblebee's deep drone, soft paws padding towards me.

Something bounces off my face. Scamp is nose to nose with me, looking hopefully from me to the tennis ball that's now beside my head. A hot lick slides across my cheek.

'No rest for the wicked,' I groan, sitting up and throwing the ball.

She races after it and returns in a flash. Buster has his head resting on his favourite cuddly toy – a polar bear he likes to carry around by its stubby tail – and looks at Scamp as if he's no clue where she's got the energy from in this heat. This is typical Scamp, though. She can never have too much attention. I call her the love sponge because no matter how much she gets it's never enough. However much she's given she gives back in truckloads, though.

Buddy has wisely taken himself inside to lie on the cool kitchen tiles, no doubt. Fifi will have followed him. She's bonded with him more than the others, calmed, no doubt, by his steady nature.

Scamp drops her ball in front of me and I do my duty. Off she runs, catching it on the bounce.

Now I'm sitting up, my eyes stray to the dirty protest envelope, sealed in a plastic evidence bag and leaning against the fence at the end of the garden. I need to tell the police about it but am too exhausted. To think I started this morning feeling good. If one more thing happens today, my brain may detonate into a mushroom cloud.

The thought is too much temptation for fate because there's a knock on the door. Not a jaunty 'shave and a haircut' knock, but three heavy thumps. Muttering many swear words under my breath, I go to answer while checking I haven't dribbled during my daydream, or got a boob hanging out of my vest top. Chances are it's Euan.

I open the door and standing there is a face from the past that sends me spinning.

CHAPTER TWENTY

It's been twenty-five years since I last set eyes on this face, but I'd recognise it anywhere. The hair, which was once cropped and neat now hangs in lanky curtains. I get the impression it's worn that way to hide behind.

Damien Francis, Leila's boyfriend, as I live and breathe. He looks like he's sprinted here, breath heavy, face florid, a couple of beads of sweat joining together to trickle down his forehead until he's tickled by them and wipes them away.

Seconds tick by before I realise I'm staring and haven't said a word. He's doing the same. It doesn't take a genius to guess what he's thinking: that the wrong sister was taken. Fifi's nose butts against my calf – something she does for reassurance when nervous.

'Wow, Damien. How are you?' Shock makes me fall back on social niceties.

'Stella, may I come in?' His words are a breathless rush. He's nervous. He's still got that distinctive clipped way of talking. I always thought it was because he was trying to hide his Lincolnshire accent. He was always ambitious and seemed to think he had to put on airs if he was going to succeed. It never won him many friends, but Leila wouldn't listen to any criticism of him – he was the one thing we disagreed on. She loved him heart and soul, though, and he felt the same. From the puppy eyes he gazed at her with to the gifts and surprises he showered on her, there was never a doubt in my mind that he'd do anything for her.

Love can become a double-edged sword, though, a blade that plunges into the heart and brings us to our knees. At first, I'd defended him against the whispers, but his refusal to be honest with the police about why he'd gone away that weekend had made me wonder if, perhaps, his love had turned to possessiveness that boiled over to violence that night. Not that there was a shred of hard evidence of that. Even so, my parents refused to have anything to do with him, and he hasn't stepped over the threshold of this house since a month after Leila's disappearance.

He's changed so much. Broken veins craze his cheeks and the sides of his nose. His eyes look watery and reddened. I'm guessing he's a heavy drinker. How different all our lives would have been if Leila were still here. If only I could turn back the clock and change what happened that night.

I send the dogs to their beds and invite Damien in. He keeps checking over his shoulder to stare at the dogs, even though they're well-behaved. He's not the calm and collected person he used to be, with crisp shirts, paisley ties, and trousers with a sharp crease; a place for everything and everything in its place.

He coughs. 'I remembered hearing from someone that you'd set up working with dogs but didn't realise you brought your work home with you.'

Ignoring his critical tone, I ask how he is and he briefly fills me in on his life in Cardiff, with a wife and two children. But obviously he's not here for small talk. A nervous energy radiates from him and judging from the speed of his breath his heart is racing. If he were a dog, I'd back away because he's too unpredictable right now and needs to be left alone. I'm stuck with him now he's inside, though, so try to take a confident but passive approach, angling my body sideways to his, as facing someone full-on can seem confrontational – and definitely so in the canine world.

'So Cardiff, eh? Are you visiting your family back here at the moment?'

'We all had to leave after what happened. You must remember? The rumours. The excrement through our letterbox. The threats to us all. My apprenticeship as a trainee accountant mysteriously ended due to "funding issues". My father was sacked from managing Peter's Pan Pizzas, and Mum's life was made such a misery in the supermarket that she left in the end. I had to change my name!'

'Of course, I remember, it was stupid of me—'

'My life is in ruins because I had the bad luck to be in love with someone who disappeared.'

'Right, well, sorry for the inconvenience,' I snap.

'Look, I'm not up for arguing. I just want to tell you to back off. Okay?'

'Back off?'

'Leila's disappearance destroyed me. I want to find out what happened to her as much as the next person – more, in fact, far, far more – but do you have any idea how long it took for people to stop recognising me? More than ten years. Ten years of people doing a double-take, saying my face looks familiar and they can't place why.'

'I know that feeling; it must be—'

'My wife has no clue about my past, and it was going to stay that way, but then… ah, then you had to dredge everything up with the documentary. Why couldn't you let sleeping dogs lie? How long's it going to be before someone we know sees it and starts putting two and two together and making five? I thought if I kept quiet and put my head down people would forget about it, move on, but because it's on Netflix it's up for ever. More and more people are watching it!

'People are starting to say I look like the bloke mentioned in the documentary. The longer it's streaming, the more people will see it. I've got a small business – this could be the ruin of it. Just contact Netflix or whoever and tell them to remove all mention of me or pull the programme or something. Leila's gone. She'll never, ever be forgotten. Never. Never. It's tragic—'

'Thanks for the heartfelt thoughts—'

'…but I'm more interested in the living. I've a wife and kids to support. I've got a life. For the first time since Leila went missing, I've found some peace and I'm not going to have you or anyone jeopardise that.'

He takes a step towards me. I put my hands straight out in front of me like a shield, trying to keep him as far away from me as possible. All the dogs are out of their beds suddenly, swirling at my feet to coalesce in a protective semi-circle. All facing Damien. Their bodies are tense. Ready to act. Scamp gives a whine of discomfort that turns into a small growl. I say nothing.

He looks down. Swallows. Wipes the sweat from his face with his sleeve. Finally, he speaks, his voice quieter now.

'Please, Stella. I've contacted the production company, complaining about including me in the documentary, but they've said it's too late. They'll listen to you, though.'

'I've no sway with them. Besides, how could they cover Leila's last movements and not include you? You were a huge part of her life. I'm sorry, but this is more important.'

He edges closer again. 'Help me. Get the programme taken off air. I can't do it without you, Stella.'

I can't do it without you. That phrase, identical to the one in the first email from Dear Friend.

'I'll think about it,' I reply. 'That's all I can tell you right now.'

Buddy's growl is so low it seems to rumble through the floor. That's my cue.

'You need to leave. Now. Thanks for coming round.'

He doesn't argue as I and my guards see him out. When he steps outside he turns to me, though. Staring. Eyes glazed. Swaying slightly.

'How can she be dead when she's standing right in front of me?'

His voice is barely a whisper but it makes me shiver.

I slam the door closed and lean my back against it while riding the wave of fear that washes through me. I'd said what was necessary to get him out of my house, but I've no intention of getting that documentary taken off air. Nothing and no one is going to intimidate me.

There's a squeak behind me. Damien's voice comes through the letterbox. 'I'm staying in town for a week, Stella. We need to talk. You need to do what I say.'

He gives the name of his B&B despite me telling him to bugger off.

There is a lot to think about, though.

I've never had the sense that Leila was hurt by someone we knew. Not really. Despite Damien coming under close scrutiny, I didn't suspect him. I felt like I'd know if it was him. Is that arrogant? To assume I'd somehow feel it if I was in the presence of the guilty party because it was my other half that they'd done it to? Probably. Damien's visit has got my mind galloping, though. Could he be the person behind the letters? Why?

The answer comes like a punch. If he killed Leila, then the best way of throwing me and the police off the scent is by creating a whole new person the investigation is unaware of. While we're busy looking for this mystery person in a car, no one is questioning him.

Even if he isn't guilty of murder, he could still be behind the emails. If they were to become public knowledge, then Damien would be free from trial by media once and for all, and he and his family could live in peace again. People backed into a corner are capable of anything, and Euan received a tip off about the first email. I must ask him who his source was.

Damien certainly seems desperate enough for any of those scenarios to be true.

That doesn't explain why he's come knocking on my door, though. Frustration could be making him impatient, I suppose.

Has he come round because his letter and email ruse hasn't worked? Now he's trying something more physical?

At the moment, there's nothing tangible to tell the police. All I have are questions and wild guesses – and a lingering fear that if I ignore Damien the intimidation may get worse.

CHAPTER TWENTY-ONE

Documentary Transcript
Title: *Missing: The Twin Who Never Came Back*

[Piece to camera. Euan is standing on a busy London street with The Shard building behind him.]

Euan: To get a more rounded picture of Leila's last known movements, we decide to talk to others who were at her father Bill's birthday party. The first person we speak to is Ryan Jonas, who Stella was seeing at the time.

Back then, he was a third-year student at Nottingham Trent University and had been dating Stella for several months. He is now a stockbroker working in the City.

[Cut to a restaurant on the thirty-second floor of The Shard. Ryan and Euan sit at a table. Through the window behind them are panoramic views of London.]

Ryan: Stella was feisty and sparky. We got on well. Was it love? Don't know about that, we were both too young, but it was definitely lust at first sight. We got chatting at the Student Union bar. They'd got a 50p a pint night and everyone was hammered, and we ended up going home together.

Euan: How well did you know Leila?

Ryan: Yeah, right, not that well, and kind of really well.

[Laughs, hand over mouth.]

That's the thing about dating an identical twin, isn't it? My mates used to joke I'd got two for the price of one, you know, all that nudge nudge, wink wink, 'do they ever swap places in bed'; stupid bloke jokes, you know? Not that anything like that ever happened. Not. Even. Close. I want to make that really clear from the start because I don't want lurid headlines.

Anyway, what did you ask?

Euan: How well did you know Leila?

Ryan: Exactly. So Stella and I had been together since her freshers' week, pretty much, and I met Leila a fair few times. She'd come over and visit at least once a month, sometimes a lot more. So I'd say I knew her reasonably well, but we weren't close-close, you know?

At first, Stella didn't even mention she'd got a sister, much less a twin. But then Leila came to visit her and it blew my mind. Stella'd warned me a couple of days before, maybe the day before, I don't really remember. Sat me down, all serious: "I have something to tell you." I thought she was going to dump me!

[Laughs.]

Yeah, no, it wasn't that, though.

Euan: Why do you think she was so nervous about telling you, or anyone?

Ryan: I don't think she was nervous per se. More that she wanted people to get to know her as an individual first. She wanted to guard that independence, you know? It's like… It's something that most of us take for granted, isn't it? Being accepted for who we are. But with twins they're a package deal. I mean, even the way people refer to them as "the twins" rather than as individuals; see what I mean? For the first time in her life, she wanted to see what it was like being just Stella, rather than "Leila and Stella" – cos that was the thing, too; she was always pegged last. It was never Stella and Leila, always Leila and Stella. Because she was the last one to be born, so was always the last to be mentioned. I mean, I don't know, but I guess that can be really grating sometimes.

Euan: Did they ever argue?

Ryan: They argued sometimes. That was weird to see, like watching someone shout into a mirror.

Euan: So they didn't get on?

Ryan: No, no, no, they were real tight, but it surprised me how much they bickered. How can you get mad with yourself? That's what I used to think when I saw them. Huh, then again, would I like me? I mean, I think I'm a pretty stand-up guy, but if there were two of me would I end up getting on my nerves? I can be really lazy at home, sometimes. Messy. That would annoy me.

Euan: What did they argue about?

Ryan:

[Cracks his neck.]

Ah, nothing important. Girlie stuff. "You've nicked my top without asking." "Why didn't you say you were going out?" I dunno.

Euan: So what can you remember of that fateful night with Leila? How did you happen to be there?

Ryan: It was Stella's dad's birthday, a big one, 50. He was having a bit of a do to celebrate, yeah? Nothing massive, but friends and family had hired the back room of a local pub, some cheesy disco tunes were played; you know the kind of thing. I'd never met the family before, so I was bricking it to be honest. It felt like a big deal. You know what it's like at that age – meeting the parents is enough to make any bloke break into a sweat, eh? So I come with Stella; we both travel from uni to be there. I've got to say the family were lovely. So welcoming.

That night was all right. It wasn't exactly rave central, and back in those days that's what I was into. Hard to imagine now but I was a skinny little thing who could dance all night long. No drugs. No funny business. Just loved the music.

Euan: You know when you protest like that it just sounds suspicious, right?

Ryan: Nah, mate, don't even joke. My work's got a strict no drugs policy. They do tests and everything, trying to clean up the reputation stockbrokers have, you know? I'd never touch drugs.

[Cracks neck.]

Euan: Sorry. Please, carry on telling me about that night.

Ryan: Stella was looking fine that night. Real hot. She'd bought a whole outfit for it, and back then hot pants were in – tiny little black shorts, right, but worn with thick black tights and DMs, so nothing too tarty. And a gold bra top thing up top. Sensational. Do you remember that? Women just wore bras back then. As tops. Bloody brilliant. I still remember the way she looked that night, clear as day. Funny the stuff that stands out and the stuff that fades, isn't it?

[Sighs.]

Bloody gorgeous she was, with this black, black hair. Pale skin, and the bluest eyes. I'm still a sucker for that combo. My wife's the same – better mention the wife so she doesn't get jealous.

[Laughs.]

But, yeah, this outfit of hers that she'd bought also included a coat. Of course, it's become famous now. Everyone knows that bloody coat.

[Cut away to a police evidence photograph of a women's trench coat in maroon mock croc leatherette, with a belted waist.]

Voiceover – Euan: The coat became a key fixation with not only the police but the press and public. It added a tragic twist to an already evocative tale. Both twins had, without the other's knowledge, bought identical coats and wore them for the first time that night. In a mix-up at the end of the evening, they took one another's – a mistake that was to possibly prove fatal for Leila.

[Cut back to Ryan.]

Ryan: It was a family fest, you know? Typical dad party. Cheesy music. Not a trace of Nirvana in sight, which I seem to remember Stella requesting from the DJ, even though I told her she'd got no chance. Everyone embraced it, though, and had a laugh. It's hard when something's catering for all ages, isn't it? I remember the missus complaining about the same thing when she was organising our wedding. Anyway, that's all I remember about Bill's do, to be honest. Nothing stood out, nothing was strange.

There was no looking back at something the next day and thinking: "Ah-ha, there's a clue to what's happened to Leila, I'd best tell the police." Nothing like that. Stella's mum was singing all the time; I do remember that. It was a bit annoying actually; she never shut up.

Then we all went back to Stella's parents' place – we were staying there. Separate rooms. Like that was going to happen. As soon as her parents went to bed, probably out like a light because they'd had a fair old bit to drink, I sneaked up to Stella's bedroom. It hadn't changed from when she and Leila had shared it as teenagers, so it was a bit weird. Posters up of Take That and Wet Wet Wet. Bloody hell.

[Shakes head.]

So in I walk, and Stella's standing in the middle of the room, swaying, staring at the coat in her hands like she doesn't recognise it. When I ask her what's up, she keeps saying: "It's not mine, it's not mine." I didn't understand what she meant at first, just thought she was wrecked from all the Diamond White ciders she'd been sinking – I'd even bought her a couple of Blastaways, which in hindsight was a mistake. You're probably too young to remember them: a bottle of Diamond White and bottle of Castaway poured into a pint glass together. Guaranteed to get anyone drunk. So there I am thinking the only action I'm going to see that night is holding a bowl and watching her puke. That's what was occupying me more than anything; so while she keeps on about the coat and going through the pockets and mumbling crap, I'm basically ignoring her and running around trying to find a bowl. I mean, it's the first time I'd met Bill and Wendy, so I'm in a stranger's house and having to search through their cupboards downstairs. Not great. I felt like a burglar.

Euan: Why didn't you wake her parents and ask them?

Ryan: What? Oh, well, it was Bill's birthday, you know. Didn't seem right. Besides, they were merry themselves.

Anyway, I find a bowl, bring it back up, but Stella's trying to come back downstairs. I block her and she gets in a real bad mood about it, starts shouting at me. I'm worried she's going to wake her parents and start a row, so all I'm bothered about is manoeuvring her back into the bedroom, where I can keep things a bit more contained, you get me? And that's what I do. Eventually. I manage to calm her drunken self down enough that she agrees to go to bed.

I stayed awake beside her all night, in case she was sick in her sleep.

Of course, when I discovered what had happened, I felt a real heel for not letting her call Leila. I thought she just wanted to talk to her, you know? I didn't realise there'd been a mix-up. I'd no idea. I didn't really drink in those days, so I could have jumped in her parents' car and done a cheeky little run round to Leila's place. But I didn't know. It's not my fault. No one can blame me for what happened.

Euan: And did people? Blame you?

[Pause. Ryan fiddles with his shirt cuffs.]

Ryan: Not in so many words, no, but Stella never looked at me the same after that. It was obvious what she thought. So in the end I cut my losses. We were only supposed to be together for a bit of fun anyway, and overnight things had got really serious. I was only a kid myself, couldn't handle the pressure of the press and all that grief.

I mean, you've no idea what it was like, especially those first hours when everyone realised Leila was missing… The whole thing was so surreal. Just twenty-four hours earlier I'd never met Stella's parents and suddenly I was witnessing the worst moment of their lives. It was… it was like watching them get beaten up, but emotional punches, you know? Every minute that passed was another blow. You could see the impact; their heads were reeling, like absolutely reeling, and Stella's mum, God, her eyes were just… There's that saying, right, rabbit in the headlights? That's what it was like. Frozen in fear, eyes massive and glassy and just bloody heartbreaking to look at. Almost like she'd taken really strong drugs, was on the verge of OD'ing or something. I dunno. I couldn't look at her, I admit. It made me want to cry.

As for Stella, she was trying to be all strong for everyone, liaising with the police, being businesslike. Because that's just Stella, you know? I don't know what she's like now, maybe this has changed her, but back then if something happened to anyone, she was always the one to take control of things. While others got all silly and emotional, she'd make sure the practical stuff got done to solve the problem. It was one of the things I liked about her, actually. To this day I'm not great with people being all crying and overemotional: makes me antsy; I don't know what to do with myself.

She did come back to uni when the new term started in the September, but of course things weren't the same. Three months had passed since anyone had heard from Leila, and Stella said she wanted to try to get some normality back in her life. She only lasted a week before dropping out to be with her parents full-time, supporting them and helping do whatever she could to find Leila. By then we were already ancient history.

CHAPTER TWENTY-TWO

The drive sweeps this way and that, the dazzling sunshine softened to green by the canopy of trees lining the entire way, until with a final turn a stately home is revealed, complete with lattice windows. It makes me think of Manderley, the house in Daphne Du Maurier's classic tale, *Rebecca*.

First impressions of the retirement village are definitely favourable, and before I've even pulled my handbrake on in the car park I'm looking around. I'd expected an institutional air but should have known that Mary would never move into somewhere like that. Instead, dotted around the grounds there is a mix of stylish bungalows and tasteful blocks of flats with balconies, all nestled between wide, open spaces, a formal garden, and trees. It should be an architectural mishmash but has been so cunningly designed that it all works as a whole. The greenery helps create a sense of peace. Windows are open, people sit around in deckchairs enjoying the balmy weather, and from the bowling green comes a gentle cheer at the match going on. Mary and I get out of the car and follow the signs for reception, gravel crunching under our feet. We pass by a group of elderly men and women doing tai chi.

There's such a sense of peace. No wonder Mary is moving here. Looks can be deceiving though, I remind myself. It's what lurks beneath the surface that matters most, not the veneer that people use to impress others.

Although I'm dreading her leaving, the move seems to have injected Mary with sparkle. I'm feeling positively dull beside her, shattered from yesterday's drama. The dog poo parcel, the email from Dear Friend, then Damien's visit were bad enough, but then I was robbed of sleep by several more silent phone calls to my home phone. I unplugged the line and managed to sleep, only for my dreams to be haunted by Leila. The darkness crowding in on us, the feeling of claustrophobia. The accusations, the shouts for help, for forgiveness, our voices harmonising so that I'd no clue which of us was saying what.

It's nice to forget about it while I'm with Mary.

At reception, the manager comes from his office to greet Mary, embracing her and kissing both cheeks. When he turns to me, I stick my hand out for him to shake before he can try the same on me.

'I'm Mary's friend, Stella.'

'Stella, yes… I'm Mr Belcher.' He encases my hand in both of his and stares intently at me. I want to yank free of him, but he lets go a heartbeat before I act. He's a tall man, big built, with rounded shoulders, as though he's spent his entire life leaning down over people. What little hair he has is thick and curly. If it were orange instead of steel grey it would look like a clown wig. He's only in his late-fifties but dresses like someone far older. Despite the heat, he's wearing a tweed waistcoat, white cotton shirt, and burgundy bow tie with white polka dots.

'Well, Mary is going to be an exciting addition to our little community, aren't you, my lovely?' he adds. Just before he turns to her, Mary catches my eye and smirks, pulling her face straight just in time.

He offers to walk us to the apartment Mary is moving into. He insists on hooking his arm through both of ours. I hate having my personal space invaded, and this guy seems to have no sense of distance at all, but maybe I'm being hard on him because I want to find fault in this faultless environment.

'Now Mary has warned me that I have to win you over, so I shall try my very best. If you have any questions, please don't hesitate to ask away. Our customers tell us that the quality of life and the sense of community and companionship that comes from living in a communal, managed development has enhanced their lives generally,' says Mr Belcher, leaning his head towards me as he talks. 'Tell me, you *are* Stella Hawkins? *The* Stella Hawkins?'

'Depends which Stella Hawkins you're talking about.' You could cut glass with my voice.

'Oh my goodness, you are! Well, as if having one star on my arm isn't enough. I watched the documentary, you know. Several times, in fact – I'm a bit of a true crime aficionado and your sister's case has always fascinated me. I have a theory I'd like to share… Ah, now just let me point out the wonderful gardens here. Day-to-day home maintenance tasks are taken care of, from mowing the lawn and maintaining these incredible flower beds – aren't they gorgeous, though? – to changing lightbulbs, as well as bigger jobs like refurbishing the lifts. There's an estates manager and other on-site staff available 24/7. This is the most luxurious assisted living development you'll find in the area, and it offers safety and security that is really valued by our residents and their families.'

The sales patter throws me off-guard, stopping me from telling Mr Belcher where he can stuff his 'fascination'. He turns a big grin on me. 'What do you think so far? Impressive, eh?'

A tight noise of agreement is all that escapes my lips.

'That lovely policeman of yours approves,' adds Mary. 'He came around himself and told me, just so he could put both our minds at ease – not that I had any fears but, look, he gave me his card and said I could call him any time with any worries.'

'He's going to regret that, isn't he?' I laugh as Mary kisses the card and pretends to tuck it in her bra.

Mr Belcher clears his throat to get our attention. 'This is the Moonlight block, where you'll be residing from now on, eh, Mary. If you'd just step in the lift and press 3 for me – thank you. So, Stella, yes, I remember your sister going missing. I was on holiday here at the time, you know. With my lovely wife. Do you feel the police really did their job? Because I think – ah, here we are, then: third floor. Lovely.'

'Mr Belcher—'

'Just one moment, dear, while I unlock. There, now, isn't it wonderful? Look at that generous bay window, and the stunning view across the trees and down into the bowling green. You won't even need to leave your home to enjoy a game, eh, Mary?'

The apartment is wonderful. The lounge is big enough to accommodate Mary's sofa and dining table, too, although she may use the other room as a dining room instead. When I ask, she says she isn't sure herself yet. The master bedroom is generous, and there's a second bedroom. Thick carpet gives beneath my feet as I walk around.

'Your dressing room?' I smile, and she nods, her eyes sparkling.

'There's a 24-hour warden available; all you have to do is press 1 on your telephone,' says Mr Belcher. He gestures like a magician's assistant. 'There are pull cords placed around the flat for assistance, too. All cleaning is done for Mary, which is nice, isn't it? I bet you'd like one of those yourself – I would!'

I make myself laugh for the sake of politeness. With Mary living here, I'm going to be seeing a lot more of Mr Belcher and need to work out a way of telling him firmly to back off, without threatening to break his jaw and make Mary's life here difficult. I start by asking lots of questions because while he's boasting about the communal lounge, restaurant, dining room and function room, he can't share his theories about my sister's disappearance. As he talks, I start herding him out of the apartment and back outside before he can notice that our visit is drawing to a close.

At reception, he wraps up his sales pitch.

'Retirement communities help to reduce the burden of maintenance, increase safety and security for the elderly and reduce loneliness. Nine out of ten of our customers say moving to one of our properties improves their quality of life.'

The line's obviously well-practised but he delivers it with such sincerity: the slight tilt to his head, the eyebrows drawn together a fraction. He's quite the actor.

He hugs Mary again. When I shake his hand, I squeeze slightly tighter than I should just to show him who's boss. It's good to get outside again.

'He's a bit much,' says Mary, taking my arm. 'But I've asked around and apparently he doesn't have much dealings with residents once they're in.'

'Phew! In that case—' I stop talking because Mary's pulled up suddenly. As I turn my head to see what's caught her, I hear her little gasp. A man in his late-sixties/early-seventies is struggling to carry gardening equipment because his right hand is bandaged to above the wrist. He's short, handsome, with a Roman nose and bright blue eyes, and powerfully built. The bits and bobs he's struggling with aren't heavy, they're just awkward with only one hand, and everything is threatening to tumble to the ground. He swears. Then catches us watching and looks sheepish.

'Sorry about that, ladies.'

'Oh, don't worry about it. You'll probably hear worse from Mary,' I say.

His head rolls back slightly. I didn't think my comment was that shocking. Mary doesn't notice, seems to have become fascinated with something that's made her turn away. The gardener starts to pick everything up, but the hoe and rake are long and the trowel and other bits so small that he's having a hard time.

'Here.' I rush forward, pick them up.

He stands up with a sigh of appreciation. 'Thanks, that's very kind. I'll be glad to get rid of this.' He shrugs his arm.

'Are you going to a gardening class or something?' I ask. 'I can carry them for you.'

'I work here. You looking to move in? You'd be a welcome addition – liven the place up a bit, I reckon.' All his words are directed at Mary; he barely even glances in my direction. I nudge her.

'Maybe, maybe not,' she replies. Over casual, I'd say.

I offer again to help him carry the equipment to wherever he needs, but he insists he's fine. 'Can't have two beautiful ladies putting themselves out for me,' he says, again looking directly at Mary. The old smoothy.

Mary seems flustered. He seems mesmerised.

We say our goodbyes and walk away. When Mary glances back, he's gone.

'Do you two have history?' I ask.

'Does the place get your seal of approval?' she asks, ignoring my question. Beneath the cool exterior she seems anxious in a way I've rarely seen, so I don't push further.

'It's everything you said it would be. The only thing that puts me off is creepy Mr Belcher. That and the fact they make an old man do manual labour on the garden. Doesn't seem right.'

She gives me one of her piercing looks. 'Perhaps he prefers to feel independent – that's the impression that I got. You don't become helpless and get thrown on the scrapheap just because you reach a certain age, you know.'

*

We're driving back when Euan calls for a chat. I put him on speakerphone to answer, and he sounds like he might explode with happiness when I tell him I'm in the car with Mary.

'*The* Mary?' he asks. It reminds me of Mr Belcher's reaction.

'Darling, other people may share my name but there's only one of me,' she replies.

'It's a real honour. Wow, I've so many things I'd love to ask you—'

I cut in. 'Maybe call later, I'm busy driving right now.'

I end the call and meet Mary's cool study.

'That was rather abrupt to a man you like.'

'Well, he's trying to get a story, make some money out of you.'

'Or he's trying to get to know someone who is close to the woman he'd like to get to know better.'

'Nah, he's a journalist; he'll be playing an angle.'

'You remind me of a little boy I went to school with who used to pull my pigtails and say mean things to me because he fancied me.'

'Oh, yeah? What happened between the two of you in the end?'

'I tripped him up.'

CHAPTER TWENTY-THREE

The dogs have settled around me in bed when the home phone rings downstairs. Typical. I run down, answer it. There's no one there. Is it a dropped call from a large call centre, or someone messing with me? It rings out again almost the instant I put it down. Still no one replies to my demand to know who's there, but I think I hear a muffled chuckle. I put the phone down and stare at it, shivering slightly in my cotton nightie. The third time it happens I ease the receiver from its cradle, put it to my ear and listen but don't speak. Breathing. Instead of returning it on its usual resting place, I put the receiver gently by the side of the phone and tiptoe up the stairs. Let them pay for a long phone call: that will teach them.

In bed, I cuddle the dogs a little closer, though, and keep my mobile phone within reach. I know how to deal with these situations, but sometimes, just sometimes, I wish I had someone to back me up. Perhaps Mary is right and Euan could be the one. Maybe I should make more effort with him. My finger hovers over the phone for a second before I start scrolling, then come to the number I need and dial it.

The engaged tone sounds out. Euan's on the phone to someone else.

*

Morning dawns, ridiculously bright and annoyingly early. With eyes full of enough grit to fill a snowplough, I creep to the phone and check. Of course, the nuisance caller has gone. When I dial the code to discover the last caller's number, it tells me it has been withheld. No surprise there.

Between these calls and the ongoing feeling someone has broken into my home, I decide action is needed. I dig out the small cameras I use to gather surveillance on clients' dogs, no longer in use now Bunny has done so well, and decide to use them like CCTV in my home. Once they're hidden around the house, I feel better – if anyone does break in, the motion detection sensors on the cameras will begin recording and I'll catch the person in the act.

Once it's a decent hour I call DCI Burns, who offers to pop round to pick up the poo parcel on his way to work.

'You'll miss the glamour of your job when you retire,' I say when I hand him the envelope.

'That and the swanky parties.' His smile fades to a frown. 'I honestly thought we'd get your sister's case tied up before I went. I hate leaving loose ends – especially this one. You need to trust DI Fremlin and his team more, rather than calling me; they'll succeed where I've failed.'

'I've looked him up, you know. He's got virtually no experience.' A quick bit of research into his background has revealed Fremlin only joined up four years ago and accelerated from constable to inspector on the high-flyer career switch programme, run by the College of Policing and often criticised by the rank and file.

'Old-fashioned policework hasn't cracked the case, maybe his new perspective will.' Burns looks beaten as he speaks, like he's let me down.

It's so tempting to tell him about the email. The words are on the tip of my tongue, but there's nothing new to say really and I don't want to hear the inevitable common-sense negativity when things are feeling good. Soon, though.

'You know I've always had your best interests at heart, ever since we met?' Burns says suddenly.

'Where's this going?'

'I noticed that journalist, Euan Vincent, has been hanging around, so decided to do some digging. He's got a few skeletons you need to know about. He's got money troubles – serious ones. By all accounts he invested everything in launching his production company and now someone is threatening to sue, and if it's successful the talk I'm hearing is that it will be a big pay out.'

'Okay.' I draw the word out, unsure where this is going.

'I don't think his motives for staying here are honourable.' After all this time, the DCI is more like a friend, and now his Labrador puppy eyes beg me to forgive him for poking around where he had no need. He's always been protective of me. 'There's some talk of a second documentary, apparently, with Netflix. Euan's been discussing it with them, telling them how the killer has been in touch with you. They reckon it might be enough to do a follow-up. He's using you, Stella, getting close so he can seal the deal – and make enough money to cover the pay out if he's sued. That's my working theory, anyway.'

'I thought you didn't follow your gut.'

'I don't, I follow the evidence and let it tell me the truth. That's what I've done here.'

I laugh. Give a shrug. 'Maybe a second documentary is a good idea. It'll keep Leila's case in the public eye. I'm using him as much as he's using me.'

'You might not be the only one he's using. Fox says she saw him with that young assistant, Asian girl, you know the one? Says they looked cosy…'

'Keshini's trying to get a job in TV, and Euan was probably telling her there's nothing doing right now.'

That's what I keep telling myself as I say goodbye to Burns and thank him for the update. But once the door is closed, I wander through to the garden and sit on the grass with my head in my hands, remembering the nagging doubt that I'd not got the whole story when I last spoke to Keshini. Thinking of all the times Euan has got me to open up about things I didn't share during interviews. How often he's called 'just for a chat'. The occasions he's seduced me and I've given in. Although to be honest it's fifty/fifty regarding who is leaping on who...

Of course he had an ulterior motive: there's no way someone fifteen years my junior would be interested in a middle-aged woman like me. He's only started this flirtation to get close to me.

A second idea appears, like clouds joining together to darken the sky before a storm.

If he really were willing to do all this to save his career and company, where would he draw the line?

Perhaps he'd consider fabricating a fresh selling point to hook investors and TV channels. Maybe he'd even go so far as emailing me pretending to be Leila's killer.

'Sorry, no sparkling water, you'll have to make do with straight from the tap,' I call across the patio. Ice cubes tinkle as I walk towards the small, round table where Euan waits.

'I'll slum it.' He leans back in his chair, all easy confidence and wonky smile.

'What would you have been up to today if I hadn't called?'

About ten minutes after deciding you might be emailing me as Dear Friend.

'Ah, nothing much, just enjoying the sea air.'

'Only you never seem to have much on these days. Thinking about it, every time I call you, you're able to drop everything. Like an obedient dog being whistled.'

His laugh is just the right side of uncomfortable. 'Well, you know I'd do anything for you.'

'Would you now? Would you tell me the truth, for example?'

'I don't—'

'Would you explain to me why you're hanging around me like a bad smell?'

He leans forward and tries to take my hand across the table. I move it out of reach. 'I know you're scared of getting into a relationship. So am I—'

'Did your fiancée really exist or was she made up to gain my sympathy?'

'Adele? Of course she's real. Was real. How could you even ask that?'

'Are you only with me so you can get a second documentary? Think carefully before you answer that, Euan, because I know about your money troubles. About you being sued. I know everything.'

Every muscle in his face goes slack then. His shoulders slump, head dropping to hide his face. Not the body language of a belligerent liar caught out. Long seconds of silence pass. His shoulders start to shake. He's crying…

'Euan, talk to me.'

Sniffs. Knuckles rubbing at his eyes like a child would. Finally, he speaks.

'Everything's such an atrocious mess. I'm going to lose everything. I'm not with you for the documentary, Stella. I promise you. But I'm not going to lie, it did occur to me that it might help swing things my way.'

'And that's why you're sleeping with me?'

His shoulders twitch as if flinching but he still speaks to his lap. 'Believe it or not, I'm with you because—'

'Don't bother.'

He looks up then, suddenly angry. 'No, you wanted the truth so listen to it. I'm sitting here, trying not to equivocate, but choosing the right words is difficult.'

'Well, it is when you talk like you've swallowed a dictionary.'

'First things first, I'm falling for you,' he says, ignoring my dig. 'Despite your truculence. Whether you believe it or not is beyond my control. I've never tried to manipulate you.'

'Oh, you've tried plenty.'

'No. When I first met you I pushed you on things, but only because I wanted to know how strong you were because the thought of the documentary breaking you... Well, it wouldn't have been worth it no matter how much money the programme made. I even argued with Penny-Sue about you on that first day of shooting. I told her my fears, told her that we shouldn't start filming if you were too fragile, that the price of breaking you would be too high. She insisted that everything was fine and that all you needed would be some charm to buoy you up if things got tough.'

That must have been the row I overheard that day.

'Turns out she was right, and I was being overprotective. It was the first sign that I'd got feelings for you. I should have known but, well, it's been a long time. There's been no one since Adele. As soon as I realised my feelings I made them pretty obvious, though.'

I'm watching his body language. When someone lies they tend to close themselves off physically. They'll cross their arms, or put their hand over their mouth, anything to create a barrier between you and them and their lies. The best liars know this, though, and can make their bodies relax. But they usually forget about their hands. They'll scratch their nose, or fiddle with a ring, or something. If eyes are the windows to the soul then hands are the doorway.

Euan's whole body is open to me.

'Even if you don't feel the same, I hope you at least believe me,' he says. 'But you're not the only reason I'm staying around here – it's because B&Bs are cheap. I've rented my flat out in London so I can pay my lawyers to fight this lawsuit before it gets off the ground. Every single spare penny I had was sunk into launching my company, buying equipment, paying the team who filmed you, their hotel bills, travel costs, it cost a fortune. Of course I've been paid by Netflix, but the profit isn't what I'd hoped and has to be invested in the next project if the company is to truly become a success.'

The tears are there again. He wipes at them, his embarrassment obvious. 'I'll lose everything if your ex has his way.'

'Ryan's the one who is suing you?'

'I didn't think it germane to mention earlier.'

'Eh?'

He gives a tiny laugh and nods. 'Yes, Ryan is suing me.'

'Euan, how did you know about the emails from the killer? Who tipped you off?'

'I can't tell you that.'

'Sure you can, if you want to stay in my good books.'

'If you insist, but you won't believe me. It was Detective Chief Inspector Burns.'

'He wouldn't.'

Euan pulls out his phone and sets it on the table between us before pressing play on a recording of a phone conversation. It's brief but there's no mistaking Burns's voice.

'Why would Dave come to you with that information?'

'You really want me to shatter confidences, don't you? He told me he's trying to get as much publicity as possible for the case before he retires, hence him abandoning protocol. Is there anything else you need to know? Ask me whatever you want.'

I stare at the phone still lying between us, silent now its sound bomb has been detonated. Thinking of Burns reminds me…

'Why didn't you tell me you'd seen Keshini and made her cry?'

'Because I'd have to break a confidence – *another* one. It's not my secret to tell; you'll have to ask her.'

'Secret?'

'Suffice to say, she's dealing with some life-changing realisations at the moment and her behaviour was a reaction to it all. A violent rejection of the truth and a desperate attempt to cling to a lie. Call her, and hopefully she'll inform you—'

'Do you want to move in with me?' Where the hell that came from I've no clue. I still don't know for certain how much to trust Euan, so it's a shock to realise I do. Us living together makes no sense at all – but it's also perfect sense. Maybe it's a case of keeping my enemies close. I honestly don't know. There are some rules, though.

'No funny business. You'll be in the spare room and pay me nominal rent. You're skint, I'm skint, we'd be helping each other.'

The biggest grin breaks out across his face, and when he slumps this time it's with relief. I'm lost in the past, though, thinking about that night all those years ago. I've always viewed it a certain way, and now the knowledge that Ryan is suing Euan has shifted something fundamental, like walking around a peaceful scene covered in twinkling snow, and only when the snow melts to reveal a deep crevasse do you realise that nothing is as it seems, and that for all this time you've been inches from death.

Because now I'm remembering how I came around from my drunken stupor several times the night that Leila disappeared. And how Ryan was never there.

CHAPTER TWENTY-FOUR

Documentary Transcript
Title: *Missing: The Twin Who Never Came Back*

Voiceover – Euan: This episode, I'll be uncovering evidence that Leila's life wasn't as happy and straightforward as it was painted at the time. Worse, I find shocking evidence that police ignored – that Leila had links to criminals and kept an explosive secret she hid even from her identical twin. All of which leads me to ask: Did she, in fact, take her own life?

[Interior. Stella's home.]

Stella: There was never a doubt I'd go to university. Getting away was my top priority as a teenager. It's strange, because Leila felt the same yet she decided to stay anyway. She once said she felt trapped in a spider's web, and no matter which direction she went or how hard she fought she never seemed closer to getting out.

It's not that there's anything wrong with Mereford, but it's natural that some people who grow up in a small town will dream of getting away. Having a fresh start. Leila had applied to do a law degree but didn't get the grades. While I went to Nottingham to study psychology, she stayed at home not knowing what to do. There weren't many options open in a place like Mereford. Most of the jobs were seasonal, for the tourist trade, and then in winter you sign on. No prospects.

[Cut to news archive footage of the seafront of Mereford in the late 1970s, with a sea of people walking along the wide pavements.]

Voiceover: Mereford in the early Nineties was a seaside town struggling to deal with change. Before that business had been booming. It was traditional for all the factories in neighbouring Leicestershire to close at the same time for the first two weeks of July. During "factory fortnight" special trains were laid on to Mereford so that families in their thousands could enjoy a hard-earned traditional holiday. Many businesses and offices followed suit, and the Leicester Mercury reported that in July 1965 alone more than one hundred thousand people left the city of Leicester to go on holiday, with a total of around £1 million in their pockets. Then there were the Nottinghamshire and Derbyshire "factory fortnights", staggered a little later. Coal mines in the surrounding counties also had set shutdowns for summer holidays, and many flocked to the coast. For most of the holiday season, Mereford was teeming and a fortune was made.

The 1980s changed all that. Manufacturing underwent tough restructuring. Many coal mines were shut down after the miners' strike. Traditions changed and more people started holidaying abroad. There was an economic downturn, and just a few years into recovery a recession hit in the second half of 1990.

By 1994 the whole country, including Mereford, was climbing out of that economic hole. There were still holidaymakers, but far fewer than those boom days. Opportunities for jobs for locals shrank.

[Cut to Stella.]

Stella: Leila didn't join the police because she really wanted to, but because it was the only decent job in the area that she stood a chance of getting. Her plan was to qualify and then transfer out of Mereford, out of the county. When she got accepted the passion came, though. By the time she finished training, she couldn't wait to start her new career.

Though identical, we had separate and distinct hopes for the future. I wanted to be a psychologist and had started my first year at university in Nottingham; far enough away from home to feel I'd successfully achieved my ambition of independence but close enough that Leila was just a two-hour journey away.

Leila stayed in Mereford, started training to join the police. That's why the police took it so seriously when she went missing; although she hadn't completed her training yet, she was technically one of their own. They knew she wasn't stupid or naïve, or likely to have simply run away to start a new life. Something bad must have happened to her to make her disappear off the face of the earth.

But I'm getting ahead of myself. When I moved to Nottingham, I'd enjoyed the physical distance between Leila and me. Being seen as an individual was a novelty to be explored and luxuriated in. It was a need that had grown during our teen years; it wasn't that we didn't love being with each other, it was something more fundamental than that: a need that all teens have to begin to stand on their own two feet and become independent. It rarely caused problems – never, really. Although there was one time when we were 11 or 12, something like that, and one of Dad's friends asked Leila where her other half was. I remember her shouting: "I am not a half, I am a whole, and so is Stella".

Voiceover – Euan: So there were sometimes cracks in the twins' relationship. I speak to their friends, Sarah and Emma, to see if they can shed more light on things.

[Cut to exterior. Café.]

Sarah: The twins weren't so goody-goody as the stories made out. What I mean is, they weren't saints, but they weren't sinners either, just normal. Now, it's like they've become these flat characters in a fiction, you know? But they were just normal. Complicated and straightforward, you get me?

Like, they partied. They were teenagers; it's only natural.

[Turns to her friend.]

Do you remember the time they got drunk and woke up in the window of the pub?

Emma: Yes! The landlord knew them – knew us all – so he let them stay over rather than risk them trying to get home in that state.

Sarah: So they could be wild, see. But no more than any of the rest of us. At that age, you do all sorts of daft stuff, don't you? If I found out my kids had done anything like that I'd give 'em what for, but when you're that age yourself it's different. Think you're indestructible.

Emma: We all did until Leila went.

Sarah: That's the thing, isn't it? See, Leila had another side, different to the one that was joining the police and being all sensible. But that's the bit that's only ever talked about, not her fun side. She could be a right laugh. Well, until she took up with Damien. Then she settled down.

Emma: Quieted right down, she did. Got a bit boring, really – not that I'm speaking ill of the dead, cos she seemed happy.

Sarah: Oh, yeah, yeah, really happy.

[The women exchange looks.]

Sarah: Well, we've never mentioned this before.

Emma: It's not like it's relevant really, but—

Sarah: There's no harm saying it now; it was such a long time ago. But the reason why Leila left the party, I reckon, was because she'd been watching Stella and Stella's fella—

Emma: Ryan.

Sarah: "I Will Always Love You", that's what they were dancing to. I know because that's the night I got together with my now husband, and we danced to it, too. It was our first dance on our wedding day. You can't beat a bit of Whitney Houston. Shame what happened to her.

Emma: Oooh, yeah, what a waste. Anyway, Leila looked upset about it. I don't know why. Maybe she just missed her own bloke or maybe—

Sarah: Or maybe she fancied that Ryan.

Euan: Was Ryan Leila's type? Were the twins often attracted to the same person?

[Indecipherable as both women talk at once.]
Emma:

[Laughs.]
You go first, Sar.

Sarah: They never went for the same type. But what can I say? There was something about the way Leila looked at Stella and her boyfriend that made us wonder. But then again, we could have it all wrong. Probably have. But she left pretty sharpish not long after and left looking a bit teary, I thought.

[Cut to Stella at her home.]
Stella: Leila absolutely didn't fancy Ryan. That's totally wrong. Who's said that? Well, whoever it is they're talking out of their backside. We were always attracted to totally different types. I went for the louder ones, was into bad boys back then, to be honest.

[Rolls eyes.]
Ryan was a nice enough bloke, and I'm sure he's all straightened out now, but back then he was well into the rave culture and

dropped Es like they were Tic Tacs. I'm amazed he got any work done at uni.

Leila wouldn't have touched him with a barge pole – not even someone else's barge pole. She liked the quieter, more studious type. The kind you could settle down with and introduce to your parents without cringing. She definitely would have ended up with a teacher or an accountant or a police inspector or something. In fact, she'd have become a police inspector. She could have been anything she wanted. She was amazing. All that future…

[Cut to photograph of Leila in her police uniform, looking serious but proud]

Voiceover – Euan: I decide to look into Ryan's past a little more. What if what happened to Leila was something to do with drugs? I find someone with an interesting story about him, but they refuse to go on record. They did, however, agree to have their words spoken by an actor.

Actor: Everyone knew this story about Ryan. He became a bit of a legend because of this, so everyone knew him by reputation and sight even if they didn't have anything to do with him. On the very first day of university, he took all of his grant money and spent it on weed to sell to fellow students. He made a fortune and didn't have to struggle for money through his whole course. He was always flush because he took his profits and reinvested, buying more drugs. Nothing hardcore like heroin or crack or something, but dope, Ecstasy, maybe the odd bit of Charlie, but I don't know that for sure. I did buy from him a couple of times, but wasn't a regular user, only recreational. Everyone did it.

He only sold to students, so we all felt safe knowing he wasn't a dodgy dealer who might break our legs if we pissed him off. But clearly even then Ryan was marked out to be a businessman and earn money.

He had a bit of a temper, too, and worked out a lot. I remember he always had big muscles, must have used weights or something, while the rest of us were typical skinny students. I suppose he could afford to join a gym thanks to his moneymaking schemes.

After Stella's sister disappeared, I did wonder sometimes… I mean, I've no evidence, nothing to base this on; it's just a thought. A shiny new police constable and a drug dealer forced into each other's company. Never going to be an easy fit, was it? I don't know, I just… it gave me pause for thought.

CHAPTER TWENTY-FIVE

Euan's breath is deep and steady, his body warm against my back as he spoons me in bed. It's not the greatest start to my new job of landlady.

The dogs have accepted for once that there isn't enough room for everyone on my double bed, so are arranged in a pile on the cool, dark wood floor. The whole room is filled with the noises of sleep, but I've too much on my mind between corresponding with my sister's killer, suspecting my ex-boyfriend, running my own business, wondering about Keshini's secret, and let's not forget that today I'm helping Mary move house. I feel like Scamp must when she finds three tennis balls and can only fit two in her mouth at once.

The new memories coming into focus through my drunken haze of the night of Leila's disappearance have been particularly disturbing.

Ryan always said he wasn't in the room because he was looking for a bowl for me to be sick in and searching for painkillers for me. But was that the reason, or was he actually not even in the house? He was there when I woke in the morning, but what about the rest of the night?

In the documentary, the police had appealed for people to come forward, warning that over time alliances shift or memories become clearer when viewed through the lens of hindsight. I hadn't expected to be one of the people seeing things afresh. Can my new memories be relied on, though, or am I misremembering?

Beside me, Euan wakes with a yawn and kisses my shoulder then announces he's going to have a shower. But he's back minutes later with a mug of tea for me. As he hands it over he leans down to kiss me. I put my hand between our lips.

'Er, don't get used to this. It was a temporary lapse.'

'I don't mind being a tenant with benefits.'

He takes a sip from his own mug. He's given himself the cracked one.

'I could come with you today,' he says. 'Help with any heavy lifting.'

'It's not the lifting that's the problem; Mary's hired people for that. It's the long meanders down memory lane.'

'It's inevitable though, isn't it? You have a clear-out and end up stopping to look through. Who doesn't want to relive their golden years and moments of glory?' He leans down and scratches Fifi's neck until she sinks to the floor and rolls on her back for a tummy rub. 'She's so trusting now.'

'A little more every day.'

'Like dog, like owner.'

I frown, but he's too busy gently scratching Fifi's chest to notice the expression on my face. For some reason, his words are niggling me, but I can't for the life of me think why.

*

The strained notes of 'Wonderwall' float from the bathroom. Euan's singing in the shower, and it's making me laugh.

Suddenly it hits me.

I'm happy.

I've never considered happiness before. My dogs are the only things that fill me with pure joy. Watching them running for the sheer love of it. The sound of Buster's feet scampering down the stairs to greet me when I come home. Scamp when she's barking with excitement about a ball being thrown or doing her comedy whining for attention. Buddy's bed head: his wiry fur poking up at all angles when he wakes. The way Fifi twists her head until it's almost upside down and groans in contentment when you hit the right spot on her neck. Those are pure hits of happiness for me. But now I'm in the throes of something different.

I hum while wrapping my dressing gown around me, then head downstairs to check emails and social media because you never truly have a day off when you run your own business. Scrolling through my inbox, I quickly spot what I'm hoping for.

Dear Stella,

I'm being such an idiot. Once again I've been thinking only of myself, talking about how hard this is for me to deal with and not considering you. You must think I'm a monster. So, here's some details about that night.

When I saw your sister's body lying limp, at first I couldn't comprehend she was dead. I thought she was passed out. Moments before she'd been breathing, fighting to stay alive. And my god, did she fight for her life – now, looking back, it's so obvious how hard she struggled against death, though somehow, I'd missed it at the time. The sound of it! It will stay with me for ever, that coughing wheeze of her final breath. At the time, though, denial had its hold over me. I watched over Leila, but her chest didn't rise again. Then her skin changed colour. So slowly. It was like watching a flower losing its petals.

I back away from the screen. Stand in the middle of the room, hand clenched over my heart, fighting down the urge to be sick, until I pull myself together and start reading again.

Eventually, I came to myself again, and all I could think of was getting rid of her body. Calling the emergency services did cross my mind, but only briefly. What would be the point? Your sister was dead because of a terrible accident caused as much by her as me – more, really – and my life would be ruined by it if I did the 'right thing'. There'd be questions, fingers pointed at me. I'd never recover from the disgrace. In that moment, a decision was made that has shaped the rest of my life: I chose to cover up what had happened.

I lifted your sister into my car and drove her to a place where no one would find her. It wasn't planned, and it amazed me that I got away with it. At first, I was constantly tense, waiting for someone to come forward with a sighting, or to say that her body had been found; but when it never happened, I thought I'd got away with it.

I'm sure you've kept things to yourself, Stella. Perhaps even about that night. So you'll understand that the real punishment lies not in the original secret but in constantly having to keep it hidden. It grows bigger in the darkness, and deeper with the passage of time. By the time the documentary aired, I knew there was only one way I'd ever be free – and that's why I wrote to you.

Your friend

Something isn't right. Something far beyond that description of my sister's last breath, though God knows that is enough to destroy anyone. I don't believe in mystical intuition, but animal instinct is another matter. Right now, if I were a dog I'd be growling, hackles raised.

We pull up at the retirement village, and I'm still struggling with that unnamed fear that slips away like a bar of soap every time I try to put my finger on it. I've barely spoken for the entire journey, but no one has noticed because I'm in the back, while Mary sits up front beside Euan. He insisted on driving, thinking my mercurial change of mood is because I'm tired, and he's been enthralled at Mary's shameless namedropping. Lennon and McCartney ('Oh, they once argued over me. They both were terribly, desperately in love with me.') Bowie ('Fascinating, brilliant man. His creative process was extraordinary…') Jagger ('Terrible flirt. Total gentleman').

As ever, how much is real and how much wishful thinking is anyone's guess, but I let the words wash over me. It doesn't cleanse my horror. It only increases the perception of the past crowding in on us all, trying to take over the future. I pull my lightweight cardigan closer around me despite the summer sun.

It's the creepy manager, Mr Belcher, who pulls me from my thoughts. He appears from the main building before we've stepped from the car, and hurries over to air-kiss Mary on both cheeks. Ignoring Euan completely, he grabs me by the shoulders and kisses me, mwah, mwah, before I can push him away.

'So lovely to see you all,' he says. He insists on escorting us to Mary's apartment to settle her in.

'I'm elderly not senile,' she says.

He chuckles as though she's made a joke. 'It would be remiss of me not to welcome you properly to your new home.'

Mary links arms with Euan and sweeps away. Which leaves me stuck with Mr Belcher. I try falling behind, expecting him to forge ahead so he can be with Mary – she's the star, after all. No such luck. He slips beside me.

'I didn't have the courage to say before, but, yes, very striking, seeing you in the flesh. Very striking. You hear of these things, of course, in the news, and so forth, but they feel like stories until there it is in front of you. In fact, it's a funny thing but I've always followed your case – your sister's case, I should say. I was on holiday in Mereford when it happened, you know, so it's always resonated with me. I have a little theory I'd like to share with you if I may.'

'I'd really rather you didn't.' The gap between Mary and Euan and me is growing. I try to hurry forward, but Mr Belcher oils his way in front of me faster than you can say 'slick'.

'No offence, but… your father. What was he really like? He always looked like he was play-acting his grief. Strange that. Did the police look properly at him?'

I square up, hands on hips. 'My father was a wonderful, loving man who wouldn't hurt a hair on anyone's head. He'd have died for his family.'

Belcher's head darts back as if worried I'll punch him. Which is a possibility.

'As I said, no offence meant. I just want to help.'

'You can shove your help. People think they can say the most insulting things and make it all okay by saying "no offence". *You* are a total prat, no offence.'

I snatch the keys from his hand with a: 'Go back to your office' and stalk off.

I don't want Mary to live in this village. I don't want her to be anywhere near that man and his strange way of staring at me as if I'm naked, as if my soul is naked. I don't want her to move at all, anywhere. She'll be further from me, and I need her close. Maybe I should ask her again to move in with me.

Euan has turned and is watching me. He's doing the squinty thing with his eyes that he does when he's appraising a situation; looking from me to the manager behind me and back again. He tilts his head as if to ask if I'm okay but doesn't speak. In answer I lift my chin, by which time I've caught them both up.

'Got the key, look! Sadly, Mr Belcher has been called away, so we'll just let ourselves into your new home, eh?'

Mary is angled away from me, though, not listening. She's rearranging her scarf. A second later I realise why: the silver fox gardener is working on a flowerbed just around the corner, almost hidden from view. The years of working outdoors have left him fit and strong; he has the kind of muscles some men half his age would kill for. His tan makes his shock of short, white hair seem even purer. As if sensing our stares, he looks up, and when he sees Mary a smile blooms. Something about the way his mouth turns up seems familiar, but the moment passes.

'Moving in day? I'll be seeing more of you then – looking forward to it.' He holds her gaze for a count of four, then returns to his flowers, but not without a long sideways glance at me, so I give him a wink of approval.

The flirting could be an interesting development. Mary is young at heart, glamorous, witty, fun – everything that deserves a little romance. It makes me realise that the urge to keep her close to me is selfish. She is struggling alone in her home. She deserves not only security but joy.

Mary takes control of the key, at last, and when we reach the front door of her flat she starts high-kicking (though only actually getting as high as her ankles) in excitement, leaning on me for balance.

'Should I be carried over the threshold, I wonder?'

'Hands off, Euan's mine, you terrible flirt.'

'That he is, my darling, that he is.'

'Only because I know you wouldn't have me, Mary.' Euan winks. Then he sweeps her off her feet and through the doorway.

Despite the laughter, that sense of wrongness looms still. That feeling of being on a stage someone has tilted, while I slide off the edge towards darkness.

For Mary's sake I keep smiling. The warmth between her and Euan casts a glow over me that I'm glad to be a part of. As he goes to the kitchen to make a cuppa, Mary pulls me into a hug.

'I'm so happy for you. I always felt that after Leila, you were left in a twilight world, Stella – no darkness because you wouldn't allow yourself to be lost entirely, but no daylight either. But Euan's brought light and warmth. He's your sunshine.'

The blush I feel creeping over my face takes me by surprise.

'Are you really going to be happy here, Mary? Alone?' I check, despite myself. 'It's not too late to move in with me instead.'

'I'm surrounded by people my own age. It's going to be wonderful, darling – besides I've a whole new audience to entertain with my stories. You know…' It's not like Mary to be lost for words. She's generally nothing if not forthright. 'Make sure you let the past go. Leila is gone. There's nothing you can do about it, and she wasn't the angel you think she was. None of us are, are we?'

The way she's looking at me makes my heart thud with paranoia.

CHAPTER TWENTY-SIX

Mary has been holding court all afternoon, sitting in her high-backed armchair, which has been placed beside the lounge's bay window. Euan's mouth is slack as he listens to her, eyes wide, like a child who has just fallen under the spell of a fairy tale.

'You see, Jane and I were both so full of frustration with the world at that stage. I only met her once but we still correspond from time to time,' Mary says. 'I felt so proud of her when she was arrested at those climate protests recently. If it weren't for my brittle bones I'd do the same. I'd go to London and stand alongside the likes of Greta Thunberg and those people bringing cities to a standstill.'

She gives that twirl of her hand that I know so well, which denotes the end of a story.

'You and Jane Fonda? Friends.' There's a reverence to Euan's whisper. He has a major crush on Jane Fonda during her *Barefoot in the Park* phase.

'Well, you see, it all started back in the Sixties. We were both so full of passion and anger at the state of the world. You know how we met? Stella hasn't told you? Oh, well—'

Around us the removal company employees unpack things, while Mary holds an audience. Every now and then she breaks off mid-sentence to give an order. I'm trying my best to help unpack, too, anything to block out the memory of the message this morning. The words are too awful to forget, though. I knew that dealing with the person who killed my sister wasn't going to be a picnic, so I keep telling myself to get a grip and pull myself together – but they are brave words shouted at a hurricane.

I try to lose myself in the comfort blanket of Mary's words. It makes me think again of what Euan said: *Who doesn't want to relive their golden years?* Mary's are so rich they're platinum. No wonder she loves riffling through them now that she is becoming too frail to get out and about much. Back in her day, she was an environmental activist when almost no one else was, when the whole world thought such people were hysterical freaks. Still, today I can only drift in and out of the stories, not hearing the gist.

I move mechanically, silently, efficiently, opening up a box and placing things where Mary wants them. Euan, however, is checking everything with Mary, which means he's done virtually nothing. Every piece triggers a new story. They get on so well. I thought she might be protective of me, but instead she's taken him to her heart as quickly and easily as I have. Even the dogs adore him.

'You're worse than us for getting sidetracked,' Mary laughs at Euan.

'Your stories are brilliant! Have you thought about writing a book?'

She shakes her head. 'I'm no good with words. Now Joe, he was fabulous at all that, that's why he was the songwriter, but me? Not a chance.'

'I'd be happy to ghost write it. I'm serious – this stuff is really popular. Come on, you've got anecdotes about the Stones, The Beatles, you've even met Elvis. And no one's ever heard your stories before, so it's a fresh market.'

She looks at him, uncertain he's serious. He clearly is. He hammers the point home.

'I have made notes,' she admits. 'Lots of notes, actually. Only, there are a few things I'd need to check with some people first.' She catches my eye. 'I'd hate to hurt people with secrets that came out, and there'd be no point in doing it if I weren't one hundred per cent honest.'

Euan's going red with excitement. 'It would be an honour to see your notes. Your book would be a chance to immortalise the best years of your life. It's as close as you can get to going back in time and living them all over again. In fact, hey, we could visit some of your favourite places. I'll take you, get some photos in situ.'

There it is again: the past invading the future. He keeps on talking, but the niggle in my brain is drowning him out. Louder and more persistent this time.

An ornament slips from my grasp and thumps onto the thick carpet as things suddenly click into place.

I know what's been bugging me about that last message from the Dear Friend. It's so obvious that it's hard to comprehend how I could have missed it in the first place.

'Stella? Are you all right?' Euan picks up the twisting glass sculpture and checks it over before passing it back to me. 'No harm done. So… you think it's a good idea, don't you?'

'What?' Dazed, I realise the conversation is still going on, ordinary and undisturbed by my revelation. Mary sighs.

'That your lovely Euan write a book all about me. Do pay attention, darling. Can you imagine!'

'Oh, the book. It's brilliant. Great.'

I nod enthusiastically, but Euan's giving me a funny look. He knows something is wrong. I can't tell him what I've realised though, not in front of Mary; I don't want to worry her.

Because along with the realisation of what Dear Friend is doing to me comes the knowledge there's nothing, absolutely nothing, left for me to work with.

I pick up another box and slit the brown tape open. The box is quickly gutted as I pull its contents out and put them away, moving automatically as my brain works in overdrive. Feeling fury and helplessness build and having to stamp it down for fear of Mary noticing.

I'd thought Dear Friend wanted to end my suffering – and his own, too – by telling me where Leila's body is. That he wanted to bring her home to rest but was too afraid of the repercussions to tell me straight away. I hadn't minded giving him personal details because it seemed a fair exchange, particularly when I was the mastermind in charge of the mighty plan to put him at ease and bring him out of hiding with the equivalent of cheese given to a wary animal.

The books I'm placing on the shelves flop over with a thump. I lift them back in place and shore them up with some bookends pulled from the box, all the time rolling my eyes at how stupid I was, thinking I was in charge of Dear Friend. How far I've strayed from reality.

Been led away from reality.

The truth is I've been played. Manipulated. Groomed by someone who knows exactly what they're doing and is loving it because, as Euan says, it gives him a chance to relive his glory days. The past is coming alive again – just as Dear Friend wants. He's reanimating the best years of his life, courtesy of me.

He's no intention of ever telling me the truth of what happened to Leila. His emails pretending to be a worried, cowardly family man are just that – a pretence. He's already growing bored of it, though, or is becoming arrogant, assuming I wouldn't notice the change in his tone in that last message.

I've been let down hundreds of times over the years. Gone along paths that led only to dead ends. It hurts every single time. But no one – no one – has ever got to me as much as Dear Friend.

*

'Hey, if you feel uncomfortable about me ghost writing that book for Mary, I can drop it. I'd never take advantage—'

'Don't be daft, I know that.'

Euan and I are standing side by side at home; him washing and me drying because only I know where everything goes, though he's learning fast.

'Well, something's clearly distressing you since I mentioned it.'

'Just me being silly. People talking about life stories, it just makes me think of Leila's cut short, you know?'

Not a total lie. I concentrate on drying off a plate rather than look him in the eye. Sud-covered hands take it from me, though, then close over mine.

Euan's got lovely hands. Strong, expressive.

As I look at them, I realise that by writing to me, Dear Friend has successfully robbed me of my only skill: my ability to read people through tiny tells. On paper, there's been nothing but lies and because my power is interpreting the physical – although admittedly dogs are my actual expertise not humans – I've missed all the clues. No wonder he fooled me so easily.

Euan folds me into a hug and I bury my face in his neck. Actually, perhaps if he knew what is happening, he could help me. The written and spoken word are his areas of expertise, after all. Confiding and reaching out feels alien to me. This is my problem and I know what to do: give the police the email correspondence between me and my so-called Dear Friend, avoiding contacting DCI Burns directly – I don't think he'll be impressed with my decision to take Euan in. Hopefully, with the extra messages, detectives will be able to get more information on the sender or ping it around with technology to pinpoint the IP address or whatever it is they need.

But I'll only do all that after checking that I'm not adding two and two and making twenty. The certainty of earlier has been tempered with doubt now there's been a chance to really think. Pesky hope has been pecking at me like a demented woodpecker. It's telling me that perhaps I've misread the situation. That perhaps

I'm being too hard and judgemental about this Dear Friend. That there's no concrete reason to believe he's reliving his glory days – and that I'm in danger of chucking away a golden opportunity on a fear-based whim. I make a show of yawning to Euan and saying I need an early night, and then trudge upstairs. A glance back shows him looking confused. Clearly he'd taken it for granted he'd remain a tenant with benefits, but right now I need to be alone.

*

Despite the dark, I walk comfortably through my home. Its every contour is ingrained in my head, no need for light to tell me the depth of the stairs I tread, the soles of my feet knowing by heart the threadbare parts of the stair carpet. I don't need to think to turn for the doorway covered in lines to denote my and Leila's growth (she always a fraction taller than me; no more than a millimetre but enough to differentiate). I know exactly where the furniture is, including the low coffee table that was a replacement for the one Mum and Dad broke when they overenthusiastically danced a jive one birthday.

Only when I'm at the table do I switch on a small lamp, and by its light turn on the laptop. As I open my emails I hear gentle padding. Buddy is coming towards me, slowly, as a slow approach will make me more likely to forgive him for not staying in bed as he was told. I smile and put my hand out, and he snuggles his face into it, running his muzzle in my palm, giving old man groans of delight at the gentle scratches I give. With the other hand I'm scrolling through my inbox until I reach Dear Friend's latest email.

The second reading does nothing to soothe my fears. There's no proof positive either – but if I had hackles, they'd be up and I'd be backing away from the keyboard again, growling.

It's not simply that he described my sister's death, it's the words he chose. ...*Moments before she'd been breathing, fighting to stay alive. And my god did she fight for her life...* How had she fought for her life if she'd been hit by a car? Somehow, the wording doesn't quite sit with his previous explanation. Perhaps he simply means that she didn't die instantly, but still I feel uneasy.

At one point he even seems to relish his description. *…I watched over Leila, but her chest didn't rise again. Then her skin changed colour. So slowly. It was like watching a flower losing its petals…*

Whoever wrote this is glorying in the memory. I can feel the triumph shining through from behind the carefully constructed sentences. It doesn't sit with the image of a scared, timid man so torn between finally doing the right thing and wanting to protect his own family.

…By the time the documentary aired, I knew there was only one way I'd ever be free – and that's why I wrote to you…

I shudder because it brings to mind a line from another of the messages. It was what was written in that first email when he acknowledged who he was.

I can't do this without you, Stella.

From the start, he's wanted to reel me in and have me help him relive the best moment of his life. The gentle creeping into my life, the manipulation, the gaining of trust so slowly, appearing to make himself vulnerable while all the time exposing my own vulnerabilities, seeming warm and wary when he was actually cold, cunning, clever… How easily I've been manipulated into believing this person wants to make restitution for his actions, and that with just the right amount of coaxing I can push him over the edge to walking into a police station. I'd even offered to meet him beforehand so we could walk in together.

What a naïve idiot!

But surely now I have the upper hand because I know what he's up to.

CHAPTER TWENTY-SEVEN

If I can keep Dear Friend communicating with me, offering up more little nuggets about his life, there's a greater chance of him slipping up and telling me something he doesn't mean to. Something that can finally put my sister's weary bones to rest. That means everything to me. Another line from the email springs out at me... *I'm sure you've kept things to yourself, Stella. Perhaps even about that night...*

If I do this, perhaps it will cancel out my own awful actions. This thought pushes me, finally, into action.

Dear Friend,

I'm not going to lie, your last message shocked me to the core when I first received it. Reading it was horrifying for me and it's taken me a while to gather my thoughts after it. But after the initial inevitable feelings for my poor sister, I was afterwards also struck by how hard it must have been for you to make such an admission. You made a mistake, and it has destroyed not just Leila's life but yours, too; I can see that now. In that respect, you and Leila are both victims of that terrible night. Try not to be so hard on yourself. You're not an idiot, or a coward, and while self-preservation may be selfish, it's also perfectly understandable. The only thing that matters is that you're trying to do the right thing now.

How are your family doing? I hope the stress of all this isn't impacting too much on them – or on your job, either.

I meant it when I said I was here for you. After our correspondence, I know now that I don't blame you for what happened or for not coming forward at first. Your messages have really helped me, so thank you so much for being so brave.

Looking forward to your reply.
Stella

Have I laid it on too thick? 'Inevitable feelings' is a bit jarring. A bit fake. What should I put instead? It seems obvious I'm lying by phrasing it that way. I tug at my hair, trying to pull thoughts from my stupid, tired, ever-circling brain. Writing the other messages was easier: at least then it felt like training; now it's stepped up into manipulation and that's beyond my skillset. Give me an aggressive dog any day of the week over this kind of brinkmanship.

I read my message again and realise I'm shaking my head. This is wrong. So wrong. I can't send this. I can't tell him he's a victim or that he's brave when I know now with every screaming part of my mind and soul that he's playing games with me.

It's past midnight and I'm no closer to knowing what to do. Every time I try to send the message something inside me refuses to go through with it.

I go upstairs. Stand outside my bedroom. Then turn right instead and push open Euan's door. When I climb into bed with him, he wakes with a sleepy smile of contentment that I'm about to smash with my sledgehammer confession.

'We need to talk…' I say.

*

Euan's eyes are puffy from sleep as he squints at the light from the bedside lamp that's just been switched on, but he takes one look at my face and sits up, trying to wake himself properly. Gives a cough to clear his throat.

'I've something to tell you,' I admit.

'You're dumping me. You've cheated on me?'

'I know you're half-asleep but don't be a dick. We'd have to be a couple for me to dump you.'

'Right. Of course. Good, good.'

He pulls me against him and rearranges the duvet around us while I begin to talk. To his credit, he listens to me without interruption; his journalist training maybe kicking in, sensing that if he does the whole tale may never come out.

Finally, there's silence. Euan kisses the top of my head then rests his chin on it.

'Right. Bloody hell. Firstly, I'm grateful you informed me. Secondly, why the hell didn't you tell me about all this earlier? But no, let's put that one to the back of the queue for now because more imperative is: what are you going to do?'

'I don't know. Go to the police?'

'Thank God – I was trusting we wouldn't have to quarrel over that. It's definitely the right thing, Stella. Deciding on the extent of this person's duplicity isn't pertinent; the only point that matters is that you need to leave it up to the experts. Yeah? The police. Accident or no, you can't deal with the person who killed your sister; it's utterly screwed up.'

'Well, I was doing quite a good job up until now. I've got some information from him and—'

'As you yourself admitted, he could be duping you, manipulating your emotions; how would we know whether he is or isn't? You're putting yourself in the firing line, and it's only going to end in trouble. I don't want you to have anything to do with him any more.'

'I've managed to look after myself for years before you came along, you know—'

'Think of the emotional damage you're doing to yourself. If he were going to confess fully and tell you where Leila's remains are, he'd have done it by now—'

'He says he's scared—'

'Of course he does. It's not up to you to find out either way. Look, you're always saying you'll do anything for your sister, but this is hopeless – you might as well bang your head against a brick wall and tell yourself *that's* going to somehow give you the clues you need to find where Leila's body is hidden.'

'I'm not an idiot—'

'Why are we even arguing about this? I'm agreeing with everything you've said yourself, but you seem determined to take offence.'

'Maybe it's the way that you say it.'

I haven't been accountable to anyone for too many years. Even if he is saying the same as me, it's different coming from someone else's mouth. I feel like I'm being bossed around and can't help digging my heels in.

Which is ridiculous, I realise with a sigh.

'Look, just shut up, stop being right, and look after the dogs for me while I go to the police station, will you?' I give him a kiss.

'I'll go one better, you stubborn bugger. I'll come with you.'

'Thank you, you obstinate old fart.'

'If I'm old, what does that make you?'

Then he's kissing me, and the dogs jump onto the bed with joyous woofs, which makes us laugh and scream, and the dogs bark and bounce even more, and the darkness I felt closing in on me is full of light.

CHAPTER TWENTY-EIGHT

Documentary Transcript
Title: *Missing: The Twin Who Never Came Back*

[Piece to camera. Euan, walking along the beach.]

Euan: After speaking with Leila's friends and my anonymous tipster, I can't ignore the signs any longer. I've got to speak with Stella's boyfriend of the time, Ryan Jonas, and ask him if there was anything going on between him and Leila – or if what happened to her might have been drug-related.

When I turn up at Ryan's home, he initially refused to speak with me again. But eventually he agreed to meet in a café and speak off camera. We sat outside, and the crew hid around the corner, using microphones to pick up the conversation.

[Caption over a holding shot of a cup of coffee.]
We apologise for the poor quality of this recording.

Ryan: Look, okay, there was nothing going on between me and Leila. Absolutely not. Capiche? I mean, she was exactly like Stella but not, yeah? It would have been a total head fuck, like cheating on my girlfriend with my girlfriend. Besides, Leila had only lived with her bloke for a couple of months, so they'd still have been in the honeymoon phase. Mind you, it's a funny business about him...

I never met Damien Francis, but he sounded dull as ditch water. Those two, they were on a trajectory: engagement, marriage, two point four children and a house with a white picket fence. Lads like me did our best to avoid all that. Stella was nice and all but neither of us wanted anything like that.

Euan: Did you ever give or sell drugs to either of the twins?

Ryan: We're done here, mate.

[Rustling, then silence.]

CHAPTER TWENTY-NINE

It's less a knock on the door more a blow to it. A single loud thud that makes the dogs jump up and bark, glaring at it in apprehension. Me, too. Another blow, a pause, then another. I swear the door shakes.

I'm here alone and have just settled down with my breakfast – later than usual – and about to check my emails in case Dear Friend has replied to me. Euan has gone out. His phone went off at 4 a.m. with someone asking if he was available to cover a shift at the evening paper in Lincoln because a journalist had called in sick. He'd had to leap straight out of bed and into the car to get there for the 5 a.m. start, but he'd been so chuffed about earning some cash, no matter how small, that he hadn't minded.

I wish he were here. Then I give myself a mental slap for wanting to rely on someone else – I've managed without for all these years and shall continue to do so. Still, having him by my side yesterday when Fox and Fremlin came over had felt good. Them dropping everything to come over despite it being a Saturday had been appreciated, although they'd looked at me like I was the biggest idiot on the planet for not keeping them informed. I'd received a long lecture about how I shouldn't reply to the mystery emailer any more and despite still having some misgivings, I've given my word.

My revelation about Ryan's cast-iron alibi disappearing, thanks to my own new recollection, had really got them exchanging glances, unspoken thoughts passing between them. When I'd asked them to keep me updated, it was Fox who spoke for the ever-silent Fremlin, snapping: 'Enquiries are ongoing, Ms Hawkins. Rest assured we're pursuing several lines and will be in touch if and when there is something to say.'

Now, another blow to the door makes the dogs' barking ratchet up from defensive to frenzied. They're better backup than Euan or the police, I tell myself, peering through the security peephole.

It can't be…

Another squint through it, as if somehow the second time I'll see what's really there rather than what I *think* I've just seen.

It's still the same person. The hair, the jawline, that way of standing with hands shoved in pockets and chest puffed out, like a cocky door-to-door salesman. It's Ryan. Twenty-five years ago I'd been drawn to his confidence, but even back then I'd known he wasn't The One. He was always too much of a bell-end for that. From what I saw of him on the documentary, he hasn't changed much. And now he's threatening legal action against Euan and the production company for their 'lies' about him, and he's being investigated again by the police.

The thought of a conversation with him should put the fear of God into me. It should, but it doesn't.

Bring it on.

The last time I'd seen Ryan was a few weeks after Leila's disappearance – exactly how long I can't remember, so much of that period has been redacted by my mind.

I open the door and his red face leers forward immediately.

'So what's this about you shacking up with the journalist? Eh? You two in it together to make my life a misery?'

Immediately, I'm on the defensive. Take a step back. Four heads crowd around my legs, peering. Ryan spots them and stands upright. Twists his neck that way he has, cracking it.

'Come on, Stella. Don't play the innocent.'

'I'm not actually playing at anything, Ryan. Nice to see you after all this time, by the way. Now do you want to calm down and explain what the hell you're on about, or shall I just slam the door in your face now and save us both some time and energy?'

'You not going to invite me in?'

'Does it look like I'm going to?'

We glare at each other. Our arguments used to be explosive, and it's amazing how easily we've slipped back into the old routine. The make-up sex afterwards was always incredible. It was, if I'm honest, the main thing that kept me with him for so long. The air between us now is thick not with sexual tension but anger and resentment.

I may not have loved him all those years ago, but I'd been fond of him and the surprising depths I'd thought lay beneath the bluff, bluster and dodgy dealings. A soft side that, at the time, he hadn't shared with anyone but me. Maybe by appealing to that side of him, I can get a confession…

'You want to calm the hell down, come in, and talk to me like a decent human being?' I ask.

Another neck crack then a nod. He steps forward, and the dogs re-start their barking. I let them for a couple of seconds. Just long enough to let Ryan know better than to start anything once he's inside. Then, with a single hand signal, they fall silent and I throw some titbits of treats at them that I've always got in my pockets.

Once he's inside Ryan seems slightly calmer, but I can see he's itching to launch into another tirade, so get my question in first.

'Ryan, what happened all those years ago…? I know—'

He gives a start. 'Know? What do you think you know?'

'God, if you'd just shut up and let me speak, I'll tell you. I've never apologised to you for the way I blamed you all those years ago, refusing to speak to you because you wouldn't let me phone Leila. None of it was your fault.'

'Of course it bloody wasn't.'

'No, and I knew it then and I know it now, and it's high time I told you as much. I needed someone to take my fears and frustrations and anger out on, and you were a convenient target. It was a shitty thing to do. Then again, I was in a shitty place, so…'

'Yeah, well.' Neck crack. 'I did try to listen to you, you know. But you were off your face. Totally wankered. I could barely understand a word you were saying that night.'

'I know. The joy of Blastaways, eh?'

'I don't give a shit about the past; it's the present that's bothering me. Why did the police come to my house demanding the "truth" about where I was the night Leila died? What the hell's made you change your mind about my alibi? And how come you're shacked up with this journalist?'

'What's that got to do with you? We haven't been dating for twenty-five years, Ryan, so…'

'It's not some petty jealousy, Stella. I want to know if you cooked up this bull about me being some kind of kingpin drugs baron together, to get publicity for your tawdry little documentary. I thought I was helping you by taking part, actually felt sorry for you that you've still not moved on from 1994; but screw you. And now you're trying to frame me for Leila's disappearance? What? Is it a way of getting another money-spinning programme made at my expense?

'Make a retraction about what's been said about me, and implied about me, or I'll sue you and that Fleet Street scumbag for everything you both own. I'll take every single thing from you that you hold dear. Don't think for a second I won't. Everything, Stella. I'll strip you bare of your dignity not just your assets.'

His blue eyes are bloodshot and bullish. Scamp starts yapping, pushing her little body between us. Buddy and Buster, calm and steady, do the same. Even Fifi presses herself against my legs but turns towards Ryan and growls. I give the command, reminding them to be quiet and still, then stare Ryan down.

'I don't respond well to threats. You should remember that well enough.'

He looks at me, the dogs, then back again. Swallows. Tries again.

'I'm just saying, Stella, that I've been treated disgracefully. I've never done anything to you or your family, but somehow my name is mud now. Wasn't destroying Damien's reputation back in the day enough for you? Now you've got to pick on me? You've no idea what I've done over the years, what I'm capable of—'

'Right, firstly I haven't picked on you. I know the documentary got a bit… carried away with some of the stuff that was said, but it was nothing to do with me. But, Ryan, you know how, in the documentary you love so much, the police say time can change the way people remember events? Well, it got me thinking that I don't remember seeing you after you put me to bed—'

'Of course you don't. You passed out!'

'I kept coming round, now and again. The memories are blurry but you weren't—'

'It must be an expensive business searching for your sister. Chasing all those…' he pauses. Searching for the right words. Or perhaps to emphasis them. '…dead ends and false leads.'

He stares me down. His jaw muscles work, clenching and loosening several times. My stomach flips. I've never seen him look so threatening. Does he know something? Is he behind the latest dead end I've hit? Is he responsible for the emails that had given me false leads?

The room seems to shrink around me, suddenly claustrophobic. I reach out and sink my fingers into Buddy's fur, instantly strengthened and reassured. Force myself to breathe slow and steady, and not give in to the bird heart fluttering inside me and trying to break free.

Ryan is still speaking, doesn't seem to have noticed the emotional punch he's landed.

'I could help with those expenses. Just change your statement to the police and pull the documentary. Or lose everything.' He's perfectly calm as he speaks. Then with a nod of his head to show the conversation is over, he saunters towards the front door – although not without keeping a wary eye on the dogs. 'You know how to get in touch, Stella. That journalist of yours certainly does.'

There's one last thing to try, to throw him off kilter. 'You can't do this without me, can you, Ryan? You need me, don't you?' I echo the words used by Dear Friend to gauge his reaction. Because it's suddenly occurred to me who might know that Leila and I had pet names for each other – him. Ryan might have overheard us all those years ago. Or maybe I told him: who can say? But it's a distinct possibility.

He looks at me. Gives a long, last grin. 'Believe whatever you need to believe, just give me what I want. I'll be in touch.'

He opens the door and slips out. I can't move because I don't know whether to run after him and demand to know what the hell he means, or slam the door shut and call the police because I'm suddenly scared.

The computer is staring at me. Calling to me. Telling me to check whether Dear Friend has tried to contact me and let slip any more information. He won't, of course, because I haven't replied to him, but it's hard not to give in to desire. Even if he has, I can't do anything about it because of the promise made to Euan and the police yesterday. Besides, I'm in no frame of mind to deal with it. Not after that awful confrontation with Ryan. As ever, my fear comes after, not during a showdown, and now I'm alone, I'm shaking.

What I need is a walk on the beach to calm me. Only it doesn't. In fact, once outside I'm more keyed up. Unable to shake the creeping feeling Ryan is watching me, I spend the whole time looking over my shoulder. Jumping at the crinkle of a crisp packet blown along the sand. Peering at shadows lurking beneath the candy floss kiosks, convinced they're a person. I even become certain a woman is following me.

The dogs pick up on my strung-out mood and play up. Fifi keeps running off and not coming back when she's called; Scamp is super clingy and spends most of the walk on her hind legs, trying to climb into my arms; and Buster and Buddy bark at everything.

My emails are still whispering to me…

Too weak to resist, I unlock my phone and check them. Within seconds I see the one I need.

Dear Stella,

Are you okay? I do hope I didn't offend you with my clumsy words. This is all so difficult, isn't it? Please forgive me for any pain I've inflicted on you.

Just let me know that you're all right.
Your friend

There's only one person guaranteed to reach me when the world starts crowding in on me and I get scared and retreat: Mary. Dropping the dogs at home, I jump in the car and feel calmer the minute she opens the door to me. Her apartment is immaculate, all the furniture in place, everything unpacked, and sparkling clean. Gone are the days when I needed to whip the vacuum cleaner out for her, which is a shame as it might get rid of some of my antsy energy.

'No Euan?' she asks, settling into her favourite armchair. It has stayed by the window, enabling her to not only enjoy the glorious view of treetops and rolling gardens, but also watch all the comings and goings. A queen holding court.

When I tell her he's working, she claps her hands. 'I'm so glad! Oh, I've clapped so hard I almost lost a diamond,' she laughs, adjusting the huge ring on her finger.

It reminds me of how Euan described her the last time we visited, on Friday, when she and he had been talking enthusiastically about writing her life story. 'That woman doesn't grab life, she hugs it to her bosom, covers it with air kisses, then presses some diamonds into its hands as thanks,' Euan had said. He understands her perfectly. When I tell her now, she blows kisses to him even though he's not here.

'You've a diamond there,' she smiles.

'Hmm, we'll see. Anyway, are you settling in?'

Of course she's already making friends and is full of gossip about fellow residents. Apparently, Mrs Merryweather, across the hall, is the widow of an investment banker and a fount of information. The two of them have clicked instantly and arranged to swim together every morning.

'That woman knows everything about every resident and staff member. No discretion, darling; it's fabulous. Did you know Mr Belcher adores acting? Apparently, he's excellent, can make anyone believe he's a totally different character, though I find it hard to believe.

'Oh, and there's a wedding next week – two of the residents have fallen in love. How wonderful! His family don't approve, but he's refused to make his fiancée sign a prenup and has already changed his will in her favour. He's threatened to disown everyone if they don't accept her! They seem a gorgeous couple, so in love, and they've asked me to sing. Who am I to disappoint them?'

'Seen any more of the silver fox gardener?' I ask. 'Come on, it's not like you to be coy. Don't you want a fancy man of your own?'

'There's nothing fancy about that man.' She winks at me but doesn't give her usual dirty laugh. The questioning look I give her is met with a sigh. 'He's your father.'

I laugh. Because it's clearly a joke, right? Even though Mary's looking at me like the world has just ended. The laugh dies of embarrassment. My heart thumps.

'Mum would never cheat on Dad.'

'Darling, of course she wouldn't; she lived and died for him and her children.'

'So wha—?'

'I gave birth to you and Leila.'

CHAPTER THIRTY

Beside me I can feel Euan shoving his hands deeper in his pockets and shifting from foot to foot as I talk to Detective Sergeant Fox. He's itching to get involved in the conversation, but on the drive to the police station I gave him strict instructions, on pain of death, to keep quiet and let me handle this. He promised, with a roll of his eyes and a muttered 'stubborn mule' as he held the door of the police station open for me.

I'm not dealing with things well. Everything is out of control. I refuse to think about Mary's confession yesterday, about being my birth mother – haven't even told Euan or Farrah about it – but it keeps leaking through every single moment, driving me mad. Dealing with Dear Friend is easier (who could have guessed that? Not me) which is why, as soon as Euan got home from today's early shift in Lincoln, he and I came to the station to chase up the police.

'How far have you got with tracking him down?' I ask DS Fox.

'These things take time—'

'Surely you've had long enough by now. It's been weeks since I passed on the first email.'

Mary's face flashes through my mind. So pale, so scared. '*Your parents were so desperate for children,*' she'd said. '*It seemed the obvious solution when I discovered I was pregnant. And look at what a wonderful family you were.*'

'*A family built on lies. Leila and I had a right to know!*' I'd shouted.

I push the memory away and concentrate on Fox's words.

'The station has recently had to downsize the number of officers at the station – in the whole constabulary, in fact. We're not the only ones; it's been all over the news about the cuts to forces across the country. It means we're overstretched to investigate everything, but I assure you we are doing our best. Cold cases are notoriously expensive and tend not to reap results, though, so prepare yourself.'

'I'm grateful, truly,' I reply. 'I mean it. The police have worked hard over the years, but all that toil has come to nothing. It's just… this lead is the first solid thing to come along in twenty-five years and you've been working on it for weeks, so I hoped, especially with the extra information handed over on Saturday…'

Mary's eyes, so full with tears, were brighter than her precious diamonds as she'd spoken. 'He was a session drummer back then. It was more than an affair. We talked about our future, starting our own band, spending our lives together, making music and love all day long, but he ran off as soon as he heard he'd be a father. And Joe would have killed me if he found out. So I disappeared for a while; your parents hid me.'

Mary. My mother. It seemed impossible she'd lied for all these years. My parents, too. Unthinkable. I turned my back, grabbing the wastepaper basket and dry heaving over it.

Detective Sergeant Fox sighs. 'Fraudsters, people like this, they're constantly developing new ways to scam—'

'Not a scam. He *is* the killer.'

'Possibly. Anyway, it is generally possible to track and trace. But if they've used VPNs, proxies or TOR nodes, anything like that will hide the original location. If they do this properly, they will daisy chain systems together. Your guy has daisy chained to several different countries, and we're having to interact with each different law enforcement agency.'

What Fox is saying flies so far over my head it might as well be a jumbo jet. Despite my best efforts to learn more on the subject, the pinnacle of my technical abilities has been setting up a Facebook page to raise awareness of Leila. I paid someone to design and make the business website for me. Fox is talking in anacronyms and going on about making multiple hops between locations, specialist software and detection tools, more daisy chains. My concentration wavers.

'Darling—'

'Don't call me that.'

'Darling, he's guessed. He's come to me, apologising for the past and asking about you. Said he'd always assumed I'd got rid of our child but that he could tell you were his as soon as he met you. I had to tell you before he did.'

'It's pretty standard stuff for fraudsters and scammers to utilise, so we'll find him in the end – it will require some time and patience, though,' Fox finishes.

'This extra information will help, surely,' I push.

'Possibly. Probably.' She's only saying that because she's seen my face darken, I'm sure. Dealing with DS Fox is so different from my chats with DCI Burns, who always makes me feel like part of the team. He and Mary are my anchors and without them I'm adrift. 'We'll go through it all and see what we can find. We'll get our best tech people on it. But you know the score by now: try not to get your hopes up too much. And, honestly, you shouldn't have engaged with the sender because you may have made things worse; he'll have felt encouraged and be feeding off the attention.'

Euan nods. 'She's fed the monster.'

I give him a warning glare before turning back to the officer. 'I know.'

I'd run from Mary's building. Me, the woman who doesn't run from anything, sprinted from the apartment like the hounds of hell were chasing me. At the car park I glanced up. Mary was standing at the window, looking down at me, her usual megawatt superstar smile replaced with an expression that made me think of that famous Edvard Munch painting, The Scream. My heart filled with such fierce love, but I didn't know how to process it – that love was for my mum's best friend, for the woman who had become a second mother to me but not given birth to me. At that moment everything had felt so topsy-turvy I couldn't comprehend. Eventually, I'd process it but not yet, not yet. I'd almost stumbled as I turned and hurried to my car, trying to weather my way through the storm of emotions raging.

Fox gives a hefty sigh. 'If this so-called Dear Friend messages again, just ignore and pass it on to us.'

'Definitely. I've no intention of having anything to do with him again. He turns my stomach.'

'Good, because the best thing you can do now is leave this in the hands of the experts.'

The experts who've got nowhere for the last quarter of a century, I think. 'Absolutely.'

'We know what we're doing. We've been doing this for years, you know.'

She gives a reassuring smile that is hard to return because 'doing this for years' translates to working leads that never come to anything.

Once we're outside, Euan pulls me to him. 'Frustrating, eh?'

'Just a bit,' I sigh into his chest.

'I know it must be so difficult for you. It's positively esoteric.' I give him a look. 'Weird, eh?' he shrugs. 'It would be driving me mad if it were me. But there's no way you could take this guy on single-handed. I mean, we all tell ourselves we'll do anything to solve a situation, but there has to be a line we won't cross. That's the reality.'

'What do you mean?'

'Telling yourself what you'd do in a situation is one thing, but being faced with it, it's different, isn't it? Making yourself deal with the man who killed your sister, well, you've gone further than most people would in reality. We say we'd do it but actually it'd be too hard, too scary, too painful, feel too impossible.'

'There are people who do it, though. People who've gone to prison to meet with the person who murdered a loved one. Parents who've forgiven the killer of their child…'

'Oh, I know, and I've met them, interviewed them. Believe me, these people are few and far between. They are made of incredible stuff, though. They're… well, like I say, they go beyond what the average person is capable of when actually placed in that situation.'

'But that's the thing, isn't it? You don't know how you'll react until you're actually living the scenario.'

'Are you having second thoughts about not replying to the emailer, Stella? I know you probably feel guilty, but seriously you've nothing to feel bad about. You've spent half your life trying to solve the riddle of Leila's disappearance, and it's finally paying off. You're responsible for this breakthrough, no one else, because you were courageous enough to agree to talk about what happened. You've done everything you need to and now you have to let it go.'

The words sink in but sit as comfortably in my stomach as an omelette made with salmonella-laced eggs. This doesn't feel like unfinished business. I've drawn a line, though, and won't be stepping across it. What will I do with all the time I'll suddenly have now?

Sort things out with Mary?

We get in the car and while indicating left, I try to imagine myself having hobbies. Gardening. Socialising. Being normal. How do people do it?

What does Dear Friend do when he's not busy taunting me or reliving my sister's death, I wonder? Has he killed before? Is that his hobby?

Could he even be lining up his next victim while the police and I patiently wait for some mythical breakthrough to appear? The thought keeps me checking over my shoulder the whole drive home.

*

The car keys are gripped between my fingers like a weapon, I realise, as I bypass the house and go straight down the side, to the high wooden gate that leads to my back garden. My thoughts from the drive home have left me on edge. Hugging the dogs will cheer me, though, and I unlock the padlock eagerly. Buddy, Buster and Fifi run over sounding, as usual, as if they haven't seen me in a year. But not Scamp. Not my love sponge, who usually leads the pack. She walks slowly, head down, tail down and only the merest hint of a wag at its very end.

'What's the matter, girl?' I ask, pushing her fur away from her eyes so I can see them better. They're sad. No, pained. Her nose dry.

I grab the other three, study them. They seem fine.

Scamp gives a little groan, then sits down heavily.

She seemed fine this morning. I cast around for a reason for the change, my eyes roaming the garden until they stop on some meat lying on the grass. Grabbing a poo bag from my pocket, I march over, scoop it up.

'What's going on?' asks Euan, confused.

'I don't know. We need to get Scamp to a vet, though – I think she's been poisoned.'

CHAPTER THIRTY-ONE

The good thing about having a best friend who is a vet is that she'll drop everything for me and my dogs. Farrah treats Scamp immediately as if she has been poisoned, pushing medication into her to counteract whatever it might be, before putting a rush job on the lab to try to identify the exact cause and give a more targeted treatment. My girl will be kept in overnight for observation.

'She's going to be okay,' says Farrah. 'There are some sick people out there, aren't there? Chucking laced meat and treats around where they know dogs are walked regularly because they've got a cob on about barking, or picking up dog do, or just a fear of canines in general. It happens more than I like to think about.'

'Has anyone else come in then?'

'No, but that doesn't mean—'

'It kind of does, though, doesn't it? This wasn't about a hatred of all dogs, otherwise the meat would have been put around the park or the beach where there's plenty of footfall. This was about *my* dogs. It happened in *my* garden.'

'You don't know that for certain. Someone could be chucking meat over the fence of lots of dog owners. Or the meat you found could be fine, and Scamp could have picked something up on her morning walk. Do you want me to let you know if anyone else comes in with pets who've suffered the same thing?'

'Yeah, please, but I won't hold my breath.'

Farrah tilts her head. 'Is everything okay? Why are you so worried?'

A forced smile. 'No reason. Honestly, it's nothing.'

Her concern is written all over her face, and I don't want to add to it by telling her I'm convinced the person who killed my sister has now tried to poison my dogs.

I'm allowed into the back, where Scamp is resting. She's too groggy to lift her head, but her tail gives a single, heartbreaking thud that seems to take all her strength. Her rich brown eyes stare into mine, begging me to make everything better.

'Hey, you, everything's going to be fine,' I croon. The black fur of her long ears looks dull but still feels silken beneath my fingers. 'You're going to stay with Aunty Farrah tonight. Just think of the luxury of a whole bed to yourself, not having to get smacked in the face with Buddy's wagging tail. Heaven! Love you, little girl. And when I fetch you tomorrow, I'm going to sit with you all. Day. Long. And do nothing but cuddle.'

With a kiss on the top of her head, I whisper goodbye as her eyes close and she sinks into sleep.

Back at home, the dogs are waiting inside, confused about being shut in on such a lovely day. I lock and deadbolt the front door before dropping to greet them.

'I'll drop by your neighbours and see if they've had any problems with rats,' Euan says.

I've no idea what he's talking about and tell him as much.

'It occurred to me that a neighbour may have garnished meat with rat poison to make it a tempting offer. Perhaps the rat took it, dropped it on your garden after having a nibble, and went off to die. It's worth asking about.'

'We know who did this. It's him: Dear Friend.'

'You're tired and stressed, and understandably so—'

'He's already been in my house, I'm sure of it.' Euan's mouth is forming a 'w'. I spit the answer out before he can ask. 'It was a couple of weeks back. Someone definitely got in, had a look around; I could just tell. The dogs scented a stranger in the house.

That's why I put some of the dog cameras around the house once I got them back from a client. Ah, I forgot to warn you about them, didn't I…?'

He starts chewing his nails as I explain how the doggie cams are usually used, and how I'd had the idea of using them as makeshift CCTV instead. 'Not that I've caught anyone inside. The most interesting thing I've seen is you rearranging your bits when you thought I couldn't see.'

A sigh is his only reply.

'Now, this so-called Dear Friend is mad at me for not getting back to him and wants to hurt me – and my Achilles heel is my dogs. This is not an accident.'

'That's… Why would he do that?'

'Because he's a killer!'

'Without evidence, it could just as easily be a neighbour sick of your dogs barking.'

'A second ago it was because they'd got rats.'

'Right, I'm going to find out what's what.'

As he opens the front door, my mouth takes over, shouting: 'Stop trying to be my boyfriend.' The door closes forcefully.

My instinct is to call Mary, but we haven't spoken since… I skitter away from the thought before making myself hold onto it… since she told me she had an intense four-month-long affair with a session drummer who got her pregnant with Leila and me. That she'd given birth and handed us over to Mum and Dad, who were desperate to be parents and couldn't have children themselves. That they'd all conspired to hide the truth not only from Mary's husband, Joe, but everyone. And now the man who'd got her pregnant was working as a gardener in her retirement village and was threatening to approach me – which was the only reason she'd decided to confess.

The anger is still there, along with a huge sense of betrayal. But I'm a grown woman, not a child, and can understand why many of those decisions were made, even if they do hurt. Eventually, I'll be able to talk about it with Mary and maybe even tell Euan, but not yet. Just a few more days, then we'll speak. Besides, right now, discovering my parents aren't my parents is actually at the bottom of my 'things to stress about' list.

*

When Euan walks through the door twenty minutes later, there's a stubborn set to his jaw that reminds me of the first time I officially met him, the time he deliberately goaded me during the interview to see how I'd handle it.

'Just because the neighbours don't know anything doesn't mean I'm not right,' he says, picking the argument up right where we left it.

'O-kay.'

'There is no proof that this was the phantom emailer. Why would he even bother?'

I should stay quiet. He's doesn't like being wrong and anything I say will only cause an argument, even agreeing with him. If it were anyone else… but with Euan it's harder to filter my feelings. 'Because I'm not playing his stupid games any more, and he realises. He doesn't want me to just walk away from him. If he is the kind of person that gets off on playing mind games, then this is exactly the sort of thing that he might do.'

'You need to stay calm and rational—'

'You're setting a great example right now.'

He throws his hands in the air, bends backwards for emphasis. 'Okay, fine, well, why don't you call your best friend, Davey-boy, and he'll lap up all your theories without argument.'

'Davey…? Dave Burns?'

'Despises me, doesn't he? Can't wait to whisper poison in your ear so he can have you all to himself. He endorses your every idea and fear, drops everything to come running like a lap dog at your whistle—'

'Whoah, don't put me in the middle of the pissing match you two have got going.'

'Who else gets the kind of attention you do? Clearly he has designs on you.'

'Ridiculous!'

'And you know what I think? I think maybe you just really enjoy the attention.'

I've been pacing, trying to get rid of my anger rather than bite to Euan's persistent prodding. Now I come to a stop so quickly that the dogs, who have been following me, slide into my legs. My words come out slow and low and dripping with fury. 'You think I enjoy the attention that my sister being snatched and murdered has given me for the last twenty-five years?'

'Yes. I mean, no. Of course not. I just think that maybe you need to let things go a bit.' He starts to gabble. 'Everything is in the hands of the police now, there's nothing more you can do, and yet now suddenly you've found a reason to draw yourself back into the drama. And I can't help but think, with my pop psychologist head on, that you need to be involved because you're a control freak. Understandably so. But ultimately? Yeah, ultimately you need to let it go.'

'Let it go. Just move on.'

He nods. I step closer, aware I'm trembling with rage now.

'Don't you dare tell me to let it go and move on. Do you know how awful it is to look in the mirror and see not just myself but my dead sister? To see her ageing but not be able to share growing older with her? No, of course you bloody don't, which means you've no idea what you're talking about.'

A dry sob heaves from me. 'You've no idea what I've been through, so don't stand there, all reasonable, and tell me to "let it go". For years this has been the only thing that has kept me going, as much as it's also what's made me want to curl in a ball and quit life.'

The muscles in Euan's jaw are working, nostrils flared, eyes down. When he finally speaks, his voice is hoarse. 'Stella, are you only living for your sister?'

'No. Not any more.'

I could explain further. Tell him that for years that was the case. That there's a reason it isn't any more. But that would mean confessing all kinds of things about my growing feelings for him that I'm not ready to face up to just yet.

He closes the gap between us. Takes my hand.

'I've…' I shake my head but keep a firm hold of his hand. 'Don't jump down my throat, but I've just got a bad feeling. Maybe I am being paranoid, but is it really paranoia when one of the worst things possible has already actually happened?'

'And you've been dealing with the person responsible for it,' he finishes. 'No, it's not paranoid. You can't blame me for being concerned for you and trying to protect you. Sorry if it comes across as a bit…'

'Patronising.'

An apologetic twist appears on his lips. 'I'll take that on the chin. Apology accepted?'

Of course it is, but there's one more thing that needs to be said as we hug it out. Unable to look at him for fear of shattering the truce, I speak to his shoulder, instead. 'Just… if anything happens to me, promise me you'll look after my dogs. Okay? You do that and they'll look after you.'

Beneath my hug his body stiffens, but he agrees. Even if it's only to soothe me, I feel better now, knowing that no matter what the future has in store the ones I care about most will be together.

We stand holding each other for a long time, swaying gently, comforting. Finally, Euan clears his throat.

'Had any more emails since the last one?' Reluctance and curiosity war in his voice.

'I haven't checked. But I should. Anything new needs to be forwarded to the police.' I hesitate. Wanting to let Euan in further but fighting against the ingrained instinct to keep everything to myself. 'We could check together, if you like?'

Pulling my phone from my back pocket, I call up my emails while still wrapped in Euan's embrace. Waiting for me like a spider sitting patiently in the corner of its web, is an email sent this morning.

Dear Stella,

Why are you ignoring me? I've hurt you so badly. There's no way you can ever forgive me – and who could blame you? Your messages have been the only thing to keep me going and without them I'm hopeless and helpless. I will leave you alone from now on, I promise. I've come to realise that the world will be a better place without me. Only you could save me and I've no right to ask that.

Please forgive me.
For ever your friend x

'He'll say anything to get a reaction from you,' Euan breathes. 'That emotional blackmail, the gaslighting, it's horrific.'

'It took me a while to realise it,' I admit. 'But he's becoming more and more blatant.'

'Yeah, this threat to take his own life – classic coercive behaviour. The sort of thing an abusive partner would do to keep you under control because they're scared you're breaking free of them. I've interviewed people who have been through it, who've almost died because of it.'

My phone pings a notification to tell me another email has arrived. Euan and I look at each other then back to the phone.

Dear Stella,

Is our game over? What a shame. It took you long enough to realise, didn't it? Honestly, I was amazed that you went along with it for so long. I suspect you're more naïve than your sister, despite the fact you're so much older than she ever grew to be – thanks to me.

I have to admit this has been far more fun than I'd anticipated. Seriously, it's beyond me how you fell for the sycophantic apologies and the grovelling, mealy-mouthed, woe is me crap I came out with. You actually believed it! Well, clearly… up until this weekend. Inevitable, but such a shame that you've decided to come clean to the cops and blow the whistle on our fun. They'll never find me from the information I've given you; it was all lies. They'll never track me down through these emails either – they've not had any luck so far, have they? It would be all too easy for me to disappear now and leave not a trace behind.

I don't think I'm ready to leave you just yet, though. I've loved our chats – so much so that I'll invite you to play again. Has that got your curiosity going, dear Stella, or are you only repulsed by me right now? Either way, you'll read on, won't you? You're the type who never backs down, never wants to admit weakness, which is, of course, your biggest weakness. That, and your drive to know the truth about Leila. So, here's my offer – you won't refuse it…

I'll tell you the truth, Stella. I'll tell you absolutely everything you want and need, right down to the smallest detail. Oooh, tempting.

The price? You do the same for me.

See, it's not such a terrible exchange, is it? It's simply a continuance of what we've already been doing; only this time I'll actually be honest.

We'll play properly, no cheating, I promise you. You'll get the answer to one question in every email you send me. One clue to know what happened, and you'll be able to put it all together eventually. And in return you will answer one question from me in every email. Quid pro quo.

Ah, but how do you know you can trust me? I promise. I swear. Believe me? I didn't think so. But then, what do you have to lose by doing this? And what do I have to gain? Tell me all about you, answer every question I ask and I'll give you your heart's desire – information on what happened that night and where your sister's body lies.

Your move, Stella.
As always, for ever
Your friend x

CHAPTER THIRTY-TWO

Documentary Transcript
Title: *Missing: The Twin Who Never Came Back*

[Euan and Stella sit in Stella's living room. She is on the sofa, he in an armchair at a right angle to her.]

Voiceover – Euan: Over the years, Stella has found herself thrown into the role of detective. She admits it wasn't one she actively sought out initially. So what set her on this path? I'd also like to dig deeper into just how far she's been willing to go to get the truth – and question whether her quest has fallen over into obsession...

Stella: I suppose I started looking into Leila's disappearance myself around the first anniversary mark. I was having counselling, coming out of the fog of grief and wanting to do something practical. It wasn't that I thought there was anything wrong with the police investigation, not at all, it was simply about raising awareness at first. Keeping Leila's name in the newspapers, in front of the public eye. People started to contact me, talk to me, and I'd pass the leads on. I was more of a conduit, really. As time passed, I got to know all of the investigating team really well, and Detective Chief Inspector Burns was very supportive and open, keeping me and Mum and Dad updated all the time. But my parents were struggling, so that's why he started talking to me exclusively and then I'd pass the information on to them and vice versa.

I dunno, it just seemed a natural progression, somehow, to go from intermediary between police and parents, and also between the public and my parents, and let's not forget the press… before I knew it, I was sometimes checking things out before passing them on to the police, if they seemed they might be something or nothing, you know?

The police do a great job, I'd never criticise them, but their resources are limited and stretched tight. They don't have the manpower to check every little lead. So I do it, and if I find anything relevant it's passed on. They need such a weight of evidence before they can justify following a line of enquiry, but I can chase up the tiniest clue or hunch and see where it might go.

Euan: How far has your search taken you?

Stella: Wow, if I counted up the mileage I've racked up over the years? No, I've no clue what the answer would be. To the moon and back? To infinity and beyond? It doesn't matter, though, does it? You know, no matter how far it is you're always willing to go further. You just do what's got to be done, don't you? No point thinking about it.

Euan: I meant more metaphorically, really. Has there ever been a time when you have really thought about it, and questioned if it's time to give up?

Stella: Let me ask you something – at what point would you give up on a member of your family? Seriously. After twenty-five years? Or what about ten? If you'd quit at ten then why not after five years, or two? Why bother at all? People who ask questions like that clearly don't have people they love – I mean the real, gut-wrenching, depths of your belly, do anything for them, die for them kind of love. Maybe it's because I'm a twin, but I can't believe other people don't feel like this about their family.

What am I supposed to do? Just shrug and then skip off into the sunset thinking: "hey, I've gotta live my life"; I'd die for my dogs for-for – for goodness sake, so what do you think I'd do for my identical twin!

[Shakes head, muttering. Indecipherable.]

Voiceover: Over the years, there have been numerous leads that have led to nothing. The vast majority have been followed-up by the police, but many have also fallen by the wayside because of a lack of resources or the lead being deemed too weak. Stella rarely ignores any.

Stella: There are some really weird ones; I mean, they go straight in the bin, ignored. The alien abduction ones, the ones where people think Leila and I swapped places and actually it's Stella who is missing… But it's like the police always say: get in touch if you remember something, no matter how small. It's my job to follow up, no matter how insignificant. It can be the most innocuous things that break cases – look at Ted Bundy; he was caught because of a driving violation; it was blocked drains that did for Dennis Nilsen. You just never know where something small might lead.

Euan: But surely that means you're constantly dropping everything to go chasing all around the country?

Stella: You do what you got to do.

[Sigh.]

You don't really get it, do you? I can see it in your face.

Euan: No, I do. Honestly—

Stella: No, just… Let me think a second.

[Pause.]

Honestly? Of course, there have been times when I've thought: what's the point? When I've wanted to admit defeat and give up. But… okay, you know how gambling addicts are when they're on a losing streak? Like, it doesn't matter how obvious it is to everyone else in the world that the best thing they can do is walk away, they are convinced that with one more throw of the dice, or turn of the wheel, or whatever, they're going to win big. All it takes is one more gamble and they're going to hit a winning streak – and what fool would turn their back on a winning streak? Well, that's me. Addicted to following one more lead, just one more, all the time, because that will be the one that will change everything.

Euan: I can understand that. It's hard to know where to draw the line. It's why people keep on doing the lottery every week, isn't it? In case the week they miss is the one where their numbers finally come up.

Stella: Ah, well, that's why I don't like to play the same numbers every week. I do a lucky dip instead – don't want to get too attached to any numbers.

[Laughter.]

Euan: Good point. I think everyone can understand that. Okay, so… What's the furthest place you've travelled to follow a tip?

Stella: I once got a reported sighting in Australia. Couldn't afford to go there, though, so hired a detective local to the area instead. It turned out to be a nurse who'd moved from England a year earlier. She did look a bit like me but was about five inches taller so… yeah, it definitely wasn't Leila.

I did go to Spain a couple of times, though, after some tourists said there was a barmaid who looked like my sister, and it happened to be a resort we'd visited as kids: a place she'd really loved and had often talked about returning to one day. That extra link made it worth checking out, see.

Euan: It must be hard. Getting your hopes up all the time, only to have them dashed—

Stella: There's no point getting emotional about it, you just have to get on with it.

Euan: How many leads have you followed over the years?

Stella: Ah, blimey, that's like the "how many miles" question earlier. I don't know. I've never bothered keeping track because there's no point. I'll follow as many as it takes, travel as far as I have to.

How many times can I keep telling you the same information?

Euan: Sorry, I mean I do get it, it's just it helps the people at home to understand, you know?

Stella: Of course. Yes. Sorry.

Euan: Can I just ask…?

Stella: Uh-huh. This must be a bad one, you're building up to it.

Euan: No, not bad at all. It's just made me wonder – have you ever been in danger?

Stella: Oh, right, yeah. I mean… yeah, yeah, definitely. There have been times where, afterwards, I've realised how bloody stupid I've been, that I've willingly placed myself in danger. Once—

Euan: How? – sorry, carry on.

Stella: I was just going to say, there was one time I arranged to meet up with this guy. Only there wasn't just one guy when I got there. He'd brought a friend. For a "party". Things got pretty hairy for a moment or two.

[Pause]

Okay, you're not going to say anything until I've told you more. Is that it? Well, he said that he'd seen someone putting my sister into their car. Unconscious, she'd apparently been. He said he'd got a partial registration number, but that he wouldn't give me the details over the phone because he was scared of this person. They'd got connections or a reputation for being a badass or whatever, I can't remember. So we arranged to meet up in a café.

Only when I arrived, the café was closed up. Turned out it had closed days before and the bloke who'd answered the phone was both the owner and the one trying to "get friendly" with me. It became obvious very quickly that he and his pal had lured me there for a good time.

They didn't know I'd gone through a lot of self-defence training after my sister. My parents had insisted on it – and if *they* hadn't *I* would have done. So. Suffice to say that a can of hairspray to the men's eyes and a few well-placed kicks and punches had incapacitated them until the police arrived.

I can handle myself, you see.

As well as completing advanced self-defence courses, stunt course, all sorts, these days I'm older and wiser, too. I'd never do anything that stupid, just arranging to meet someone alone in the middle of nowhere…

Euan: Are you sure? Because you keep saying you'll do whatever it takes—

Stella: Yes, but within reason. Okay? I'm not stupid.

Euan: Not stupid, at all, just, well, maybe a bit blinkered, perhaps? What would you say to that description?

Stella:

[Laughs and sighs.]

Yeah, okay, that could be fair comment. But there's no one I have to answer to but myself, so it's not like I have a husband and children I'm abandoning while I go gallivanting around.

Euan: You'll agree to blinkered, then. What about obsessed?

Stella: I prefer dedicated.

Euan: To bringing the person responsible to justice?

[Pause]

Stella: Not… not necessarily. Everything I do is for Leila; it's not really about the person responsible, not any more.

Finding Leila's body, or what's left of it, would be a blessing. It wouldn't end all the questions, of course not, but it would be an ending, of sorts, to be able to lay her to rest. Even if the killer is never found, that would be enough. I think. Yeah, I often think that: that I'd give anything to be able to bury her.

[Pause.]

Euan: You mentioned questions. What sort of questions do you have?

Stella: Just thinking of every awful thing that could have happened to her. All those different scenarios running through my head and I've no idea which one is even close to being near the truth. And just…

…

…

…

Wondering if she cried for me. For us. You know. If she died knowing what was going to happen to her. Did she call for us? For me. We were one soul in two bodies; she must surely have screamed for—

Sorry, can we stop? I need a break.

CHAPTER THIRTY-THREE

Euan and I stare at the email on my mobile phone. Euan's face is reddening. Even the tips of his ears are starting to brighten.

'The sick bastard. He wants to feed off you like some kind of grief vampire. He'll never tell you the truth.'

It's surprising how calm I feel as I put the phone away and sit down.

'Don't worry, I won't be part of his sick game. Taking it away from him is the only power I have, and it's exactly what I'll do.'

'For all we know the police could be arresting him right now.'

'I'd give anything to see the look on his face at that moment.'

We agree that the only sensible way forward is for me to inform the police immediately. In a stab at diplomacy, I call Detective Sergeant Fox rather than DCI Burns – after Euan's comments, I'll be making sure to keep them separated.

I forward the emails to the police, and while I'm on the phone to Fox, Euan rants in the background about how I should be assigned a couple of protection officers.

'I'd love to but there's no budget; there's just not enough officers,' Fox tells me.

'I'm tough enough to look after myself.'

'No, you're not – no, she's not!' Euan shouts towards the phone.

I put my hand over it. 'What were you telling me earlier? Take your own advice and calm down.'

As soon as I'm off the phone, I let him hug me, knowing that it's as soothing for him as he wants it to be for me.

'We're doing everything we can. As long as we're sensible, we'll be fine,' I say into his neck. He gives me a little squeeze and rubs my back, and I mirror his movement. 'I'm outgunned, outmanoeuvred, totally beat. Time to let the experts take over.'

From the feel of Euan's body against mine I can tell he's comforted. He hasn't known me long enough yet to realise I'm lying. Dear Friend is a monster. Now that my worst suspicions have been confirmed nothing will stop me from doing what needs to be done. Not fear. Not scruples. Nothing.

I need this to be over. For Leila – and for me. After years of dealing with this, I'm at breaking point. I know the killer is going to try to gaslight me into believing things that aren't real, but I've no choice but to play the game because there are bound to be kernels of truth hidden beneath the layers of lies. My job hasn't changed from when we first started exchanging messages: to search those truths out like a shell game.

So while Euan nips to the loo, I type out a quick reply to Dear Friend.

Okay, I'll play. But you've got to get the ball rolling by giving me something first. What really happened to Leila that night? It wasn't an accident, was it?

The sound of the bathroom door opening comes as I press send and quickly shove my phone into the back pocket of my jeans. Euan flops beside me on the sofa and yawns.

'Christ, what a day. I'm exhausted, fancy coming to bed? I've got to be up in,' he checks his watch, 'urgh, six hours.'

It's tempting. To curl up in the comforting warmth, to pretend nothing else exists outside Euan's arms. How quickly I'm becoming used to relying on him. But a buzz from my back pocket reminds me that can't happen. Not any more. I have to start pulling away from him again.

I wrinkle my nose.

'I'm going to watch a bit of telly to unwind. You go up. See you tomorrow.'

There's some panel show on the box. Comedians playing one-upmanship, the scores arbitrary. I'm not listening to them; I'm straining my ears, instead, for the sounds of Euan settling down. The whirr of his electric toothbrush; the minutes passing as he flosses. Splashing when he washes his face with some exfoliator or other and slathers moisturiser on; the pad of his bare feet along the landing from bathroom to bedroom. A creak; he's getting into bed.

The credits on the programme are rolling when finally there's a click, barely audible over the low hum of laughter from the television, but enough to tell me he's switched off the bedside lamp. Dear Friend and I won't be disturbed.

Dear Stella,

You want to jump straight to the nitty-gritty, do you? Unimaginative but understandable, I suppose. You mustn't be greedy, though, and expect to have everything you want simply fall into your lap. After all, if I spill every detail to you immediately you've no reason to come back to me. Quid pro quo, Stella, that is the deal.

I will answer part of your question: was it an accident?

Payment up front, though. And all I want to know is what your birthdays feel like now you're alone.

Always,
Your friend

It can't be as simple as this, can it? All my fears about handing over gut-wrenching information suddenly seems a total over-reaction. There really is nothing to lose. With a shrug I type out a reply.

Birthdays are, as you can imagine, tough. But to be honest, I've reached an age where I don't really celebrate anyway – once you hit your forties it's really not such a big deal. I miss Leila, though, and do spend the day thinking of her and wishing she could be with me.

Is that enough information, I wonder? Maybe not. So I make one confession that I think will sate his curiosity.

It's probably the day that is hardest for me. Far harder than Christmases or anniversaries.

Your turn now. Tell me what happened.

I can't bring myself to type 'Dear Friend' under any circumstances, nor can I be bothered to sign off. There's no point in pretending our messages are nuanced or serve any deeper purpose than to give each other exactly what we need. With no further thought, I press send.

I'd go to bed but I'm too tired to move. Emotional exhaustion has drained my batteries and for the first time in a long time, I cry. Like I did in the old days immediately after Leila's disappearance. I curl up on the sofa and let the pain and frustration overwhelm me. Scamp tries to lick my face free of the salty tears, but they fall too fast even for her. Buddy and Buster lie either side of me, pressing their bodies against mine, as if to tell me they are there, as always, for me. Giving me their strength and their love. And that's how the three of us stay for a long time before I finally stand and wash my face free of the salt that has dried on my skin and made it tight. Then I look into the mirror and see Leila staring back at me. Haggard from waiting.

'I'm so sorry I've let you down,' I whisper.

Too weak to resist, I go to Euan's room and slide my body against his back, slip my arms around him. His hands steal over

mine, pull my arms tighter around him and he sighs in contentment, leaning in against me, toes rubbing over my feet. I lose
myself in the sound of his peaceful sleep, in the circle of warmth
he creates, until he slips away at 4 a.m.

*

As the sun invades the horizon, sending spears of light to pierce the
darkness, the dawn chorus begins. I'm sitting outside, a blanket
draped over my shoulders, my knees drawn up so my feet can
rest on the edge of the patio chair. My guilty fingers steal over my
laptop's keyboard, trying and failing to formulate answers to Dear
Friend's latest message. He's annoyed, has made it clear I'm on a
final warning because my last email disappointed him so much.

Dear Stella, he wrote,

*Imagine my deep disappointment when I opened your last
message. I'd made this offer of exchange in a spirit of generosity, only for you to provide me with a few scant lines written in
seconds. No thought put into it. No truth behind the words. Is
this all your sister is worth to you?*

*I'll give you one last chance to give me what I want. Don't
fob me off with snippets you'd be happy to share with a woman
behind the till in Asda. We've got shared past, a history that should
be respected. Tell me how you really feel; reveal the pain you've
never shown anyone else.*

*If you don't, then this will be the last you'll hear from me – and
you'll never get the answers you want.*

For a moment I wonder if that would be so bad after all, to
never know. But I've spent twenty-five years with this hanging
over my head and dictating my life. Drive like that doesn't simply
disappear because I want it to.

At 8 a.m. Mary calls me, which is uncharacteristically early for her. I send the call to voicemail, feeling guilty but unable to cope with anything other than these messages. Besides, if I speak to her now she'll know I'm trying to hide something and I can't let anyone know. Otherwise I might be talked out of what I'm doing, which is, I'm all too aware, foolhardy and reckless. It also feels inevitable, though, and there's no way anything will make me stop.

I need to be honest with him… but without telling him everything. There's no need for the ugly truth of Leila's last night to come out.

Fair point, I type.

Okay, here's the truth. I don't like my birthday, for obvious reasons. In fact, most birthdays are spent in bed, feeling sorry for myself; the only day I give in to the feelings of not being able to face the world.

The first birthday after Leila disappeared everyone understood how tough it was going to be – or they said they did. They came up with a well-intentioned plan to throw a party for us both. Said it was to celebrate her life. The thought of it was so wrong. How could we celebrate her life when she wasn't with us any more? I didn't argue, though. I was willing to do whatever it took to make things better for my parents, and they seemed to like the idea of a party for Leila (and it was clear that's what it was. It certainly wasn't about my birthday, that was just the because, but that much was a relief for me). So I made all the right noises and let everyone get on with it.

But as the date grew closer, I started getting panic attacks. It was the thought of everyone looking at me and comparing me to Leila and finding me wanting. Knowing that at least some of the people in the room might be thinking: 'why wasn't she the one that got taken away? If we were going to lose one of the twins I'd rather it had been her'. Others thinking how freaky it was that even though Leila wasn't with us any more it was like the ghost of her was still to be seen. I don't know, it's hard to explain, but I hope you'll give me credit for trying, at least. And the worst thing? It was that during all of that the one person I always turned to during tough times wasn't there. I'd have given anything to take her place and have her back in the land of the living.

At first I managed to hide my panic attacks from people. The sweats, the heart palpitations; the conviction I was having a heart attack that was going to kill me. But the closer our birthday got the worse they grew. Two days before the party Mum found me curled up in my bedroom, literally biting down on my duvet to try to keep the cries down. The party was cancelled. But the way Mum and Dad looked at me was like I'd let them down. Like I'd stolen a chance for them to celebrate Leila.

That was the worst birthday, of course, but the ones that followed weren't much better. Mum and Dad stopped all celebrations, none of us wanted them for mine or theirs. We never ate Black Forest gateau from Marks & Spencer again because it was what Leila and I always had for our birthday cake, thinking it the height of sophisticated decadence.

Even now my birthday is something I refuse to acknowledge. Friends know better than to ask me to do anything on the day because celebrating without Leila feels so wrong. I still wake up and expect to see her. Still miss us exchanging our presents, just the two of us, before going downstairs to see our parents because we wanted a few minutes alone to mark just how special we were to each other, just how remarkable it was that we were two people made from one whole, identical in thought and feeling and looks. We savoured it, especially on our birthdays. And now I'm alone. I'll never get used to that feeling, and every birthday just underlines that now I'm only half.

I hope that answers your question. Your move.
Stella

Closing my eyes, I take deep, controlled breaths to quiet my heart. After a minute, I'm good to go. Feed the dogs, have a shower, clean my teeth. It's gone 10 o'clock now, and I'm running so late, but still check my emails. I thought he'd make me wait, toy with the power he has over me, but Dear Friend has come back quickly.

Dear Stella,

Thank you for your beautiful message. You've no idea how much it meant to me. I could tell how hard it was for you to open up about things you've buried so deeply that they've never seen the light of day. I don't think we're done with that yet, though, are we? You've still some secrets left up your sleeve, I can just feel it.

In return for your generosity, I will, of course, answer your question, though I will spare some detail in order to save your feelings.

A scoffing huff escapes my lips. But I read on. Of course I do.

CHAPTER THIRTY-FOUR

There was truth in my description before. It was raining so hard that night and the lights suddenly all went out. All I was thinking about was the argument I'd had with the missus that day, her nagging me about working all the time, how she didn't believe I was working, that I must be having an affair. I wasn't – but I was having a lot of fun with the ladies, and why not, after all I'm a hot-blooded bloke.

My wife couldn't understand that and kept shouting down the phone that she'd get a divorce if I didn't change my ways. As if. Then I saw your sister, my headlights picking her up easily in her bright red coat, her wet hair plastered against her skull, giving it such a look of fragility. I picked her up, and she knew what was going to happen. When I kissed her, she responded. Then the silly bitch blew hot and cold. You can't do that to a bloke; it was giving me ball ache. All I did was try to persuade her and she totally overreacted. What happened after that wasn't my fault. None of it was my fault. But I've had to pay the price every single day since and I'm sick of it.

I know this isn't enough for you though, is it? You need to know all the details to quiet your imagination. You need to know why, and how long it lasted, how I felt, and how she reacted and what she said and did, and where she is and… I could give you more details, if you like. I can tell you e-v-e-r-y-t-h-i-n-g. But for now I'll stop. Too much information at once is like giving too much water to a man who is dying of thirst – you'll drink in so much it will make you sick. Far better to take a sip at a time.

There's so much more to tell, though, Stella.

Just think, everything you want and more is at your fingertips. What do you need to ask next? I feel for you, having to prioritise. I'm in the same quandary myself, wondering what to choose next from the box of delights. I think I'll go for…

How did it feel having to play your sister in the reconstructions? Tell your dear friend all about it.

<3 ;)

I shove the laptop away from me and swear. A lot. I'm up on my feet, wanting to kick something, wanting to run away, wanting to scream. The dogs back away from me, cautious, and their fright doesn't calm me but does make me shut up, and I make do with trembling in place, fists clenched, because they don't deserve to have their anxiety triggered by me or this twisted bastard.

He deliberately targeted Leila and murdered her. She didn't stand a chance.

My hands are in tight fists, but I already know the question I'll ask next. What I need are hard facts, not emotions. Things that can be passed on to police to narrow their investigation down.

I think back to the row I had with Euan, and everything I held back from saying even during the height of my anger. There are no longer secrets between Dear Friend and me, though, and no desire to keep things hidden. Finally, here is someone I can be absolutely honest with, without fear of judgement.

Dear Friend,

I begged to do the reconstruction. It was the first practical thing I could do, and it helped me deal with my guilt – yes, I was plagued with guilt, not that I expect you to understand why. Honestly, I thought something almost magical would happen by retracing my sister's steps. There would be an ah-ha moment where what had happened to her would suddenly become clear to me, like in black and white Sherlock Holmes films, where all he has to do is cast his eyes around a room to be able to explain from a series of clues too tiny to be noticed by anyone else, including the bumbling police. I'd be the special one who would see, though, who would feel, and crack the case wide open. A sixth sense that would lead me.

Every step I took I tried to feel Leila with me. There was nothing. No trace. I wanted to keep on doing what she'd done, trying to feel what she'd felt, hoping that if I could embody her enough I'd somehow bring her back or get a flash of intuition about where she was. I'm her identical twin; I knew everything about her. I should have known this, the single most important thing that had ever happened to her. But I didn't. I'd felt it when she'd fallen off her bike years before, but nothing as my footsteps echoed down her street and the camera panned along beside me.

I walked on with no clue how Leila's own journey had ended. Mine came when the director called, 'cut'.

Doing the reconstruction didn't screw me up. Lack of insight did.

You know, at first when she disappeared we'd get regular reports of sightings of her and get excited… until we realised they were people who'd actually just seen me walking around buying a pint of milk or whatever. It wasn't so bad here, but when I went back to university it was nuts. I actually started calling the police every day to let them know what I'd been up to, so they could discount any sightings of me.

Now tell me, what road did you pick Leila up on? And what time? Two questions, I know, but such easy, short answers that surely it doesn't really count as cheating, does it? You're in charge, so only you can decide.

Stella

Goodness knows how long I've been staring blankly across the garden since sending the message. A look at the clock tells me it's almost 1 p.m. and the poor dogs are pacing, desperate for their walk. I need to call Mary back, too. Despite everything else going on – or perhaps because of it – it's time to talk to her and start getting to know her in a different way. Maybe I can begin the process while on the beach, while the dogs play. As I clip on their leads, I listen to my voicemail from her. She sounds on edge, a false ring to her cheerful tone.

'Darling girl, it's only me. Do give me a call back when you receive this. Please. I know you're busy but I… well, I need to speak with you.'

The dogs start barking – a heartbeat before there's a knock on the door. My heart is thumping and I have a horrible thought that it might be *him* at the front door, dissatisfied with my reply. Wanting to see for himself the impact his words have on me. For once I don't give the dogs the command for quiet before answering, determined that whoever is on the other side should know I'm not alone. Not for the first time I curse the fact mace or pepper spray isn't legal for civilians to carry in the UK, and instead grab a can of hairspray that lives near the front door for occasions such as this.

I unclip the dogs again and wrap a lead around my right fist as a knuckle-duster, then open the door. Ryan is standing on the doorstep looking as red and sweaty as ever.

CHAPTER THIRTY-FIVE

I push the door shut but Ryan pushes back, shouting something I can't catch over the dogs' din. They're worried, scared, and in full-on defensive mode, trying to wriggle past me.

'Bugger off, Ryan, or I'll set the dogs on you!' I shout, bracing against the door. My feet are sliding though, no match for his strength. I lean in to the ever-widening gap and spray the canister towards his face. There's a satisfying coughing and spluttering, but no scream of pain or lessening of pressure.

'Stella! Let me in! I just want to talk!'

'I'll call the police!'

Scamp is growling and snarling now. Trying to wriggle through to the outside. My feet slide further and I fall, full-weight, against the door, banging my head before slipping to the floor. I'll be pushed aside now; Ryan will step over me like a piece of rubbish. Will he hurt my dogs? I try to stand, but I'm woozy and it takes two goes. In the time it takes, the door opens wider and I cry out in fear.

The dogs don't attack. They're wagging.

'What the hell's going on? I just saw someone run off.' Euan's worried face leans over me, then he's leading me to the sofa. 'Are you okay? Should I call an ambulance?'

'I'm fine.'

He strokes a finger across my forehead and shows me the blood on it. 'So I see. Are you going to be okay while I see if I can find this bloke?'

'Don't be stupid. Besides, I know who it was. Ryan.'

'Ryan your ex? Ryan who threatened you the other day. Ryan who is suing me. The—' Every muscle tight, in fight mode. He's moving towards the door. I grab his arm and hang on tight.

'Hey! Leave it, just leave it! I'll call the police in a bit just… right now I need you to stay with me.'

It grinds my gears a bit to come on all helpless female, but if Euan catches up with my ex right now it probably won't end well for either of them. If a spot of play-acting can keep him safe then so be it.

*

Euan managed to find some steri-strips in the first aid box and has done a good job of cleaning up the small cut on my head, which sits on top of a proper bump that stands proud. He still keeps mentioning hospital, but it's not worth it because I don't even have a headache. I will have an impressive bruise, though. I report the incident to the police and they say they'll send someone round, though it may not be today. In the meantime, Euan continues to cluck around me, so I send him to fetch some ice cream to cheer me up.

'Ben & Jerry's praline and cream, right?' he checks. It's impressive how well he already knows me and we've only been together five minutes.

With him out of the way, I know I've at least half an hour to myself before he gets back. So, of course, I whip my phone out and check for new emails.

Dear Stella,

I do love watching you during the reconstruction. You look so determined! I think that's probably your defining trait – you're even determined to make me bend the rules by answering two ques-

tions instead of one. Naughty, naughty. They showed that road so many times in the documentary, using that reconstruction clip over and over, showing you walking down it. If it's any consolation, you were perfect in the role, right down to stopping where I picked her up near the phone box, just after the lights went out across the town. It was such perfect timing for me.

It happened right by the corner. I almost skidded my Nissan Bluebird and hit the lamp post there. It was a decent car but had no power steering, so was like steering a tank.

Send me some photographs of you and Leila together. I want ones that have never been released, from your private and personal collection. Just the two of you. It would be lovely if you could include some from your birthdays, so I can bring the memories you shared with me to life. It would make my day. And don't forget – lots of details because unlike you I can handle them.

Your friend

The air turns blue for several minutes while I swear out my anger. Fine, I'll dig out some photographs, ones I've deliberately kept sacrosanct because there aren't that many of us. We were young in the days when people weren't photographed constantly from every angle, when each one was a precious memory to be treasured even if it was out of focus. With each email this Dear Friend seems to dig a tiny bit further, asking for more emotion, more investment, pulling me into deeper water with him so slowly, it's hard to notice that suddenly my feet are no longer touching the ground and I'm beginning to drift far from shore.

I can't deal with this right now. Not immediately after so much drama. The dogs are yawning and pacing, still stressed out themselves. I hunker down to their level. Scamp is straight over, wagging with such nervous energy that her whole body is going from side to side and she's jumping up to lick my face and offer me comfort. She hates me being upset. Buster trots over to me and stands by my shoulder, rubbing his head against me. It takes a couple of soothing chucks to coax Buddy and Fifi over.

'I'm sorry,' I hush. 'Everything's okay now. Don't worry.'

Their solidity, their gentle eyes, give me such comfort. They've still not been for a walk yet today. Some fresh air will do us all good, I decide, getting everything together and leaving before I can dissuade myself.

Yep, it's scary out here. I feel exposed just being on the pavement outside my own house, but that's why it's important I do this before fear can settle into my brain and make me want to stay at home instead.

Hitting the beach, feeling that fresh breeze riffling through my hair and clothes, everything seems lighter, brighter, easier. Families laugh and shout as they jump in and out of the rolling waves. Others play ball games or hunker behind brightly-striped windbreakers. It's normally quieter along this section of the beach, where dogs are allowed, but it's such a lovely day that tourists are out in their droves. As incongruous as my thoughts are, being surrounded by normality helps burst the bizarre bubble that has formed around me. It makes me feel more like myself, and to think rationally. Dear Friend is adding more detail to his descriptions, but he's right, I need to know more. I need to know everything. What did he do to Leila once he had her in his car? How long did she suffer? Was she awake and aware for it? Did she manage to injure him at all?

'Stella!' The call comes from a few feet away. I've been so lost in thought I hadn't even noticed Ryan approaching. Now he's standing, waiting for my reaction. The dogs are messing about in the sea, chasing each other, too busy to notice what's happening.

'Don't—'

'I'm not going to come any closer.' He holds his hands up as I fumble for my phone. 'I'll stay here. Keep calm. You have my word. Just… please just listen to me for one minute before you call the police.'

His voice stops me pressing the call button, even though I've dialled 999. It's different than before. Low, gentle, reasonable. My eyes run over his body. Muscles relaxed, eyes wide, mouth slightly open, hands raised in a gesture of surrender but fingers not fully straightened to make the gesture forced or aggressive. He's calm.

My defences don't drop though; my finger stays over the call button.

'What do you want, Ryan?'

'To apologise for being a dick.' He screws one side of his face up in an expression I'd forgotten about but that instantly comes flooding back now I've seen it. It's the face he pulls when he's really sorry.

'So an apology will make it all better, will it?' I gesture to my bruised forehead.

'I did that? Christ, I'm so sorry.' Arms move forward, palms turn skyward. Open and entreating before they fall by his sides. He's hiding nothing. He doesn't step towards me, though, instead keeping his word to maintain distance. 'My stupid temper. It gets the better of me sometimes.'

'You always did have the self-control of a toddler.'

'The wife says the same. She's the reason why I'm here, actually. When I told her what I'd done she went a bit ballistic. Look, there's a lot I need to tell you. Would you be willing to listen? I'll sit down – no threat, see?' He sinks to the sand, sitting cross-legged: a childlike pose which seems so at odds with his burly frame. I stay standing but tell him to go on.

'It's hard to know where to start, but the wife told me to start at the beginning to try to make things simpler, but I feel like I should start in the here and now and work my way backwards…

'So to start off, I can't apologise enough for hurting you just now. I hope you'll forgive me, but if you want to report me to the police, I won't blame you and I'll take it on the chin because I shouldn't have tried to push my way into your home. I've never been like that before, never raised my hand to a woman – you can ask Her Indoors if you like; I can call her now. No? Well, anyway, I'll let you decide what to do. I, er,' he peers forward, trying to get a better look, 'I hope that doesn't feel as bad as it looks.' He does the twisty face again.

'Stupid thing is, I only came round to yours to apologise. It's just I was so worked up that I got a bit carried away and before I knew it things had got completely out of control. Again.'

I raise an eyebrow.

'Pretty stupid, eh?' he nods. 'I'd found something out, see. It's all tangled up with the documentary, so it's hard to explain everything. When that came out it caused a lot of trouble for me because of the drugs stuff. Come on, Stella, you know I wasn't as bad as they made out. And I might have been a dick back then, but I'm all right now. My wife would kick me out if I didn't keep my nose clean. She's a good woman.'

'They did make out you were a bit of a drugs lord,' I concede. 'But I didn't get to see the documentary until it was aired, so I'd no idea. I did speak up and say it was unfair though – to the production company and to Euan.'

'Yeah, Euan. When did you two—?'

'Er, no, we didn't get together until after the documentary, and we weren't in cahoots over anything, before you start that again. Now, I'm here to hear your full confession, not the other way round, so…' I make a chivvying motion with my hand.

Before he carries on, I look for the dogs. They're still splashing around. Buster has a piece of seaweed he keeps flinging in the air and catching.

Ryan starts talking again.

'After the documentary came out, people starting pointing the finger at me and work began questioning me, saying I wasn't a good example to junior members of staff and brought the company into disrepute, and then the wife and kids started getting hassle. Thing is, you've no idea what I've done, what I'm capable of these days; see, I work with an anti-drug youth group helping them get information and rehabilitation, and that'll probably have to stop now. I was furious. Justifiably so, I still believe that. But what isn't justified was what happened next. I'm so sorry, Stella…'

What on earth has he done? My heart beats faster, trying to race ahead to what he's going to tell me, imagining his words: *'I'm so sorry, Stella. I pretended to be Leila. I've been toying with you, and pretending to be Leila's killer just to mess with your head a bit. Payback for the trouble you caused me.'*

But what he actually says takes me by surprise.

'I hired a lawyer to sue the production company and get them to pull it. When the lawyer told me I probably wouldn't win because, technically, they hadn't actually said anything that was wrong – which I still don't think is right – well, I hired a private detective to dig around. She started looking at Euan, and then when it became obvious you two were together, she started digging for dirt on you, too. I threatened Euan, told him I'd tell you what I'd found out about him being on the verge of bankruptcy, that he'd been in big trouble and desperate even before me and my lawyers got involved. He said you already knew.'

Huh, Euan hadn't told me about any confrontation between him and Ryan.

'I told the PI to keep going, to do whatever it took. And that's what she did. You've got to believe me, though, that I'd no idea she was going to take things this far without running it past me first.'

'Running what past you?'

Could the PI be behind those messages? But why on earth would she do that?

'She's been following you. She even broke into your home a couple of times to try and find dirt to use against you.'

'She's done *what?*' I explode.

'I know! It's unforgiveable, and the second I found out I felt sick. I sacked her on the spot. That's why I raced to yours just now, but I was still so keyed up by the whole thing, so filled with adrenaline that—'

'That you acted with the emotional maturity of a toddler. Like usual.'

It hadn't been my imagination. Someone had been in my home, going through my things, violating my privacy.

'Did this woman poison Scamp?'

'What? No! She didn't do any harm to your dogs. Not as far as I know anyway. She told me she always made sure they weren't in the house; otherwise it would have been too hard to get in.'

'Right, and I'm supposed to take the word of a burglar?' It feels right, though; which means I was spot on about Dear Friend poisoning Scamp. Who else could it be?

'Honestly, Stella, you saw how worked up I was with you when I came round, so just imagine how I was with her. Put it this way, I'd be surprised if she withheld any information from me.'

'She's definitely been sacked and won't be coming anywhere near me again?'

'The message was received loud and clear,' says Ryan.

He hands over the woman's details so I can report her to the police, without me even having to ask for them. It's very reasonable of him… which means it's time to strike.

'Ryan, what really happened the night Leila disappeared? Every time I woke up you weren't there.'

'I was – I swear! You just can't remember.'

'Come on. I know you're keeping a secret about that night.'

'I've never lied about what happened. I sat with you the whole time, making sure you didn't choke on your vomit. The only time I left the room was to—'

'Yeah, yeah, to get a bowl and some headache tablets. But I know you've been holding something back, Ryan.'

He protests again. I play the most obvious card in my deck, though there are others if it comes to it. 'Tell me everything and I'll withdraw my complaint to the police about this.' My gesture takes in the fresh bruising. 'If you don't, I'll make sure they pursue you and charges are pressed.'

Blackmail is the resort of the lowest of the low, but what choice do I have?

His head hangs down. 'Everything I've told you and the police is true, but…' His voice is low and scratchy, barely audible over the rushing wind and the roar of the waves. Something hits the sand beneath him, causing the tiniest puff of grains. A drop of water. Ryan Jonas is crying.

He is a fool sometimes. He's got a quick, occasionally unreasonable temper. But I've never seen him cry before.

I shiver, chilled to the bone by the kind of cold that summer sunshine can't touch.

'That documentary stirred up a lot of mud at the bottom of the pond, didn't it? Thing is, there's something I need to tell you about that night, Stella. I've never lied – but I haven't been completely honest either.'

There it is again. That chill striking at my soul.

CHAPTER THIRTY-SIX

I've gone completely still, and there seems no sound but him and the waves, as if the whole world is holding its breath along with me.

'Remember I wanted to leave the party and you said you had to go to the loo again first, so I was waiting outside for you. Watching that storm felt exciting. Then Leila came out and stood beside me. There was no one else around and she started flirting with me, saying about how I was so straightforward and easy, why couldn't other people in her life be more like that. I didn't know who she was on about, but afterwards, well, after what happened I wondered if she meant her fella, cos… Stella, there's no way of telling you this without hurting you, so I'm just going to come out with it. Leila and I, we went round the corner, checked no one could see us, and we hid in the shelter of that bit of the building that goes in and out – you know the bit I mean? It gave us a bit of shelter from the wind and rain and we were both drunk – I certainly was – and we… we kissed.'

The nausea that hits me is dizzying. What if that wasn't all that happened? What if they arranged to meet up later, him sneaking from my room to have sex with my identical twin? What if he'd met up expecting sex and when she turned him down things got ugly? Maybe it had been an accident; maybe it had been a crime of passion.

'There's more, isn't there?' I say. 'Tell me or I'll push for your arrest.'

Ryan wipes at his face with the back of his knuckle, leaving a trail of sand across his cheek that's stuck to the damp tracks of his tears.

'I've never told anyone this because I've always persuaded myself it wasn't important. Telling people the truth would just mean everyone thought badly of me and Leila, and it's not like I had anything to do with whatever the hell happened to her later that night.'

'Ryan.' The words are a growl of warning.

'Thing is, though, I also convinced myself that afterwards I didn't see something I really should have mentioned to the police. And I can't keep it secret any more because everything's bubbling out anyway and it's time to tell the truth. I only kept quiet to maintain my reputation but that's screwed anyway now, so I've nothing to lose. I'm a dick, Stella.'

I don't argue. But I don't speak either, not daring to derail him when he's so close to telling me his secret.

'Just before you came out of the loos I thought I saw, parked across the way, Leila's car. I could be wrong. But I don't think I am, and all the years passing haven't made me any more convinced of it. Her car was there, tucked around the corner with a prime view of me and her. If it was there then that means whoever was driving it must have seen us kissing. And the only other person who ever drove her car was—'

'Was her boyfriend, Damien. Her fiancé. If he saw you both, then that gives him a motive, Ryan.'

All these years, Leila's boyfriend had been under suspicion but there'd never been any real evidence against him. He'd protested his innocence, and I've often defended him, felt sorry for him, even – but was he really guilty the whole time?

Is he behind the emails, then? Perhaps he's taunting me as a way of punishing Leila for being unfaithful. More likely he's trying to put me and the police off the scent by pretending to be a stranger who accidentally killed my sister.

Whatever is going on, there are questions he needs to answer.

'Did you kill my sister?' My fists hurt from hammering on the bedroom door of the B&B. 'I know you're in there! Did you kill my sister!'

It flings open to reveal Damien blinking furiously. In the days since I last saw him, he's travelled even further from the man who dated Leila and was always neat enough to make Marie Kondo look untidy. Sweat patches stain his crumpled off-white T-shirt, and his jeans have grubby marks on the hems and around the pockets.

I shove the door wider open, but don't step inside because I don't trust him. A little way down the corridor a man pops his head out of his room to see what's going on, meets my glare and disappears back inside.

Damien seems to refocus. Looks at me, furious. 'After all these years now you're chucking this at me, too? What's brought on this change of heart? Desperation, that's all.'

'That, and the fact I've been speaking to Ryan. He's told me, Damien. I know you saw him and my sister together on the night she went missing.'

He goes through white to the dingy shade of grey of an ancient face cloth.

'I—' But that's as far as he gets. No words left.

Caught.

Damien famously lied about having to go to a work do instead of coming to Dad's birthday party, then there's the controversy over the fire exit near his room having a broken alarm, which would have allowed him to sneak out.

'Detective Burns always believed you were guilty, but I'd had doubts. I was as taken in by you as Leila must have been: no surprise there, I suppose.' I'm hugging myself, I realise, disgust making my flesh crawl. 'What? Did you suspect Leila was having an affair, so decided to pretend to leave town so you could catch her out?'

He's glaring at the floor, but it doesn't hide the tiny twitch below his right eye. I'm on the right track so keep pushing. That kiss with Ryan had been a one-off, though. I didn't doubt the truth of that. Still, perhaps Damien had sensed my twin wasn't happy with him; maybe they'd been arguing, and he'd become suspicious.

'You saw her with Ryan, didn't you, then drove to the flat you and she shared and waited for her? Which meant she must have made it home.'

That twitch again. A vein on his temple is throbbing.

'Maybe you let her in before confronting her and she then ran from the flat and you mowed her down.'

No reaction. Okay, scrap that: the whole car scenario could be made up by Dear Friend – aka Damien.

'No, you killed her in the flat then used her own car to dump the body somewhere before driving home and—'

'Do you honestly think I could hurt her? Even after that?' He talks to the floor.

'If you didn't, why can't you look me in the eye?'

'Seeing you is like someone driving a stake through my brain, it's so painful. An aged, fake Leila sent to mess with my mind. Almost her but not quite. I'd give anything to swap you with her.' He drags his eyes up to mine as if they weigh a ton. 'Do you think I'd kill the most amazing person in the world? The best thing to ever happen to me. The person I should have spent my life with; who I'd given my soul to? People talk about you and her like you were two halves of a whole, but you weren't – she was my soulmate, my twin flame. It makes me sick the way you've highjacked her loss and made it all about you.'

He spits with the force of his words. It lands on his chin, glistening. He doesn't wipe it off.

'If you hate the sight of me so much why are you hanging around here still, Damien? You said your piece to me last week. Staying in Mereford isn't going to make it any more likely the documentary gets pulled.'

'Why? For the same reason you stay in that house stuffed full of torturous memories. Because you can't resist the pain.'

'Stop talking rubbish. Why were you spying on my sister the night she went missing – and why didn't you tell the police the truth about where you were?'

His silent sneer, once again directed at the floor, is my only reply. The truth is close, I can feel it, but he's buried it so deep that I've no clue how to uncover it. He won't even look at me! I want to grab his face and force him to speak. It won't work, though. Anger, accusations, logic, police interrogations and public condemnation haven't got to him.

There has to be a way.

Then it comes to me. My stomach twists at the thought. It's too awful, too weird, to even contemplate, but I find myself stepping forward until I'm over the threshold of his room, which reeks of stale sweat. Softening my combative body language, I reach out to stroke his arm the way Leila used to. He recoils. Then catches hold of my hand and brings it to his lips, kissing the palm. I repress a shudder.

'You can tell me anything, Damien. Baby.' My voice is gentle and warm. When he looks at me, I channel Leila's look of love by picturing Euan standing before me. In response, his eyes glow, lines disappear from his face; he stands taller as I place my other hand over his heart and step in towards his body the way a lover would.

'You've been so brave, Damien, keeping this quiet, but now it's time for us to talk honestly, isn't it? Just the two of us.'

He seems totally lost in the past as he gazes at me, one hand clutching mine, the other running up and down my arm. Pulling me closer until he's touching my back, almost embracing me.

'Oh, Leila, I did see you with Ryan that night, saw him drooling all over you but I knew it was nothing, baby. I'd only gone away because you'd said you were getting bored of us, so I gave you some space by going to the hotel; it was the only thing I could think of to keep you.'

I want to close my eyes to shut out this sick game I'm playing. Does Damien seriously think he's talking to Leila or is he trying to psych me out?

'If you love someone, that's what you do, baby: set them free so they'll come back. I knew that whatever you did and whoever you did it with, you would always come back to me because what we had was unshakeable. Seeing you with Ryan only confirmed that – what I saw was lust, infatuation at most. Nothing to put us in danger once you'd got it out of your system.'

'It must have hurt, though?' I squeeze his hand and smile an apology.

'Of course I was hurt, but it didn't mean I wouldn't forgive you – by the time I reached our flat I'd already done that. You must know that, surely, baby.' He's mad, quite mad, but I'm not going to break the spell as he continues. 'I made a decision then, knew exactly what was needed: a grand gesture. I planned to tell you that I knew, get you to sit down and tell me everything and then, if you'd have me, I'd suggest we set a date for the wedding.'

'You still wanted to get married?' My voice is weak with amazement.

'Of course!' He laughs as though it's obvious. 'Then we'd have moved away for a fresh start – you deserved more than a flat with black mould growing up the lurid pink walls. I'd have followed you anywhere. It would all be left in our dust we'd leave so fast. Finally, no more reason to be jealous of Stella and her fresh start in university.'

Confusion darts across his features at my name. I move my hand from over his heart to stroke his cheek and cup his jaw gently, and it seems to soothe him.

'I knew you were just acting out, rebelling against all the crap surrounding us. It had nothing to do with *us*. Our marriage would have marked a fresh start, with complete honesty. I didn't want to go forward with any lies hanging over us. If you said no then I'd wait because there was no way you and Ryan would become anything serious. Once it was over, I'd be waiting to pick up the pieces and start our future.'

He's got that look people get before they kiss. Bending his head towards me. I lurch away, can't help myself.

'What… What's going on?' He blinks, seems to be back in the present, reluctant and confused. I've got to push on before he stops talking altogether.

'You're claiming you weren't jealous at all? Didn't want to punch Ryan, even?'

Rapid blinking. A frown. 'Such a provincial reaction, Stella. Listen to what I'm saying: there was nothing to be jealous of.'

'If all this is true, why didn't you answer the door to Leila when she got to the flat?'

He shakes his head, eyes lost in past pain. 'I've gone over it a million times in my head, and I can only think that there'd have been no reason for her to knock because she didn't know I was waiting for her. I sat up all night, waiting, only leaving first thing in the morning to go back to the hotel.'

That explained why there was no sign of him by the time Ryan and I went inside the flat.

'So if she did make it back, she'd have looked for the key, found it missing—'

'…and walked to the phone booth to call you, Stella. I had been listening out for her arrival, of course, but I'd expected her through the door, you know. The sound of the wind and the rain was so loud that night that it easily would have drowned out the noise of her standing outside, searching for the key.'

I can tell he's imagining the scene, just as I am. That he's pictured it so many times, torturing himself with 'if onlys'. Does that mean I believe his crazy story of not giving a toss about Ryan and Leila kissing? Maybe. Or maybe he went berserk and killed her, and this is a lie he's told himself so often he believes it – because it's hard for me to take the word of someone who has been talking to me as if I'm my dead sister come back to life.

'When she went missing why didn't you say anything?' I ask. 'Ryan didn't speak up because he was being a selfish arse who didn't want to look bad, but—'

'Of course he was. I didn't know that at the time, though. Initially, I wondered if she was holed up somewhere waiting for him. I had this horrible idea of them setting up some kind of secret love nest together, but it quickly became obvious this was for real, that Leila had disappeared, and so I made a decision to keep quiet so her reputation would stay intact. Imagine what people would have said about her. The press would have painted her as some scarlet woman. I wasn't having that. If it means going to prison to protect her then so be it.'

He's bonkers in his own way. The fire of obsessive love still glints in his eyes for Leila. Whether that makes him more or less likely to have killed her or to have sent me emails is no clearer. There's no actual evidence against him still, though none exonerates him either, so I'm no wiser than before this confrontation.

His poor wife…

CHAPTER THIRTY-SEVEN

'It didn't even occur to you to text me, did it?' Euan's pacing and the dogs are trotting between him and me, not knowing what to do with themselves.

I lean against the back of the sofa, watching him go back and forth. 'I've told you everything now – Ryan's promised he'll call the police and make a new statement telling the complete truth, so they'll be questioning Damien again, for sure. There was too much going on for me to stop and call you. And I won't apologise for that, not given the circumstances.'

'Just think for a moment about what ran through my head when I got back from the shop with the ice cream you asked me for, and there's no sign of you. You'd just been attacked, then you disappear. No note, nothing. I was out of my mind, was about to ransack the house for clues and call the police.'

'You didn't need to, I was fine—'

'I didn't know that. You didn't even pick up when I called you.'

'You're not my keeper.'

'No, I'm you're partn—'

'You're my tenant. We have fun together. Don't make this more than it is, Euan.'

His head rears back. I'm shocked by how much I've just hurt him. By how much my own heart squeezes in protest. 'Look, if it makes you feel any better, Mary tried to call a couple of times and I didn't answer her, either.'

'Trust me! Trust someone, anyway. I could have gone with you but it didn't even enter your head, did it? Just don't forget you're not alone in this.'

'*Of course* I'm alone in this. I'm less than alone; I am halved. Until I find a way to be whole I can't be anything other than alone.' Even as I'm saying it, I'm arguing with myself. Really, I should have thought to leave him a note. 'Anyway, I can't ask you along. You might break a perfectly manicured nail.' It's supposed to lighten the mood but comes out sounding like a criticism.

He narrows his eyes. 'Are you still getting emails? You are; you're writing to him still, aren't you?'

'Where did that come from?'

'You're being groomed!' he shouts. The dogs scatter, hiding in their beds. 'Can't you see that he's played you perfectly. He's got inside your head and now you don't have the strength to break free. It's coercive, emotional abusive. Gaslighting.'

'You think I've got battered wife syndrome?'

'Sometimes you're so old-fashioned.'

'Because I'm old, Euan, far older than you.'

'Yeah, let's argue about the stuff that really matters and forget that you've put yourself in mortal danger by emailing a murderer. That you run around all over the place confronting people. It needs to stop, otherwise you're going to get yourself seriously hurt, killed even.'

Everything's too complicated. There are no right answers any more. So instead of trying to come up with some, I launch at him. The argument ends with us having sex, but it still lingers in the air later, like the smell of gunpowder after fireworks. We can't go on like this. I'll have to ask him to move out. I can't afford to grow soft and reliant on anyone or become distracted by his and Mary's talk of finding a happily-ever-after.

*

Unable to sleep, I curl up on the sofa, the dogs arranged around me while I hunch over my laptop, writing using only the light from the screen. With all the drama of the day, it's only now, far past midnight and with Euan asleep in bed, that there's free time to reply to Dear Friend. Reading this new message alongside the others, it doesn't seem likely that Damien is behind them – not after our encounter revealed how unstable he is. The words seem too lucid, too calculated for them to be written by the person I spoke with earlier.

In his last message, Dear Friend told me he wants photographs that have never been published before; the ones I've always saved from the prying eyes of the world. I hate him for that. One more reason to despise him. One more hurt to throw on the pile.

It sickens me as I attach a picture I took on my phone of one of the photographs. It's of Leila and me cooking. The kitchen wallpaper on one wall has brown and orange flowers on it, the colour palette of the Seventies still being felt even though this must have been around 1980, and the kitchen units on the walls are wooden and painted orange. Row after row of cookbooks lined the shelves. Along one wall is the fake pine cladding that was just starting to come in. I remember holding it in place as Dad (because that's who he will always be, regardless of genetics – same with Mum) hammered it in – we were always called in to help with the DIY projects; generally to stand until we ached holding something heavy in an awkward position.

Although I can't remember why we were baking that day, it must have been for a special occasion, as just in view on the counter is a box of After Eights. The wafer-thin mint chocolates were considered the height of sophistication back then. We're about six or seven years old and covered in flour, and we're con-centrating on the two bowls in front of us – we had to have one each. Mum is watching over us, the softest smile on her face. Food was always at the centre of our home. Mum worked part-time and spent the rest of the time looking after the family, and all our food was home-made. Back then ready-made meals from shops seemed like a fancy treat.

'Wait and See Pie', that's what Mum always used to say when Leila and I were kids and we'd be hopping around her asking what was for tea.

I write down these wonderful memories, as delicate as butterfly wings, and share them with a monster who only wants them so he can pull them apart. Nothing is held back. All so that I can write this:

If you won't tell me where Leila is now and don't have the common decency to tell me what you did with her, then at least tell me why. You say it was her fault but that sounds like bullshit and excuses. You said you'd tell the truth, so do it.

Tell me WHY. I need to understand – and you're right about one thing: I need to know everything.

Despite exhaustion and the small hours of darkest night, sleep won't come. I close my laptop but keep checking my phone for notifications because I know whoever Dear Friend is he feels the same as me. He's been waiting for my response all day, refreshing his emails impatiently, wondering what I'm doing that can be more important than this. He's sitting somewhere even now, checking, reading, smiling that he's finally got a response from me. I close my eyes and can feel him, out in the darkness yet so close to me that we are breathing in sync.

Euan will be getting up in a couple of hours, maybe less. Still, I don't slink back into his bed. Not long to go now. My phone vibrates to life.

Dear Stella,

You're getting to know me so well! I can't hide behind a mystical pull, not really, or some kind of instinct. I could claim that it's

Leila's fault. That what she was wearing was too short, too tight, too provocative for me to be able to resist, that she must want the attention, really, if she's going to wear outfits like that. That as a man I am helpless to resist a woman. It's all her fault really.

I could say that. It would be enough for most people. Not you, though, eh?

Leila died because I wanted something and she refused me. I was in a crappy mood and wanted sex, and she dicked me about, so I crushed the life from her with my bare hands. Sometimes I know it was an accident. Sometimes I know I enjoyed the sense of power that comes from being completely in charge.

Now you know – and I bet that knowledge doesn't help you one bit.

You once told me a bit about your favourite Christmases. I want more. Send me pictures.

Your friend

Sick bastard loves power. That's why he's buggering about with these emails, a lion toying with a gazelle. There's no point in holding back, though. He certainly isn't, and I feel he'll know. So I type into the blackness, and think of Leila, named after the inky night, and how I wish I could light some of that darkness like the stars I'm named after. Instead, Dear Friend is a black hole devouring us both as he feeds on our memories.

I choose a precious photograph that's never been seen in public before: one I hid under the bed when the documentary team came to the house.

Here's a picture of Leila and me one Christmas, in our burgundy velvet pageboy outfits. I've never shown it to anyone outside the family before. You can see from the photo that we thought we were the absolute bee's knees. See how she's leaning forward, laughing, eyes closed, while I am being a proper poser, hands in pockets, one foot forward to really show off the burgundy patent leather shoes I'd recently been bought. They made click-clack sounds like high heels when I walked, even though they were flat and Mum wouldn't let us have heels because they'd 'ruin our feet'. Our pageboy suits, though matching, were not identical. As ever, Mum had wanted them to have slight differences to encourage our individuality, and she'd made them herself – just imagine the time and effort taken to design them and make them so beautifully. Looking at them now I'm struck by the love and dedication poured into them. So while both were in the deepest red berry crushed velvet, my knickerbockers had a gold button at the knees, and gold smock work across the shoulders of the waistcoat. My shirt was pale pink with a lace ruffle spilling down its centre, and a tiny velvet bow at my neck. Leila's was the same colour but had gold piping around the bottom of her knickerbockers and trimming the edge of her waistcoat. The ruffle on her shirt, which was white, was shorter but fuller, more of a cravat, and she also had lace trim at the wrists. Even though we were only about six, we were a super-fashionable New Romantic dream as we stood in front of the white-painted living room door, beside the sideboard. Peeking out you'll see Dad's guitar, the red electric one he loved but rarely played. Instead, he'd often play his classical guitar. He agreed with The Rolling Stones's Keith Richards that playing a classical guitar made him a better electric guitar player.

Your turn, you sick shit. Where is Leila? What have you done with my sister's body?

I'm shaking as I press send. As the screen momentarily darkens, I see my reflection; my lips are pressed into a tight, pale line, a sheen of sweat across my face as though I'm coming down with something.

Above me I can hear the sound of Euan moving about. I hurry to the kitchen, turn on the radio, and start cooking him a full English breakfast, desperate to seem normal. The delight on Euan's face when he sees it brings me joy and pain. He eats quickly, apologising. As he stands to leave a new song plays.

'The Boo Radleys, "Wake Up Boo",' we say in perfect unison.

'I'll let you have that one,' Euan says. 'Loser buys a takeaway curry tonight? Don't forget I'll be home later than normal; meeting with Glenda, my agent.'

Kissing him, acting normal, feels like an out-of-body experience.

The door is barely shut when my phone buzzes again with a notification. Dear Friend is as keen as me to get this done. He seems to barely be able to disguise his excitement, the emails increasing in speed, him asking more from me, our relationship spiralling like dirty dishwater down a plughole.

Dear Stella,

Always so blunt. Has no one ever told you that patience is a virtue? Swearing at people won't win friends now, will it?

What have I done with your sister's body? Well, first let me tell you something for free: she fought despite her injuries, Stella. Not enough to challenge me, but I thought you'd like to know that little snippet and hug it to your heart. I bet you'll fight until the end, too. You really are identical.

That still not enough detail for you? How about I tell you how I punched her in her face. I split her nose open and made her head bounce on the floor. When I screwed her, she played dead until I strangled her, and then she tried to gouge at my eyes, but her gamble to try to fool me, lull me into a false sense of security to drop my guard, then make her escape, didn't work. Then I got rid of her. She might have really been dead by then. She might not. Honestly, I wasn't bothered enough to check. I'd done with her, had my fun, felt the power, and now she was as spent as an empty crisp packet.

As for where she is... well, that's a different question, isn't it? So to answer it now wouldn't be playing according to the rules we've set down. Perhaps if you answer my next question adequately, I'll tell you. I want to know about the worst argument you ever had with Leila.

Your friend

I'm strung out and exhausted. I can't tell him that. It's too personal, too much. He wants me to not just bare my soul but to slice it open so he can examine its entrails.

No one, not a single living soul, knows about my worst argument with Leila. The one I had that night. The one that changed everything for ever. The reason why she took the wrong coat and didn't bother checking.

The reason why she's dead.

CHAPTER THIRTY-EIGHT

The cursor in the unwritten message flashes at me, a lighthouse beacon warning me I'm too close to the rocks. Leila and I never argued growing up. We'd bickered sometimes but it had never been anything major. The night of Dad's birthday party had been different; the memory of it has me shaking, my stomach churning like a stormy sea. Shipwreck is imminent.

Dear Friend always sniffs out how to hurt me the most, but he's excelled himself with this question. He knows I'm sitting in the newborn light of dawn waiting with him in our own personal darkness of the soul. Trying to find the words. Another message flashes up, encouraging me.

> Don't be coy, Stella. Tell your dear friend everything. Trust me.
> Or it's game over.

I've never told anyone about this. It's my biggest shame. I can't tell him, I can't. Maybe I can make something up about a catfight over a Sindy doll or something.

But he'll know. He's got an instinct for these things and seems to have got under my skin so well he can sense my weaknesses.

I rub at my eyes, trying to clear the brain fog of uncertainty. There's no point complaining. I need to put my shoulders back and get on with it. Punch through the pain to get closer to the finish line. So, with a guilty look over my shoulder, even though I know Euan is at work, I start to type.

Slow. Reluctant. Each word dragged from me.

Dear Friend,

The atmosphere had been odd all day. Mum was frazzled from being pulled in all directions, trying to put the finishing touches to plans for the party while also not wanting to neglect Dad during the day. Leila and I were the same, so we were all stretched thin on jolly dad-sitting duties, then whizzing over to the Richmond Caravan Park for ballroom preparations. It meant we were all tense but refusing to admit it in front of anyone else, for fear of looking like a potential party pooper. Leila was distracted, but no more than the rest of us, I thought. It didn't help that it was so airless that day, so unbelievably hot, that people were breaking a sweat just breathing the hot, heavy air into their lungs. The forecast for the storm was welcomed by everyone, hoping it might freshen the atmosphere.

Ryan and I were supposed to arrive early but took advantage of our only chance to be alone. Made love, then watched Beadle's About *before finally moving, which meant the party was going quite well by the time we arrived. Fat drops of rain sploshed us as we stepped inside, and Mum sent us straight outside again by the French doors at the bottom of the ballroom.*

'Quick! Help me get the food inside before the heavens open and it all gets ruined!' she said.

The wind picked up suddenly, coming from nowhere and tossing the paper cups from the trestle tables, and straining the string that held up the 'Happy Birthday Bill' banner stretched between two trees. The fat drops were exploding more frequently across the surface, leaving dark stains on the tablecloths and shining on the clingfilm stretched over countless bread rolls buttered that morning on a production line of Mum, Leila, Ryan and me after we'd ushered Dad from the kitchen. Fillings slapped on:

tuna mayo; cheese and ham; ham and pickle; salmon; chicken and salad.

'What about vegetarians?' I asked.

'They can just take the chicken off the bap and eat the salad,' Mum said.

Bowls of crisps: salt and vinegar, plain, and prawn cocktail. Foil-covered jacket potatoes prickling with cocktail sticks with cheese and pineapple. And a couple of quiches from Marks & Spencer, no less. Mum had made a guitar-shaped birthday cake that took four of us to move inside as the rain began to pelt and the first thunder rolled.

I barely saw Leila that night. That photo of the two of us? The one so famous because it was taken an hour before she disappeared? She and I had finally found ourselves standing side by side after singing 'Happy Birthday' to Dad with everyone. Leila had looked distracted but when I asked her if she was okay, she insisted she was, and when I pushed, she said it wasn't worth talking about, not with so much going on at the party.

It was a good night, all told. Dad had a whale of a time. Everyone was dancing. We even all sat on the wooden dancefloor to 'Ooops Upside Your Head', shimmying back and forth and thumping the ground, feeling the thunder outside shaking the building. Dad and Mum had to be helped up, already a bit the worse for celebrating.

Of course, I told the police about all this after her disappearance. Every dull, everyday detail. But not what I'm about to tell you.

I'd come out of the Ladies' loos and Ryan wasn't where I'd left him. It was so hot I was desperate for my drink and he'd disappeared with it, even though we were supposed to be leaving. I searched around, pushing through the sweaty bodies, extricating myself from a bear hug from Dad, telling me he loved me. With no sign of Ryan, I decided to get some air outside. Went through the double doors that were shut tight against the rain hammering to get in, and hugged tight to the wall outside, watching the lightning strobe across the sky. The water was coming down too fast for the drains to cope and edged towards my Doc Martens. I shuffled my feet as far back as they could go. Even though I'd only nipped out for a minute I wished I'd put my coat on – the red trench coat I'd bought specifically for that night. The one Leila had, coincidentally, bought, too.

I turned to go back inside just as lightning flashed, and there were Leila and Ryan kissing. If it hadn't illuminated at precisely the moment that I turned, maybe I wouldn't have noticed them. Maybe none of the things that followed after would have happened. Like dominoes falling, one event led to another to another to another, and so we all toppled.

I didn't march over and confront them. You've guessed that. You probably want to know why, and honestly, it's impossible to explain, apart from I had a feeling like I was the one in the wrong. As though I was spying not on them but on Leila. Like it was something she had to do, and although I didn't understand the reasons then, I would eventually.

So I scuttled away as if I was in the wrong. Went back inside and headed straight to the bar. The Blastaway was downed in thirty seconds flat. It didn't quench the raging thirst, so I got another – and a tequila chaser. Shot followed shot as the resentment grew. I'd slid back into the shadows as if I was having some kind of out-of-body experience; like I was watching myself with my boyfriend. I'd slunk away like I was in the wrong when it was them not me who were the problem. How dare they do this to me? How dare Leila?

Eventually, I had the blurred courage to try to find Leila. She was in the Ladies, putting on her amethyst shimmer lipstick. With a sneering comment about how Ryan must have wiped it all off for her, I told her I knew, and slut-shamed her.

'Sorry,' she said. But the way she looked me in the eye it was obvious she wasn't. Not a bit of it. 'It's not as if you're serious about Ryan, though.'

She gave a little shrug. The tiniest movement, as if a gnat was annoying her between the shoulder blades.

'What, so you've done me a favour? Thank you for bringing forward the inevitable,' I shouted.

The worst thing, which made me even more furious, was that I knew she was right. Being the other half of me, and knowing me as well as I knew myself, didn't make it better, though. It made it worse.

I'd been moving my hands to press them together into a sarcastic praying position, a namaste thanks for her betrayal. Instead, egged on by alcohol, I slapped her. That sound! So disappointing compared to the crack in films; so insignificant considering the fissure it opened between my sister and me. It wasn't enough.

Here's my confession, Dear Friend. My deepest, darkest secret dragged out into the light is this: at that moment I wished with all my heart just to be free of this person who mirrored me, who felt the same as me, who knew that stealing my boyfriend didn't matter because I didn't love him at all; I didn't even like him, only stayed with him because the sex was good and he was exciting to be around. That wasn't the point. Even though she was right, she was completely wrong. Even though she was wrong, she was utterly right. So, I told her the one thing guaranteed to devastate her.

'I wish you were dead,' I slurred.

I stumbled away, couldn't face the consequences of what I'd done. She caught me up by the coat rack, and I picked up both coats and chucked one at her. Didn't even bother checking which was which. It didn't seem important at the time; just one more thing we shared that I didn't want to. One more thing that I'd got that she'd taken from me – that's what I thought in the heat of that moment, even though it wasn't true and we'd never argued before. Not really. All I wanted was some space for independence. Just for a while.

And that was the last thing I said to Leila. The last time I set eyes on her was her running to the minicab she'd called, hugging the coat around herself, and looking over her shoulder at me as she slammed the door shut.

A lifetime of shared experience, of unique love, of thinking the same things and breathing one another's air, became worthless because my sister died thinking I hated her, when nothing could have been further from the truth. Because that's sisters. No matter what you say or do, no matter what you put each other through, you always love each other, you're always there. Hurting and helping. Sisterhood.

Did Leila realise that? Did she know in her heart of hearts that nothing she could ever do would make me turn my back on her because we were tied for life? Or did she die hating me for hating her?

Ryan got me home. I was too drunk to even speak properly by the time he found me, so the confrontation between him and me never happened. If I'd have cared about him more, I'd have told him in the morning, hangover or not; screamed and ranted probably. But Leila was right, I wasn't bothered enough to do that. He didn't matter to me. All I wanted to do was talk to Leila and heal our rift, somehow, but it was already too late because you'd come along.

There you go: that was the only proper argument Leila and I ever had. Our worst and only.

Now you tell me where she is. Answer my question or I won't be giving you any more answers. I'm tired of your dodging.

I hit refresh. A new email appears, but it's a marketing shot, not Dear Friend. I should do the washing-up which has been sitting in the sink soaking for hours since Euan left for work. Apart from a quick walk in the park for the dogs, I haven't moved from the sofa since, even though the sun is shining, because I'm waiting for Dear Friend's next demand.

The phone rings: Mary's name appears along with a photo of her smiling at me. It's early for her and I feel bad that I haven't got round to calling her, but still I let it ring out and go to voicemail. *Later*, I think. Still ignore it when she calls again seconds later. Then the home phone rings. When the answer machine kicks in a familiar, unctuous voice fills the air.

'Mr Belcher here. Please call me urgently regarding your friend Mary Bird.'

I snatch the phone up just in time. 'What's happened? Is she all right?'

'Ah, oh, er, yes, darling Stella. I'm afraid I'm the bearer of bad tidings. You've lost so much already and now—'

'Just tell me.'

'Of course, of course. I'm so very sorry but your friend died. She was found this morning, having passed away peacefully, in her sleep, in her favourite armchair.'

The winged one by the window. The one she waves at me from. Oh my god. Mary, no.

The manager's fake grief annoys me as we stand in Mary's apartment. He didn't know her. No one here had got the chance to see what a wonderful person she was, apart from maybe her neighbour friend, who is standing in her own doorway across the hall, dabbing her eyes. I'll go speak to her in a minute.

I'm completely devastated. If only I'd answered the phone and spoken to Mary, told her how much I loved her. If only we'd sorted things out. Once again someone I love has died thinking

I hate them. The thought makes me wonder if I should try to get to know my biological father.

'Is your gardener about?' I ask Belcher. 'He and Mary had become quite close. Can you let him know what's happened to her, please?'

'Really? That's, er, sweet. Of course, I'll let him know as soon as he returns from holiday.'

He starts wittering on about something but I tune him out. Can't take my eyes away from the armchair. I rub my hands over the heavy brocade upholstery. How often I've hugged her while she's been sitting in that chair. I can almost hear her telling one of her 'is it or isn't it real' stories about someone famous, then asking me to fetch her a cup of tea or a cheeky gin because all that talking has made her parched.

Perhaps she was sitting in her chair on the lookout for me. I can see her, craning around, impatient, having left me so many unanswered messages, and heartbroken to think her revelation might have destroyed our relationship.

'How did Mary die?' I ask. Knowing the answer but needing to hear it again.

'She passed away in her chair here. Must have fallen asleep and slipped away – we're, er, we're just sorting the death certificate now.'

'Are you okay? You seem on edge…'

'Me? No! Just saddened by this dreadful loss. Still, if there's an ideal way to go, that's it, isn't it?'

I make a noise of agreement. Still too numb and confused to cry, I can at least find comfort that Mary, who was always such a fighter, didn't have to fight at the end.

*

The inside of the car is stuffy and baking even with all the windows open, but still I sit in the car park, looking up at Mary's window, unable to move. The only thing I've done is break the news to Euan as soon as his shift ended at noon, and stopped him from coming straight back.

'Being here isn't going to change anything,' I said. 'Besides, don't you have a meeting with your agent this afternoon?'

'I can postpone, she's incredibly loquacious – talks for Britain; I'll be stuck there forever—'

'Mary, of all people, would understand you have to look after your career.'

'And what about you?'

'I don't have a career.'

He'd sighed about 'using levity to disguise pain' before promising to keep the meeting brief and be home as soon as he could. When he does get home, I'm going to have to tell him the truth about Mary's relationship to me, and I'm not sure I have the words or strength. Maybe tomorrow...

I will myself to turn the engine over. Go home. Instead I stare at my hands on the steering wheel and remember how Mary's neighbour, Mrs Merryweather, had gripped both my hands in hers. Her skin like paper, joints swollen with arthritis, felt like Mary's. Eyes wide with sincerity as she poured platitudes over me. *She loved you like a daughter... So few visitors, so I couldn't help noticing ... Anxious to get hold of you. Not herself... Mustn't blame yourself.*

I should have called her. I should have explained that, although it would take time to recover from the sense of betrayal, I still loved her and always would. She was my second mother in every sense.

But I'd been too wrapped up in myself and what's going on with Dear Friend to have room for anything else. Even now, almost despite myself, I pick up my phone and check my emails.

He's replied.

Will Dear Friend finally tell me where my sister's body is?

CHAPTER THIRTY-NINE

Dearest Stella,

I can do better than tell you. I'll show you. You'll finally know every detail of what happened to your sister and her exact location. No lies, no half-truths; it will be utter honesty between us. You've earned that with your last magnificent email.

Of course, there is a price – a high one – to reflect how valuable the information is.

You've always said you'll do anything to know the truth, but now you have to decide if you really mean it. The time for bluffing one another is over; we both know that. If you really want to know all the answers then come and meet me – I'll let you know where and when.

But don't forget we're playing 'show' not 'tell' now.

Your move.

In anticipation

Your friend x

The breath has been knocked from me. I double over, head hitting the steering wheel, my fist kneading my solar plexus to Heimlich manoeuvre the horror from my body. Leila's killer has made the ultimate offer. My life in exchange for knowing everything of Leila's death.

I'll have the answers to all the questions that have suffocated me for twenty-five years. Is it something I'd really die to know? What's the point of knowing only to take it to the grave with me, unable to share it with anyone? No chance of justice being done.

But a lifetime of torture and guilt and wondering finally over.

For twenty-five years I've dreamed up every scenario possible, and plenty of impossible ones, too. I've dreamed of what happened to my sister and woken with sweat-soaked sheets clinging to me, unsure if the nightmare is a product of an overactive imagination or some weird twin 'knowingness'. I've come up with explanations that put the most twisted of imaginings of online conspiracy theorists to shame.

Now there is the offer of real, solid knowledge. An end to the torture of wondering.

The tightness is lessening now. I can sit up straight, still massaging my chest. Breathe a little fuller.

But don't forget we're playing 'show' not 'tell' now. Do I still want to 'play'?

He wants me to walk willingly into his trap: a meek lamb stepping up to the table to offer its throat for slitting. Presumably, he'll 'show' by doing to me exactly what he did to my sister. Not at the place he attacked her, though; it's too public. Where then?

At the burial site, almost certainly.

I'd always thought the worst moments of my life were those twenty-four hours around Dad's party. The row with Leila. The discovery that she'd gone missing. The realisation that I was to blame. Now I'm not so sure. I think this may well be even worse. Because the culmination of all that grief and years of searching and refusing to give up is that now I get to die.

Goodness knows I've sacrificed enough already. I've given my whole life over to finding Leila. I've turned my back on friends, refused to let in love, let slide the opportunity to have children, in order to devote myself to this mission. Now he wants to kill me.

I won't do it. Nothing is worth giving my life for.

I go to delete the message but it glares back at me, goading me. I've come so far, sacrificed so much, only to give up now? My life seems a fair exchange, really. Death at the hands of the man who took my twin's life has an inevitable symmetry about it. There's no Mary to mourn me. No family. Euan will look after my dogs…

Poor Euan. It's only now that I have to let him go that I admit to myself I really do love my posh southerner with his fancy vocabulary and encyclopaedic knowledge of Eighties and Nineties music. Despite all the other drama in my life, he's made me the kind of happy that has me smiling to myself, that makes me hum as I walk to appointments, or grin and call out greetings to people I barely know. The kind of happy that turns into something long-term. It's terrifying.

For decades I've kidded myself that I'm a fearless creature, fully prepared for anything, but it's a lie; I've spent my whole adult life avoiding letting people in, and it's fear that's done that. I don't let anyone get too close for fear of them leaving me like Leila did, or hurting me the way the person who took her did. It's what my parents did, too. They closed down and shut everyone out, myself included. Euan has got closer to me than anyone has since Leila, though. I didn't realise how small I'd let myself become until he came along and made me grow. I think, hope, I've done the same for him.

We *could* be together. Dear Friend will have to get his kicks elsewhere, once I stop replying to him. Euan and the dogs and I could move somewhere new and build a life. There's nothing to stop us, nothing at all, except…

I shouldn't have let Euan in, I think, punching the steering wheel in frustration. Not because I'll get hurt, but because he will when I make my deal with the devil.

Of course I'll make that deal.

To not know what happened to my sister would be to continue the insanity of not knowing, of the madness of circular thinking, of constantly wondering, of filling in the gaps with the worst possible imaginings. You can't simply switch off obsession; it always ends in self-destruction. There's only one way to stop this. I knew it from the moment I got Dear Friend's offer, or perhaps even from the very first time he messaged me. I will see this game to its conclusion. I've never backed down from any challenge, just like I've never abandoned my sister.

I feel strangely calm as I send the email telling Dear Friend that we can meet whenever and wherever he wishes.

There's nothing left for me to do but wait now I'm back home, because there's only so much a person can do to prepare for becoming a murder victim. My thoughts aren't full of wondering what will happen; I'll know that soon enough. All loose ends must be tied up, though, before I die, and it makes me think of Keshini. I never did get around to calling her to discover her secret. There's no curiosity as I call, only a sense of ending things. She picks up straight away.

'There's something I need to confess,' she says. She's as nervous as if her secret were as big as mine, but luckily it's more life-affirming than that: she's realised she's gay. Apparently, she'd confessed tearfully to Euan that she and her parents had a frank conversation where she'd told them about her seemingly irrational behaviour, and they'd helped her come to the answer she'd always known: that actually she'd been struggling with huge feelings for someone – me. Her confusion made her reject the fact even while knowing it to be true, and instead she'd clung onto proving how much she wanted Euan. Even after she'd realised in her heart that it was women she was attracted to, she had been determined to prove herself wrong. Like so many of us do about so many things, she'd lied to herself until it was no longer possible.

'Eventually I accepted my attraction to you, but there was still no way I could face telling you – I'd had a hard enough time telling myself. There was only one time I tried—'

'That time I was on a date with Euan? My birthday.'

'That's right. I was crying because I was so nervous! Anyway, it's out there now and I feel better for it.'

'I'm so glad. If I hadn't been so distracted, I'd have seen the signs,' I reply.

Or would I? I wonder after saying goodbye. Look how long it took to realise Euan's feelings for me were real. Some body language expert I turned out to be.

It's too late for beating myself up about anything now, though. Instead, I sit on the sofa worrying that time is ticking on and if Euan arrives home before I have to leave, I'm not sure I'll have the strength to lie to him. All I can do is wait with my dogs and try to squeeze a lifetime of love for them into however long I've got left. I stroke Scamp behind the ear, cup her head in my hand and marvel at all the love it holds and all the cleverness, crammed into one small space. The phone pings, making us both jump. It's a text, though, not an email. There are enough words showing in the notification for my heart to jolt.

It's impossible. It absolutely cannot be Dear Friend sending a message from that number.

Opening it, my worst fears are confirmed. There's a time, a location. It's clearly Dear Friend.

I double-check the name of the sender, thinking my eyes must be deceiving me.

It can't be. It can't.

It's Mary's phone number.

He must have killed her.

That bastard. Dear Friend has outmanoeuvred me at every turn. He'll do it again. But even knowing this, I need to see him. I need to ask questions. I need answers that I'm willing to die for to know the truth.

Shakes gone, I send my reply.

'I'll be there.'

The phone pings almost instantaneously, and seeing Mary's name appear fills my mouth with saliva as if I'm going to be sick.

'Get in the car right now. No calling, texting, emailing anyone. I'll know if you do. Turn left out of your drive then left at the bottom of the road. More instructions to follow.'

Mary's image beams at me above the text.

*

As I drive, the messages come like rain pelting me. Like those fat drops from the storm the night of Dad's party. Innocent looking individually, but together they have the power to flood and destroy.

Each one changes the location I'm heading for. I'm circling around the whole of Mereford like an open-topped tourist bus, heading towards the sea then away, in and out of town. Whether it's to toy with me or make sure I'm not working with police to have someone waiting to pounce on the killer when we meet up, I don't know. At one point I'm lured past Leila's old flat, which makes me wonder if I'm being taken to random places or ones that have special meaning to the killer and that night. Will he monologue and reveal all before killing me, like an episode of *Scooby-Doo*, I wonder. Hope.

Sending the messages from Mary's phone is the cruellest way to pull my strings and make me dance while a noose tightens around my neck. Dear Friend has murdered my sister, killed my parents with their grief, and now taken Mary before I got the chance to know her as a mother.

Who'd had the opportunity to kill Mary and snatch the mobile from her room and now use it against me?

Another message arrives. I frown, then go around the one-way system and head out of town. Before long, the traffic and tourists and CCTV cameras and any possible help have been left behind. Now there's only my little car barrelling along narrow country lanes, changing direction as instructed, as random as a pinball.

*

I pull into a lay-by, as per my latest instructions. I'm halfway down a narrow country lane in the middle of nowhere. I've one bar of service and my 4G coverage has been downgraded to Edge.

The phone buzzes.

'Get out of the car and wait.'

I do as I'm told, checking all around me. The only features on the flat land are scruffy fields of scrub and a row of tall poplar trees that stand to attention on my right. The road seems to peter out further ahead, where I can see a lake and signs warning that there's no fishing allowed – no fly-tipping, either, though judging by the burnt-out mattress beneath the sign, no one's taking much notice. There are no anglers in sight, nor is there any passing traffic. There isn't a single person around. No one is lurking in the hedge or the field or even up a tree. I'm all alone. The strong September breeze flying across the open land has knives in it. Summer is almost over, the circle of seasons turning again and pulling me with it.

I walk around, nervous, always checking over my shoulder. There is one surprise I have up my sleeve and I pray it will be enough: I've brought the dog surveillance cameras with me.

They're small, portable, triggered by movement and the recording is saved so that what happens to me will be there for all to see, once someone decides to check the feed. I haven't alerted anyone to it because I can't risk someone arriving to save me before I know about Leila – that's what this is all about, after all. I don't want to die, but I'm willing to if it means the person who took my and Leila's lives will be caught, and this should do the trick. I've been practising the self-defence moves I know, too, to make sure I'm not rusty when Dear Friend strikes. Now all I can do is wait. Behind me the metal of my car bonnet makes a noise as it cools and contracts.

There's the hum of an engine going slow, a hiss of tyres rolling on tarmac. Something is coming. It pulls into view around the corner. A beat-up, white people carrier I've never seen before, possibly a Ford Galaxy, with tinted windows and a wing mirror held on with silver tape. Slows. Stops. Engine still ticking over. A beat-up rust wreck: the registration number obscured with mud I'm willing to bet Dear Friend rubbed on. The person behind the wheel is obscured by lowering sunlight across the windshield.

I wait for his next move, every muscle tense.

I think I'm prepared.

But you can't prepare for everything.

CHAPTER FORTY

Nothing prepares you for the fear of hearing an engine being gunned, the squeal of tyres as they head towards you, the desperate calculations as you realise there's nowhere to escape. For the pain of bouncing off the bonnet.

No chat, no preamble, no chance of defending myself.

I lie with my head twisted awkwardly, body splayed. Breath won't come. Winded.

Heavy footsteps. Heavy breathing. Shoes come into view, stop in front of me. Brown. Dark leather, highly shone beneath a film of dust.

Breathe, breathe, breathe!

A big gasp comes. Oxygen flooding along with relief. Then realisation. This is what happened to my sister. Now it's happening to me.

Hands reach down. I strike, scratching to get his DNA beneath my nails. He shouts in pain, a bleat of agony that spurs me on. I try to pull out some of his hair, but it's so short my fingers slide across it without gripping anything.

I'm fighting for my life. Hands around my neck, squeezing. I look straight into eyes so familiar and want to scream at his treachery.

'I told you I'd show you, Stella. Die happy, you stupid bitch.'

All the worst nightmares I had about Leila are going to happen to me.

*

My eyes open. Darkness. Yet instantly I know I'm naked from the way the air moves over my skin and the hairs rise freely. I give a start and pain fractures me, sending me tumbling into a deeper blackness.

*

When I come round again I move more slowly, trying to fight the fear. Am I being watched? Is he nearby, waiting to torture me before he ends my life? No. The darkness is still, without movement or breathing close to me, and no prickling sense of someone nearby.

There's nowhere for my head and legs to unfurl from the foetal position I'm curled into on my left side. The space I'm in is tiny. Claustrophobic. I run my hands around me, above me, below me. Fuzzy material brushes against my fingertips in every direction, apart from immediately in front, where there is a long line of something cold and smooth – metal, I guess – running the length of my box-like prison.

Every part of my body hurts. Even breathing is painful. I think some of my ribs might be cracked, and my left leg broken. The throbbing pain between my legs is the worst… I feel torn and… wet. Blood? Pee? Blood; I can smell it.

'Keep it together, Stella.' The sound of my voice makes me feel braver, as if I'm not alone. As if it's Leila speaking.

Adrenaline is quickly making the pain lessen like magic. It's helping clear my woozy thoughts. It's awkward but I manage to twist enough to get my hands up and around to the back of my head. They come away sticky and smelling metallic after exploring a wound where the skin has split wide. An aching jaw, bust lip, flattened nose that makes breathing hard.

So this is what happened to Leila.

The blackness is less dense as my eyes adjust. Little slivers of grey become apparent in the darkness. My fingers explore what feels like large screws sunk into, what… plastic? I try to push my fingers into the crack, but they're too big and the space won't budge. I try pulling at it and feel my nail tear.

'Where the hell am I? Come on, Leila, give me some answers!'

The boot of a car. The realisation comes from nowhere. With it a bolt of panic. *Push it down, Stella, feel the fear later, like you always do.*

I wonder what the plan is for me. What will be done to me next? And all at the hands of… *that man.* I can't, won't, think of him by his name because it hurts too much. All those lies. All that trust invested in him. He'd fooled me utterly – and Mary, too.

Or had he? Had that been the reason behind the flurry of calls to me before her death? I'll never know, but I suspect that Mary was sharp enough to become suspicious – perhaps that was why he killed her, or perhaps that had always been his plan, in order to hurt me as much as possible, a cat clawing a mouse's entrails out one by one.

The screws I'm picking at won't give at all. But I don't scream in frustration or pound on my prison walls, for fear it will alert him – he's probably close, waiting to dispose of my body, so I need to start planning how to fight back when the car boot opens.

There's water under my body. Not much, but it seems to have come from nowhere. Hang on… no, it's seeping in from outside, leaking through the seams around the car boot.

No, no, no.

I put my hands over the worst bits, as if to hold it at bay.

Stay calm, hope help's coming, try to help yourself. I fight the panic and try to think.

There's no chance of breaking the lock on the boot open. Maybe the seats will be weaker. With no space to turn to kick them, instead I brace my one good leg and both arms against one side of the trunk and push my back against the back of the seats as hard as possible. They don't give. I push and rock, but there isn't any sense of movement, not so much as a creak against the catches holding them upright.

The water is rising. It's slow but steady, covering one arm now, and I have to lift my head awkwardly.

No one is coming. This is down to me. I shouldn't have done this. I should have called someone to let them know what was happening. But this had been my one and only chance to discover the truth, and maybe even catch the killer myself. I'd had to try – for Leila's sake. I couldn't risk the police's involvement somehow stopping me finding out her resting place.

Now our bones will be together.

The end point is racing towards me. I'm doing this for my sister. Sacrificing myself so that her killer can be brought to justice. Hoping that not only can I find peace by knowing what happened to her, but also that somehow the killer will be caught by my sacrifice. If my dead body is found fast enough, the police will find his skin under my nails, and that will nail the bastard, along with the recording of my attack.

That gives me strength. I'll go to my death bravely, won't let that evil man rob me of my dignity. I'm here because I chose to be.

My dogs leap into my mind. They are my family. My world after losing my sister and parents. They love me, rely on me; how will they manage without me? I should be home with them, not…

Fresh weakness sweeps through me, bringing a tidal wave of tears. Scamp, my clingy, wonderful girl, so full of love, so in need of it that no matter how much I give her she soaks it up and wants more. My little love sponge. Never seeing me again will destroy her. Solid, reliable Buddy will seem to take it in his stride, but it'll come out in little ways: barking at strangers, the fear of traffic returning; he'll begin to make a mess in the house again like he did when I first got him as a rescue dog. Buster will sit by the front door, ever watchful for my return. And Fifi, who has finally begun to accept she doesn't need to be afraid any more, will hide her belly once again and refuse to come out of her basket.

This can't happen.

Screaming, I lash out at the prison I've willingly climbed into. I've always been the same, recklessly willing to jump into any situation, telling myself I won't be out of my depth.

There's a movement. A sudden tilt that throws me against the back of the trunk. Water rushing in now. There's no room to kick or punch, but I do my best in the tiny space. Fists soon bruise, nails tear as I scratch, knuckles and fingers bleeding. Scrabbling at the lock, or where the lock probably is, somewhere in the middle, but it's sunk so deeply into the plastic that I can't reach it. How long have I been here? Someone must notice I've disappeared soon and call the police.

They won't get here in time, though. This is where I die, then. Just like my sister. Now I know, and the knowledge I had always thought would make things better doesn't. It doesn't give comfort or power or soothe me. I don't feel closer to her. What was I thinking, doing this? This was all my sister felt: horror, terror, desperation, hopeless, helpless.

Acceptance.

This was what I agreed to. It's what I'd wanted. I lie back. Try not to allow the panic to take control as the water rises. Pretend my family is with me. Buster's gentle nose-nudges of comfort. Scamp's soft fur to bury my face in. Buddy's steady gaze to keep me strong. And my sister's arms around me, holding me close and telling me we'll be together soon.

Leila, I'm sorry but I don't want to die.

I push and push against the back seat, my back battering against it in time to my hammering heart, my one good leg bracing. It's no use. The water is around my neck, lapping my chin.

An idea. Reaching blindly, I pull at a section of the fuzzy material, moving my fingers along until I find a piece that gives.

Coughing and spluttering, I pull out the car jack housed beside the spare wheel.

Running out of time…!

My hands slip and slide; I'm flailing uselessly, not making an impact on the metal of the boot. Too much water. Can't keep on. I scream, and water rushes inside my mouth, up my nose, down my windpipe.

CHAPTER FORTY-ONE

Documentary Transcript
Title: *Missing: The Twin Who Never Came Back*

Voiceover: So far, everything you've seen was on the original documentary. This episode we'll be exploring the incredible aftermath of its screening, and the drama that was triggered. We reveal the inside story to the deadly conclusion of the mystery of the vanished twins which began twenty-five years ago.

[Cut to news footage and shots of newspaper headlines.]

History Repeating Itself. Missing Twins Double Mystery
Tragic Stella Took Her Own Life, Claims Psychic
Mereford Mourns for Murdered Twins

[Cut to archive news footage. Grainy long-lens video of Euan, taken the day the story of Stella's disappearance broke.]

Newscaster's voiceover: Euan Vincent's tread is heavy as he walks along the beach, a lost soul trying to come to terms with the twist of fate that has led from him reporting on a mystery to being in the centre of it. His relationship with Stella Hawkins was a fledgling one, but sources close to the couple say they were "head over heels in love".

Now, he appears lost. Sometimes he pauses and seems to lean against the bear-like dog by his side. Buddy doesn't mind. He stands patiently, waiting for his master to regain his strength. Man and dog united by grief. Euan sinks his fingers into the thick fur, seeking comfort from the warmth. Then Fifi gently nudges him with her nose, hitting the back of his knee. Euan turns and sits on the sand, almost collapsing, and it's Scamp and Buster who whimper and put their heads on his knee.

Everyone in the bustling seaside town of Mereford is questioning how two sisters could go missing twenty-five years apart. Some suspect foul play, while others believe that Stella may have ended her own life.

A neighbour agreed to speak with us, on the condition she wasn't named or pictured.

Neighbour: She was obsessed with what happened, and it's all got too much for her; it's obvious, isn't it? Nice enough woman, kept herself to herself, like, but… It's that Euan I feel sorry for now. She took him in and then broke his heart with what she's done. It was always going to end in tears with her. I've been taking food round for him, but he's never in. I'll keep trying though. He's a lovely man…

Newscaster: Not all the townsfolk agree, though.

[Cut to High Street. Shoppers walk by in the background as different people are interviewed.]

Off camera – journalist: What do you think has happened to Stella Hawkins? Do you have a theory?

Interviewee 1: Someone's done her in – and it's got to be the same person who took her sister. Stands to reason, doesn't it? They need to look at friends, family, someone who knew both those poor girls. I'm locking my doors and keeping alert from now on.

There should be some kind of enquiry into the police handling of this. Top brass hauled over the coals.

Interviewee 2: Dunno. Maybe she got sick of everyone talking about the past and has run away, like, for a fresh start. That enough? Only I want to get home for me dinner.

Interviewee 3: The boyfriend did it. It's always the boyfriend or husband, isn't it? He looks dodgy. Something a bit too slick about him for my liking.

[Cut to more long-lens footage of Euan, this time walking along a street. He stops at every lamp post and attaches a poster.]

Newscaster voiceover: Calls for an urgent enquiry are growing, along with fear in this small seaside town. Just as Stella Hawkins used to cover the town in posters about her sister, Leila, now Euan puts them up about Stella. The whole town is as desperate for answers as he is – with many asking: if someone has targeted both the Hawkins' twins, just who might be next?

[Cut to close-up of poster with photo of middle-aged woman smiling at camera. Beneath is writing.]

MISSING.
HAVE YOU SEEN THIS WOMAN?
ANYONE WITH INFORMATION ABOUT STELLA
HAWKINS SHOULD CONTACT...

[Cut to archive news footage of vigil at St Hildred's Church, which is on a roundabout where four roads come together to create a cross. Flowers are piled beneath two poster-size photos: one of Stella, the other of Leila. They spill across the base of the cenotaph commemorating the fallen heroes of WWI and WWII. Crowds of people stand with their heads bowed, some holding candles.]

Voiceover: The news that Stella's body had been discovered in the trunk of a submerged car broke two days after her disappearance. Her vehicle had been sunk in a lake six miles outside of Mereford. The location had once been a brick pit where, around a hundred years earlier, clay had been scooped before shaping and firing. When the clay was exhausted, the empty pit was left abandoned and the deeply scarred land filled with water to create a lake. They are common in Lincolnshire, with many becoming popular with anglers who fish for the pike and carp released into them. But a handful have been left, and it was one such that the killer used as a dumping ground.

When the people of Mereford and surrounding area heard about the discovery of the body, it wasn't long before the community pulled together to stage a vigil – not only to pay their respects to the twins, but to demand justice. The service was attended by hundreds and the world's media gathered to cover it.

[Archive news footage shows Euan.]

Voiceover: Euan's form, even from a distance, looked grief-shattered. Bent over, hands covering his face. It was like the nation saw that picture and wanted to give him a hug.

CHAPTER FORTY-TWO

EUAN

All four roads leading to St Hildred's Church have been closed to traffic. The church stands on a large roundabout, within easy walking distance of the town centre and the seafront. It's the perfect location for a gathering. The crowds bathe in the buttery light of the late summer's evening, curious tourists joining locals to fill pavements, flow into the intersecting roads, gather in gardens and balconies. People hold single flowers, bouquets, candles, cards.

They're all here to say goodbye to Stella.

Euan stands between two poster-size photos of her and Leila, surrounded by piles of flowers, and scans the crowd. Some wear 'Justice for Stella & Leila' T-shirts, and matching baseball caps to keep the glare of the lowering sun out of their eyes. There are only a handful of faces he recognises. Farrah has placed herself at the front, and instead of giving in to tears over the death of her best friend, she gives him the kind of look that could freeze lava. They exchanged words yesterday when she confronted him about how shifty he looks since Stella's death.

'You're swinging between heartbreak in public and antsy in private, Euan. You don't ring true – and I've told the police as much,' she said. Her words had been enough to make sweat trickle down his back, but he'd blustered his way through.

She's not the only one who has flagged him up to the investigating team. He knows for a fact that the now-retired Detective

Chief Inspector Dave Burns also threw Euan's name into the ring after hearing of Stella's disappearance, while sunning himself at his new home in Northern Cyprus, because Fox and Fremlin had told him as much. Bloody Burns had never hidden his dislike of Euan.

Nerves and anger rage through the journalist at having to attend this memorial, vigil, whatever the hell it's supposed to be, but he knows all eyes are on him, so he makes a conscious effort to stop grinding his teeth, unclench his jaw, and do the deep breathing exercises he learned for relaxation back in the day when he'd first become a presenter.

Behind him he can feel the dual stares of Fremlin and Fox, assessing him, seeing how he's coping. His heart starts to patter, fighting against the deep in and out of breath he is forcing on his body.

Time has run out, though. He steps up to the microphone and begins to give the performance of his life.

The atmosphere shifts to expectation. The crowd go silent, apart from the occasional sniff and sob. All eyes gaze up at him. He clears his throat and speaks.

'Stella Hawkins was a brave and wonderful woman who—'

That's when the singing starts.

A group at the edge of the crowd drown out his words as their voices swell. He turns to DS Fox.

'Is that…?'

'"Who Let the Dogs Out",' she frowns.

Men brandish cans of lager and shout the song out, laughing, as they push and shove their way through the crowd. One kicks at some flowers laid on the pavement, sending petals flying into the air.

Fury explodes through Euan's veins. After everything Stella has been through, how can people be so disrespectful? He clenches his fists and marches towards them and into the brawl. He's barely reached them before he's punched, head knocked sideways, hard, he sees stars. And someone familiar. Someone hurrying away, their head down. Walking towards a plain, pale blue van with mirrored windows.

'Stop him! No!'

No one hears over the yelling. Another punch lands. Euan fights to get away, to reach the man, to stop him getting to the van.

Because inside the van hides Stella.

And the man heading towards it is the person who believes, wrongly, he has murdered her. If he sees her, this time he'll make sure no mistakes are made.

Hands claw at Euan's shirt. He feels it ripping, buttons popping. He takes a step. Then another punch lands. He sinks to his knees.

Stella! Must save Stella!

It's the last thing he thinks before a kick to the head knocks him out.

STELLA

Like some kind of Bond villain, I watch an array of screens showing live footage of the vigil. From the outside, the van looks normal, apart from its small, mirrored windows at the back and along the sides, but inside it's decked out with equipment that must be worth a fortune. When I said that to Euan this morning, he'd pointed out its most valuable load was me: the woman everyone – including my killer – thinks is dead.

I really had almost died that night. But Euan had got home and spotted the note I'd left, telling him to look at the feeds from the Doggy Cams, and after a call to DS Fox, they'd worked out where I was and rushed to the location. When Euan pulled me to the surface of the lake, I was blue and lifeless. He refused to talk about it, but Fox had told me how Euan had worked on me non-stop until I took a choking, gasping breath on my own.

My first words when I came around in hospital, several hours later, had been the name of my attacker. The shock on people's faces proved how cleverly he'd hidden in plain sight. The problem was he'd done a disappearing act now – which was why we'd come up with the idea of leaking news of my death and staging a vigil, in order to draw him out from whatever stone he'd crawled under.

It's feels horrifically cruel sitting so close to friends who are genuinely grieving for me. There's Farrah, clearly suspicious of Euan, little realising the reason he seems shifty is because he's hiding the massive secret I'm alive. Guilt weighs heavy at not telling her what's happening, but the fewer people who know the more likely this crazy gamble is to work.

'Are you okay?' asks Pete, an officer who has been assigned to stay with me the whole time. He's a tall, broad man who reminds me of a bull, with his thick neck, sloping shoulders and thatch of thick brown hair. I get the impression Euan helped choose my protection officer and picked the biggest bloke in the station.

'Kinda. People from school, university, the local shop, clients and colleagues, friends and distant relatives, they're all here,' I reply, stunned. 'See her? That young woman crying and being held up by her parents? Her name's Keshini; she's come back from London for this. It's heartbreaking watching everyone and being within touching distance of them.'

'Once we catch that bastard, they'll understand why this was necessary.'

I hope so.

As well as the cameras set up by the police, the screens also show feeds from the media, which has attended in droves. Looking at it all is dizzying, trying to concentrate on each person on every screen impossible, so instead I try to relax and use instinct and peripheral vision, much like a dog hunting might do.

'Hold on. Can you zoom in or something?' I point to the screen. There's a man: his face is obscured beneath a baseball cap with a local nightclub logo across it and he keeps his head down.

Pete's thick fingers fly. 'Hang on. It's a feed from a broadcaster, so I can't control the camera. Let's see if I can get him on our cameras…'

Agonising moments of tapping and squinting and sighing. Finally: 'Got him! Ah, no, not him.'

The disappointment weighs me down like trying to swim with rocks in my pockets.

My eyes flick from screen to screen, desperately searching. The pressure is getting to me. To spot *him*. But we can't even be sure if he's coming. We hope but we don't know anything. After twenty-five years of waiting, catching Leila's killer has come down to a punt, nothing more.

Noise swells outside the van. What's happening? There's a knot of people singing something. On screen, I see others seem to be taking offence, squaring up to them. I can't hear what's being chanted. Then I make out a chorus…

'Why are people singing "Who Let the Dogs Out"?' Pete asks.

I scoot closer to one screen and stare at the baying, barking, laughing, shoving figures intent on causing trouble at the peaceful vigil.

There! A face I recognise.

'Oh my…! It's the puppy farmers.'

'Who?'

'I recognise him – and oh, yeah, him, too. I broke into their place a few weeks back and got their illegal business shut down. They've been pretty peed off with me ever since.'

'You seem to pee off a lot of people.'

Fifi's old owner is there, too. I knew he was dodgy! It's no surprise he's mates with these others.

The fight is growing. More people in the crowd getting involved. A can of lager flies from the pack of troublemakers, and almost hits an old woman in a wheelchair. Other people are reacting, anger spreading, the whole vigil falling apart and turning into a seething mass. The police swarm forward, trying to get it under control before it turns into a riot, but there are so many people it's hard for them to quash the trouble.

Euan is in the middle of the fight. Someone punches him and he almost goes down.

'No! Help him! You've got to help him!' I shout.

The officer hesitates.

'If you don't, I will.' Though what I can do limping along on crutches with my broken leg and cracked ribs, already bruised and beaten and a little high from strong painkillers, I'm not sure.

Pete looks at the screens once more, then outside through the mirrored windows as the crowd roars and swells. More officers are running to the scene. They've no shields, no riot equipment; this wasn't how anyone imagined a peaceful memorial would turn out.

'Looks like it needs all hands on deck,' Pete says, 'but I can't leave you.'

'I swear if you go out there, I won't go anywhere. I'll be safe in here. They need you.'

A moment of thought then a nod. 'Okay. But you definitely stay here, understood? Don't move. Don't speak to anyone.'

'Of course.' I cross my heart.

'Lock the doors if you don't feel safe.'

*

People are scattering in all directions. Some running towards the fight, yet more hurry away, while others simply try to defend themselves as chaos descends like a rainstorm. Alone, I watch the screens, my bird's-eye view making me feel even less a part of the action. Innocent people are out there being hurt because of me, and it kills me not to be able to go outside and try to bring a stop to it. I can see Euan square up to Fifi's owner, who shoves him back. No!

Turning from the screen, I look through the window instead, pressing my face against it to bring myself closer to him. Euan falls. Attackers surround him. I can't see a thing.

There's a man hurrying towards the van. I stare past him, see DI Fremlin trying to reach Euan's side. But the man is heading right towards me, obscuring my view.

'Move out of the bloody way,' I mutter, dodging right and left to see beyond him. His head is down, his hands in his pockets.

The fake nonchalance draws my eye. He might as well be whistling as he walks as quickly as he dares without arousing suspicion from anyone watching, baseball cap pulled right down. He's almost on the edge of the crowd now. Almost free.

It's *him*. I whimper, duck down instinctively. Fear frozen. He's been here all along. Among the grieving and the fearful, he has walked free and unstoppable as he hides in the crowd.

I dare a look at the screens, searching for someone to come to my rescue again. DS Fox will notice his act and arrest him. But all the police are involved in the fight; no one is looking at the people leaving. The whole point of the vigil has been forgotten thanks to the stupid puppy farmers. Outside, the roar of the crowd rises and the chorus of 'Who Let the Dogs Out' soars once again.

I try to think but my mind is as frozen as my body. Someone's got to do something. But there *is* no someone. There's only me. Broken, beaten, raped, almost killed by the last encounter. I want to have the strength to confront him, to tackle him, to bring the bastard to justice, but all the front that's been driving me this far abandons me. I've nothing left but terror now I can see him.

Everything I've been blocking out comes flashing back in strobes of horror. Flying over the car's bonnet. Fighting for my life. The burning pain of trying to pull oxygen into my lungs as he squeezed my throat closed. Waking in the back seat, his face over me, the weight of his body pressing down, suffocating me. Cutting my own lip as I bit down on it against the tearing pain below. The blessed release of a hard blow to the head sending me reeling into darkness. The fear of waking in my own car boot and being overwhelmed by water.

I'd died. He'd murdered me. Just like Leila.

My body is shaking now, shivers that have nothing to do with cold or the freezing sweat running down my body. With me, fear always comes afterwards, but everything I've been forcing myself to think about later has created a debt that my whole being demands be paid – right now. My heart feels like it'll burst through my chest like an alien, and the darkness closing in pulls me back to the car boot, the claustrophobia, water in my lungs. He's going to see me through the windows, let himself into the van and hurt me all over again, and this time I've no fight left and this time he'll kill me and this time Euan will be destroyed.

I won't risk my life again. I want to live.

I want to build a future with Euan. Grow old with him and do all the boring things that make a life. Doing the washing and drying side by side, sharing details of our days; worrying when he's ill and nagging him to go to the doctor, even though he won't want any fuss; arguing and calling each other all the names under the sun, then making up.

The urge to stay alive lends me courage to raise myself up enough to peer through the window.

He's getting closer. Looking around. Like he hasn't a care in the world. Then his eyes turn to the van, meet mine.

He's seen, he must have seen, and I slide from my seat to the floor, losing the use of my body. The real fight begins then, as I try to overpower my fear in order to stay sane while I wait for the thunk of the van's rear door opening.

It doesn't happen.

Of course, he can't see anything but his own reflection in the mirrored windows. Am I safe then? Hampered by the cast covering my left leg from toe to immediately above my knee, I pull myself from the back of the van towards the front and drape over the front seat, keeping low. He's still the picture of innocence, and no one's taking any notice of him. He doesn't even look up at the sound of a child crying as her parents hurry past.

He's going to get away.

My mobile! I suddenly remember it, dial Euan but he doesn't pick up. Everyone who could help is fighting just a few feet away from me. They can't hear their phones over the chaos. I could dial the emergency services, but by the time extra officers arrive he'll be long gone.

I've got my rape alarm on me. Okay, so I could open the door, maybe even send him flying with it if I caught him. Let the rape alarm go off; people would hear it and come running.

Would they hear it?

Would they get to me in time?

Would I actually hurt him by hitting him with.the door, or would I just be opening it to virtually invite him in? Once he sees me he won't let me live.

He's passed the van now and is moving in front of it to cross the road. I peer over the dashboard at his back, holding the steering wheel to steady myself. Something tickles one hand.

It's the keys, dangling from the ignition.

He can't get away. He mustn't get away.

Scrambling forward, I flop awkwardly into the driver's seat and my cracked ribs make me cry out loud. My bad leg is on fire as I pull it into place with my hands until I'm sitting properly in place. It's a good job Pete's so tall, the seat pushed back as far as it will go, or I'd never be able to get my broken leg in.

He's walking away. Hands in pockets. Shoulders relaxed. Head down. Doesn't give a toss about me or Mary or Leila.

He has to be stopped.

Everything is whiting out, blood pounding in my ears; all that exists is him and me, and I'm turning the key, the engine roaring to life, the accelerator pushed to the floor, the van lurching forward.

For Leila.

He turns. He sees the van.

For Mary.

He looks through the windscreen and his eyes widen in recognition, growing bigger and bigger.

For my parents.

My foot is hard to the floor.

For me.

A thump as I hit him and he's carried along with the van.

Screams. People scattering.

For every unknown victim.

A second impact. Shockwaves through my body. My head hits the steering wheel as we slam into the cenotaph.

Shaking, I lift my gaze. There he is, former Detective Chief Inspector Dave Burns. Trusted friend. Ally. Dear Friend. Killer. Trapped between the cenotaph and the van's bonnet. He's still staring at me, and for a split second something passes between us.

Then his mouth is as wide as his eyes and he's screaming, screaming, screaming as people run towards us.

CHAPTER FORTY-THREE

Documentary Transcript
Title: *Missing: The Twin Who Never Came Back*

[Montage of archive video footage from the time of arrest, plus headlines from the time.]

Voiceover: The world's media had attended the vigil, and the moment of arrest of former Detective Chief Inspector David Burns was caught on camera for everyone to see. The dramatic footage has now become famous around the globe.

After a touch-and-go first week in hospital when his life hung in the balance, Burns eventually recovered, although he is now in a wheelchair as a result of crush injuries to his legs. He was immediately charged with killing Mary Bird and Leila Hawkins and the attempted murder of Stella.

Coming up, we talk exclusively to Stella and Euan about the terrifying night she died and came back to life – and Detective Inspector Nick Fremlin tells how he headed the operation that netted a killer cop.

[Cut to interior shot of a large conservatory, which has views across a garden filled with mature deciduous trees, a generous lawn and a riot of colourful flowers. Three people are seated. Euan and Stella sit on a sofa, surrounded by dogs, while beside them in an armchair is DI Fremlin. He is picking a dog hair off his otherwise immaculate suit when the interview begins.]

Off camera – Interviewer: DI Fremlin, tell me, how did you realise the full extent of Dave Burns's depravity?

DI Fremlin: My team first became suspicious when the doctor called out to produce a death certificate for Mary Bird noticed her eyes looked slightly redder than expected. What happened next was a mixture of gut instinct honed by years of training and good old-fashioned police work, and I'm very proud of my team. One of my officers, Detective Sergeant Alison Fox, had already been working with internal affairs on a hunch that Burns was more involved in the disappearance of Leila Hawkins than evidence suggested. When Mary Bird's death was flagged up as suspicious, DS Fox came to me and we immediately suppressed that information from the rest of the station and outside, in case Burns was somehow also connected with it. This was particularly important, as a neighbour of Ms Bird's reported seeing someone who matched Burns' description.

Unfortunately, Burns was one step ahead of us, moving swiftly against Stella before a post mortem could confirm Ms Bird's elevated carbon dioxide levels, which proved suffocation as cause of death.

Interviewer: Let's hear from Stella herself about that night… You must have been terrified!

Stella: I think I was too busy trying to stay alive for that.

Euan: Well, I've never been more scared in my life! You died that night, you really did.

[He turns in his seat to face her.]

The memory of pumping your chest and getting no response. The minutes ticking down, your face blue… that will live with me for ever.

Interviewer: How did you find her?

Stella: Well, I'd hidden some cameras to capture my attack and left a Post-it on my laptop, so that when Euan got back from his meeting he'd see it. And you did, didn't you?

Euan: I'd had a long meeting, and as soon as I got home I could tell Stella wasn't there. I called her phone and she didn't answer, and I remember thinking to myself: She won't have done anything stupid, will she? Then I saw the note with my name on, on top of her laptop. When I opened it up there were instructions for me to watch the cameras, Doggy1, Doggy 2, and Doggy3—

Stella: I use them for helping with dog training, usually.

Euan: Right. Well, I do as I'm told and can see the cameras have been hidden in bushes around a lay-by, and there's live footage of a man getting into a car and driving away. It was dark, so I didn't recognise him, but of course, now I know it was Burns. I'd no idea why Stella wanted me to see it, so rewound it so I could see what had happened before that and… and…

Interviewer: You saw the attack in full, didn't you? Stella, do you want to pick up the story here?

Stella: There are bits I remember, but most of it I was unconscious for, so… Let Euan tell you. What I will say is if Burns had just killed me, instead of deciding to take his time attacking me, I wouldn't have been saved.

Euan: I've never felt so helpless. All I could do was watch as Stella was mown down. She was thrown like a fish into the air, over the bonnet then *crunch* to the floor.

Stella: When I was younger, I'd done a course with a stunt person, who'd advised me how to fall in order to limit injury. He'd even shown me the best way to be hit by a car, by timing a jump onto the bonnet and keeping hands either side of my head to protect it from hitting the windscreen. It's only because of that I'd been saved from more catastrophic damage by the car.

Euan: Even then you somehow had the presence of mind to fool him by playing dead, to get him closer and fight back.

Stella: Well, no, that makes it sound really impressive. I was actually winded and couldn't breathe until he reached me.

Euan: And while you're fighting for your life, who do I call to come to your rescue? Dave Burns.

[Shakes head.]

I dialled 999 then thought: "No, Dave will pull out all the stops to save her." I'd no bloody clue it was him I was watching.

[Both wipe away tears.]

Anyway, his number came up as not available, so I called Alison – Detective Sergeant Fox – instead. While I screamed down the phone, she stayed calm, got me to forward the recording to her and she recognised it instantly. Good job she was born and bred in this area or things could have been very different.

Interviewer: You arrived minutes before the emergency services, Euan, is that right?

Euan: Some long grass had been crushed down by tyres and because it was so dry they hadn't sprung back into place. So I followed them to the lake and ran straight into the water. The hot summer and lack of rain made it far shallower than normal, so I spotted Stella's submerged car almost immediately through the murk. The trunk was wide open, revealing...

[Voice catches.]

Stella's lifeless, naked body.

Interviewer: It's okay. Take your time.

Euan: She was dead. Cold and blue when I broke through the surface. I don't know how long I performed CPR, pumping her chest and breathing for her, until she spluttered back to life.

Stella: You saved me.

Euan: You saved yourself. If you hadn't put those cameras out, you'd never have been found. If you hadn't managed to get that trunk open yourself, I wouldn't have reached you in time.

Interviewer: Ah, yes, tell us about how you opened the locked boot.

Stella: This is actually something people should know, in case they ever find themselves in this situation – okay, it's unlikely, but still. Over the years I've done a lot of self-defence classes and reading up on things, and years ago I read how using a car jack can force the lock. I just set the jack on the bottom of the boot then wound it up so it hit the top of the boot, then kept on winding until the lock couldn't take the force any more. I must have passed out just as it finally burst apart. Too late for me to get out.

Interviewer: All that while water filled the space – that's incredible.

Stella: Yeah, well…

[Shrugs.]

I do honestly think that if I hadn't spent so many years preparing for worst-case scenarios, I wouldn't have got through this. I almost didn't get through it.

[Cut to police evidence photographs of Stella's wounds. Her left leg broken; her face swollen. Bite marks puncture her skin in various places.]

Interviewer: For a horrifying couple of hours, Stella, you remained unconscious while medics treated you. Because your attacker was still at large, your transfer to hospital had been kept strictly a secret, and you were kept under guard the whole time. As soon as you came round you named your attacker, but it was too late.

Now, DI Fremlin, at this point Burns had already fled the country, right? He'd found himself an apartment in Kyrenia, North Cyprus, which overlooked the historic harbour and spectacular castle that dates back to Byzantine times. From what we understand, the town has a lively British ex-pat scene. So he thinks he's safe and no one knows he's a killer.

DI Fremlin: That's right. He hadn't even bothered lying. We'd all known he planned to move there when he left the job; he'd spoken of it a few times. Once again, he was playing mind games and hiding in plain sight, you see? It was only when we went to arrest him that we discovered he'd chosen that location because the Turkish Republic of Northern Cyprus, to give it its correct name, isn't recognised as a country in its own right by any other nation than Turkey, which makes extradition from it tricky.

Clearly, Burns knew that even if anyone ever investigated what he'd done, he couldn't be arrested in Northern Cyprus, and it would be time-consuming for the UK police to go through formal channels to force him back into the UK– which would buy him enough time to go on the run.

Interviewer: And this was why you decided to fake Stella's death and hold a phony memorial? To lure him out?

[Fremlin nods.]

Tell me how on earth that audacious plan came about…

DI Fremlin: It was Stella's idea, initially. She said he'd relax if he thought his plan to kill her had worked. To be honest, I told her it wasn't procedure and she'd been watching too much television, but then this one…

[Jerks head towards Euan.]

…piped up with examples where law enforcement agencies in other countries had faked someone's death in order to draw out a killer.

Euan: As a journalist, I'm always on the lookout for weird stories, and I remembered this case I'd read about recently in America. Texas, I think. Police realised this guy's wife was planning to have him killed, so he and the police faked his death to prove it.

An undercover cop met the wife and pretended to be a hitman. It was all arranged. The poor husband had to carry on like normal, even had to sleep under the same roof as the person planning to have him killed. Can you imagine? To "prove" to the wife the hit had taken place, the police put make-up on the man's face, got him to pose as if dead in a shallow grave, and took photographs.

[Cut to book about this case.]
[Cut to image of a man with a bullet wound to his temple. The blood and the grey pallor all look disturbingly convincing.]

Euan: Only last year, a Russian journalist faked his death with the help of Ukrainian authorities. He did it to draw out people who wanted to kill him. Obituaries were published; people around the world were shocked by his so-called death. If I remember right, not even his wife and children were in on the plan. Then the next day there was a press conference where the truth was revealed.

DI Fremlin: With permission from my boss, I decided to go ahead with the ruse that Stella was dead. We moved her to a safe house and issued a press release. Then DS Fox called Burns and played her part beautifully, informing him that Stella's body had been found and the townsfolk were planning a memorial for her and Leila. It was a delicate balancing act between encouraging him to come, telling him he'd be missed because he'd been such a key part of the investigation into Leila's disappearance, but not making it obvious he was the sole reason the event was taking place. If he suspected even for a second it was a trap, he wouldn't have come; but Fox appealed to his vanity. Burns said it was unlikely he would attend, that it'd be too much toing and froing when he'd only just left the country, but that he'd think about it – he even tried to get Fox to investigate Euan, saying he had money problems and a terrible temper.

Still, Burns was more cautious than we gave him credit for. We'd set up alerts to let us know if he came back into the country, but he used a fake passport bought earlier in case he had to go on the run. That meant we had no clue when he entered the country. Even so, we thought we were prepared for him, with handpicked officers in the crowd looking for him.

Interviewer: What on earth made him come, do you think? He was home free!

DI Fremlin: It's basic psychology. Attending the vigil was a big risk, but so was putting himself in the middle of the investigation, befriending Stella, and let's not forget how emailing her pretending to be someone else was either breathtakingly stupid or incredibly arrogant, too. There's an established pattern of risk-taking here. Men who commit crimes such as this are often increasingly reckless – it's part of the thrill.

Stella: Someone like him can't resist seeing the fruits of his labour, the pain and loss he's created; he's a sadistic bastard.

Interviewer: So there you are, imagining you've thought of every angle and then… a mass brawl breaks out.

DI Fremlin: That's correct. The now-notorious riot at the vigil was the final act in a campaign waged against Stella by criminal elements in the community. When we arrested the troublemakers from the vigil, a group of them who had previously been arrested for illegal puppy farming confessed to being behind a hate campaign of silent phone calls. They'd also sent a letter pretending to be from Stella's sister, and later sent dog excrement to her, and even poisoned one of her dogs.

Interviewer: All this going on while being cyber stalked by a killer cop intent on killing you, Stella.

During police interviews, Burns refused to answer questions, only ever replying "no comment". When he lodged a plea of not guilty, an audible gasp rang out in the courtroom.

[Cut to archive news footage of Stella Hawkins on the steps of Lincoln Crown Court, in the grounds of the ancient Lincoln Castle. She stands

between two columns of the Gothic building, behind her is the huge wooden door at least twice her height. She is flanked by Euan Vincent and Farrah Sykes, and she looks at each, seemingly for reassurance, before reading from a piece of paper. Her voice is clear and strong.]

Stella: Even now, Dave Burns is playing power games. Despite overwhelming evidence, and surely against the instructions of his lawyer, he has refused to admit to what he has done. There can be only one reason for this: to get time in court so that he can make me suffer once again, by giving me no other choice but to testify against him. If he hopes to intimidate me then he has failed. If he hopes to evade justice, he will fail in that, too.

He messed up by not caring enough about me to even bother checking whether I was alive or dead when he pushed the car into the lake. He'll regret that. I'm ready to face him. I'm ready to find out why he did all those terrible things.

I've no further statement at this time. Thank you.

[Flash photography. Clamour of journalists shouting questions as she walks away and gets into a waiting car.]

CHAPTER FORTY-FOUR

On the third day after the vigil, I finally get out of bed and, with the aid of crutches and an overly attentive Euan, I make it downstairs to instead lie on the sofa, a thin blanket over me against the chill of early autumn. Not that I need a blanket once the dogs settle around me: Buster by my head, Scamp to my right, Buddy to my left and Fifi curled by my feet, all keeping me warm.

I've barely moved since my confrontation with Burns. I feel broken not just in body but mind. All those years of keeping my emotions at bay is catching up with me. I wish the clock could be turned back for so many reasons, for Leila, Mum, Dad, Mary; my regrets piling up like the leaves starting to fall from the trees.

A knock on the door has the dogs jumping to the floor. I struggle, force myself to stand, still not able to relax around visitors.

Euan comes in, followed by DS Fox and DI Fremlin – Alison and Nick, as they've asked me to call them these days. 'After all we've been through, I think we can be on first name terms,' Fox said. I got the feeling it's an honour not given to many people. She reminds me a bit of me. Now, though, she has the strangest look on her face. Nick Fremlin is the same. Sombre but also relieved. He's no longer the stuffy politician police officer of our first meeting.

'Stella,' he says, 'we can't be one hundred per cent certain yet but—'

'You've found her?'

'We've found her.'

My soul is lightened. I'm almost floating. Fremlin rushes forward, catches me where I sway, and helps me back onto the sofa.

'A lifetime of searching is over,' I say.

'The state of you, though… was it worth it?'

'I wouldn't change a single thing that happened.'

His eyes have swollen. He's not the only one. I pretend not to notice everyone spending some time clearing their throats and staring out of the window, while Euan quietly sits by my side and puts his hand beside mine, barely touching. He knows instinctively just how much fuss I need, not overwhelming me with more because touch sometimes scares me after my ordeal.

When I'm finally left alone again I pull out a tiny compact mirror. All I can see are partial sections of my face, just as I like it. I move it around, looking past the swelling and bruises to find patches of my lost twin.

'Leila, you're free now. You can rest in peace at last.'

Framed in the rectangle, Leila's smile blooms in the reflection.

CHAPTER FORTY-FIVE

Documentary Transcript
Title: *Missing: The Twin Who Never Came Back*

[Montage of headlines.]

Killer Cop in the Dock
Fling Started with a Fag and Ended in Murder
Sixties Singing Sensation Murdered Over Misunderstanding

[Cut to archive news footage of reporter outside Lincoln Crown Court.]
Voiceover: A documentary crew have been given unprecedented access to the six-week trial of Dave Burns at Lincoln Crown Court. Using six remotely controlled miniature cameras positioned around the courtroom, film-makers have been able to capture the notorious case as it played out. Keshini Naidoo, a spokesperson for the production company behind the ground-breaking project, said: "It seems only fitting that this case, which has played out so publicly, should be captured this way, and we're honoured that the judge agreed with our request."

[Cut to interior shot of the court.]
Voiceover: Witnesses gave testimony, evidence was set out, the prosecution had laid out their case well. When it came to the defence, they had only one card up their sleeve: to get disgraced former Detective Dave Burns onto the stand. It was clear from

the start he was going to relish his moment to share his story. But would it really be enough to clear his name?

[Cut to courtroom footage of Burns sitting in his wheelchair on the witness stand. He appears relaxed. When he speaks he looks at Stella Hawkins.]

Defence barrister: Tell us, in your owns words, if you will, how you came to meet Leila Hawkins.

Burns: I gave a lecture when she was on her training course – not to her class, to some others. Afterwards, I had a fag outside and that's when I met Leila because she'd skulked around the same corner for a sneaky cigarette, too. There'd been an instant attraction between us, even though she was only 19 and I was 35. She was up for it; I started flirting. By the time I'd thrown my butt on the floor and ground its glow out with my foot, we'd arranged to meet up for a drink in my room, as I was staying overnight.

I hadn't realised she lived with someone until after we'd shagged. The way she spoke about her bloke gave the impression she was sick of his puppy love, which bordered on obsession. She wanted to break free of his clinginess, to kick the puppy and have some fun, and I was happy to provide it, no strings attached.

Back at the station, we were both professional and grown-up enough to act as if we didn't know each other. What had happened was a one-off.

Then came that night.

I'd had a row with my wife. She'd been nagging on again about my long hours. I was sick of it, so went back to work, even though I was knackered and angry, and only just reached my desk when my direct line rings and it's Leila, in a payphone.

"I've lost my house keys. Any chance you can help me out?" she asked.

I knew what she meant – she didn't say it in so many words but wanted to know if I fancied meeting up for some fun.

It was chucking it down; my car's wipers couldn't clear the windscreen fast enough. When the street lamps went out, electricity lost across the town and beyond, I almost changed my mind but felt bad about leaving her in the middle of a storm – cos I'm a nice guy, see?

So I pick her up from the payphone and she's soaking the seats, which pisses me off a bit because it was a new car. Then she asks me to break into her place. No chance – and I told her as much, so then she says, all reluctant-like, "you could take me to my parents' place". So when I suggested an alternative she jumped at it.

At that time, me and a couple of mates shared a shag pad between us. A slightly seedy former holiday let a few streets away from the station that we clubbed together to cover the cost of full-time, so we could have fun without wives or girlfriends finding out. After all, Mereford gets some tasty holidaymakers who are up for some slap and tickle, especially after a few drinks. The joy of working odd hours and shift patterns is that it's easy to have a bit on the side.

Defence barrister: I think we get the picture, Mr Burns. Please continue.

Burns: All right, but don't forget our agreement. This is my time, I'm telling my story, my way.

Right, so it doesn't take much to get Leila to the flat. A bit of, "ooh, it's late, you don't want to wake your parents; they'll be dead to the world after celebrating all night" does the trick. I remember, when I checked under the plant pot she told me it wasn't a secure place to leave a key, and I said you'd have to be stupid to rob a place owned by coppers. What I didn't tell her was that the key being there meant that no one else was using it, if you get my drift.

But as soon as we get inside things go downhill. I kiss her and she starts complaining that the doorknob's digging into her back. When we go into the lounge properly, she says: "You can get off now, if you want."

Like it's her place to order me from.

"Let me get warmed up first. Come on, you weren't shy before," I say.

Defence barrister: Mr Burns, I want you to think carefully about the testimony you're about to give.

Prosecution barrister: Objection. Leading the witness.

Judge Tallis: Sustained.

Burns: She kept pushing me off, though, saying she was upset, that she wasn't in the mood, that she'd had a horrible row.

"I'm not your boyfriend," I snapped.

"Clearly. He'd be nice to me. I don't even know what I'm doing here."

She was really getting my goat, blowing hot and cold, saying no and meaning yes – you know what women are like. Plenty of others over the years had changed their minds once I'd used a bit of persuasion.

She pushed me off, trying some self-defence moves she'd just learned that sent me stumbling.

Defence barrister: I really must remind you that this testimony may harm your defence.

Burns: That's my decision, right? I've promised to tell the truth, the whole truth and nothing but, so… So I figure she likes it rough, eh? I easily pinned her down to the floor, but accidentally – *accidentally* – smash her in the nose with the heel of my hand. And she blows it all out of proportion, saying she's going to report me at work. Lodge a formal complaint! Says she'll tell them about my "inappropriate conduct" at the training centre, too.

She started to walk away. I grabbed her. Not to do anything bad, just to stop her, to get her to listen to reason, to think. She started screaming blue murder. The little hell cat bit me. I managed to get her into a choke hold. To show her who's boss, to calm her down. And it worked. Worked so well she passed out.

And then we did what we'd come to the flat to do. But she wanted it. She loved it rough. I could see it in her eyes, feel her body respond to it.

I didn't know she was dead until it was over.

Not my fault.

Defence barrister: Your honour, I'd like to request a break, please.

Voiceover: When the court reconvened, it became clear Burns was now acting for himself, as his barrister had stepped down. The jury were informed Burns had been told he could change his plea to guilty but he had refused to do so. He made it clear he was happy to continue and returned to the witness stand.

Burns: Where was I? Yes, so, there I was with a dead body on my hands. I panicked for a moment, then forced myself to think like a policeman. As long as the key wasn't under the flowerpot, I knew no one would come in and disturb me, so I cleaned up then carried Leila outside in the blackout, while the raging storm kept potential witnesses indoors.

I took her to a lake I'd played at as a lad. Weighed her body down with some nearby rocks, waded out into the water, and watched her body disappear. No one ever went there apart from to illegally dump rubbish, so I was fairly certain she'd never be found.

Being assigned to the investigating team was a coincidence. At first, I was terrified people would put two and two together. Then I realised what an advantage working on the case gave me. My boss, DI John Glossop, was an old-fashioned cop even in the 1990s, who hated "the politically correct brigade" with a passion, believed transparency was less important than looking after your own, that good policework was more about following gut instinct than evidence, and if someone looked guilty then they probably were. So it hadn't been hard to get him relentlessly pursuing Leila's fiancé, Damien Francis.

Did you know sixty-one per cent of women killed by men in the UK are killed by a current or ex-partner? I didn't either when

I killed Leila. But it's spouting rubbish like that that got me my reputation for being a good copper. I built a reputation for being exceptionally hard-working, fair, pursuing evidence, and being particularly understanding of vulnerable victims of crime. It's how I landed promotion after promotion. No one realised I was so good because I knew just how true that statistic was for myself.

I tried to reform, tried to move on. But Stella Hawkins was always there, a loose cannon I had to keep an eye on. I could never move away, never start afresh, because Stella refused to give up.

After twenty-five years she finally started to give up hope, though, and I began to relax because everyone had forgotten about her and Leila. I decided to retire and told my boss. The following day, I got a call from someone saying they were making a documentary…

Can I have a glass of water, please? Thanks.

[He takes a sip.]

I agreed to take part to find out if the documentary makers had found any fresh leads. After it aired, I tried to stay calm, tried to think of an exit plan. Then that letter had arrived, pretending to be from Leila, and Stella was so disturbed. It wasn't like her to let things get to her, but the combination of the anniversary, documentary and that letter had made her vulnerable – and it inspired me to strike at her by emailing.

In an attempt to throw her off the scent, I pretended to be the hit-and-run driver overcome with remorse, planning eventually to guilt-trip Stella into stopping her relentless pursuit of justice. I had to be careful she didn't guess it was me, though, so wrote in this over-wordy way – actually, I based myself on that journalist, Euan Vincent. It totally fooled her, she'd no clue who the emailer was. But even when I'd claimed to be suicidal, she'd tried in her amateurish way to trick "him" to confess to the police. What a bitch.

Shout from the gallery: Bastard!

Judge Tallis: Order! Silence in the court, or you will be removed.

Burns: As I was saying…

[Takes another sip of water.]

In the end, Stella forced my hand. I'd no choice but to get rid of her. After weeks of working on her, she was finally ready to walk into my trap as a willing victim. At first, I'd been frustrated that Stella refused to feel sorry for the remorseful, suicidal hit-and-run driver I'd created, then frustration turned to anger and I'd made her spill all her emotional baggage just to hurt her as much as possible. I knew how private she was, and it was a blast getting her to share all those private moments.

But just as I thought everything was in place for me to kill her, a diamond-encrusted, over-the-hill, D-list, celebrity-shaped spanner was chucked in the works.

Mary Bird.

I'd only popped around before work to her new flat to check it was secure, so I could keep Stella onside. Gave her my card just to be polite, saying she could call me any time, but it was a surprise when she actually did and asked me to come round because she needed to talk to me. Mary had sat in that chair of hers like it was a throne as she smiled up at me in a flirtatious way that made me feel sick.

[He puts on an exaggerated falsetto voice.]

"*Darling,* I need to ask you something… I'm writing my *memoirs* and have a piece of information I think will send readers *just wild.* A publisher is interested and they've told me fresh information about Leila will guarantee *incredible* sales of the book thanks to renewed interest in the case after the documentary. Isn't that *marvellous* news?" she said. "But I first wanted to check with you – and then Stella – to see if it's all right. You see, a few months before Leila died she was unfaithful to Damien." She paused for dramatic effect. Stupid cow. "I've never said anything before because it isn't relevant to her disappearance; they *split* well before anything happened to her, and I've no idea who it was."

But it *was* relevant – and I knew Mary's book might jog other people's memories of long-forgotten sightings of me and Leila together at the training centre, or at the hotel where we'd had the one-night stand. Then questions would start to be asked…

There was something else, too. Something she was holding back, I could tell. You don't spend years investigating people without developing a nose for a secret. Of course, it was only once I was in prison I found out her big secret was that she was the twins' real mum.

I was right to kill her, though. I told the daft old bat not to mention anything to anyone else until I'd had time to look into its possible relevance. As soon as I was alone, I bought my plane ticket, bringing forward plans by a week or so, and sneaked into the retirement village the following morning to take care of the problem.

That just left Stella, and that was easy. Arrange the meet, run her over, get rid. I admit I lost control, though. Standing over her, I felt fury like never before. All those years of trying to move on from 1994 and she'd never let me. When she fought back, all that frustration at her and her bloody sister detonated. What did she expect?

I was surprised by how quickly they found Stella's body, but it didn't bother me. I knew the water at this time of year would have quickly destroyed any DNA evidence I'd left behind. I thought being invited to the memorial showed no one suspected me. There's no fool like an old fool, eh? I was so close to getting away with it all, and my stupid pride was all that tripped me up.

So there you have it: my story in full. I've been the helpless victim of female treachery and manipulation from start to finish. I lied, but so did every single one of them, Your Honour.

Voiceover: The court descended into chaos at that point, and Burns was led away. The jury took just half an hour to come back with their verdict of guilty.

When sentencing Burns, the judge was damning of the former policeman.

Judge Tallis: Your testimony had nothing to do with trying to prove your innocence; it was purely a tool for you to further hurt people you have already injured. You have consistently blamed everyone else for your actions, while taking no responsibility at all for yourself. As a police officer, you were in a position of trust, which you chose not only to disregard but to use to your own sick advantage, to gain the trust of all three of your victims before you struck without any show of mercy or restraint.

I have no hesitation in handing down the maximum sentence possible under the circumstances.

Voiceover: More women have now come forward to make complaints of sexual assault against Dave Burns. A team has been set up specifically to investigate these historical crimes.

At least his last victim, Stella, has a happy ending. She and Euan Vincent met during the making of the original documentary and are still together now.

Euan has quit journalism and wrote the tell-all biography of Sixties songstress Mary Bird, which he described in the foreword as a "labour of love", following the discovery of extensive notes she'd written herself. *Let Me Tell You a Secret,* named after Mary's big hit of 1968, spent several weeks topping the *Sunday Times* bestseller list, and included several revelations – including that she was, in fact, the birth mother of Stella and Leila Hawkins.

Stella is said to be slowly getting to know the man she now knows is her biological father, a man who only came on the scene just before the murder of his former lover.

Stella sold the family home in Mereford, and she and Euan have relocated to a more rural Lincolnshire setting, citing a desire for a fresh start with their four dogs. She still runs a dog training business.

There have been rumours of Hollywood interest in making a film version of their story, but those close to the couple say they would never agree to that.

A friend who asked not to be named told us: "They want to leave the past behind."

EPILOGUE

The face of a murdered woman stares back at me from the mirror.

There she is. Leila. Dead but alive.

Only it isn't her. It's me. I reach out towards the reflection, taking in the whole face. The grey at the temples and along the parting. The fine lines around the eyes. The slight sagging along my jaw. And at the same time I see the way I was – we were – and reach out to stroke her cheek as her eyes warm. Even after all these years when I see myself, it's my dead sister who looks back, but it's no longer something that fills me with fear or shame. It's good to have her back with me.

Euan appears behind her and I turn as his arms enfold me.

'Happy birthday, Stella.' He kisses my forehead, and I breathe in the familiar smell of aftershave and fresh air he always seems to carry with him. 'Are you ready to go to the cemetery?'

It's going to be a tough day. First, we'll spend the morning by the grave of Leila and my parents, who are buried side by side. Afterwards, we'll scatter Mary's ashes by the sea, as stipulated in her will. Tonight, though, Euan has promised to cook something for me and make me celebrate – and for once I'm not going to argue.

It's taken time to recover from my attack. The physical complications were bad enough but it's taken longer to get over the emotional ones left over from the rape, the lies, everything… With Euan's patience and understanding we're getting there.

'I just need to grab the flowers, they're on the side, then I'm all set,' I say. 'Did you get the Black Forest gateau from Marks & Spencer, like I asked?'

'Would I dare not?'

'I should think so, too.'

It's what Leila and I always used to have on our birthday and now, at last, I can face eating it again and lose myself in happy memories of years gone by, remembering my sister with a smile. The problem was never that I thought she wouldn't forgive me for my actions that night, it was that I couldn't forgive myself. Now, though, I think I've atoned. Leila is lying beside my parents just as I promised them all.

Euan and I settle the dogs, putting the radio on for company for them before we leave. Music fills the air.

'Ain't Nobody, Chaka Khan,' Euan blurts out.

'Ah, it's Chaka Khan and Rufus, so you lose.'

'Come on, I beat you!'

'You got it wrong…'

'Actually, isn't it Rufus and Chaka Khan? So…'

As we bicker happily, we step outside, into the sunshine and a bright future awaiting us.

A LETTER FROM BARBARA

Thank you for reading *The Girl in the Missing Poster*! If you want to keep up-to-date with all my latest releases, just sign up at the following link. Your email address will never be shared and you can unsubscribe at any time.

www.bookouture.com/barbara-copperthwaite

Two years ago, I was watching a lot of true crime documentaries. A lot. Square eyes amounts. Six months prior to that, in August 2018, I'd fallen ill, and the consequent chronic fatigue that struck was so profound I couldn't walk sometimes; I didn't have the strength to stand beneath the shower, I had to sit; I couldn't concentrate enough to read a book let alone write one. By February 2019, I'd improved enough to actually read! I could even watch TV that required more than two brain cells, and that's how my true crime documentary addiction started. Right near the end of one about TV presenter Jill Dando's murder, her brother, Nigel, said something that instantly hit a nerve with me:

'I just wish someone could explain to me – or a judge and jury – and tell me why they killed her. It makes no sense to me. It will never make sense to me.'

I rewound it, grabbed a notebook and jotted it down. I was struck by the incredible sadness of never knowing and couldn't help thinking: What if the killer is watching this programme too? What if s/he got in touch and tried to explain? What then? It was like someone had thrown open a window in my brain and scenes and scenarios flooded in…

I started writing immediately, even though all I could manage was a couple of paragraphs a day, at best. I got frustrated often, remembering the person I used to be and wishing I could work and think like before. Sometimes it felt like it would never be finished – yet somehow I reached the end, growing stronger with each month that passed. Now, pretty much two years to the day after I was first struck by the idea, *The Girl in the Missing Poster* has been published. There is a sort of symmetry to that which I think would please Stella Hawkins.

And that line from Nigel Dando? It's been used in the book in full as a little tribute and thanks. I hope one day his sister's mystery is solved.

While we're on the subject of reality, all the crime statistics used throughout the book are correct at the time of writing. And those two crazy stories about faked deaths in order to trap killers? Yes, they're real, too.

I'd love to know what you think of *The Girl in the Missing Poster* so, please, if you have a spare minute leave a review on the site where you bought it. That way I can read your thoughts because it's you, my lovely readers, you have helped me through one of the toughest times of my life. Thank you for everything.

Barbara

PS If you want to get in touch or find out the latest on what I'm up to, there are lots of ways: Facebook, Twitter, my blog, and website, as well as Goodreads. I sometimes run competitions, so be sure to pop in!

AuthorBarbaraCopperthwaite

BCopperthwait

barbaracopperthwaite.wordpress.com

www.barbaracopperthwaite.com

ACKNOWLEDGEMENTS

The lone twin network is a UK group specifically to support those who have lost a twin. I was keen to accurately capture the uniquely painful experience of becoming a twin-less twin and reached out to them for help. Anyone interested in finding out more should read *The Lone Twin*, by Joan Woodward, or visit *The Lone Twin* website.

www.lonetwinnetwork.org.uk

I also received expert help from former Chief Inspector Stuart Gibbon, of GIB Consultancy, who checked over all my policing facts. He's brilliant to work with! Anything wrong is down to me and my dramatic licence.

Also, big thanks to Jason Lane-Sellers, who explained to this Luddite technophobe how anonymous emails work. Then there's Rosalind Lavigne, True Crime TV producer, whose help with how true crime documentaries are put together was invaluable. Thanks to the No.1 Freelance Media Women for putting us in touch with one another.

Tough times test us all, but it can also be when you discover how lucky you are. That was the case for me. So my biggest 'thank you' has to go to my partner, Paul, who did his best to hold me together when my health fell apart – because without his love I can't imagine how I would have managed.

Thanks also to my family, Rory, Rona and Ellen, for having faith in me, and especially my mum, who will always be my Number 1 Fan! And my friends, Julieanne and Emmi, for chats even when I could barely speak.

Huge thanks to the incredibly supportive book community I'm lucky enough to be part of, including: The Savvy Authors, The

Psychological Suspense Authors' Association, Book Connectors, book bloggers (especially Shell Baker, Anne Williams and Linda Hill) and The Book Club, Lost In a Good Book, Crime Book Club, and UK Crime Book Club.

Now it's time for me to thank Bookouture, my wonderful publisher. It's hard to put into words the gratitude I feel for the genuine care, understanding and patience you've shown me. My fabulous editor, Jessie Botterill, has pushed hard for *The Girl in the Missing Poster* to be the best story possible, showing unfailing faith and enthusiasm for it. Thank you! Then there is the PR & Social Media team, Kim Nash and Noelle Holten, who have the fastest fingers in the West when it comes to social media!

I must give special mention to my fellow Bookouture authors, who are always there for each other whether it's to laugh, cry, advise, support... Angie Marsons, you helped me take those first tentative steps back into writing. I will never forget that kindness and it made such a difference to me. Susie Lynes, thanks for your friendship and advice – and jokes. And Anna Mansell, you've been with me practically every step of this rollercoaster writing experience, celebrating highs, suggesting wine during the lows. Couldn't have done it without you, mate.

I can't go without thanking my dogs, Scamp and Buddy, who get cameos in this book, as well as Buster, who is gone but will never be forgotten. Thanks for inspiring me, and I'm sorry writing this book took me away from my real job, which is throwing tennis balls and feeding you treats.

Finally, thank YOU for reading *The Girl in the Missing Poster*. I really hope you enjoyed it! If you did, please let me know by leaving a review. And don't forget, I sometimes run competitions across my social media, giving away the chance to have characters in my books named after you. One such lucky winner was Penny-Sue Wolf, whose name I'm sure you all recognise...

Printed in Great Britain
by Amazon